Retur
Falcon

E.M. Phillips

For my Family

For Dawn, who has read & critiqued all my scripts,

For Neli, who always finds what I want, when I want it,

For Graeme, who has patiently led his technically inept
mother through the mysteries and pitfalls of IT

Bless them all

Acknowledgement and thanks to:

Sandra Jacques, for her editing skills.
Dick Purdue, at Indian Lake, NY,
for checking my American 'voice.'
The US Veterans' Association.
The Imperial War Museum, London.
The IWM Air Museum at Duxford.
Sgt. White's notes from his B17 mission diary of raids
over Germany 1943/44

Cover photo by Dennis Bright

Return to Falcon Field

E.M. Phillips

Return to Falcon Field

Published 2009 by Sagittarius Publications
62 Jacklyns Lane, Alresford, Hampshire SO24 9LH
Tel: 01962 734322

Typeset by John Owen Smith

ISBN 978-0-9555778-5-7

Printed and bound in Great Britain by CPI Antony Rowe, Chippenham and Eastbourne

PROLOGUE

HAWKSLEY MANOR, HAMPSHIRE

February 1944

In the drawing room of the old house the young woman sat, eyes closed and head resting against the high back of the tapestry chair. Beyond the deep casement windows a late afternoon sun cast shadows across the lawn and already there was the chill of frost in the air.

The slate clock on the mantle struck three and the woman shivered. Rubbing her arms she rose and walked toward the window, some sixth sense telling her they were coming, even before they were within sight or sound.

She pushed the French windows wide and stepping out crossed the paved terrace. Crushed by her footsteps the wild thyme that grew between the flags released a faint fragrance into the still air and she smiled in remembrance. *Just waiting for a nice fat goose* he'd teased her the first time he smelled it.

She leaned her hands on the stone balustrade and waited. Minutes passed before she heard the faint but steady thrum of engines, the thrumming changing to a full-throated roar as they appeared, flying beneath the thin evening cloud, casting giant shadows over the fields. Wings and fuselage glinted in the dying sun as vibrations from the powerful engines set the casements behind her rattling. Then one thundering pass overhead until they were almost out of sight and the huge 'planes turned, breaking off one by one into a long slow descent towards the runways and out of sight.

Straining her eyes she counted them in: the first dozen flying in ragged formation, then half a dozen stragglers coming slowly in ones and twos. When the count stopped far short of the final tally, she stepped back into the room and closed the doors. He would ring soon, she comforted herself, her heart taking up an unsteady rhythm. He always called her once the de-briefing was over, but he wouldn't speak then, nor later, of the crews who hadn't made it back.

She left the chill of the sitting room and went into the little study where a log fire burned; where tonight she would smooth the care and the weariness from his face and eyes and they would talk, and make love, and be quiet together.

Sitting by the desk she rested her arms on the leather top; watching the telephone, waiting patiently for it to ring.

5

Part I

I'll be seeing you in all the old familiar places

That this heart of mine embraces all day through...

1

BRACKET SOUND, NEW ENGLAND

August 1965

Ryan Petersen helped his neighbour load the last of the wooden crates into the van then turned away, letting his gaze pass slowly over the old plank houses ranged around the sweep of the bay. The afternoon sun blazed down, sparking the shingles and gilding the treetops; at the end of his wooden jetty the tall mast of the *Dancer* dipped and rose in the swell of a passing launch

Locking the back doors of his van securely Al asked, 'You reckon that's about the lot then, eh, Prof?'

'Yeah, all but our hand luggage and a couple of cases; everything we'll really need when we get there, but I'll be glad when this lot arrives and I can get my own books and things around me. Thanks a lot for taking it to the freight depot for me.'

'Well, you been a good neighbour and done more than a few favours for us over the years. I guess you'll be glad to get away for a while – helluva long way to go, though, England. Young Joel looking forward to it?'

Ryan grimaced. 'Not so's you'd notice. He's at an awkward age for moving to a new place.'

'There's no awkward age Ry; all boys are like that all the time – I know, I got three. Still, nice you got your mom comin' along to help out.'

'Yeah,' Ryan's tone was dry and non-committal, 'be a lot more help though if she hadn't cancelled her flight and decided to take an ocean cruise.'

Al gave him a quick, complicit grin. He shook Ryan's hand vigorously and clapped his shoulder. 'You take care now; you and that boy.'

'Will do. See you, Al.'

Ryan turned back into the house, ignoring his son's sulky face pressed to his bedroom window. He hoped he was doing the right thing in taking this year in London; exchanging his comfortable settled post in his familiar college for the unknown campus of a British university, but anything was better than staying here, conscious all the time of the sympathy, both spoken and unspoken of friends and the accusing stares of less compassionate acquaintances. Give it a year and pretty near everyone would have forgotten what happened last fall.

Frowning a little he wondered again if he should have stuck out, refused his mother's offer to follow them over and gone it alone with Joel. Abby, his daily housekeeper who cooked most of their meals and kept Joel in order, would have been his choice to travel with them, but she had her own family to care for and couldn't be spared.

He pushed a hand through his thick thatch of silver hair and made a mental note to get it cut soon as he hit London. With all this hassle of the move it was one of those things he'd not found time for. It wouldn't be a good start to arrive at his new post looking like something out of a Pete Fonda road movie. London may be swinging, but the academic scene might still be a tad sticky over little things like hair on the collar. A ratty looking Professor of European Literature mightn't go down any too well with future colleagues.

*　　　*　　　*

After supper and with his son at last in bed he sat in the cooling air of evening, watching the moon make a pathway across the water. Tomorrow he and Joel would leave this house. In less than forty-eight hours from now his ears would hear the English voices so familiar to him twenty years before; his palate adjust again to English food. In the weeks before his mother's arrival he would be living in a stranger's house, in a country with too many memories, in sole charge of a son he loved but didn't understand and sometimes didn't even like overmuch. He sighed and pushing from his chair went to his bed pretty well convinced that he was making a mistake and should have stayed put right here in Bracket Sound.

*　　　*　　　*

As the cab gathered speed down the street next morning Joel sat bolt upright, stubbornly refusing to look out of the window and return the waves of friends gathered in neighbouring porches. Who wanted to live in a crummy place like London anyway, he thought mutinously, the summer vacation wasn't over yet and there were still a trillion things him and Jake wanted to do before school started again.

The cab turned the corner and they began the climb through the trees. Ryan could feel his son beside him rigid with misery and resentment. He wanted to hold him close, say, 'Don't worry, it'll be

10

all right; England will be fun and you'll get used to it real soon,' but he could feel the barrier around the boy, palpable as a wall and he couldn't quite manage the words, or even touch him, and they rode in silence to the airport.

*   *   *

An hour into the flight Ryan gave up watching the younger stewardess's legs, even though they caused the first real flutter of good old fashioned lust he'd felt in a long time. But enjoyable and welcome though such carnal stirrings were, this was neither the time nor the place to indulge. With a faint sigh of regret he did his best to block out Joel's audible perusal of a heap of comic books bought at the airport and began a desultory scan of the Literary Reviews in the New York Times.

After reading his comics twice, cover to cover and half a dozen visits to the john Joel finally gave in to exhaustion and fell into a doze against his father's shoulder. Ryan put down the Times and leaning back closed his own eyes, pondering once again over what in hell had made his mother cancel her flight for the extra expense in time and money to book passage across on an ocean liner. Nothing but plain damn contrariness, he thought irritably. She didn't even like the ocean, wouldn't as much as set foot on the deck of the *Dancer.* Now it would be a good three weeks before she caught up with them and he'd have all the hassle of fitting Joel's winter outfits and organizing his new school around his visits to his own new College and preparations for the coming semester. He wrinkled his brow; no, that wasn't right; over there they called them something else and had three of them instead of two...he sighed and returned to the Times. Oh well, *que sera, sera...*

When they landed it was raining, a steady downpour that turned roadways into shallow rivers. Standing outside the passenger hall at London Airport Central, shivering in his linen pants and jacket and polo sweater, Ryan regretted his thick plaid hunting jacket was packed away in his luggage in the optimistic expectation that late August in England should be reasonably warm. Beside him Joel stood silent; a small forlorn figure in Levi's, sweatshirt and denim jacket, a Boston Red Sox ball cap pulled low over his forehead, his face peaked with cold.

A sudden gust of wind blew stinging rain in their faces; Ryan snarled 'The hell with this!' and putting thumb and forefinger to his mouth let go a piercing whistle; seconds later a cab swung alongside

11

the curb, sending a spray of dirty water across the paving. Shouldering his suitcase Ryan took his son's arm and raced him across the forecourt, his flight bag bumping wildly against his skinny legs.

'Where to, guv'nor?' the cabby twisted around in his seat grinning cheerfully at Ryan where he sat brushing rain from his shoulders.

'Marlborough Street, Chelsea – d'you know it?'

'Know everywhere guv'nor. Have to else I'd never keep me licence.' He swung the cab out into the traffic. 'Come from some place warm'n dry have you?'

'Yeah,' Joel's voice was an aggrieved pipe, 'now I'm wet'n cold!'

In an effort to comfort the miserable little bastard, Ryan said, 'It gets better. When the sun shines in England in the fall it's almost like being back home.'

'Your dad's right, sonny,' in his rear-view mirror the cabby raised enquiring brows at Ryan. 'Been here before have you, guv'nor?'

'Yeah, came over with the Air Corps in 'forty-two – stationed in Hampshire and used to come up on leave.'

'Good place London was then – friendly,' the cabby hunched eloquent shoulders, 'different now, full of ruddy foreigners who don't even stop to give you the time of day.'

'Is that so?' Ryan grinned, remembering how friendly most people had been in his time, especially the girls. Those, he thought nostalgically, had been the days of wine and roses, of warm beer and wet streets, US Forces canteens and the back rows of movie theatres. The days when girls wore stockings and those cute little lace garter belts, the pantyhose that now de-sexed every woman yet to be invented…

Dragging his errant thoughts back and settling into the leather seat he put an arm around his son's shoulders. 'You see that little piece of blue up there?' he pointed out of the cab window at a minute azure patch showing through the heavy cloud. 'Give it some time and that will be all over the sky and the sun will shine. That's how it is here.'

'Heck, *every* day?'

'Nah, mostly it's fine and when it isn't you just put up your umbrella and wait for that patch of blue to get bigger.'

'An *umbrella*?' the boy ruminated in silence for a minute then asked plaintively, 'Do I have to have one of them?'

'*Those,*' Ryan laughed, feeling suddenly light-hearted. 'No, you can be one tough Yankee and get wet!'

*　　　*　　　*

By the time the cab dropped them in a quiet tree-lined street off the Kings Road, it had stopped raining. Leaving Joel sitting despondent on his flight bag Ryan ran down the basement steps of the narrow Georgian house, where, following the trusting Elliot's instructions he rummaged behind a large flowerpot full of trailing plants, emerging a few seconds later with a set of keys in his muddied hand.

'Jesus!' Cursing the wet and the dirty sleeve of his pale grey jacket he climbed back up the area steps. Fitting the key into the Yale lock he swung the house door open and stepped into a long black and white diamond tiled passage, half way along which rose a steep carpeted stairway.

Joel trailed moodily behind him, dragging his bag along the tiles. 'Why don't you go see what's up top,' Ryan suggested, and when his son had clumped up the narrow staircase and was out of his hair, he made a leisurely exploration of the house at ground level.

At the front was a dining room, behind that a small study that with the addition of a day bed doubled as an extra bedroom. The house felt chill, but in each room and in the long hall were radiators. These were the size of tank traps and as of now cold as a Christian Brother's heart, but at least come winter proper gave some hope they wouldn't freeze to death. At the end of the hall was a small kitchen, the cupboards well stacked with tins and basic foodstuffs. Immediately before the kitchen a narrow door opened onto a flight of stairs down to a basement and a comfortably furnished bedroom doubling as a sitting room. A door at the rear of this led to a postage stamp-size paved courtyard while a bathroom, a galley kitchen and a small utility with a sink and taps in one corner completed the unit.

Just as well about that sink, Ryan thought, his mother wouldn't survive without a washing machine. He sighed. One more darned thing to go on his List of Things to Buy. Still, the place would give Hannah her own space; close but not so close that she need be breathing down his neck all the time; she even had her own front door leading off the main room and opening onto the railed area steps.

Returning to the kitchen he washed the dirt off his hands, found and set to half-heat the central heating switch he found hidden in a cupboard then climbed to the second level. On the turn of the staircase was a bathroom with a shower over the bath: a further turn and two steps up brought him to a landing and a door opening onto a long sitting room that ran the depth of the house from front to back.

'Hey, dad,' Joel clattered down from the top of the house while Ryan was at the rear window looking down into the small walled garden, 'come on up – you can see right over all the roofs to a sort of park place. Can I have that little bedroom at the top – not the big one, I guess that's yours – I can put the bed right up against the window and watch the sky.' Not waiting for a reply he turned and thundered back, shouting: 'I can move it now!'

'Wait!' Ryan sprinted up behind him, visions of someone else's furniture being manhandled straight through the window lending him speed. Arriving at the top he leaned against the door of the small attic room to catch his breath and take in the reason for his son's sudden metamorphosis from apathy to excited action.

It was really no more than a dressing room, linked to the master bedroom by a communicating door. In the sloping ceiling a long skylight reached to within some three feet off the floor, leaving just enough space for the bed, now jammed against one wall with a small table beside it, and a high wooden chest set against the opposite wall. Ryan began to chuckle.

'Gee, dad, what are you laughing at?'

'There's hardly room for all your mess in your big bedroom at home and I'm wondering what this place will look like when you've been here a while. You'd have more space to move around if we made that downstairs study into a proper bedroom.'

'I won't *make* a mess here! Please, dad, *please* help me put the bed under the window, then when it's dark I can open it an' put my head right out an' see the stars!' Joel bounced on the bed and gave his old wide smile and Ryan felt a sudden heat behind his eyes. It seemed a very long time since he'd seen that smile.

He dropped onto the bed, pulling the thin undersized body into his arms, hugging him close. Joel's chest gave several spasmodic heaves and he wound his arms tight around Ryan's neck. 'Think you'll like it here?' Ryan asked quickly.

'Dunno, maybe.' The reply was muffled in his shoulder.

'OK, let's get this bed moved then we'll go find somewhere to shop for bread and milk and stuff for breakfast. I guess we can eat out tonight and save messing with supper.'

'Yeah,' Joel loosed his arms and brushed a furtive hand across his eyes. 'You think they got hamburgers here?'

'Maybe, maybe not; never did have when I was here before – but come on, we'll sort out this room of yours then freshen up and get going around town.'

After he had climbed from the window, checked the safety of the leads and sturdy railed parapet, then rearranged the room to his son's satisfaction, Ryan allowed himself a cautious sigh of relief. Perhaps after all he really had made the right decision. Perhaps here in this big anonymous city where nobody knew them, they could both start getting their lives back on track.

Following Joel as he went hopping down the stairs he began to feel a resurgence of hope and optimism. Things had to get better for both of them.

They just had to.

*   *   *

They bought salami and ham, cheese and rye bread from a local delicatessen; milk and butter from a dairy on the corner of Lincoln Street then walked down the Kings Road to Sloane Square. Joel's eyes stretched wide at the sight of bizarrely dressed men, and girls in the very briefest of mini-skirts, some with long shiny boots rising up to their thighs. Nobody dressed that way in Brackets Sound. When a young man with bright red hair frizzed and bushed about his thin, bespectacled face passed them wearing a military jacket with gold epaulettes, stalk-thin purple velvet flares and silver high heeled boots, Joel breathed, 'Gee, did you see that, dad; did you *see* that? It's just like 'Frisco on TV only here it's for *real*!'

Give it a few years and you could be looking the same, Ryan thought but only advised, 'Don't stare, kid; he thinks he's normal and you're the funny one.'

They chose one of several cafés in which to have an early evening meal, returning afterward to their new home tired, and in Joel's case, ready for bed.

Bathed and in clean pj's, his damp hair flattened to his head and eyes limpid with sleep, he looked nothing like the sulky obstreperous little thug who had tried Ryan's patience all through the long vacation. Lying back with hands behind his head he stared through the window at the moon struggling through the clouds. 'I'd sure like to go out into space like that Russian guy,' he said, 'Jake's dad says that by the time we're all grown up we'll likely just take a rocket up there like it was a 'plane? Whadaya think about that, dad?'

'I wouldn't take a bet on it. Seems to me there'll need to be a whole lot of work done first. Now settle down; it's late.'

'Yeah, I guess,' Joel raised up on one elbow, eyeing him cautiously. 'Are you going downstairs now?'

Ryan's ear detected a slight tremble in the words and a little gulp at the end. 'I was. Why?'

'Oh, nothing...'

15

Joel wriggled down the bed again and, remembering what it had been like to be ten years old and in a strange place, Ryan suggested, 'How about if I leave this door to my room open a chink and go lie on my bed for a while?'

Joel was nonchalant. 'OK; if you want.'

For a moment Ryan hesitated, then bent to kiss the top of Joel's head. Joel said 'Aw, *dad,*' rubbing at his crown as though he'd dripped molten lava onto it. Ryan grinned and tousled the damp hair, ''Night, goofball!'

Long after Joel slept Ryan lay on his own bed, staring up at the intricate plaster mouldings around the ceiling. He moved restlessly on the unfamiliar bed. It was five years since he and Ellie had lived as husband and wife. He was no monk and during those years there had been a few other women, all short term and none he loved or had loved him. Then in the months following Ellie's death he hadn't wanted a woman. Shock and guilt had dampened down the all too ready fire.

But now he had uprooted himself from his safe and familiar world old needs were beginning to surface. Uninvolved short-term sex wasn't the answer he knew, he'd tried that and it didn't work all that well. But it was impossible now to imagine finding someone he'd want to share the rest of his life with. He had lived too long without love, so long that sometimes he wondered if the love he had once found in this country all those years ago had been real or just an illusion; a consequence of war, born of fear and a desperate need for comfort and hope for the future.

Eventually he made his way downstairs and switched on the Elliot's out-of-the-ark TV, where some crazy guy in a fez was doing magic tricks that went wrong. He was funny but not so funny as Burns and Allen or Bilko, and after a few minutes Ryan switched it off again. Going into the kitchen he rummaged in his flight bag for the bourbon, then carrying the bottle and a glass returned to the big feather cushioned couch in the sitting room and prepared to make a night of it.

*   *   *

Within the week their crates had been freighted over and they could unpack all those items that go to make everyday life comfortable: books and records, games and familiar clothing, all smelling of pine and ocean and home. Father and son began to settle down together and sixteen Marlborough Street started to feel less strange and more

16

like a real home.

*   *   *

The cease-fire between Ryan and his son lasted all of two weeks: weeks in which they explored together their new territory. Together they toured the various museums, took in the odd movie or went up river by motor launch. On those occasions when the boy had to wait in the porter's office while Ryan met some of his keener future students in the college library, or was invited by a handful of his future colleagues to their favoured drinking places, they would spend the rest of the day at the Science Museum; Joel's favourite and a place of which he never seemed to tire.

It was the most time they had spent alone together in all of Joel's ten years; although exhausting it was kind of fun and Ryan began to wonder if they needed Hannah after all.

But that was before war broke out over the Big School Uniform List.

*   *   *

His colleague Artie Samuels had suggested he register Joel at an International School in Kensington his own girls had gone to during his own exchange year in London. At least half the pupils were American, he said and the school had the advantage of being only a short 'bus ride away from Chelsea. When they visited toward the end of the first week Joel appeared reasonably impressed with the place and unusually co-operative, until the moment they arrived at the outfitters and Ryan handed over the uniform list.

With Joel lumpen as a dead cow a harassed assistant did her best to fit him with the required regulation gear of shirts and ties, short grey pants, full length grey raincoat and heavy overcoat for the winter. By the time they reached the final insult of a pink and grey circled cap, pink and grey striped scarf and grey blazer with a pink badge, Joel was scarlet with suppressed rage and the assistant limp from nervous exhaustion.

Now the clothes that hung in the wardrobe had become weapons with which to wage war. With Hannah due in at Southampton the day after next, and only a week or so before his first morning at school, Joel was at his infuriating worst. Raging noisily across the breakfast table against the humiliation of a darned school uniform with pink bits all over it and the ultimate indignity of those short pants, he was

17

pushing Ryan's patience to the limit.

'It stinks! Nobody but a dork wears short pants for school; heck, I haven't worn *them* since kindergarten!'

Ryan kept his temper in check with difficulty. 'You wear them all summer on the beach.'

'That's different; that's what all the guys back home wear in summer.'

'OK. So that's what all the guys here wear for school in summer *and* winter.'

Close to tears Joel yelled, 'I don't care– they suck. I'm not wearing short pants *or* stupid coats an' caps with pink bits!'

'You are and that's an end of it. Now quit squawking and finish your breakfast.'

Joel shoved his plate half across the table, slopping milk and cereal over the cloth then sat back with folded arms. Ryan ignored him and continued his own breakfast in silence, but after a minute or two the boy began to kick, softly but rhythmically at the table leg.

Thud, thud, thud went the sneaker against wood. Ryan felt the dull nausea of an approaching sick headache and what patience he had stretched paper-thin. Thrusting his own plate aside he stood, and leaning across the table said with deadly calm, 'Just one more kick and so help me I'll skin your goddamned ass.'

'I don't care; I hate this place. I hate it, I hate it, I *hate* it!' Joel screamed at the top of his voice and very slowly Ryan counted to ten.

'No you don't. Right now it's me and the clothes and going to a strange school you hate, and all the kicking and yelling in the world won't do one bit of good, nor change one single thing. I'll still be here, so will the clothes, so will the school. So why don't you just give it a break before I do something we'll both regret.'

Joel opened his mouth on another threatened yell but Ryan had had enough and his patience snapped. Crashing his fist down on the table with a force that set the china rattling he roared at full pitch, 'Go to your room – *NOW*!'

Lips quivering Joel slid off his chair, shot around the breakfast table and scampered from the room. Ryan waited until he heard him scramble to the top of the house and the slam of his bedroom door then slumped back in his chair with closed eyes. *Shit*, for a moment back there he'd sounded just like his own old man!

He gave himself ten minutes to cool off and do a spot of constructive thinking about how to turn a pretty lousy start to the day into something positive and useful…

OK, he decided, first both he and Joel needed to get out and cool down; second he needed a car; should have sorted one soon as they arrived. Hannah would be pretty frosty if she had to train it from Southampton. Combining the two needs now would save face all around.

He pushed from the chair and crossing the room flung open the door. Calling up the stairs with what he judged to be just the right mixture of political amnesty overlaid with menace he demanded, 'Joel, you come on down here – right now!'

His son's rebellious face appeared over the top banister. Ryan stared at Joel until the boy's defiant expression crumpled and he began to snivel and slide hand over hand down the rail. 'Go wash your face,' Ryan ordered as Joel hit the first landing. 'We're going out.'

While he waited he wondered where to start looking. He wasn't particularly interested in cars *per se* and no expert at what went on under the hood. Back home he left all the technical stuff to Clem at the garage. He didn't want to be conned into buying some banged-out load but where in hell did he start looking anyway?

When he'd been in this city back in 'forty-two, he remembered, just about every GI in the country had soon clicked that any London cabby could be relied on to know where pretty damn near everything could be found, from a salt beef sandwich to a cut price hooker. Maybe that might hold good for used car dealers as well. At least it was worth a try.

When Joel finally appeared he looked subdued and red-eyed, but with a stubborn set to his mouth that said pretty clearly he hadn't yet thrown in the towel. Two can play at that game thought Ryan. Opening the front door he motioned him out. 'You step over the line just once more,' he warned, 'and I'll make you *sleep* in that uniform. You hear me?'

'Yeah, I hear you.'

'OK,' Ryan put a hand on his shoulder and shoved him down the steps. 'Now you just keep your mouth buttoned. I have some serious business to do and I don't need you messing things up.'

In Sloane Square he flagged down the first cab that happened along. Drawing alongside, the cabby leaned over asking the standard, 'Where to, guv'nor?'

Ryan was easy, affable, playing the lone Yank asking a favour. 'Hi, I need some wheels in a hurry; you know where I can get a decent used car?'

The answer came promptly. 'S'good place off the Cromwell Road; know it well – I got me sister a tidy little banger from there a few months back.'

'OK is it?'

'Yup, real kosher.'

'Then lead me to it.' Opening the door he bundled Joel inside; the boy grumbled under his breath but, 'Remember – button it,' Ryan told him. Joel obeyed, but sat on the tip-up seat as far removed from him as possible and glared ferociously out at the passing crowds.

Turning around in the teeth of the traffic the cabby left the main road to drive through a maze of back streets, eventually drawing up before a used car lot with a red board over the entrance gate bearing a gold crown, beneath it the legend "Coronet Automobiles – We Have The Car That *You* Want To Buy"

'Here you are guv'nor. Decent place this is. Nice bloke runs it, name of Jerry Kingsley; sells everything from Mercs to Austin Sevens. He ain't cheap and he's a bit sharp, but he won't sell you a dud if you tell him Alfie Blume says "hello."'

'Is that all?'

'Yus – he'll know.' He leaned to take the fare. 'Thanks guv'nor, best of luck.' He drove off chuckling. Slinging his jacket over his shoulder Ryan threaded his way through the cars on the forecourt and with Joel trailing behind walked into the one-storey pre-fabricated office.

A slender, curly-haired young man came smiling from a desk at the back of the room; he wore a black Beatles jacket, narrow trousers and shoes so highly polished you could see your face in them. One real cool dude, Ryan thought and hoped his cars were as good as his dress sense. 'You Jerry Kingsley?' he asked.

'That's me, squire.'

'Alfie Blume said to tell you hello!'

'In that case I'll do me best for you. What you looking for?'

'Something with plenty of leg room; classy but not flash. And no more than a hundred and twenty quid max. So what have you?'

For a moment Kingsley studied him in silence then flicked a swift wink at Joel, who was at the desk fiddling with a plastic dog with a nodding head. 'I got just the thing. Come in Wednesday, a Jowett Javelin. She's a classic…not a scratch or flake of rust on her, real leather up'olstery …' eloquent hands described the car's lines in the way another's might the curves of a woman.

'Yeah,' Ryan was cynical, 'but does it go?'

'Like a dream. Come and see – she's out the back.'

They followed him out of the rear of the office into a yard, where a sleek, black, highly polished car gleamed in the morning sun. Joel breathed an ecstatic 'Hey, *man!*'

The urbane Jerry Kingsley patted the hood with a loving hand. 'Ain't she a beaut?'

Trying to look knowledgeable Ryan walked around surveying the large chrome hubs, worn but well-kept leather upholstery, the polished walnut dash. 'How much?' he asked eventually.

'To you, a hundred 'n ten nicker – it's a bargain.'

'You reckon? Does it bleed oil?

'Nope'

'Guzzle gas?'

'Bit thirsty,' he was faintly contemptuous, 'if you want forty to the gallon mister, you buy a Mini!'

He was pushing it a bit, but Ryan admired his cheek. He lifted the hood like he knew what he was doing, while Kingsley watched with shrewd confident eyes. Ryan said eventually, 'Make it ninety.'

The young man narrowed his eyes. 'A straight hundred sounds better.'

'OK.' Ryan felt for his chequebook. 'You've got yourself a deal.'

He looked startled. 'Don't you want to take 'er for a run first?'

'Nope, if Alfie says you're OK, I guess that's good enough for me – you take a cheque? You can call my bank in Chelsea if you like to make sure it won't bounce right back!'

'You trust me; I trust you. I'll get 'er filled up while we sort out the insurance and do the business – the first tank's on me.' Jerry Kingsley grinned as he led the way back to the office. 'Around here customers like you don't grow on trees. Yesterday it took me an hour and cost me ten fags to sell a thir'y quid Austin to a bloke in a pork pie hat, plus-fours and an Oxford accent you could strangle a cat with…' he signalled to a pimply youth, who dropped his cigarette butt under his heel as they appeared and begun assiduously polishing a black Rover. 'Syd, fill up the Jowett and don't leave no finger prints – this gen'man's from the FBI and you never know what he might get you on!'

Ryan followed Kingsley to his desk where he wrote his cheque. Finishing he handed it over with a smile. 'Thanks.'

Kingsley grinned. '*Mazel tov,* I wish you well to drive her, and good motoring, squire.'

*   *   *

Nosing the Jowett out into the morning traffic, Ryan registered that there was one hell of a lot more of *that* since he last drove the London streets and it was several minutes before he felt able to relax his hands on the wheel.

'Gee dad, can't we go faster?' Joel ventured.

He was sitting low in his seat, clutching the plastic dog with the nodding head. He'd been so quiet that Ryan had almost forgotten he was there. One up to the heavy father routine he thought, and couldn't help a smirk of satisfaction at coming out on top this time. 'Not in this town,' he answered, 'and what are you doing with that thing – you didn't snitch it, I hope?

'The guy at the car lot gave it me.' Joel leaned his copper coloured head against Ryan's arm. 'It's a great car isn't it, dad?'

'Yep, she sure is.'

He leaned a little harder. 'You still mad at me?'

'No, but don't do it too often or you'll know what mad really is.'

'That school stuff,' he ventured, 'its really more sort of red than pink, isn't it?'

'Yeah, it's red all right. Now let's get ourselves out of town and let this baby go a little.'

Ryan drove toward what he hoped was the way to Kew. The morning was fine, he felt alive for the first time in weeks and his son was OK, at least for the time being.

It was going to be a great day.

2

MARLBOROUGH STREET, CHELSEA

September 1965

Saturday they drove to Southampton to meet Hannah.

Overnight it had rained, but by the time Ryan left the outer limits of the capital the sun was out and they drove on through a bright September morning. Traffic was light and the Jowett ate the miles. Running smoothly past the smart houses and leafy manicured landscape of Surrey they came at last into Hampshire's lush pastures, where sheep and cattle grazed alongside fields of blackened stubble left after harvest. Ryan remembered how it had been when the farmers fired the stubble and the smoke drifted over the airfield; how for hours afterward their uniforms had held the acrid pungent smell. "The unique and quintessential fragrance of an English autumn" their RAF flight controller had called it. Ryan grinned at the memory: a poetic old guy, Alec Marshall.

Only half listening to Joel's intermittent chatter he fell silent, memories crowding in on him as he drove over the intersection where taking a right turn would have led him to the New Forest, to the open sandy heath, to brackish ponds deep within oak and beech and pine and the spread of the Beaulieu river as it wound toward the sea...

By the time he drove down the broad Avenue leading to the Southampton Docks he knew why he had taken a chance and come back to this country after so many years. It hadn't only been to leave bad memories behind in Bracket Sound and breathe easy for a while; hadn't really been to give Joel and him a break. Oh, sure, those were valid reasons and they sounded good, but none of them was strictly true.

On this bright September morning he knew exactly why he had come back to England. He had come to lay the ghosts that had haunted him on and off, for more than twenty years; to make the journey back in time; say goodbye to Falcon Field; write finish to the love that was Claire; discover if she at least had managed to find the happiness that had eluded him.

He made a silent vow that once Hannah was settled in he would take a break one weekend. Not to stir things up, just to see if the runway was still there and the row of trees at the far end that always threatened to take the asses off the gunners in the ball turrets as the big ships lifted into the air. Make a few discreet enquiries; view from a safe distance the Manor, perhaps unseen catch a sight of her... yeah, he drew a deep breath, he'd take that break sometime soon.

*   *   *

Joel stood at the barrier, hopping from one foot to the other in his excitement, making Ryan aware of how much it would mean for him to have his grandmother join them. Although she lived the far side of Boston and Joel didn't see all that much of her in school time, now he'd been parted from Abby, Hannah was going to be a pretty important person in his life.

'You sure she's coming, dad?' Anxiously he scanned the passengers as they left the customs counters and began to flow down the long arrival shed towards them, some followed by porters pushing a mountain of luggage. One of those, Ryan thought, would be attached to Hannah, who would have packed two of everything to cover the whole year, from winter snow to summer sunshine.

'There she is!' Joel yelled suddenly, his excitement threatening to levitate him over the steel barrier that penned them. He jumped up and down, waving frantic arms above his head, 'Gran'ma, gran'ma!'

Ryan scanned the crowd and gave his long slow grin. Yes, there she was, at her back a straining porter barely visible behind a trolley loaded with his father's old leather cabin trunk and a couple of large suitcases. Tall, big boned and, despite her years, still with that leggy Irish walk, she was with a little stretch of the imagination and a decade or two – or three, Maureen O'Hara and Katie Hepburn rolled into one handsome package.

In the split second before she looked up and saw them Ryan felt a great rush of warmth, realising with surprise overlaid with a kind of grudging relief, that he was glad to see her. Glad that Joel would have a woman again in his life and glad that he would once more have someone around who could make him laugh; even if between times he would still want to strangle her for the irritating manipulative mother she was.

As she reached them and bent to let Joel leap and hang around her neck, she looked up at Ryan and gave back his smile. 'How you been doing, Ry?'

'OK,' he said impulsively, and not quite truthfully. 'Just fine, Ma, we've been doing just fine.'

*   *   *

Hannah sat with Joel in the rear seat as Ryan drove, her arm around her grandson, listening indulgently to his chatter, asking the questions she knew he wanted to answer. Every now and then through the rear view mirror her eyes met Ryan's and she'd give a small enigmatic smile. She hadn't missed the sudden warmth in those brilliant blue eyes, nor the old crooked smile as he kissed her cheek, and she wondered if she might at last be about to get just a mite closer to the son she'd lost so many years ago.

Her younger son's death she had eventually learned to accept and live with; the wall of suppressed hurt and anger Ryan had erected around himself had been much harder to accept and damn' near impossible to live with.

It had taken something more than even war, she reasoned, to turn her son into a stranger and over the years since his return she wondered often if it had been a woman who had shattered him; leaving him unable to pick up all the pieces so that he never quite fitted together again. It seemed more than likely and might have accounted for the hasty and ultimately disastrous marriage made so soon after his return home.

Covertly now she studied his face in the mirror, noting the lines of tiredness and strain around his eyes; guessing shrewdly and accurately that being in sole charge of his son had not made for an easy few weeks. It was a good thing she hadn't been longer in coming to sort things out...

Resolutely she pushed aside her doctor's warning, the professional advice that she should stay put in Boston; the absolute veto on the long flight. She just had to hope her medication would do its job, keep her on an even keel and give her enough energy to deal with the pair of them.

*   *   *

Installing himself as guide and general information bureaux, Joel took his grandmother over every inch of the house while Ryan lugged the trunk and her cases down to the basement. By the time he'd brewed a pot of coffee and broken out a fresh pack of cookies, she was in the sitting room with her shoes off, her still shapely legs stretched along the couch.

25

'Nice house,' she said as Ryan put the tray down on the marble slab table, 'but it could do with a good cleaning.'

He looked around the room. 'I haven't gotten around to finding a cleaning lady yet.'

'I'll tidy up, but a cleaning lady you've got to have.' She sat up and took the cup he handed her. 'I'll ask around the neighbours. How are they – friendly?'

'No idea; haven't gotten around to finding about them, either.'

'My, but something or some*one* must have kept you busy then.' Hannah glanced back at Joel, who was lounging over the back of the couch. The tops of his ears reddened and she gave him a long thoughtful look that made him wriggle. 'Joel, honey,' she said firmly, 'you go on downstairs and open up my big blue valise and see what's packed right at the bottom – and do it real careful, I don't want you mussing up all my clothes.'

Joel was through the door almost before she'd finished speaking. She listened to him thunder down the basement steps then turned to her son. 'I figure you got five minutes to say what's been going on around here with you and that boy, so shoot!'

He shot, succinctly and with feeling: about the short pants, the cap with the pink bits, the tantrums. Everything the unholy little shit had been getting up to...

Ryan thought she was never going to stop laughing; she was still wiping her eyes when Joel hurtled back into the room carrying a large model of a Pioneer rocket. 'Look what I got!' his eyes were shining. 'Gee dad, isn't it just great to have gran'ma here?'

'Yeah,' Ryan watched Hannah reaching for another Kleenex and wished he'd kept his mouth shut. 'Yeah,' he repeated. 'It's great, just great!'

*   *   *

Joel's bedtime that night was a civilized affair, Hannah shooing him through bath, prayers and into bed in double-quick time. With his eyes on his book and his ears tuned to the sounds from the room above him Ryan listened intently, picturing the scene: Joel snuggled down into the covers, thumb in mouth, Hannah's long thin hand stroking his hair as she began to sing, her voice filled with all the haunting melancholic humour that was at the core of all Ireland's sons and daughters, wherever they were, and regardless of how far removed from home. It was in Ryan as it had been in Niles, overriding their father's cool Scandinavian pragmatism and their middleclass

American upbringing.

> *'Mellow the moonlight to shine was beginning*
> *Close by the fireside young Eileen sits spinning...'*

As the rich musical voice drifted down the stairs Ryan lay his book down on the arm of the chair and sat back, remembering Niles and himself in their shared double bed in the tall brownstone house near the park, curled back to back while their mother sang them to sleep; a thread of memory that had run through childhood and all the years of growing up; of school and college and war. He'd remembered it in the still hush of an English summer evening, while the woman he loved slept in his arms; in the brief respite before bone weary sleep between missions; in a dead man's bed beneath the eves of a French farmhouse in winter.

He thought of Niles, his other half, his good companion, lying in his soldier's grave, of the stupid wasteful deaths of war and the devastating death of love. Of how he had let it change him and age him...

Hannah came down the stairs and he hastily snatched up his book and held it before his face.

'He's almost asleep – better go on up and tell him goodnight.' She paused. 'Ry, you clever enough to read that close to your nose?' she asked, then as he slapped the book shut and stood up she smiled and touched his hand. 'You sure do look like your poppa when your feathers are ruffled.'

'I sure do feel like him sometimes.' Impulsively he bent and kissed her cheek. 'Back in a minute,' he said, 'and I could do with a cup of coffee.'

When he reached Joel's room the boy was already asleep. Ryan sat down on the bed for a few moments to watch his sleeping face then unplugging Joel's thumb from his mouth, kissed the crown of his head and went back downstairs where the smell of fresh brewed coffee was already beginning to permeate the house.

*   *   *

Tired from her travels Hannah went early to her own bed but Ryan stayed, stretched out on the big chesterfield, a glass and a fresh opened bottle of bourbon within reach on the low table; pipe, tobacco and Zippo ready to hand. Tonight sleep would only come with the help of at least half the bottle and he knew that tomorrow he would feel and look like hell, but that was the way it went when old memories began to chase around in the mind. Although whisky failed to blot those out completely he'd found by experience that taking enough of it was one sure way to make them bearable.

The clock on the mantle chimed fifteen after midnight, the strokes loud in the silent house; the only other sounds the faint hum of traffic from the Kings Road and an occasional murmur of voices as people passed beneath the open window. Suddenly from nearby came the hesitant strains of a guitar as some unknown hand picked out the melody of *Love, love me do*. More music Ryan thought and smiled briefly as the fledgling musician went wildly off key, paused then started again.

Love, love me do, you know I love you...In the pool of light from the single lamp at his side he lay still, letting imperfectly buried memories stir and take shape; picking at the wound, dreading but needing the memory of a thin face, a wide mouth and very round, mint green eyes; hair the colour of chestnuts breaking straight from the shell, a dusting of freckles over a tip-tilted nose: Ellie, bright and beautiful, before her mind darkened and her looks were eroded by sickness and drugs...

He dug deeper, dragging guilt and remorse into the quiet room, only to swerve away from the still figure on the hospital gurney; the green eyes closed in death, the bright hair tangled with the weed and mud of the river bed.

Jumping up he crossed to the window and pulled down the sash, cutting out the sound of the guitar. Savagely damning Hannah and her singing, he returned to the couch and reaching for the bottle re-filled his glass.

*   *   *

He slept at last, face down on the couch, a cushion pulled over his head. When he next came to consciousness it was to lie only half awake in the grey morning light, while from the tree beyond the window the harsh chorus of a flock of starlings drilled remorselessly into his head.

With temples hammering and mouth foul and thick from tobacco, he lay with closed eyes, struggling to break the thread of his dream...Ellie, looking back over her shoulder and crying as she ran, himself running on leaden feet trying to catch up with her before she was gone...falling, falling...turning over and over into the water as he leaped with frantic outstretched arms to grasp and save her...

But it hadn't been like that. Ryan sat, cradling his head in his hands. He hadn't tried to stop her, hadn't been there; in fact had never ever been there for Ellie when she needed him.

He stumbled to the bathroom, cleaned his teeth then stripping off his crumpled sweaty clothes stepped under the shower, turning it to cold and letting the water cascade over his head, shuddering and gasping as the icy needles pounded his skin; scrubbing at hair and body as though by punishing himself he could erase the hideous memory of that day.

Stepping out at last and wrapping a towel about his waist he climbed quietly to his room and careful not to disturb his sleeping son dressed quickly then ghosted downstairs and out into the rear yard.

It was still early, not yet seven o'clock. He filled his lungs with the damp morning air and made a conscious effort to dismiss the depression left by the dream. He'd come through it all, hadn't he? Still had a life to live, even if he couldn't see his way past the next twenty-four hours. He was back in good old grey drizzly England again and he'd be crazy not to take the first opportunity to set the record straight. There may be, even after all these years, something left from that dichotomous time of beauty and carnage, love and hate. Someplace worth a re-visit, some person who might ask, "Hey, you remember when?" See, even at a distance, that someone with the laughing eyes who, despite war and the consequences of war, had made the world an almost perfect place.

He took another deep breath. Just one visit, that was all, one trip to get the past all cleared up and out of his mind then maybe he could work out some kind of a future worth the having.

*　　　*　　　*

If Hannah noticed he was hung over and particularly vulnerable that morning she didn't comment; accepting his excuse that he had work to prepare she tactfully suggested she and Joel should go to church, then go sightseeing afterward. Relieved Ryan escorted them to the bus stage before returning to Marlborough Street, where he swallowed a heavy dose of Aspirin and crashed straight out onto his bed.

*　　　*　　　*

He awoke late afternoon. Through slit eyes he could see his mother was stood by the bed holding a couple of seltzer tablets poised over a glass of water. As he groaned and struggled up onto one elbow she dropped both tablets into the glass and handed him the fizzing mess.

'Can't think what you've done to get so all tuckered out,' she said with a bland smile. 'Drink this and see if you turn back into Dr Jekyll.'

He drank the seltzer shuddering then stood, smoothing his hair and tucking in his shirt. He said shortly, 'I'm fine.'

'Maybe you should have come to Mass with Joel and me.'

'Don't start that, ma. You go your way and I'll go mine. I don't mind you taking Joel to Mass with you sometimes but don't you brain-wash that boy.' He picked up his brush and began to punish his hair. 'Right now he has a good open mind and I aim for him to keep it that way; make his own choices.'

Hannah didn't answer, just picked up the empty glass and left the room, only pausing at the doorway to say over her shoulder, 'You shouldn't drink, Ry; it gives you pink eye and makes you scratchy as a dog with fleas!'

Ryan waited for the door to close then examined his eyes in the mirror. He scowled and turned away with a light shudder. She was right as usual, darn her.

*   *   *

As Hannah was more than willing to take on the job of taking and fetching Joel to and from his new school Ryan left her to it, and on the first morning of the school term escaped to the civilised environs of the university to work on his timetable for tutorials and lectures. He got a kick to find his name already on the door of his room: Professor Ryan L. Petersen. It made him feel he belonged and he began to look forward to the start of the University year.

Homeward bound that afternoon and half way down a narrow one-way street, a clapped out but nippy Ford in front of him stopped suddenly and without warning, dead centre of the roadway.

'Shit!' Ryan hit the brake hard and screeched to a halt inches away from the rear fender of the stalled car. Immediately another car braked behind him then another and horns began to sound. Shaken by the near miss he leaped out and slamming his door stalked up to the Ford demanding, 'How the sweet Jesus did you manage *that*?'

'I didn't *manage* anything!' A woman struggled from the driving seat and traded glare for glare. 'And if you can't be halfway civil, just shove off and let me find a *gentleman* who'll be some help!'

He looked into her snapping dark eyes then down at the oil seeping from beneath the car. 'I reckon you'll need more than a gentleman to get this heap going again.'

She said, 'Bugger!' then her face crumpled and for a moment she looked as though she was going to cry.

By now the cacophony of horns operated by impatient motorists was approaching the sound barrier and despite the fact that she'd insulted him, the old macho protective bit rose to the challenge. 'Look, before it gets real ugly, why don't you get back in and steer and I'll get a couple of these guys to help push you into that alleyway over there. OK?'

Clearly unimpressed she sniffed. 'Thanks – but it's not an alleyway, it's a mews.'

Having put him in his place she slid back behind the wheel, a manoeuvre that had her skirt ride up displaying a pair of very shapely legs. Ryan managed a long and appreciative look before she flushed, pushed her skirt down over her knees and slammed the car door on him. He grinned, said, 'Don't leave the handbrake on now, will you?' then went to the back of the car, where a couple of very fast movers from the TR2 stuck behind his own car were already flexing their muscles. Together they pushed the Ford into the mews then the pair from the sports car shook hands all round and left Ryan to restart the Jowett and continue his journey. But on a sudden impulse he gave a valedictory blast on the horn and waving the line of cars behind him on, turned into the mews. Stopping a few yards behind the Ford he switched off his engine, climbed out and strolled with his lose rangy walk toward the dead car and a closer look at the owner of those legs.

She wasn't bad he thought, even though her short curly hair was all over the place and she was looking mean as an ill-tempered camel. Beneath the scowl she had a cute face and great eyes and her long bare legs really were out of this world. But on closer inspection he saw they ended in a pair of Jesus sandals beneath an ankle length cotton skirt with a loud and eye-wrenching pattern. An embroidered, off the shoulder peasant blouse tucked into a wide belt with an ornate silver buckle covered a pair of shapely but disappointingly small breasts, the whole strange ensemble topped by Gypsy Rose Lee earrings and a raffish looking fringed green wrap flung about her shoulders and knotted carelessly at the neck.

Despite the crap clothes and the slender, almost boyish figure, she was still pretty edible and Ryan felt another definite carnal stirring of the loins. However, an even closer inspection disclosed a wedding ring, while a steely glint in the eyes and a determined tilt to the chin all added up to a tough cookie. Disappointed, he decided she was not at all his type; a pity, but there it was, he didn't go for tough women, particularly married ones.

She climbed out and stood beside her car, biting at her lip and looking around distractedly. 'I have to get home. My daughter will wonder where I am...'

After her bad-tempered snarl and that explosive "bugger" Ryan was surprised to hear the cultured tones of the well educated Brit coming from someone who at first sight looked like she was straight off the front line of the chorus in Carmen. He gave her the once over again and sighed. 'Tell me where home is and I'll take you – '

'There is no need,' abrasive again, she interrupted his half-hearted offer of help to give him a disdainful look, 'she is with my neighbour and I can telephone.'

'How will you get home?'

'There are things called buses and trains – you may have noticed them,' she gave the Jowett a meaningful look, 'but then again, perhaps not.'

Great legs she may have, but he didn't take that sort of put down from any woman. Ryan stalked back to his own car, got in, fired the engine and started to back up. She began to walk alongside and as he reached the road called, 'Sorry – thanks for your help.'

With clipped New England freeze-dried courtesy he answered, 'My pleasure ma'am, think nothing of it.'

She rolled her eyes heavenward. 'Over here, Yank, we only call the Queen ma'am.'

'Well now,' he answered with biting sarcasm, 'over *there*, that's what we call a lady – ma'am!' and accelerated away before she could get in another snappy back answer. Smart-ass he thought, his temper simmering, a pity because those legs really were quite something.

*　　　*　　　*

By evening he was still turning the encounter over in his mind, annoyed and irritable he'd let that Calamity Jane get to him. By now he thought sourly, she was probably telling hubby all about how she'd put some rude Yank in his place.

He sat by the fire while Joel chattered to Hannah and played with his rocket and the Action Men he'd brought from home. Absorbed in his own thoughts it took a while to register that both Hannah and Joel were being unexpectedly enthusiastic about the journey to and from his new school, so enthusiastic that Ryan forgot the sassy woman for a moment and began looking for the hidden agenda that had to be in there somewhere, and as patience wasn't Joel's strong point, he soon found it.

'We went up top on the bus – the school's real close. With that tower thing at the corner you can almost see it straight off if you sit in the front. It's easy isn't it, gran'ma …just a coupl'a stops,' Joel beamed at Hannah, his confidence so obvious that Ryan immediately smelled conspiracy. Joel paused to fix guileless green eyes on his face and give an angelic smile. 'So now I know the way I can go on my own – can't I dad?'

'Are you kidding? Of course you can't. London's a big place and you have to cross a mighty busy road before you even get to the bus.'

Joel blinked, confidence wobbling but he hung on in. 'If gran'ma takes me to the stop I can go on from there; I know where to get off.'

'Sure, why not,' Hannah gave Ryan the kind of bland look that confirmed his suspicion they'd already fixed things up between them, 'he'll be fine by a couple of days. It's only a short ride and the bus stops just along the street from the school.' She smiled at Joel. 'I'd still pick you up, mind.'

Joel's face flooded with gratitude. 'All right Gran'ma, so can I do it the day *after* tomorrow, dad?'

'I said no.' Ryan put the boot in quickly. What the hell; he might not have much authority but what he did have he intended hanging on to. 'We get this week over first, so I can see if you behave yourself before we make with the independence; we'll maybe talk about it again then.'

Joel muttered, 'Talk, talk; always talk!' he looked appealingly at Hannah who shrugged and gave him a sympathetic smile. Turning his head he gave Ryan a duplicitous sidelong stare before some instinct for self-preservation kicked in and he wheedled humbly, 'Then can I go on my own *next* week?'

'You've a whole seven days of keeping out of trouble to get through first,' Ryan snapped, 'manage that and you should get a citation from the President, step out of line once and I kid you not, *I'll* take you to school – every day until we get back home to Bracket Sound!'

Hannah ruffled Joel's hair with a sympathetic hand. 'Guess your papa's got you there, boy,' she said and shot Ryan an ironic look. Jesus, he thought, what was it with her that she always put him in the dog-house, he must have been smashed when he agreed to have her come to England. If he'd brought along Lady Macbeth to housekeep it would have been a more even fight.

Later he went out into the garden to smoke a pipe and think again about the Calamity Jane's legs, wondering idly how they'd look in one of those cute mini skirts and if her husband appreciated them as much as he had. He heard Joel splashing around in the bathroom and felt a sudden twinge of guilt over his son's bid for independence. If he hadn't still been annoyed by the brush-off he'd received earlier from Calamity Jane he might have seen the funny side of those two ganging up on him; been more ready to bargain, instead he'd cut his mother and Joel down in the same way as that darned woman had him.

After a while Hannah came out to join him and they sat together on the wooden bench for a few minutes in silence. Finally Ryan said dryly, 'Nice try ma, but don't do that too often. Joel doesn't need any help from you to be a pain in the ass.'

'And you don't need any help to make like a bear with a sore head. Maybe I shouldn't have gone along with him, but I guess he needs to feel *someone* is on his side. For a boy without a mother you're a tough kind of father to have.'

'For a boy *with* a mother Lars was a tough kind of father to have.'

'Sure he was, but he cared about you and loved you – only like you he just wasn't any too good at showing it.'

'Damn right he wasn't,' he said with feeling, 'the only time I got any warmth from him was when he belted my butt; that warmed me all right.'

'Then don't make the same mistake with Joel. He doesn't cut up because he's a bad boy; he does it because he needs you to take notice he's around; see he's someone worth loving. You got to trust him, Ry and you have to talk to him about Ellie and what happened. I hate to think what he's got locked away in that head of his. It won't come out for me but it might for you.'

Ryan suddenly lost it. 'God damn it all to hell, ma, what am I supposed to do when he dodges any mention of his mother – ram it down his throat? Don't you think I got enough crap in my own head without stirring his?'

She sighed. 'Well Ryan honey, you are supposed to be all grown up, so I guess I think you should have the guts to find some way to help that son of yours let it all out. Then perhaps he can stop worrying and being a pain and just have fun again like a boy should.'

If there was one thing he hated it was being cornered. *Talk to him. Trust him.* How could he? He couldn't even trust himself. 'I'll think about it,' he said grudgingly, 'but don't expect miracles.'

She said cryptically, 'They happen.'

He gave a brusque shake of the head. 'Not for me they don't.'

3

MARLBOROUGH STREET, CHELSEA

September 1965

It took Hannah less than a week to get to know the neighbours, join a Bridge club, fix up a cleaning lady, a middle-aged diminutive cockney named Doris, discover that the thirty-something woman on the corner of Marlborough Street was single and a doctor at UCH, and invite her to dinner.

Ryan watched his mother pull out all the stops. The dinner was great and the Doc a real looker. If to Hannah's intense and obvious regret they didn't strike any immediate romantic sparks from each other they certainly sparked something else, but were both old and experienced enough to keep it under wraps for that evening at least.

After their guest returned to her own house Ryan sought refuge from his mother's disappointment in the downstairs study. Life, he thought, might just be about to take a turn for the better. Deliberately he shut his mind to the possible consequences of starting something on his own doorstep with a woman he'd only just met. He wouldn't push it, but after his long enforced celibacy knew if the offer was made, and he was pretty sure it would be, there was no way he was going to refuse.

*   *   *

A couple of days later they met up again and over a drink in the corner bar shared a laugh at Hannah's abortive matchmaking. Charlotte, ("call me Charlie") Lawrence, was a psychiatrist at University College Hospital, with a long-term businessman lover at present on temporary loan to his firm's Bangkok office. By the end of that week, like two drifting sticks coming together in a stream, Ryan and Charlie had moved into an amiable relationship: sensual, romantic even, but practical. She had a long lovely body that he explored with the thoroughness and appreciation of a man who'd been too long without a woman, and she was fun. It was quite a while since he'd made love laughing but in the weeks following that first evening in her bed they did a lot of that. Afterwards, they would lie back on the pillows and smoke a joint, then make love again before he dressed and went home.

Charlie asked nothing more of him, nor he of her. Without spelling it out, each knew that when her lover returned Ryan would step out of the frame and stay out. Civilised that was Ryan and Charlie.

The comical aspect of him with his mixed up head and murky past screwing with a lady shrink didn't at first register. When it did Ryan found it kind of appropriate; the therapy was great and he figured that it beat lying on a couch and just talking.

*   *   *

The university year started, Doris came on two mornings a week to polish furniture and vacuum carpets as though her life depended upon it; the household settled into a comfortable routine and Joel had achieved his heart's desire and now travelled alone to school each morning; more, he had a special friend, a small girl by the name of Nicole. Ryan raised no objections when Hannah let him go to tea with her on a few evenings after school. It kept the boy out of his hair and gave him an opportunity to slip along to Charlie's in the early evening while Hannah was fetching Joel home from whatever corner of London the child lived.

Although for the first weeks of the university term good manners meant Ryan had to attend a series of getting-to-know-everybody drinks evenings organised by the wives of other dons where there was generally at least one determined academic, male or female and usually from a science faculty, which said a lot, to button-hole him and describe in detail the beauty and/or brilliance of one or more unmarried daughters. But altogether and taking these flaws into consideration, life was pretty good. He found his feet quickly at the college and thanks to Charlie, was able to resist any temptation to sample the charms of the daughters, concentrating instead on getting to know his students; their needs, strengths and weaknesses, and enjoying the academic round.

There was only one thing still nagging at the back of his mind and towards the end of October and when the first feeding frenzy surrounding a new and unattached male on campus had faded, he finally did something about it.

*   *   *

On a crisp bright morning he drove out of London, a road map spread on the seat beside him, the weekend stretching ahead free of all company but his own.

Once clear of the sprawling capital the road unfurled, familiar and remembered. As towns and villages flashed past he discarded the map altogether and navigated from memory. Almost he could feel the bounce of the jeep over patched bomb-damaged roads, hear the raucous voice of Mike Hogan raised in song above the roar of the engine: "*Oh, how I hate to get up in the morning/Oh how I hate to get outa bed*" and Bernie's riposte, "*Outa who's bed, buddy?*"

For over a year a forty-eight hour pass had meant just one thing to most of the bomber crews: get to London, get a woman, have some fun and if you were very lucky, get laid, but by the summer of nineteen forty-three the camaraderie of Rainbow Corner and the less wholesome pleasures to be found around Piccadilly and in the back streets of Soho, had ceased to be a part of Ryan's life. By then he'd been spending all his brief respites from war in a small discreet hotel in Bloomsbury, in the arms of the woman he loved more than life itself.

*　　　*　　　*

Now the Jowett was running past tall hedges on the long road from Winchester. Slowing down as he passed through the village on the edge of the Hursley Forest he recalled this was where he and Claire had taken refuge in the church one afternoon, from a squadron of German bombers heading for Southampton docks.

Nothing had changed overmuch he thought, as he picked up speed again on the wide straight mile down towards Romsey, the war might never have touched the place except for the memorial cross with its sober engraved lists of killed and missing sons.

Once around Romsey and out past the Salmon Leap he put his foot down hard on the gas and headed for the Forest. As the miles sped by he began to sing aloud: '*Gonna make a sentimental Journey, Gonna set my mind at ease… Gonna make a sentimental journey, and revive old memories*,' until an uncomfortable tightening of the throat made him falter and stop.

He was almost there.

In the distance he could see the sharp right turn that led to the long lane, the high hedges of hawthorn either side. Memory took him down to the guard post at the end, the flat tarmac of the runway, the squat control tower, the line of vehicles: supply and crash and fire trucks and the inevitable meat wagons with the painted Red Cross on top and sides. Dominant over all else the huge hangers, within and before them ranged the great menacing birds of prey.

Peaceful, tranquil Hawksley's very own Wing of B17s.

*   *   *

He left the car at the cut-in and walked the final fifty yards to the entrance of Falcon Field.

Coarse grass grew in thick tussocks between the broken slabs of the concrete around derelict buildings, the runways pooled with rain-water. To the far left of where he stood at the site of the guard post were clustered the remains of the Nissan hut offices of the US Station and Group Commander. Beyond these the sparse remains of cook-house, mess halls and row upon row of the dozens of other huts and buildings that once housed the US bomber and ground crews alongside the handful of RAF men and women who had helped keep the B17s in the air and for whom this place had for a few crazy years been home.

Above the control tower a tattered rag of windsock stirred in the light breeze and Ryan released a pent-up breath, Jesus, what a mess. The few brick or corrugated iron buildings still left standing had shattered windows, with crumbling walls or rusted iron sheets, while wooden doors hung drunkenly on broken hinges or lay rotting in the grass.

Someone should have cleaned this place up, he thought sadly, not left it lying abandoned, like a discarded mistress way past her prime.

Scrunching over broken glass and splintered wood to the runway he faced the long line of trees that rose like a great wave before the rolling bracken and gorse acres of the New Forest. Closing his eyes he dug deep into memory...

Propellers fired and turned, the thunder of their engines drowning the birdsong as the *Boston Babe* taxied preparatory for the long run to take off. Then the slow lumbering start, the full-throated roar as he pulled back on the stick, the nose lifted and they were airborne. The voices over the headphones: *'Tail to turret – reckon you're gonna get us there an' back, Ry, before all the turkey get's et?'*

'Just cut the crap and keep your eyes on your guns Manny, or you'll be having your Thanksgiving dinner in Paris, France!'

Ten of them there'd been in the old Fortress, the names forever in his memory: Pilot and co-pilots Ryan Petersen and Mike Hogan, forward and below them in the nose, bombardier Glen Scott, behind,

38

navigator Ed Walker; Bernie Schultz in the upper turret and further along radio operator Art Lingren and his dorsal gun, with Pete Palmero in the ball turret. Then along the catwalk to Charlie Segar and Ray Berger wisecracking and cussing along at the waist guns; Perry Manaserro in the tail... Hoagy cracking the latest Goering joke over the intercom, the staccato blasts as guns were checked in the empty skies over the English Channel then, all banter over, they were flying in formation and in total silence over the water. Ryan felt again the tangible tightening of nerves already stretched fine as the coast of France drew closer, the awareness that the ground batteries and the Luftwaffe would know they were on their way, and be ready and waiting with the welcoming party...

Opening his eyes he came back to the present, to the deserted runway and the broken buildings. Turning around slowly he faced the lane where he'd left the car. From where he stood it was just two miles to the village of Hawksley and as the crow flew over Belstead Wood, just one mile thirty-two yards and a five-barred gate from Hawksley Manor and Claire Louise de Lacey; one time lover of Ryan Petersen, mother of Rupert and wife of Brigadier Geoffrey Howard de Lacey, M.C. and Bar.

*   *   *

Skirting Hawksley he drove on to the next village and The Bull Inn at Stafford Lay; a great pub he remembered, where the acid-tongued but soft hearted Nellie Parsons had welcomed the American invasion; reasonably tolerant of their high spirits and the occasional fights that broke out, so long as they kept the bar busy and the money ringing in the till.

Nothing here had changed thought Ryan, as he stopped on the forecourt and stepped from the car. Still the same long wooden benches either side of the studded oak door, the Inn sign hanging slightly crooked; even a black Labrador lay sleeping in the shade of the plane tree, just as Dick Wardell the shepherd's wall-eyed collie Fly had more than twenty years before.

Ducking his head under the lintel, where gilt lettering informed patrons that the landlord was one Nathaniel Marsh, Ryan stepped through the door and down the worn wooden step into the bar. Immediately the particular rich English country pub smell of smoke, ale and the sharper tang of spirits caught at his throat.

A young couple wearing shorts and sweaters sat at a table in one corner, their bulging haversacks on the floor beside them. In the

39

opposite corner an old man smoked his pipe, knotted brown fingers curled around a tankard of dark ale on the table before him, a small brown rough-haired mongrel at his feet.

Suddenly, despite the familiarity of his surroundings Ryan felt an out of place stranger. Nodding briefly at the hikers and the old man he walked self-consciously to the counter and hitching a foot on the brass floor rail began feeling his pocket for his pipe, looking up as a young man came through the curtain at the rear of the bar.

''Morning, sir,' the barman gave him a cheerful grin. 'What'll it be?'

'Scotch on the rocks, I guess.'

He looked shocked. 'You want *ice* in your malt?'

Ryan found his tobacco and began filling his pipe. 'I sure do; is that a problem?'

'Ah, a Yank!' the barman winked and setting the glass down leaned an elbow on the bar counter invitational to a chat. 'I remember your lot from the war – always wanted their beer cold and their Scotch iced. Old Nellie Parsons who owned this place then called 'em uncivilised heathens to their faces!'

'I remember Ma Parsons– I've seen her come from behind that flap to break up a fight and belt the beejesus out of a half-dozen of us guys.' Ryan shook his head reminiscently. 'Scared the hell out of us until we got used to her – she still around?'

'Nah, she's been over in the churchyard these seven years.' The barman grinned. 'My dad was the pot man in them days, now 'e's the landlord. I was just a nipper – used to hang around waiting for your boys to drop me chocolate or some gum. My dad hated that gum – walloped me good and proper he did when he found it stuck under me bed. "Eddie," he said, "you swaller any of that stuff an' it'll stick yer insides together like glue!" Hey, remember that song: *Does your chewing gum lose its flavour on the bedpost overnight?*' He guffawed and hitched his elbows more comfortably on the counter. 'What brings you back here then, mister?'

'Just thought I'd have a look around,' Ryan was carefully non-committal. 'Would you have a room for a couple of nights?'

'The season's over now sir, so you can take your pick. If you'll 'ang on a minute I'll take you up.'

*   *   *

Ryan unpacked his bag in the long low ceiling room. Stretching full length on the bed he found it deep and firm and the pillows soft, so guessed he'd maybe sleep easy that night.

He washed up and brushed his hair before returning to the bar for a lunch of bread and cheese, then sat over a beer to make some kind of plan for the rest of the day. Maybe he'd go out into the Forest proper, he thought, over to Brockenhurst, or to Buckler's Hard and see if anyone was sailing.

A surge of nostalgia for Brackets Sound and the *Dancer* washed over him and from the corner of his eye he could see Eddie, ostensibly polishing glasses but watching him closely; when Ryan turned to look at him he asked, 'Made up your mind where to go today, sir?'

'Not really – thought I might take a look at the water; I'm kind of missing that.'

'Do a lot of sailing, do you?'

'Yep, a fair bit.' He added incautiously, 'but sailing isn't what I came for.'

Casually Eddie began to wipe his damp cloth over the bar counter. 'Looking up old friends then are you, sir? Where was you stationed during the war then – that big base over Beaulieu way?'

'No, we were the early birds – the big bases came later. We took over from the RAF's Lancasters at Falcon Field.' Ryan grinned reminiscently. 'They left some of their ground crew and WAAF's behind for us tho' – nice guys, great chicks!'

'Ah, 'awksley. I remember that – your lot give a big Christmas party in the old village hall one year, didn't you? Must have been 'forty-two or three – '

''Forty-two.'

'Yeah, that's right. It was all the nippers from 'awksley and 'ere and Everberry... never forgot that party, we didn't. See, we'd been rationed so long us younger ones 'ud never seen so much grub all at once – sick all next day some of us was!' He laughed and slapped his hand on the counter. 'You lot was devils for the girls though, wasn't you? My dad used to lock my sister in her room of an evening if he knew you was throwing a party for big boys an' girls,' he winked. 'He didn't know she was out of 'er window and over the lavy roof when there was a dance on. Went barmy 'e did when she got a bun in the oven; still she become a GI bride and lives in California now she does – you been there?'

'Once or twice,' Ryan finished his coffee and stood up. 'Not sure if I'll be back for dinner – that OK if I just show up late?'

'Sure, and if you're in after midnight, me dad'll leave the side door on the latch. Cheers, sir, and enjoy your day.'

Enjoy? Ryan thought as he settled into the car, not quite the word he'd have chosen for this wallow in nostalgia. Pulling out the choke and turning the key he sat uncertain for a few moments, allowing the engine to idle. On the village green directly opposite the Bull stood a signpost, the right arm pointed towards Brockenhurst, the left towards Hawksley.

He said aloud, 'Get it over with, you dumb ox!' and swinging the wheel to the left, put his foot on the gas and took off down the lane.

*   *   *

Reaching the village he passed the first of the cottages then slowed the car, idling along the one street and reading the names above the row of small shops. Only two had changed purpose and as far as he remembered the remainder still had the same names above the windows. He braked suddenly and killed the engine, staring in dismay at the smart blue doors and white painted window frames of a low red brick building. On the wall by the entrance hung a board with *HAWKSLEY VILLAGE HALL* painted across the top and bore notices giving times for Dramatic Society, Parish and Women's Institute meetings; thumb tacked to one door was a brightly coloured poster for the village Playgroup.

For a few minutes he sat rubbing a hand over his chin, wondering what had happened to the old hall; that small squat building with peeling paint, fretted bargeboards and grubby windows criss-crossed with brown tape.

Ridiculously disappointed and put out he slumped in his seat, remembering the first time he'd stepped into that old unlovely wooden building, with its corrugated iron roof and draughty doors; back in nineteen forty-two when they'd all worked their butts off to throw that Christmas Party.

Back to that first, never to be forgotten moment when the inner doors had opened and Claire de Lacy stumbled through them to fall into his arms and into his heart...

4

HAWKSLEY, HAMPSHIRE

December 1942

Captain Ryan Petersen leaned against the doors, smiling at the volume of laughter from fifty or so kids at the Mickey Mouse cartoons Sergeant Duffy was showing on the shaky screen. Remnants of the party littered the long tables, only the paper napkins and plates and emptied juice cups remained, every crumb of food and every last spoonful of ice cream had vanished, devoured by their small guests.

Suddenly he became aware that someone on the other side of the doors was trying to open them; he moved quickly to one side and a woman in British Red Cross uniform half fell through the opening.

'Gee, ma'am, I'm sorry,' he caught at her arms to steady her. 'Are you OK?'

She gave a gurgle of laughter. 'I'm fine, thank you; it was my fault, I expect I pushed too hard. I thought it had jammed – it does that sometimes.'

Still holding her arms Ryan Petersen gazed down into a pair of the clearest, largest grey eyes he had ever seen and felt his heart do a sudden crazy back flip. At that moment there was a concerted yell of laughter from the children and she raised her voice to speak above it. 'How much longer before they finish, do you know?'

He found his own voice, 'Just coming up to the end now, ma'am.'

'Oh, good, it's Nanny's day off – I have to collect my son and I'm on duty at the hospital in an hour.'

Ryan couldn't take his eyes off her. Only a half-head short of him, she had a smooth bell of mid-brown hair, a smile that could melt a glacier and a sensational figure. Her voice, low and slightly husky, was definitely classier than anything he'd heard so far in Hawksley. A light sweat broke out under his collar and he asked hastily, 'What do you say I fetch him for you?'

'No, I don't want to spoil it for him; I can wait a little longer.' She waved to a small boy perched on a windowsill, who gave her a beatific smile from lips sticky with candy. She blew a kiss and the boy blew one back with an elaborate puff of the cheeks. 'That's my Rupert.' she said, and Ryan grinned.

'He's cute, but I have to tell you he's already chucked-up twice!'

'Chucked what?' For a moment she was puzzled then her face cleared. 'Oh, you mean he's been sick; how disgusting.' She laughed outright. 'Nanny will feel vindicated; she said he shouldn't come and now I'll be in hot water because I let him.'

Ryan reassured her quickly. 'Believe me, he wasn't the only one – and he went right back and ate some more.' Cheers and whistles rose to a sudden deafening crescendo as the film flickered to an end with Pluto chasing a cat into a diminishing circle of light. Hastily pushing open the door again he motioned her outside. 'I guess you'd better wait out here, ma'am. Sergeant Duffy will quieten them all down before their minders arrive.'

Laughing, she put her hands over her ears against the din of excited childish trebles. 'How will he manage that?'

'Back home the sergeant has eight kid brothers and sisters. He knows what he's doing when the going gets rough.'

Taking her arm he steered her into the deserted vestibule, pushing the door closed with his foot, determined to get this woman alone for a few minutes and find out as much as possible about her before that hoard of Norman Rockwell urchins burst from the hall. Smiling down at her he offered his hand, 'Ryan Petersen, ma'am.'

'Claire de Lacy.' her handshake sent a long lick of fire snaking up his belly. 'I daresay we shall meet again sometime as my mother-in-law is planning a simply enormous New Year Dance. She's very anxious to have as many of your countrymen join us as can be spared from the aerodrome.' She grinned mischievously, confiding, 'I think she has a secret passion for Glenn Miller and I wouldn't be at all surprised if she wasn't looking to pick up a few tips on how to jitterbug!'

'Gee, how old is your mother-in-law?'

'I've never dared ask –'

She broke off and Ryan turned, trying to mask his irritation as the outer doors of the hall swung open to admit a man and woman, closely followed by others, arriving singly and in pairs to collect their children. Claire de Lacy gave a smile and slight shrug of what he hoped was regret, before turning to greet several of the new arrivals by name while he stood aside and watched.

Obviously married, with a child of around six, maybe seven, a house large enough to hold a "simply enormous" New Year's dance and attendant mother-in-law, this woman, who was making his body warm dangerously and his heart beat faster with every passing second, was definitely out of bounds...

Sergeant Duffy poked his head around the door inviting, 'Come and get 'em, folks!' Ryan sighed and levered his shoulders from the wall. *OK. So she's married, but that doesn't stop a guy talking to her, does it?*

He smiled at her over the heads of the crowd, stepped back into the hall and made straight for the small boy with hair sticking up on end and socks hanging around his ankles. 'C'mon, soldier; your mommy's here so let's go get her!' He swept him up on to his shoulders and the young Rupert squealed with delight, holding on tight with a fist full of hair as Ryan strode back across the room. Stopping before her, he said, 'One cleaned-up boy, ma'am, safely delivered '

'Thank you kindly!' Laughing she held out her arms as Ryan bent his back to let the child slide from his shoulders. For a minute she held his gaze over her son's tousled head. 'Thanks again. Don't forget that New Year's dance. We shall expect to see you then, Captain Petersen.'

'Ma'am, I wouldn't miss it for all your tea in Boston Harbour,' as she turned to leave he raised his hand, 'I'll see you…'

'Pop, you dirty old dog!' Scottie came from behind and hit him in the back. 'You should be ashamed; an old man like you making it with a classy doll like that.'

Ryan gave him an amiable grin, 'Twenty-five may sound old to a little squirt of nineteen, but I've been out there pitching a long time while you probably haven't even got to first base yet. So go find yourself some popcorn and the funny papers and leave the serious stuff to the men.'

*   *   *

When Claire returned from the hospital that evening, Nanny Elgin was lying in wait in the hall and launched straight into the attack. '*Mrs* de Lacy, I have to tell you that Master Rupert's been sick all *over* his best shoes – and I've had to *burn* his socks!' Her voice rose to an indignant vibrato. 'I said he shouldn't go – all those rough village children – '

'Don't be such a snob, Nanny.' Claire was too tired after her hours on the ward for diplomacy. 'It didn't do him any harm when we had all the 'rough' evacuees here, did it? He had the time of his life and cried buckets when they left. Anyway he'll meet tougher – and rougher, characters when he starts prep school next year. Their vowels may be more refined, but they'll still be disgusting little savages under the skin.'

Nanny stood her ground. 'But eating all that unsuitable food – little wonder he was sick.'

'It does no harm for a greedy seven-year-old to suffer the consequence of making a pig of himself.' Claire pulled off her cap and threw it on to a chair. 'I'm going up to bathe and change before dinner. Perhaps you'd tell my mother-in-law I am home.'

She climbed the stairs slowly, already regretting her hasty tongue. Poor nanny, she really mustn't get on the wrong side of her or she might up and leave, then where would they be? Nanny and cook were the only living-in staff they had now, managing with just Polly from the village to clean and a part-time gardener for the grounds. Thank goodness the Min. of Ag. had taken over the East and West wings last year. At least the responsibility for keeping those parts of the house cleaned and heated had been taken off her hands.

Since Geoffrey had left for North Africa almost eighteen months ago the running of the house and the Home Farm had fallen heavily on her shoulders. While Marion did what she could around the house and Old Elias did his best to run the farm with the help of his two young sons, since Cowell the Estate manager had been called up Claire had to face a weekly struggle with the farm accounts and the myriad Ministry forms and directives.

I'm still young, she thought resentfully, sitting in her few inches of cooling water and trying to imagine a sumptuously deep and deliciously hot pre-war bath. Twenty-seven isn't old but by the time this war is over I shall be a worn out hag.

She smiled to herself. Judging by the look in that young man's eyes today the ageing process didn't seem to have progressed too far as yet. She thought about his height and the smooth tanned skin, those amazing blue eyes and the thick blonde hair that had shone pure silver under the light. Beneath the easy laid back charm he had about him a very definite air of being in command, of being his own man. She liked that.

Aware the water was now several degrees below tepid and she had goose bumps all over from the cold air filtering under the door she pulled the plug and stepped out, shivering and reaching for a towel. She should be thinking about Geoffrey in far off North Africa, not one of those young men who, if rumour was to be believed, were simply sex on legs and a menace to British womanhood. But that, of course, might just be wishful thinking!

Wrapping the towel about her she scurried along the passageway. God, but the house was freezing. Without fuel to run the central

46

heating boiler or the comforting fires they used to have lighted each evening in the bedrooms, they really would have to find some way to deal with the draughts that whistled beneath doors and around the big casement windows. She hurried into a long wool dress: war or no war, Marion still expected her to dress for dinner, even if dinner was no more than Spam fritters lurking under watery parsley sauce, or the eternal casserole, made from whatever one or other of Elias's boys had managed to shoot or trap that morning...

Please, she prayed silently as she brushed her hair; let it not be tough old pigeon or rabbit stew *again* for dinner tonight!

*   *   *

Ryan lay stretched on his bed with hands clasped behind his head and a cigarette between his lips, going over in his mind the events of the afternoon. *Claire de Lacy*...what a woman! He wondered how old she was, what her husband did and if he was around at all. Can it, he told himself, she's married, and you don't want to have her old man coming after you with a shotgun.

But it was no use. The memory of those eyes and the low voice with the husky little catch in it just wouldn't go away. He crushed out his cigarette and turned restlessly, hunching on to his side and staring at the blacked-out window. If the weather held they'd be flying again tomorrow; which might just be the mission when the *Boston Babe* flew through one ground barrage too many, so there was no guarantee that he'd ever see her again.

If he didn't make it back he wondered if she would miss him at the New Year's party.

*   *   *

'Right, so it's Brest again gentlemen,' Wing Commander Miles Townsend, the British Met Officer, took over from old man McIllhenny. 'You will be pleased to know that the weather will be delightful, with no more than a balmy sea breeze over the channel and a little altocumulus at around 600 feet over your target...'

'"Brest again, gentlemen – and the weather will be de*light*ful"' Hoagy mimicked. 'That guy slays me!'

Pete Palmero groaned. 'Not titty again; last time over there I nearly got my fuckin' ass shot off. For Christ's sake, haven't we bombed goddamned France enough? When're we gonna get a crack at Germany?'

'Don't be in too much of a hurry we'll be there soon enough.' Ryan's voice was heavy with sarcasm. 'Remember, it's a hell of a lot further home from Germany. France'll just do us fine for now. Count your blessings while you can.'

*   *   *

The raid on Brest was bad. Within minutes of their rendezvous with their fighter escort over the channel they were intercepted by a squadron of F.W.7s; the rattle of their guns and those of their own Mustangs soon joined by heavy anti-aircraft fire from the ground on the approach to the French coast. The *Babe* was in the centre of the group and in a great spot to be caught by the ack-ack guns. Ryan held tight formation through the flack as tracer bullets sheeted across the sky, seeing from the corner of his eye one of the FWs shoot past on his starboard side, a Mustang on its tail. Easing his oxygen mask from his cold cheeks he glanced around at the other Forts and returned a thumbs-up with Tom Nielsen on his port side. They were almost at target; all Scottie had to do was let go his bombs onto the right spot and they could get the hell out of it.

Puffs of smoke, harmless looking as candyfloss were exploding around them and the aircraft rocked continuously. Concentrating on holding course on the rapidly approaching target, Ryan was jolted by the sudden *whumph* of cannon shell and a split second later felt the hit. The aircraft heaved, staggered and dipped to starboard and even as he righted it, a heart-stopping bubbling scream sounded from the nose then quickly petered out. The skin crawled on the back of his neck as his fingers, numb with cold, found the switch on his mask. He cleared his throat, 'Pilot to navigator.'

'Yeah, pop?' Ed's voice was laconic.

'You OK?'

'Yeah, but it was fuckin' close and I guess Scottie's been hit.'

Ryan signed to Hoagy to take over the controls and for the space of a few seconds sat immobile, thinking of all that could be happening in the bomb bay beneath them. He said tersely, 'OK Ed. Get in there now and let me know what the damage is. If there's any fire, deal with it. We're over target in under five and those bombs have got to go.'

As he pictured the navigator worming his way forward into the cramped nose his mind raced over a half-dozen horrifying possibilities: Scottie was dead...fire had broken out ...the landing gear was wrecked and he'd have to land the ship on her belly...the bomb release had buckled, the bombs were stuck and they were all dead meat. He took a deep breath and spoke with a calm confidence that almost had him convinced.

'Pilot to navigator – you there yet?'

He could hear Ed's heavy breathing, then, 'There's a fucking great hole in the deck – '

He interrupted crisply, 'How bad?'

'It's big, man, but *big*! No fire tho' and all the bomb release gear looks OK. Scottie's out of it ...not shrapnel – looks like he got it through the fuselage with machine gun fire an' he's taken it in the leg.'

'Does he have a pulse?'

'Hold it while I get my glove off...shit, but it's too cold to feel a fuckin' thing...I think he's OK – just passed out with shock and he's bleeding a lot. Want me to take over?'

All their guns were blazing now as the FWs swooped like hawks through the formation. Ryan twisted his head around, registering the gap on the port side where Nielsen's craft had been. As he looked the space was filled by the *Alabama Blue* with Tod Parker jabbing his thumb down to where a Fortress spiralled earthward, slowly and gracefully like in a silent movie. Ryan counted three chutes open before the plane exploded and a wing ripped off, slicing through the cockpit of a diving Focke-Wulf and turning it into a blazing fireball.

His mouth dried, filled with the smell and taste of rubber from his mask, but his mind was clear and already grappling with the task ahead. 'You get him out of there,' his voice was level, 'then check the bomb doors. Artie, come forward and see what you can do for Scottie and if it needs it get a tourniquet on that leg fast.' He grimaced at Mike's raised brows, his hand hovering again over the switch on his mask.

For a long agonizingly tense couple of minutes there was silence over the RT apart from the navigator's laboured breathing, 'OK, Pop, he's out an' I can see Artie coming. Everything's ready to go.'

'Know what you're doing?'

'Yeah, no sweat.'

'Then it's all yours.' He put his hand back on the controls. 'Target coming up *now*... Watch your leader.'

'OK, skipper...steady, steady...Holy *shit!* ' The plane staggered as a shell exploded alongside; for the first time the navigator's voice rose. 'Fuckin' hell, pop, I said steady! Now left...more...a bit more...*now*, keep her *real* nice and straight...'

Down in the nose, hand around the bomb release, thumb over the button, Ed's stomach slid and slipped like wet Jello. He began to hum:

'*Since I kissed my baby goodbye*' while the sweat ran down his face and froze in the icy air that poured through the open gun ports and the jagged hole in the deck.

*   *   *

They lost eight Forts in all and the *Boston Babe* returned home a deal less pretty than she set out. The calm, clear voice of the WAAF R/T operator acknowledging Ryan's homecoming call with: 'Hello, C Charlie, hello C Charlie, this is Juno answering ... receiving you loud and clear, strength niner, over...' sounding like the heavenly choir to the anxious crew. After a bumpy landing and an exhausting de-briefing, Ryan logged the flight then crashed out on his bed, blanking out how close they had come to disaster. To remember was to threaten nausea and a return to the momentary but shaming gut-wrenching funk he'd felt when they were hit.

*   *   *

He jack-knifed up on the bed his forehead beaded with sweat and his mind still in the damaged fortress, *Shit!* How long had he been asleep? He peered at his watch. Christ – only an hour! He swung his legs off the bed and stood swaying for a moment, then crossed to the door. Hazily, he thought he'd go see how Scottie was. First though he needed a drink, but going into the crowded bar was beyond him right now. Walking down the hallway to Mike Hogan's room he poked his head around the door. 'Got any rye in here? I'm clean out.'

'Sure, come and join the party.' From the depths of the single armchair Hoagy gestured towards Manny and Ed, sprawled across the bed, glasses in hand. Manny raised his in salute.

'Hi ya, pop – the smell from the mess hall's not that hot so we reckoned a drink or two first was a good idea.'

At the mention of food Ryan's stomach heaved. 'Think I'll take a rain-check on eating tonight and go see Scottie instead.'

'You'll be wasting your time; he'll still be out to lunch.' Ed drained his glass and held it out. 'Another, Hoagy, I ain't legless yet!'

'No, and you not going to get it tonight,' Ryan intercepted the shot Mike was about to hand his navigator. 'The guys are already halfway to getting the old ship patched up. If we fly again tomorrow I don't want some boozed up fink navigating me all the way to France and back.' He ruffled Ed's curly head, 'Nice work today kid; you did well.'

50

'Just don't do that to me again, pop, I fuckin' near wet my pants over that bomb release!'

'You and me, both, Ed.' Ryan sank onto the bed beside him, listening to but not joining in the banter. He allowed himself a couple of drinks then got back on his feet. 'Think I'll go and check on Scottie all the same. Any of you guys coming with me?'

'Nope,' Manny gave him a sly grin, 'we all know why you're so hot to go, Ry...reckon you're hoping to get another shot at nursie-nursie!'

Ryan grunted. 'Nah, she'll be home fixing her old man's supper by now,' he straightened and buttoned his jacket, 'see you later, boys. Enjoy your hash.'

He returned to his room; splashed cold water over his face and cleaned his teeth. Picking up his brush he began to smooth his hair, all the while eyeing himself in the mirror. *OK, so Scottie won't be around for hours, but what the hell, you only live once. So, Mrs Claire de Lacy, if you're still there, here I come...*

Picking up his trench coat he left the room, whistling *Lili Marlene* and thinking it was kind of handy to have a good excuse for taking a jeep off base without having to bribe the sergeant mechanic in charge of the pool.

*   *   *

The corridors of the small cottage hospital were hushed and quiet and Ryan trod them warily, wondering if Scottie would be guarded by the kind of dragon he'd encountered back home on his one and only visit to a hospital. On that occasion he had been the patient, with a fractured collarbone gained in an over-enthusiastic tackle during an ice hockey match with a load of gorillas from Carmel. A nurse came suddenly from a side room and asked pleasantly, 'Are you lost?'

'I guess so. The old guy at the door said to come this way – I think!' He grinned. 'All these corridors look alike. I'm after Sergeant Glenn Scott.'

'Oh, yes, he's in here.' She walked a few feet and opening a door beckoned him in. 'He's still sleeping off the anaesthetic I'm afraid, but you can stay a few minutes.'

Ryan thanked her then looked around the small room, bare apart from the narrow bed, a hard upright chair and wooden locker. The bedclothes were raised over a metal cage to protect Scottie's wounded leg and he looked curiously small and vulnerable beneath the white covers. Like a kid, Ryan mused, but at just nineteen that was about all he was – a kid.

As the nurse closed the door he drew the chair up to the bed to sit gazing at the boy's pale unconscious face. Poor little bastard; he sure looked rough. He took one of Scottie's hands in both of his own and raising it resting his chin on his clasped hands. 'It's OK, kid, you've still got both your legs and you'll soon be back dropping your bombs short,' he said aloud. 'When you wake up again just think about that Purple Heart and you won't feel a thing!'

There was no response to his words but he continued chatting. 'Wonder who we'll get to replace you; whoever it is, lets hope he's got a better aim than you...only kidding, pal. You're pretty damn good for your size and we'll miss you...we'll surely miss you. So get back to base real quick...'

*   *   *

On her way home Claire thought she would look in once more on the American boy they had brought in that afternoon. By the time she came on duty tomorrow he would have been moved to the larger and much better equipped US Military hospital some twenty miles away in Lowood. With her fingers on the door handle she glanced through the round glass view window and paused: someone was with him. The visitor's head was bent over the hand clasped in his own; she couldn't see his face but there was no mistaking that hair. She smiled. It was the American captain she'd spoken with at the children's party.

At the sound of the opening door he looked around and made to rise, but she motioned him to remain seated, whispering, 'It's all right. I only looked in to see if he was awake yet.'

'No, ma'am: still out of it, I'm afraid.'

'He will be transferred to Lowood first thing tomorrow for more surgery on that leg – no broken bones fortunately but it's a nasty wound and the bullets went deep. Will any of you be able to visit him over there?'

'I guess we'll manage between missions.' His mouth broke into the slow lazy smile she remembered from the previous day. 'I'll miss the little runt.'

She laughed. 'When they first brought him in he kept asking for 'Pop' Petersen.' She gave him a teasing look. 'Why did he call you that?'

'Well, now, I'm the oldest guy in the crew you see. Scottie here started it and I guess it kind of stuck.'

He let go the boy's hand, tucking it carefully under the coverlet.

'I'd better leave now.' He glanced at the cloak thrown over her nursing uniform. 'If you're on your way home, ma'am, can I offer a lift?'

'Oh, that would be wonderful. No petrol to spare for the car I'm afraid: I usually walk. I just have to pop over to the nurses' home to change – it's a hanging offence to be seen outside of the wards in this outfit.'

'I'll be out front in the jeep.'

'Give me ten minutes then...' she turned at the door, adding, 'Pop!' with a mischievous smile

*   *   *

Ryan took a deep breath and waited for his heart to stop banging about in his chest. She really was something else again; he hadn't felt like this since High School when he'd borrowed pa's old Chevvy to drive down to the shore and neck with little Mary Lou Cassidy.

Outside the hospital he sat in the jeep, gazing up at the cold night sky and waiting impatiently for her to reappear. In his top pocket was a letter from Ellie, full of hometown gossip and sexy reminders of when they'd been together, although she'd never let him go all the way like some girls would. But then girls like Ellie would always hold out for that ring on their finger before they'd give in. He thought about her for a minute or two; how her hair shone like burnished copper in the sunlight; the pale freckles over that tipped up nose, the wide green eyes and the feel of her breasts under the soft sweater...

Then Claire de Lacy was walking towards him, smiling and looking a million dollars. As he jumped from the jeep all thoughts of Ellie Sullivan were abruptly severed as he took her hand in his.

5

HAWKSLEY, HAMPSHIRE

October 1965

'Can I help you, sir?'

Startled, Ryan looked around into the concerned face of a young Police Constable. For a moment he was completely disorientated and stared back uncomprehending as the constable bent closer to the open car window. 'Are you all right, sir? Not ill or anything?'

How long had he been sitting here? The man probably thought he was a nut case! Ryan pulled his wits together. 'No. Thanks. I was just...' he gestured at the village hall. 'It's different...not as I remember...'

'Ah, yes, sir. I'm told the old one was hit by a buzz-bomb in 'forty-four, so thanks to that old Hitler, Hawksley got a nice new hall.'

'I kind of liked the old one.'

'Can't say I knowed it then, sir; I only come here from Fordingbridge a couple of years back.' He glanced at his watch. 'Well, if you're sure you're all right, sir, I'll be off to my tea.'

'Yeah, sure; sorry if I gave you a problem.'

'That's all right. Enjoy your visit, sir.'

There it was again, he thought, watching the young man pace away. Enjoy, enjoy...he gave a short laugh and started the car. Driving on through the village and turning left at the T-junction he cruised slowly down Sweetwater Lane, slowing the car to a crawl as he reached the tall wrought-iron gates.

On either side, topping the stone pillars reared an ornamental lion, between its paws a shield with the de Lacy coat of arms. Beyond the gates a tunnel of Chestnuts faded away down the long drive, their branches touching, shielding from the lane the handsome Jacobean mansion.

Ryan remembered with a stab of nostalgia how the leaded windows caught the afternoon sun; spilling an uneven pattern of light over the grey flagged hallway and bringing to life the heavy wall tapestries. For a few moments he loitered, slipping the clutch and creeping at snail's pace past the gates, then suddenly impatient with this mawkish wallowing in the past, sent the car surging forward again.

At the end of the lane he turned to retrace his route. About to re-pass the gates he slammed on the brakes. Set to one side and slightly askew, which was why he'd missed it the first time, was a green and gold notice board.

HAWKSLEY MANOR
HOUSE AND GARDENS OPEN TO THE PUBLIC
SAT. SUN. AND BANK HOLIDAYS, 10am to 4pm
APRIL 1st TO OCTOBER 31st
ADMISSION 5/-

He sat staring stupidly at the board. He'd heard things had gotten tough in Britain since the war, that death duties and all the taxes their socialist government had dreamed up had stripped the landed gentry of most of their cash, but *this*...he glanced at his watch and felt a sudden irrational disappointment: it was ten after four, too late to do anything about it today. He pulled himself up sharply, what the hell...he couldn't just pay his money and stroll around the place like some culture hungry tourist.

Suppose you were to walk right up there, what then? he jeered silently. *For Chrissake, she thinks you're dead, remember? You're the guy who flew off one morning and never came back. And what about her old man – yeah, what about Brigadier Geoffrey Howard de Lacy; how would you introduce yourself to him: 'Hi, buddy, you don't know me but I'm the guy who slept with your wife while you were screwing your leaves away in North Africa – you don't mind, do you "old boy"?'*

With sweating hands he gripped the wheel; easing the long nose of the car out of the narrow lane he turned it again towards Hawksley. He'd get the hell away from here; drive down to Beaulieu; spend an hour or two by the water, then return to The Bull and have a leisurely evening meal and an early night.

Tomorrow he'd get himself back to Chelsea and forget all about the de Lacys and their bloody Manor. It had been stupid to come, stupid to think he might get a glimpse of her and double damned stupid to think that if he did it would make a flying fuck's worth of difference to his bloody awful life.

*   *   *

A Barn Owl hooted. Ryan lifted his head from the pillow and listened for the call to be answered, rewarded after a few seconds by a long *whoo*. Restless he pushed back the bedclothes and reached for the switch on his bedside lamp, flooding the room with light.

Sitting on the edge of the bed, cold in his silk pyjamas he thought again about his brief aborted visit to Hawksley that afternoon; remembering a chill New Year's Eve when moonlight sparkled on snow, an orchestra played "They Didn't Believe Me" and he held Claire de Lacy in his arms for the first time.

He leaned forward clasping his hands between his knees. What a night that had been: the huge hall, a Yule log burning in the cavernous stone fireplace, the walls covered with holly and ivy, a great fir tree in one corner, decorated with tinsel strands, silver bells and ribbons. In the gallery overhead a small orchestra had struggled valiantly to emulate Glenn Miller, but finally given up in favour of more traditional old-fashioned quicksteps and waltzes.

He had stalked her, Ryan remembered, like a feral cat and once he'd captured her had kept her close, savouring her hand in his, the sweep of her long gown around his legs, the slip of silk beneath his fingers. A singer had joined the orchestra; he had a good tenor voice with sexy undertones that sent all kinds of feelings pulsing through him...

And when I tell them, how beautiful you are
They'll never believe me, they'll never believe me...

That was the moment he decided there were altogether too many other people around them, and bending his head to hers asked: 'Can we get out of here for a while?'

She'd looked up at him very thoughtfully for a moment then smiled, and when they reached the far end of the hall drew him towards a door in the corner.

'Through here; ten minutes only. It's almost midnight and we shall have to be back before then.'

Ryan remembered he'd grinned and said, 'Ten minutes will do,' not knowing then that even a lifetime wouldn't be enough.

6

HAWKSLEY MANOR,

New Year's Eve, 1942

She said, 'I must go back.'

He held her closer. 'Not yet.'

Moonlight streamed through the long windows of the gallery, throwing sharply contrasting pools of light and shadow across the polished floor. Dancing in and out of the shafts of light they moved effortlessly, like people who knew each other well and had danced many times together; not strangers who had scarcely met, knew little about each other, and where one at least was living only for the moment.

It was tantalising, erotic. Ryan wondered how much longer he could hold out before he kissed her. Clasping her hand close against his heart he smiled as the music changed. 'Who's idea was that?' he asked and she gave her throaty chuckle.

'My mother-in-law – she will always see that is slipped in somewhere. The Merry Widow waltz is a part of her salad days.'

'Is that so? It makes a guy wonder what she did with them then!'

Slowly he spun her away from him then drew her back; into his arms and into the waltz. Looking down into her eyes he sang softly:

> *'Lippen Schweigen s'flüstern Geigen*
> *Hab Dich lieb*
> *All die Schritte sagen bitte*
> *Hab mich lieb,*
> *Jeder Druck der Hände deutlich mir's beschrieb*
> *Er sagt klar,*
> *S'ist wahr, s'ist wahr*
> *Ich hab Dich lieb…'*

The waltz quickened and he swung her, light in his arms; spun faster and faster until he wasn't sure whether the room was moving around them or they around the room. He willed the music to go on, delaying the return to the crowded hall, the rowdy whistles and cheers that would usher in nineteen forty-three; for the time denying all thought of a return to war, conscious only of the woman in his arms.

The music ceased. She stood still in the circle of his arms smiling up at him. 'You sang that as though you knew the language, not just the song.'

'I teach European Literature to undergrads: it helps to speak at least some of the lingo.'

'And you can dance a Viennese waltz, too – a man of many parts!'

Yeah, he thought, and some of them are giving this man one hell of a problem. Close by an owl hooted suddenly, she grimaced and said, 'Those wretched things get into the attic to roost and keep me awake at nights.'

'He's only calling for his mate.' Ryan moved his hand slowly down her back, felt with a sudden turn of the heart the electric shiver of her response and bent his head towards hers. But at the last second before their lips touched she took her hand from his shoulder and pressed it gently against his chest to move his suddenly urgent body away from her. 'Not a good idea, that.' Her voice was unsteady and slightly breathless. 'I must go back. I shall be missed.'

'If you go back *I* shall miss you.'

She shook her head, her eyes solemn, 'But I am the hostess of this party and I must not stay here any longer. In a few minutes it will be tomorrow.'

He looked down into her eyes, holding her gaze. He asked, 'Do you know what I've learned over these past months?'

She answered lightly, 'No. What have you learned?'

'That there is no such thing as tomorrow: only today.'

She gave a rueful little smile, 'but tomorrow always comes.'

For a moment the temptation to kiss her anyway was almost overwhelming, but he knew that in a very nice, very oblique, very English way he had been put in his place; that despite the unmistakable response of her body she at least had kept her head and managed to retain the illusion of the good hostess indulging the whim of a guest.

He gave a wry, defeated smile, raised her hand, kissed her fingers and released her with a slight, mocking bow. 'Then I guess it had better be Auld Lang Syne with all the trimmings!'

'I rather think it should be just that, Captain Petersen.' She led the way to the door at the end of the gallery then stood for a moment with her hand on the heavy brass handle. Her voice softened, 'but thank you for a lovely, special dance. I enjoyed it very much.'

He bowed again. 'Thank *you*, ma'am; it was my pleasure.'

He followed her through the door, into the sudden blast of laughter and music. Eyeing her slender back in the midnight blue silk dress that did amazing things to that already sensational body, he reflected that war and the likelihood of a sudden demise was making randy dogs of them all. No wonder Uncle Sam's invading forces had gained the dubious and not altogether unfounded reputation of being, as Ivy Wastel the village postmistress had complained in his hearing, "ready and willing to jump anything in a skirt". He reflected that men away from home and under daily threat of death would always behave badly, and there would always be girls willing and able to help them do so.

All the same, there had been more to his dance with Claire de Lacy than a desire to indulge his own baser feelings and needs. He sighed as he linked hands for Auld Lang Syne with Homer Orbach, the *Boston Babe's* temporary bombardier from Tennessee. Although it had been a bonus to discover her husband was safely out of reach in North Africa, she was still married and that should, must, make her unavailable to him or any other Johnny-come-lately.

*   *   *

Caught up in the hurly-burly of welcoming in the New Year, the conga-lines snaking around the hall and the noisy Paul Jones, they hadn't danced together again that night, only passed close several times, exchanging brief smiles before they were swept apart. When it was all over, "Auld Lang Syne" sung again, the lights dimmed to allow the guests to slip through the heavily curtained doorway and out into the crisp white night. Unwilling to take the transport back with the rest of the merry well-oiled crowd he had lingered in the shadows of the stone portal, hoping she would show herself once more so that he might make a personal goodbye beyond that formal handshake while the older Mrs de Lacy looked on. But as the minutes ticked by without sign of her he realised he was waiting in vain.

'Are you taking root, sir?' He saw a young WAAF sergeant was standing looking up at him. Glancing at the flash on her sleeve, then back at her face he recognised her as one of the girls from air control in the tower. She settled her cap asking, 'It's Pop from C Charlie, isn't it? I talked your kite into base the other week after you'd caught a packet.'

He gave her a speculative look, noting the *retrousse* nose, the short upper lip showing a glimpse of small even teeth, the softly rounded figure in Air Force blue, and gave his lazy smile. 'We sure were glad to hear you.'

'Always nice to be appreciated, sir,' she smiled back then looked around the deserted courtyard. 'I must fly – I seem to have missed my lift.'

He hesitated then thought, *Why not*? Offering his arm he said, 'Me too, so I guess I'd better walk you back. It's not safe for you to be alone with all these Yankee wolves around!'

She gave a gurgle of laughter. 'What about you?'

'Me?' He grinned amiably. 'You're safe with me, sergeant; I'm housetrained.'

She answered 'If you say so, sir.' and taking his arm walked with him down the long drive, the snow crisp beneath their shoes, a bomber's moon riding high above the trees.

For a long time afterward he remembered that walk back. Sergeant Robyn Graham had a soft Highland accent and a great smile, like someone had thrown a switch and lit her up from inside. Depressed and out of sorts over his failure to dance again with Claire, her youthful high spirits and ingenuous company were irresistibly appealing.

'Do you have a boy friend?' he asked as they approached the lane leading to the base.

'Yes, sir, he's a fighter pilot and we're going to be married next week by special licence.' She bounced a little, like a puppy eager to please. 'We can't afford a big do so the wedding breakfast and the champagne will have to wait until later.'

'Congratulations.' He smiled down into her shining face, ruefully saying goodbye to the lecherous thoughts he'd been harbouring of necking a while with her in the little cut-in under the trees. 'You've got it right, sergeant – live for the day.'

'Oh, not only for the day, sir,' she was earnest, looking up at him with a self assured smile, 'for *all* the days; the war won't last for ever you know.'

When they reached the guard post, had shown their papers and passed through, he walked with her to the area situated at the far end of the camp and isolated from the men's quarters by a high linked fence. Halting outside the gateway he took off his cap and bending, kissed her briefly on the lips.

'Thanks, sergeant, for keeping a lonely airman company.'

She grinned and mimicked his accent. 'You're welcome, sir!'

'Goodnight, Robyn Graham; enjoy your honeymoon.'

'We will, sir – and thank you for walking me back.' She opened the door, whispered 'Goodnight, sir,' and blowing him a kiss through the wire stepped noiselessly out of sight.

*   *   *

Ten days after the walk on that New Year morning, the pilot of a Dornier bomber came out of the clouds on a surprise raid to test the defences along the south east coast of Kent. Chased by a Hurricane he jettisoned his last bomb. It fell on a small seaside hotel, killing outright Robyn Graham and her new husband as they slept in each other's arms.

7

HAWKSLEY, HAMPSHIRE

Late October 1965

In his room over the bar of The Bull Inn Ryan closed his eyes in a spasm of pain. The return to old haunts after so long was becoming more emotionally charged than he'd expected. Why had he recalled that incident so clearly...the feel of crisp snow beneath his shoes, the moonlight glittering on white hedges and the small figure bobbing along at his side, so confident of her future happiness...*Not only for today, sir...for all the days...*

Since his arrival at the Inn that morning, past and present had begun to merge into each other, allowing deeply buried and painful memories to surface, threatening the defences he had so carefully constructed over the years. Wearily he tried to reason what made anyone even try to take over and run their own show when God, the Fates, or what you will had such a nasty habit of taking charge and leading every poor sap down whatever crazy paths they wished.

He turned out the light and humped back down under the bedclothes. Well, he had to face it; a man could only chase a dream so far. Even if he found Claire, what could he do? No, it was all beginning to hurt too much. Tomorrow Fate was going to lead him right back home to Chelsea, and more basic therapy from Charlie.

*   *   *

But by the morning and after a good night's sleep the cowardly urge to abandon his search was replaced by a determination to give Hawksley another shot and the hell with the consequences. Leaving his bed he padded on bare feet to the window and pushing it wide leaned on the sill. Now that he could think more rationally he realised that with the place open to every Tom Dick and Harry it was unlikely any member of the de Lacy family would be in residence. But even if there was no hope of seeing Claire he could return to London knowing he had confronted and hopefully laid to rest at least one ghost from the past, even such a relatively minor one as driving once more up that long familiar tree-lined carriageway to view Hawksley

Manor in all its Jacobean glory.

In the back yard below the window, Eddie was sluicing a bucket of water over the cobbles. A pale sun had done little to banish the early morning frost and the air was sharp and invigorating. Ryan's mind took another of those disturbing leaps it had been making recently, this time back to a crisp New England October morning and a similar cloudless sky, when a younger Ryan in a new charcoal grey suit and sober tie, filled with misgiving about the wisdom of what he was about to do, but too hopelessly needy and involved to have resisted that inexorable progress towards Holy Matrimony, knelt with his bride before the altar rail of the Church of the Immaculate Conception. An hour and a full Nuptial Mass later he'd done it, and with Ellie beautiful in white lace walking beside him down the aisle he knew that he had just made what was possibly the biggest mistake of his life.

Suddenly impatient with the morbid stupidity of his thoughts, he turned back into the room and taking up his shaving kit made for the bathroom. After a short tussle with a recalcitrant water heater he managed to run a bath of sorts, wondering as he lowered himself into the tepid water, when the English would get around to fitting showers as standard with their room lets. Bathing quickly and towelling dry with a rough towel that smelled of fresh air and lavender, he shaved with more than his usual care and returned to his room.

He dressed in yesterday's grey cords; broke a new pale blue shirt from its cellophane wrapping, swearing aloud as he jabbed his thumb on one of the half-dozen pins needed to keep its pristine packaged shape, added a tie then changed his mind and chose another then changed his mind again, replacing both with a dark blue paisley cravat he'd bought in the Burlington Arcade. Tucking it into his open shirt collar he grinned at his refection; what a laugh Abby would let loose if she could see him now!

We miss you, Abby – how about taking a holiday here in England- perhaps next spring? I guess the Elliots and that husband of yours could get along without you for a while. Joel and me will walk you down the Kings Road; take you shopping and send you back home with one of those silly pancake hats and an Ossie Clarke suit – or even better, buy you a pvc mini skirt and an authentic SS Obenfurher's cap from Carnaby Street...

He laughed out loud, knowing she would never come. 'Breakfast!' he told his reflection firmly and picking up his tweed jacket went down the narrow turned staircase towards the tantalising smell of frying bacon and freshly brewed coffee.

*　　　*　　　*

At a few minutes after ten there were already several cars and a coach parked on the gravelled area beside the house. He cruised first around the fountain on the front drive and past the open front door, where he could see a middle-aged woman seated at a table presiding over a cash box and a stack of leaflets. After making one more circuit to check he'd never seen her before, he parked alongside the other vehicles in the car park then scrunching back over the gravel climbed the steps, two half-crowns ready in his hand.

'I'm afraid you've missed the start of the first tour, sir.' The woman glanced up with a smile from her task of placing coins in a cash box, 'Will you wait? It only takes about half-an-hour.'

'Sure, I'll take a stroll around outside if that's OK.' Ryan looked past her into the hall. 'Does the tour take in the whole house?'

'Oh, yes, and you are free to go anywhere in the grounds but the stable yard and cottage: those are out of bounds.' Her gaze lingered on his face and he saw her expression sharpen for a moment before she smiled again. Fingering the pile of what he could now see were guides to the house and grounds she asked, 'Would you like one of these?'

'Of course,' he forced himself to return her smile and fished in his pants pocket for sixpence. Not that he needed any guidebook; he knew every inch of the place by heart. One thing was for sure, there would be no chance encounters today. He thought sourly that he need not have tormented himself with what he should do were he to come face to face with Claire, or anyone else from the past. It was possible the family no longer owned the place; even supposing they did they'd most likely be shacked up somewhere abroad until the last visitor had buggered off back to Texas or Tunbridge Wells or where the hell else they'd come from.

He made his way around to the back of the house via the terrace, pausing for a moment to stoop and brush a hand over the thyme which grew between the flags before descending the broad stone steps down into the formal gardens, the beds still hedged with box and filled with late flowering roses.

Passing through the opening in the eight foot high yew hedge he traversed the narrow paths around the walled fruit garden, then skirting the tennis court walked towards the lake lying cold and still under a pale sun. For a while he stood on the bank watching for any sign of the Golden Orf that in summer moved lazily through the

64

water, but on this chill morning they were well below the surface and out of sight beneath the reeds.

Leaving the lake he took the gravel path leading to the stables, pausing on the way at the iron courting gate that gave access to the big meadow, on the far side of which stood a five-barred gate, beyond that the broad sandy ride through Belstead wood.

He considered walking across the meadow to the woodland, but the grass was long and wet and spending the next hour or so with soaked shoes and trouser cuffs wasn't on. Turning around he began setting the geography of the grounds in his mind's eye.

To his left lay the railed parkland, dotted now with grazing sheep; to the immediate right but still out of sight were the stables, the stable cottage where old Elias, his wife and sons had lived, beyond that the big hay barn and open-front sheds that had, in his time, housed tractor and farm equipment and a cumbersome old-fashioned band saw. After a momentary hesitation he chose the right hand path alongside a hawthorn hedge that would take him on the permitted side of those "out of bounds" stables and cottage, wondering if either or both of old Elias' offspring were still living there; how many horses were now in the stables and who rode them.

Reaching the end of the hedge he turned on to the wide hard standing before the broad carriageway running between twin paddocks and beneath the arch into the stable yard. He smiled to see the clock in the gable over the arch was still broken, its hands at a remembered quarter after three...

From the corner of his eye he caught a movement and for a moment took a step back in time. Bemused, he stared at the jet-black, big-boned hunter grazing the short paddock grass. Impossible, he thought; it couldn't be.

Heedless of trespass he walked over to the rails and leaning his arms on the top called softly, 'Sampson?' The horse lifted his head and snickered and Ryan let go a long breath. 'Geez – it really is you – hey, come over here Sampson you old devil, and tell me hello!'

The animal plodded over to where he stood and put his nose in his hair, blowing and nibbling gently as he had two decades before. The signs of age on that noble, once proudly held head; the hollows above the eyes, the sunken cheeks, were unbearably moving, so much that Ryan felt his eyes warm dangerously. As Sampson snickered again and blew into his shoulder, Ryan laid his head against the stallion's neck, talking softly, his hand rhythmically stroking the still glossy coat.

Suddenly the horse gave a shrill welcoming whinny and Ryan

spun around, almost falling over a wheelchair parked no more than six inches away from his legs. Fleetingly he wondered how the man seated in it had come upon him so silently, even over the smooth tarmacadam of the path, until he saw the wheels were fitted with unusually thick pneumatic tyres.

The newcomer looked up at him, his expression neither welcoming nor hostile, and as Ryan gazed down into a pair of pale blue, blandly enquiring eyes beneath a leonine head of pure white hair, his stomach did a rapid kind of sideways dip.

It was a face previously seen only in photographs and the portrait that had hung in the dinning hall of the manor. Then the hair had been black shot with grey and the lines on the craggy face less deeply scored. *Holy mother of God,* Ryan felt a bubble of hysterical laughter rise in his throat. *Geoffrey Howard de Lacy...so we meet at last!*

De Lacy's eyebrows rose fractionally and he asked with polite irony. 'Perhaps you would care to tell me from where you have sprung – and why you are canoodling with my horse?'

Recalling that meeting later Ryan didn't know how long he stood looking down at the apparition in the wheelchair, only conscious that Sampson was nudging his back and with the footrest of de Lacy's chair practically touching his ankles there was no way he could get out of this particular situation with any kind of dignity. At least he thought, collecting his scattered wits, so far as the owner of Hawksley Manor was concerned he was merely a trespasser whom he was undoubtedly about to see off.

Summoning a smile he spread his hands in apology. 'I'm sorry, sir, I guess I shouldn't be here at all, but I was just looking around until the next tour of the house was due and kind of lost my way.' He rubbed Sampson's nose again. 'I saw this old boy and came to talk to him.'

'And did he tell you his name?'

Ryan's uneasy stomach glissaded to somewhere around his kneecaps while sweat gathered at his hairline. He hesitated then compromised with a half-truth. 'I recognised him. An old guy used to exercise him back during the war. I often met them when they were out on the road.'

'Uh, huh, that would have been Elias; he might have been old but he had a good touch with a horse – helped me break this feller. We'd just got him going nicely when I had to go overseas.'

'Yeah,' Ryan rubbed Sampson's nose again. 'He was a great ride...' as the words left his mouth he realised his second mistake and added hastily, 'I...guess; from what I saw of him!'

The light blue eyes narrowed as if de Lacy had registered the correction, but he only put his hands on the wheels of his chair, backing slightly but not moving so far that his captive could easily walk away. As Sampson gave another shove he observed in a neutral tone of voice, 'He'll have you over if you're not careful. He's become demanding in his old age – as do most of us, eventually.'

'That so?' in control again Ryan kept it light. 'I can't wait; it'll be one way of getting my own back on my son, who's giving me a hard time and doing all the demanding right now.'

'Ah, there you have the advantage of me. I don't have one of those, demanding or otherwise.'

Ryan opened his mouth then shut it again quickly. What the hell was de Lacy talking about? Hadn't he carried this man's son on his shoulders, taught him to swim in the lake, taken the lead rein of his pony and run alongside him around the paddock where Sampson now grazed?

Suddenly he wanted out of here and away from this weird old guy who was obviously a whole heap of sandwiches short of a picnic and whose eyes had never for a moment left his face. He took a hold on his nerves and tapped the guide book; 'Sorry again if I was trespassing, sir; guess I'd better be getting back to the house, else I'll miss my tour.'

De Lacy smiled suddenly and turned his chair towards the stable yard. 'Then I mustn't delay you further. I am told it is a rare treat and not to be missed.'

'Goodbye, sir; it's been nice meeting you.' Sweating again but this time with relief, Ryan began to walk back in the direction he'd come. He had almost gained the safety of the hawthorn hedge when de Lacy answered him in a benign voice that was almost, but not quite, devoid of mockery, 'Goodbye, Mr Petersen, it's been nice meeting *you* – at last!'

Ryan kept walking; along the hedge, past the tennis courts, through the gardens and straight to where he had left the Jowett. Climbing in he fired the engine and with a scattering of gravel turned and sped down the drive and out through the gates.

And all the way on that drive back to Stafford Ley and the Bull he could feel those parting words stuck like a rapier between his shoulder blades.

*   *   *

Arrived at the Inn he went swiftly up to his room to sluice his face with cold water at the washstand. Picking up a towel he started to dry his face then stopped suddenly to peer even harder at his reflection, turning over again in his mind the last words Geoffrey de Lacy had addressed to his retreating back.

He turned every look; every nuance of the few words exchanged between them over and over in his mind and was still baffled. Even if the man *had* discovered his existence, either through gossip, or more likely his son's sour-faced old nanny, there was no way that from any description given twenty years before the man could have instantly recognised him, an unheralded stranger.

Again he leaned his hands against the basin and stared into the mirror. The face looking back was light years away from youth: weather-beaten, lived in, cynical; cheekbones more prominent, mouth harder; the thick silver hair longer now and cut by an artful and ruinously expensive Mayfair barber, flopped in casual fashion across his forehead. The narrow blue eyes, all there was of Hannah in that face, stared back at him, bemused and uncertain.

A very different face from that of the young Ryan Petersen, who had ridden Sampson in all his magnificent power and glory across the gorse and heather of the Forest on that unforgettable winter's day in nineteen forty-three.

8

HAWKSLEY, HAMPSHIRE

January 1943

Claire heard the thunder of the approaching 'planes and crossed to the window to watch their return. Ink black against the pale grey of the winter sky the stragglers came in twos and threes behind the main force and she hoped as she had done in the weeks since New Year, that the *Boston Babe* and all her crew had returned safe and sound.

Ryan Petersen hadn't been particularly subtle about engineering all their "casual" meetings, she thought with a smile. Her walk to and from the hospital over much the same route on four consecutive afternoons a week had made such encounters fairly easy. That she looked forward eagerly to these meetings with the quiet American caused her only the occasional twinge of conscience. Geoffrey, even on home ground, had hardly been the most attentive or faithful of husbands and she was under no illusions about how he might be spending his spare time in Alexandria. The meetings with Captain Petersen had lifted her spirits, making her feel young and attractive again – and, yes, desirable. It was proving very good for her self-esteem to have a man look at her with admiration in his eyes – and such eyes. Sinful eyes, she thought, and with a sinful mouth to match them.

'Back again, thank goodness; poor lads, they don't have much rest, do they?' Her mother-in-law came into the drawing room, shivering and pulling her cardigan more closely around her. 'I only hope they return to find warmer quarters than ours. Yesterday I even found myself wondering how I could appropriate some of that coal the Ministry people had delivered last week! We really should think about closing up everything downstairs but the small sitting room and study, then we could at least heat a couple of rooms properly.'

'Better forget about the Ministry coal,' Claire smiled. 'I'll bet that woman in charge counts every lump. Tomorrow I'll get Polly to help me move the small pedestal table from the hall and we can have our meals in the study instead of that draughty dining room.' She linked her arm with her mother-in-law's. 'Come into the kitchen now and I'll make a pot of tea to warm us, then before I go on duty this afternoon

I'll call in and ask Elias' boys to fell the old beech that was struck by lightning at the end of summer. It will still be a bit green but should provide enough wood to keep us warm until spring. I'm free all over the weekend so if they get a move on first thing in the morning, we can take the long trailer down and pick up in the afternoon.'

'I thought you had earmarked that time for the farm accounts.'

'I had, but those can wait until Sunday.'

'Don't overdo it, Claire dear. I worry about you.'

'You shouldn't; I'm as strong as a horse. Which reminds me…if this thaw keeps up the ground should be soft enough by morning for Elias to exercise Samson. I promised Geoffrey I'd try and keep him up to scratch but he's really too strong for me. If Elias wants company I'm quite happy to take Dolly for a hack.'

Marion gave her arm a gentle squeeze. 'Yes, my dear; get out and away from this place and the hospital for an hour or two; it will do you good.'

There are a number of things other than keeping the horses exercised that would do that, Claire thought as she filled the kettle and set it on the range. Another party like they'd had for the New Year for instance, and a chance to let down her hair once again with the handsome Ryan Petersen. She wondered what it would have been like if she'd let him kiss her that night. She had a sneaking suspicion it might have been a far cry from any such embrace she'd ever received from Geoffrey, who's sole contribution to romance had been to occasionally climb into her bed and ask, "How about it, then?"

To which enquiry, she remembered with a stifled laugh, she'd invariably given the standard answer of, "Yes, all right," if in the mood or "No, not tonight," if she wasn't. Either way he hadn't seemed to mind. Sex with Geoffrey had been infrequent, quick and seldom passionate, but with nothing with which to compare the experience, she had always accepted as normal the infrequency of his demands and her response, or lack of it, to them.

Scarcely out of the schoolroom and starry-eyed at the proposal of the considerably older, distinguished and then attentive Geoffrey, she had rushed into marriage with scarcely a thought for the future. But the totally inexperienced young woman she had been must have fallen far short of *his* expectations. Never the most patient of men, once the necessary son and heir had been achieved he quickly returned to enjoying the company of a variety of willing and considerably more experienced lovers.

Claire rested her hands on the wooden handle of the kettle and stifled a sigh, how far away and unimportant all that was now and how little she cared.

*   *   *

Marion noted the shadowed look in her daughter-in-law's eyes, while her sharp ears heard the almost inaudible sigh. It must be four months at least since the girl had received a letter from Geoffrey. Of course the mail was unreliable but it was more likely to be a lack of thought or interest on her son's part than any inefficiency of the BFPO's mail delivery.

She loved her son, in a dutiful, motherly way, but aware of his deplorable morals and lack of commitment to home and family, there were times when she found it very hard to actually like him.

Married at twenty to the now deceased General Edward Howard de Lacy, she had suffered a similar fate to that of her daughter-in-law. There was something very wrong with the de Lacy men, she thought; their wives could be ravishing beauties but the grass on the other side of the fence was always greener. Studying Claire's closed expression now as she prepared the tea, she wondered if her daughter-in-law had already begun to look elsewhere for the love and companionship that had been denied her for the past ten years.

*   *   *

They were stood down for the best part of a week; five days respite from flying. Five days, Ryan thought, to wipe the war from his mind, five days in which to get to know Claire de Lacy better.

Hoagy, Ed and Pete had already left the base for London, the jeep well stocked with nylons, perfume and candy from the PX. Charlie and Ray had got their feet under the table of a farm in Stafford Ley, where there just happened to be a couple of land girls, while Perry, Homer and Art were on the trail of a bevy of WAAFS from the base.

Having declined the offer to make it even numbers on the trip to London with Hoagy and the boys, and resisting the lure of the WAAFS, Ryan waved the last of his crew away and turned his steps towards Hawksley. Fired by thoughts of Claire he quickened his pace as he passed the guard post and strode down the lane.

The increasing warmth of her greeting when they met, the way her eyes lit when she smiled were giving out all the right signals. "Leave it alone, pal," Hoagy had counselled, "Come up to London with us and get yourself a piece of ass like you used to – you ain't goin' no place with a dame like that!'

But now he couldn't bring himself to join the hunt around Piccadilly and Shaftsbury Avenue: avoiding the hookers, looking for the girls willing to be nice, and maybe a bit more, to a guy in exchange for being given a good time. His meetings with Claire had cured him of all that.

In all his twenty-five years he had never been so obsessed with one woman. And it wasn't only the desire to get her into bed driving him. He wanted to hold her hand, to walk and talk with her properly, to know all about her; not have just a few minutes polite conversation on those occasions when he had managed to waylay her. He wanted to discover for himself what music she liked; did she laugh at the Marx Brothers? Cry at the movies when the lovers were forced to part? What books did she read? Did she love her husband?

There was a hint of rain in the air. He pulled up the collar of his trench coat and glanced at his watch: a quarter after two. If she were going on duty today he'd be just about in time to catch her. He left the lane to climb the stile into Belstead Wood and strode swiftly along the broad ride towards the five-bar gate at the back of the manor, already feeling the familiar heat begin to invade his loins again.

*   *   *

He had been sitting on the gate for about five minutes when he saw her crossing the meadow towards him. As she came closer he jumped down from his perch to salute her, before snicking the latch and holding open the gate.

'Hi there; like some company?'

'Of course,' she smiled up at him. 'I heard your squadron come back.'

'It was a short run.' He fell into step beside her. 'I wanted to ask you...that is, I thought...' he cleared his throat. 'It's just that we're stood down for the next five days and I wondered if I could see you; take in a movie maybe...' he tailed off and gave a sudden, self-conscious grin. 'Hell, why pretend; I'm asking you for a date!'

She gave him a thoughtful look.

'I'm honoured, but should a married woman accept?'

'Oh, sure – if you like we can take young Rupert along as a chaperone.'

'I don't think that would be a good idea, this week they are showing *The Hunchback of Notre Dame*.' She looked him up and down. 'Do you ride?'

'Ride what?' he was puzzled, 'a bike?'

She laughed outright. 'Not a bicycle – a horse! There is a big fellow needing exercise and I can't handle him. We could ride tomorrow.'

'Oh, sure,' he laughed with her. 'I spent a couple of vacations from college working as a cowhand and you don't get far on a thousand acres without a horse.'

'You don't look like a frustrated rancher.'

'I'm not. A pal from my college's folks had a ranch in Oklahoma; I lit out there on a few vacations to get away from my family for a while.'

'Why?'

He walked in silence for a few moments. 'Things were always a bit strained with my old man,' he said eventually. 'Pa and me – it was a relationship that never happened; we never really hit it off. It was a relief when I got my Masters and could live on campus all year round. When I go back I won't stay home. I'll finish my Ph.D. and be able to do what I was aiming for before Uncle Sam decided he needed me – find a good university, teach French and German Literature to graduates and earn enough to buy my own place.'

'Gosh! You don't exactly waste time, do you?'

'Nope; I'm a fast mover.' He gave his sudden disarming grin. 'How's about our date with this horse – do we both get to ride the same one together?'

She chuckled. 'No, we don't. I usually exercise my old mare Dolly; she's getting on but enjoys herself more if there's someone to ride alongside. I hope you have a strong pair of wrists; Geoffrey's hunter Samson is only seven and full of himself.'

'I've those all right.' He gave her a sideways glance. 'That takes care of one – how's about the other four?'

'The other four what?'

'Now you're doing it!' he grinned again, 'the other four days I have on leave.'

She said regretfully, 'I'm afraid I have too much work to do on the farm this weekend.'

'Great, I'll help.' He wasn't to be deflected. 'Just lead me to it.'

She hesitated, but only briefly. Why shouldn't she spend some time with an attractive man? She wondered cynically who was showing Geoffrey hospitality in far off Alexandria. Whoever it was, it was sure to be both female and willing.

'Well, ma'am,' he watched her face, intrigued by the sudden glint of steel in her eyes, 'do I get the job?'

She laughed. 'On one condition – that you stop calling me ma'am.

My name is Claire, remember?'

'Sure thing; and mine's Ryan.'

She said recklessly. 'Come to lunch tomorrow – after our ride; then we can go logging. Rupert will be delighted to come along and get in the way.'

He raised a quizzical eyebrow, 'How about your mother-in-law?'

'She'll be delighted too, and she *won't* get in the way!'

When they reached the hospital gates she turned, holding out her hand.

'Tomorrow, then: ten o'clock? Oh and you'll need some old clothes for the afternoon – logging is dirty work and you are bound to end the day absolutely filthy.'

'I'll find some gear somewhere.' He raised her gloved fingers to his lips. 'Old New England custom,' he explained in response to her smile, 'it's what a gentleman does when he says goodbye to a married lady!'

'Quite,' she said and turned away but not before he had seen her blush. He watched her out of sight then slapped his open palm against a handy fence post. 'Yeah, *man*!' he exclaimed aloud and wheeling, strode back to Falcon Field with a light step and an even lighter heart. Now all he had to do was find some suitable civilian kit and wait for the morning.

*   *   *

'Ask the sky pilot,' Perry advised. 'He's the only one near your size who spends his spare time trampin' the countryside in clothes even a bum wouldn't want to be buried in!'

'Yeah,' Ryan grinned. 'I'd thought of him but you can bet he'll make me pay some kind of a high price.'

Drawing blanks elsewhere he ran the chaplain to earth in the mess bar, sitting with his long legs propped on a stool, reading a week-old New York Tribune and smoking a pipe that should have carried a health warning. Glancing up as Ryan sat beside him he said succinctly, 'I haven't seen you at Mass for a month, so whatever it is you're wanting you can't have it.'

'Aw, come on, father, I have a tough job on tomorrow and I need some of your skid row gear for the day.'

'Only if you're not set on doing anything real dirty, like chasing some girl through a swamp. My clothes may be old but they're clean and I only wear them for lurking in the bushes to watch the wildlife around here; gonna write a book about it when I get back home.'

'I'll buy a copy.' Ryan hitched onto the table. 'I need to help some folks with getting in the winter firewood – and I'll have O'Casey launder your gear after. Be a pal, father, I can't go logging all duded up.'

Father Ramsey sucked on his pipe. 'OK – but that'll be a buck and a half for the comforts fund.' He held out his hand.

'Shyster,' Ryan dug in his pants pocket. 'You wouldn't like a pint of my blood as well, would you?'

The chaplain grinned. 'That's what comes of not sayin' your prayers. Take what you need from the suitcase on top of my wardrobe...and see I get it all back.' He returned to his paper, 'have a nice day, Ry – and keep away from the girls while you're wearing my pants!'

Ryan reckoned a buck and a half was a high price to pay for the loan of an old checked logger shirt, a pair of sweats, a yellow and brown hunting jacket and mountain boots, but fair trade for a day spent with Claire de Lacy.

9

HAWKSLEY MANOR

January 1943

Ryan let down both stirrups then tightened the girth another notch while the big hunter rummaged thoughtfully in his hair. Eyeing the saddle dubiously he offered, 'This sure is one strange looking contraption – a man can't get to sit right in it – and I don't call that little bitty raise of leather a pommel – where in hell am I supposed to hitch my lariat?'

From her seat on Dolly, Claire gave a gurgle of laughter. 'You'll find it hard to ride like the Lone Ranger in an English saddle!'

'Gee, I just hope I can sit down afterwards 'cause it doesn't look any too comfortable to me.' As Ryan swung onto Sampson's back the horse rolled his eyes then side stepped and did a hefty experimental buck. 'Hey, put a lid on it!' Ryan pulled his head round hard and sat deep, letting him feel his weight. 'Try that again pal and I'll have your neck on the sawdust before your ass has time to raise an inch.' Samson snorted and shook his head, then stepped out docilely beside the older more biddable Dolly.

So, Claire de Lacy grinned to herself, Captain Petersen could be mean and masterful as well as charming and courteous – quite an intriguing combination might *that* turn out to be!

*   *   *

They rode through Hawksley and Stafford Ley and towards the open forest, Ryan keeping his eager mount under tight control until they reached the heath, then leaving Claire and Dolly to enjoy a sedate canter he pulled the peak of his cap low over his eyes and set the powerful horse in a flat out thundering gallop through the gorse and heather. Getting the measure of the unfamiliar saddle and Samson's stride he leaned forward along his neck, urging him over a wide stream which the horse took unhesitatingly with one effortless leap, then pushing him on again until the wind made his eyes stream and face throb with the cold, so that finally he had to reign in and turning, make his way back with smarting eyes and reddened skin to where

Claire waited.

'Wow! This sure is some horse.' He rubbed his face with his hands to bring some feeling back into it before swinging from the saddle to loop Samson's reins over a limb on a fallen tree. Helping Claire to dismount from Dolly he first tethered the mare then taking off his scarf spread it along the rough bark. 'Better give him – and me – a breather before we go on,' he said.

Claire sat down, pulling off her headscarf and shaking her hair free. 'It looks as though Sampson has met his match. It must have been quite a shock to find a cowboy on his back.'

Ryan grinned, his blue eyes sparkling. 'Not exactly a lady's ride when he feels his oats, is he?' Shrugging off his trench coat he draped it over the shoulders of her tweed jacket. 'Here, take this, you're shivering.'

'Thank you, but won't you be cold?'

He sat beside her. 'Hell, no, right now it feels like I've a little piece of heaven that'll keep me warm enough for a good while yet.'

Her cheeks pinked. 'You are quite a flirt, aren't you, Captain Petersen?'

'Ryan, ma'am,' he corrected.

'Claire, 'she countered and tucked in the corners of her mouth on a smile. 'Are you married, Ryan?'

'No.'

'I'm sure there must be a girl that you left behind.'

'Sort of…want to see?' he fished in the pocket of his Eisenhower for his wallet. 'Her name's Ellie Sullivan and she kind of thinks we're walking out – you know, going steady.'

She took the photograph he tendered and studied it. 'She's very pretty. *Are* you "walking out"?'

'Well, now,' he returned the photo to his wallet. 'It depends what you mean by that.' He gave his slow wicked grin. 'Back home if a guy takes a girl to a movie a few times and necks a little when he kisses goodnight, to her that's going steady – but that's not necessarily the same thing to him; he's most likely only there for the kissing and the necking and anything else he might hope to get!'

She protested, 'That's hardly fair – it must be difficult for the girls to know when there is a difference.'

He turned towards her and leaning an elbow on his knee looked straight into her eyes. 'Ma'am,' he said softly, 'If this guy kissed you I reckon you'd know if it was for real or not.'

She sat immobile, half hypnotised by those brilliant eyes, then Dolly whickered and she came to with a guilty jump. 'I don't know how we got on to the subject of American mating rites, but I think we'd better leave it at that!' She stood. 'We should go back now or Marion will think we've got lost.'

'I'm sorry.' Taking her gloved hand he held it between both of his. 'I didn't mean to hit on you like that – honestly. But you are a very beautiful woman and I'm a long way from home and, well, for a moment there I guess I just got carried away.'

Gently she disengaged her hand from his. 'I think you may consider yourself forgiven,' she said and handed him his coat. She watched him button it, then as he whipped the belt around his lean frame felt a new and extraordinary sensation stir deep down inside her, followed rapidly by an almost irresistible urge to run her fingers through that shiny hair and kiss the long mouth. Looking up he caught her gaze and she turned away hastily, fumbling with Dolly's reins and making a muddle of untying them from the branch.

'Here, let me...' He took the reins from her nervous fingers to stand looking down on her for a long minute; then, 'Oh, Mrs Claire de Lacy,' he said softly, 'you surely shouldn't look at a man like that!' and dropping the reins caught her to him and closed his mouth on hers.

*   *   *

In all her twenty-seven years no man had ever kissed her like this, with such slow aching passion; with lips and teeth and tongue; a long persuasive kiss that deepened slowly, demanding a response. For the first time ever she wanted to make love – make it now with this man who was turning her bones to jelly and arousing amazing sensations in places she hadn't even known existed before this moment.

He released her at last on a long sigh and cupping her face in his hands looked deep into her eyes, saying huskily, 'This is a wild way to fall in love!'

She said, 'Don't say that – you mustn't.'

'Why not, it's true. I think I fell for you the first time I laid eyes on you and I haven't gotten you out of my mind since.' His arms wrapped her, held her. 'I wake with you every morning and go to bed with you every night...if that isn't love I sure as hell don't know what else you'd call it.'

Her lips trembled. 'Perhaps it's just that you are lonely and a long way from home.'

'No.' he shook his head. He stood her a little away from him and placing his hands on her shoulders stared intently down into her eyes.

'Now you tell me if you feel the same way – or not.'

'And if I do feel the same, what then?'

'Then I'll know I'm the luckiest guy alive – and I want you Claire de Lacy, so much I could be about to bust.'

She began to laugh helplessly. 'Then that makes two of us – but what a thing to discover on a freezing day in the middle of a blasted heath.'

He cupped the back of her head with both hands, tangling his fingers in her hair. 'When I make love to you properly for the first time it won't be on this or any other blasted heath, but at the Ritz, in a bed the size of Times Square, with flowers and champagne and Richard Tauber singing *Lippen Schweigen*!'

She kissed his mouth and ran her hand over his face. 'It won't last, it can't; you know that, don't you? The war will end, Geoffrey will come home to his wife and you will go back to your Ellie, who thinks you are walking out…'

He pulled her hard against him. 'The hell with all that,' he said roughly, 'there is no Geoffrey, there is no Ellie; there is only today and you and me.'

*   *   *

It took Marion de Lacy less than five minutes to get the measure of the young man who had disappeared so suddenly with Claire during the New Year Dance, and now magically re-appeared at the luncheon table. He was politely deferential to her – and flirted covertly but outrageously with Claire whenever her own attention was distracted for a moment. She knew when a man was setting out to charm and if she were a proper mother-in-law, she thought tartly, she would nip his charm in the bud right away and send him packing. Then she looked at the bloom on Claire's cheeks and the sparkle in her eyes and remembered a passionate long ago love affair when she had been a lonely young woman married to the faithless Geoffrey's equally faithless father. So long as they were discreet and there was no hint of scandal, she thought with sudden compassion, she would not interfere, but turn a blind eye for as long as possible. Claire was a sensible, balanced woman; she would know that any affair must end, that was the inevitable conclusion of all such liaisons when there were husbands and children to consider. Although Geoffrey might allow his wife to leave his house he would never allow her to take his son with her.

And Claire would not abandon Rupert, even for such a man as this.

Ryan knew he had been checked over, evaluated and more or less approved of, and wondered why this tall aristocratic woman was allowing him to make love to Claire right under her nose. He felt slightly uneasy and was relieved when the meal ended and Rupert appeared in the doorway. Tightly bundled into a thick sweater and dungarees and clutching a sturdy pair of boots to his chest the child announced importantly, 'Elias says we are ready to go and if I'm not a con-danged nuisance I can steer the tractor!'

Claire laughed and held out her hand. 'Come here, darling. Say hello to Captain Petersen – you remember him from the party?'

He leaned against her shoulder. 'Yes, I remember – he helped me to be sick!' His smile was a carbon copy of his mother's. 'Hello, Captain Petersen.'

Ryan smothered a snort of laughter. 'Yeah, and hello to you, Rupert; I'm going to help your mommy get in the firewood, so maybe you can show me where to change my gear.'

'Change your *gear*...' Rupert rolled the unfamiliar word around his tongue then offered generously. 'You can change it in my room if you like and I'll show you my airplanes.'

'I like – that's if the ladies will excuse us.'

'Of course,' Marion smiled. 'Don't let him talk all the time,' she warned, 'or you'll not get through before nightfall.'

*   *   *

Not since basic training had Ryan sweated so hard. Logging was tiring, backbreaking work. While Elias' sons and Ryan chopped and sawed the branches of the fallen tree into manageable lengths, Claire and the old man chained the denuded trunk to the tractor and Elias drove off, leaving them to heave the remaining wood into the long trailer. When Elias returned they had filled the trailer and a filthy, but happy, Rupert sat on Elias's knees on the tractor and drove them back to the Manor, while the rest of the workers sprawled exhausted across the timber, picking splinters out of their hands and twigs and an assortment of creeping wildlife out of each other's hair.

Back at the machine shed old Elias surveyed the results of their labour and rubbed his hands. 'Tomorrow when we gets the saw to them there branches an' trunk Missis will 'ave all the firing she needs 'till spring –'

'And heat enough water for a good hot bath,' Claire added feelingly.

Conscious of the warm mess and the hot shower he took every morning at base, Ryan gave a wry smile. These people had to struggle so hard for so many of the things he took for granted. Tomorrow, he thought, he'd bring some tinned goodies from the PX for Claire and the *Grande Dame* and candy for Rupert...Smiling at Claire across the piled logs he moved his lips silently, *I love you*...and she smiled back, miming a kiss.

Somehow, somewhere and soon, he determined, he would hold Claire de Lacy in his arms and the war could take a back seat. From the corner of his eye he saw Elias' boys wink and nudge each other and realised he was gazing at Claire like a lovesick kid. He felt himself colour and turned hastily to Elias, offering, 'If you could use another hand tomorrow I'd like to help – just give me an axe and I'll chop all the logs you can want.'

Elias spat on his leathery palm and shook his hand. 'Done, mister,' he said, then gave him a sly look adding, 'an' I reckon that might earn you another bite to eat up at the 'ouse while they'm 'aving thur Sunday dinner – in't that right, missis?'

'Yes.' Claire blushed scarlet. She put her hands on Rupert's shoulders, trying to look formal and failing dismally. 'We'd like that very much, wouldn't we, Rupert?'

'Yes, we would.' The boy twisted his head to look up into her face. 'But you've gone awfully red all of a sudden, mummy.' Turning back he stared at Ryan. 'So has Captain Petersen...' He looked worried and asked urgently, 'Are you both going to be poorly, mummy? When *I* get all hot like that Nanny makes me go to bed.'

Ryan breathed, 'Oh, *Jesus!*' Old Elias cackled and spat.

'Ar, you'm right there, young master,' he wheezed on a laugh. 'I reckon as bed's the proper place for folk as is getting a fever!'

*   *   *

Three weeks after Elias' prophetic pronouncement they became lovers for the first time. Not at the Ritz or in a bed the size of Times Square, but in a plush but discreetly anonymous Bloomsbury hotel, where the bed was a predictable four-foot six. But they had the flowers and the champagne and Richard Tauber singing *Lippen Schweigan* on the chaplain's portable gramophone, for the loan of which Ryan had been rooked a further two dollars.

With Claire supposedly visiting one of her many London friends and Ryan escaping a forty-eight in company with his crew, alone and away from all responsibilities and cares they could pretend that they were young lovers on their honeymoon.

Making love for that first time was as though there had never been another woman in his life or another man in hers. Claire, spread in abandoned voluptuous delight, wondered with hazy ecstasy how long it would be before she lost her senses completely. Breathless, she gasped, 'So this is being ravished!' and felt his chest shake with laughter.

'Sure it is.' His lips browsed her breast, over her belly, then lower still, setting every nerve end in her body jangling. She gasped and caught his head in her hands.

'Oh, my *God,* are you supposed to do *that*?'

'Yeah, it's an old Viking custom!'

She arched against him, her senses tumbling wildly out of control and with one swift movement he slid up her body murmuring, 'and *this* is another one!'

*   *   *

Much later he raised himself; holding her face between his hands and stroking his thumbs across her cheeks he said huskily, 'Gee, I've found an English rose who makes love like an angel.'

She gave a shaky little huff of laughter. 'I don't think angels make love – even if they had the parts I doubt they'd know how.'

'Well one of them just knew all right,' he kissed her eyes. Tasting salt on his lips he said, 'Hey, I didn't mean to make you cry.'

'I'm not crying – I think my eyes are just leaking with happiness! I've never felt like this before.'

'Nor have I,' in the half light he saw her smile, 'honest Injun I mean it, I haven't, not like I feel with you.'

'Is love always this wonderful?'

'It will be – for us...' his voice faltered and she touched the corners of his eyes with gentle fingers.

'Are you leaking with happiness too?'

'Some.' He lay back against the pillows; drawing her head onto his shoulder he stroked a hand down her long smooth back. 'You are one dangerous lady to have around when a man is supposed to be fighting a war.'

She smiled up at him. 'We'll fight it together,' she said, 'for as long as it takes.'

He gave a contented growl deep in his throat. 'That's my girl.'

Long after she slept he lay awake staring into the shadows. No matter about Geoffrey, no matter what anyone thought or said, he wasn't going to let this woman go from his life without a fight. Setting his jaw determinedly he tightened his arms possessively around her.

Somehow, in some way, he would make the impossible possible.

*   *   *

Twenty-two years, five months and three weeks later, he stood in a bedroom above the bar of the Bull Inn and stared at his reflection in the mirror. Summing up aloud the thoughts and desires of the young Ryan Petersen of so many years ago he took himself to task with a few well-chosen words, 'Arrogant, stupid and abso-fucking-lutely *insane!*'

10

MARLBOROUGH STREET, CHELSEA

October 1965

Exhausted and disturbed by dreams filled with images of Claire he awoke next morning with a dull headache and an erection he didn't need. Cursing, he hurtled from his bed and after a cold bath and a hasty breakfast left the Bull with no intention of ever returning again to Hawksley. It had all been a terrible costly mistake. He would never even get the chance to see Claire again. Not while that cold-eyed man stood, or rather sat, in the way.

Driving furiously and fast in an effort to exorcise the memory of his disastrous weekend, he only came to his senses when he was stalled by the traffic at Barnes Bridge. Hunched over the steering wheel, waiting for a young, unruffled constable to sort out the chaos, he reluctantly acknowledged that he should have gone back to the Manor; should have at least tried to find answers to the three big questions that would probably haunt his brain to the end of his days: How come de Lacy was in a wheelchair, where was Claire, and why his denial of Rupert?

Perhaps, thought Ryan, after he had gone from her life and despite all opposition she had left Geoffrey, taken the boy and simply disappeared to another part of the country, or even abroad. He could go on making those kinds of guesses, he thought irritably but the only place he might find the answers was with that cool-eyed man back in Hawksley. And that he couldn't do, at least not yet, and given the way he felt right now, probably never…

*   *   *

He was hours earlier than Hannah could have expected him and nobody was home; even Charlie's place was closed and the blinds drawn. Ryan sat in the car outside number sixteen drumming his fingers on the wheel, wondering what to do next. It felt a long time since breakfast at The Bull and an unpleasant gnawing ache was just starting to gripe his guts. The idea of lunch in a crowded London Pub didn't attract and after a few minutes' deliberation he fired the engine again and turned back towards Richmond and the river in search of some quiet pub or restaurant.

Traffic was still heavy and as he reached Hammersmith Broadway a battered old Ford with a vaguely familiar number plate cut in front of him. Cursing and jabbing at the brake he slowed, and as he was forced to tag along behind remembered where he'd seen it before. Oh, great, he thought with heavy sarcasm, if it ain't Calamity Jane!

Not satisfied with cutting him up she was stuck right in front of him as traffic stopped and started in a spasmodic nose-to-tail crawl. Her body language, what he could see of it, was mirroring his own, shoulders hunched and hands drumming an irritable tattoo on the wheel. As they crept at snail's pace over the river his annoyance was beginning to fuse with a mild curiosity about the final destination of this aggravating female and almost without realising what he was doing he followed her out of town.

When she eventually stopped in the car park of a small waterside pub just past Richmond, he slid the Jowett in on the far side of the parking lot and waited while she went into the lounge bar. She reappeared a few minutes later carrying a full glass to a small table by the river. Setting down her glass she settled on one of the iron chairs. Making no attempt to drink her wine she sat motionless, just staring at the water.

Intrigued, he watched to see if she was meeting anyone, but when after several minutes she was still alone he left the car and walked into the pub. Inside it was warm and cosy; a coal fire glowed in an inglenook fireplace. A large yellow mastiff stretched before the brick hearth watched him with one lazy eye as he crossed to the bar. It was early, with perhaps no more than twenty people dotted around the tables. When the barman came to serve him Ryan ordered a pint of bitter then jerked his head casually towards the door. 'I'll have the same lunch as the young lady out there; I can wait and take both if that's OK.'

'Right, sir, two Ploughman's it is; won't be a couple of ticks.'

Ryan paid for his beer and meal, watching her through the window while the order was filled, wondering how he should play this particular situation. On her previous showing any approach was likely to result in his either being cut dead or down to size; not, he thought grimly that he'd let her get away with it a second time – and anyway, what the hell was he doing putting himself in line for another snub from this sassy dame? He began to feel annoyed with himself for giving in to the impulse that had landed him in a strange pub and undoubtedly about to get his come-uppance from this ill-natured female, however much he might load on the charm.

Although sunny, it certainly wasn't warm enough to lunch *al fresco,* and he wondered why she chose to eat in the open air instead of the cosy bar. Sure she was done up nice and warm and of course she may just be an open-air freak. He moved nearer to the window and took a closer look.

Today she wore a high-neck white sweater and scarlet military style jacket, those classy legs hidden beneath narrow-leg navy pants. In this more conventional get-up she looked one hell of a lot more edible than in the Gypsy Rose Lee gear. Ryan let his gaze rove from head to feet and back again…very slowly. From out of nowhere came that old familiar kick inside.

Surprised to find that it was not only his interest that was being stirred he thought with wry amusement that forty-eight hours of dredged up memories of making love to Claire were beginning to play hell with his libido, putting him back to where he was before Charlie: on the prowl again and desperate for some female company. Were it not for the mystery surrounding that lone figure in the wheelchair, he thought resentfully, the memory of Claire might at last have been laid to rest, leaving him to move on and make what he could of the rest of his life.

Not that he was figuring on Calamity Jane filling any gaps he mused, as he collected the two plates of bread, cheese and pickle from the bar, just that eating lunch while speculating about the body that might go with those legs had to be preferable to eating alone. Holding the plates in one hand and his glass in the other, he hesitated for a moment at the doorway, suddenly at a loss on how to make his approach: then his mouth curved in a smile…he'd go for his old college days' routine and see if she had a sense of humour. Settling his shoulders into a cowboy slouch he crossed the grass towards the figure by the water.

She didn't hear him coming so when he slid a plate under her nose and did his best John Wayne, 'Saw you park your horse right over there ma'am, and figured you might like some company eatin' your grits!' she jumped like a startled faun and let rip an unladylike, 'God *almighty*!'

'Not quite, but close.' He sat down opposite and raised his glass. 'Hi.'

She gave him an evil glare. 'Do you have some mission in life to hassle strange women?'

'Nah,' he shook his head, 'apart for those who either break down inches from my fender or cut me up in their beat up cars.'

'Some of us can only afford crap cars,' she said haughtily, 'and that monstrosity *you* drive would be more at home on the Brookwood circuit. Now will you please leave me alone to eat my lunch?'

Ryan ignored the insult and the request. Hell, he thought, but she was one aggravating woman – and why was he sitting with his butt on a cold iron chair, his arms on an even colder table, trading insults with some sassy Brit when he could be snug in the warm bar? Come to that, why had he followed her here anyway? He took another long look which she met with stony indifference. A wicked desire to tip her over the edge into outright temper made him smile; still in John Wayne mode he invited 'Lady, how about we just mosey on over to that little old log cabin there and eat up our grub in the warm?'

Close up her eyes were a wonderful glossy brown with little gold flecks and right now those flecks were near molten with fury. For a moment she teetered on the brink, then conquering the threatened outburst with an effort shrugged and looked away. 'You please yourself where *you* eat, Yank,' she said dismissively, 'but I'm staying right here,' and began on her bread and cheese.

There was a long silence. This was one picayune way to behave towards a woman, he thought: busting in on her meal then doing his best to rile her because *he* was feeling bruised and out of sorts. What happened to the old Ryan who knew how to treat a lady? Perhaps he *was* in need of some of Charlie's professional advice. Apologizing wasn't easy, but he managed it.

'I guess I was out of order there; I'm real sorry, ma'am.' She looked up with the faintest of grins and he added hastily, 'OK, so over here that's what you call your Queen. '

'And over there that's what you call a lady,' she countered, then gave a real unexpectedly gutsy laugh and held out her hand. 'I'm Julia Frazier, and you are who…apart from John Wayne?'

'Ryan, Ryan Petersen, glad to know you, Julia Frazier.' He took and kept hold of her hand. 'Hell, you're freezing. Why sit out here and get hypothermia when there's a fire in the bar?'

'Because there is – was, no one else out here, and today I prefer my own company.'

He stood up. 'The hell with that; you need a seat by that fire and a bowl of hot soup else you'll be cluttering up a bed in your local hospital…' She opened her mouth to protest and he sighed. 'Now don't give me hassle, Miz Frazier; I get enough of that at home.'

'I'll bet you do.' She glowered as he handed her the glasses and picked up both plates, but after only a brief hesitation, followed him across the grass to the Inn. Her back, he noticed as he stood aside to let her enter, was ramrod straight and quivering visibly with what was most likely suppressed fury.

There was a table free by the side of the fire and leaving her there to get over her strop he went to the bar and ordered the soup.

*   *   *

Julia Frazier propped one elbow on the table and resting her chin on her hand watched the persistent Yank through half-closed eyes. She was furious with herself: first for almost letting him get under her guard, and secondly for allowing him to order her about in that high-handed fashion. Bloody men, she gritted, give them half a chance and they would invariably become either maddeningly macho and get fresh, or start in with the looking-after-the-little-woman routine. Irritatingly this one had managed to combine the better aspects of the two. However, she allowed herself a small smile; as soon as he'd said his name she knew she had one card up *her* sleeve which should shake that superior air of impregnable male calm.

*   *   *

When he returned with the soup she accepted it with a frosty 'Thank you,' remaining silent until she had finished, then made equally short work of the remains of her bread and cheese. Mopping her last piece of bread around the bowl she said conversationally, 'You need not have tried so hard to get acquainted, Mr Petersen; we would have met sooner or later. I know your son…and your mother, and I've heard all about *you*. In great detail I may say.'

She sat back, observing his startled expression with malicious pleasure, but he recovered swiftly and she had to give him points for that.

'How come?' he asked and she gave a little crow of laughter.

'You should have just seen your face!' She pushed aside her plate and rested her arms on the table. 'I teach at the International School and as Joel and my daughter Nicole seem to like each other's company I see quite a lot of him – and of your mother when she fetches him home.'

Ryan regarded her with mixed feelings of admiration and pique. So this was the woman whose house Joel had been visiting. Just my luck, he thought, all she had to do was tell Hannah he'd picked her up in a bar and he'd never hear the end of it. 'So where's your daughter today

88

while you're high tailing it out of London?' he asked, needling her a little.

'With your mother and your son; they're doing the rounds of the museums.'

Some devil inside him made him push harder. 'What's wrong with your old man looking after her while you have a day off?'

An angry flush spread from neck to hairline and her eyes positively flashed fire.

'Try getting your facts right before you sound off; I don't have a husband. He died five years ago. Today would have been his fortieth birthday, so I have a very good reason for wanting to be on my own.' Two huge tears hung trembling on her lashes for a few seconds, then spilled over and ran down her burning cheeks. 'Sod you, Yank!' Rummaging blindly in her pockets she produced a wisp of lace-trimmed cotton that wouldn't have wiped the nose of a gnat and began dabbing ineffectually at her eyes.

'Oh hell; here, use this.' Ryan pushed an almost clean handkerchief into her hand, conscious that they had suddenly become the focal point of every single person in the bar, most of the men looking as though they'd like to punch his nose good and hard for making a lady cry. Embarrassed he turned his back on them and leaned forward, shielding her as much as possible while she mopped at her tears. 'I'm real sorry, Julia Frazier; I've had a rough couple of days but I shouldn't have taken it out on you.'

She blew her nose vigorously like a kid and he found that pretty cute. She sniffed, looking up at him with her big wet eyes, 'Did you have a rough couple of days the first time I laid eyes on you, because you were bloody rude then as well.'

He said humbly, 'I know; I'm a heel. Look, how about we get out of here – go for a walk alongside the river? You can kick me in the water if you like.'

She hesitated then agreed. 'All right,' she stood up hitching her bag over her shoulder and he followed her to the door. As he opened it and stepped aside she swept out imperiously, treading heavily and deliberately on his foot as she did so.

He yelped loudly and followed her out of the door as fast as his throbbing big toe allowed.

*   *   *

They walked, or rather she walked and Ryan limped, along the towpath for perhaps five minutes without speaking. He was in no

89

hurry to chat. Despite her attack on his foot he was kind of tickled by her exit from the bar and after all his doom and gloom over the abortive journey to Hampshire he needed a laugh or two. Eventually she broke the silence; turning to him with a rather tentative grin to say, 'Pax?'

'Oh sure, I'm a nice guy at heart.'

She grinned. 'Your John Wayne take-off was good. You could be a pro.'

'You must have a bad effect on me. I haven't done anything like that for years – not since college when I did it to get started with the girls. My Charles Boyer had them all over me like a rash.'

'I'll bet.' She grinned again. 'How's the foot?' Ryan gave an exaggerated wince.

'It may not be broken.'

'You did ask for it. What were you doing there, anyway?'

Taking care that neither of his feet were anywhere near hers he admitted, 'I followed you.'

'Why?'

'Darned if I know,' he shrugged. 'You cut me up around Hammersmith; I got stuck behind you and kinda took it from there.'

'Impulsive, aren't you?'

He said dryly, 'My middle name' and she gave another of her quirky little smiles. 'That's not what your mother thinks.'

'What does she think?' he asked, making a mental note to give Hannah a hard time of it for gossiping when he got the chance.

'That you don't get out enough and that you…' she went slightly pink and finished in a rush. '…that you should get out more!'

'Lady, you are one hell of a lousy liar,' he growled, 'the second part of that should be "and you drink too much."' He levelled a finger. 'Now you listen to me Mrs Julia Frazier: just you don't believe everything my mother tells you. I may over do it once in a while, but not as a habit, and my mother would think the Pope was an alcoholic if he had two swigs instead of one at the communion wine!'

She began to laugh then, so much that she again had recourse to the handkerchief still clutched in her hand. Sitting down on one of the wooden benches by the towpath she dabbed at her eyes while he towered above her with drawn brows; but her laughter was infectious and eventually he gave in and joined her on the bench. 'OK,' propping his arm on the back of the seat he turned towards her, 'seems you know a lot about me and my family, so how about filling me in on you and yours.'

'I told you: I teach at the International.'

'And...'

'I'm a widow and have a ten-year-old daughter. What else is there to know?'

'What do you do when you're not being a schoolmarm?'

'Quite the interrogator, aren't you? One time I thought I could be a concert pianist but I wasn't that good – you know what they say: "Those who can, do those who can't, teach". So a couple of evenings a week I teach the piano to kids who'd rather be doing something else with their time.'

'Doesn't sound much like a barrel of laughs.'

She gave a dismissive shrug. 'It helps pay for the groceries.' She stared into the middle distance, her expression blank and uncommunicative.

Jeez, he thought, but she changed moods quicker than any woman he'd ever met. He asked: 'You always been this hard to reach?' and watched the slow flush spread from neck to hairline before she stood, turning away from him.

'I'm getting cold again. I think it's time I returned home.'

He wasn't about to be put off that easily, 'Where's home?' he asked as they began to walk back along the towpath.

'Battersea,' she tipped her nose in the air. 'It's a dump. Anything else you'd like to know?'

Yeah, he thought, a whole lot of things: like how a dame who looks and talks like you is so impoverished that she lives in a dump, drives an unreliable heap of scrap, needs two jobs just to get by and freezes a guy at ten paces? Also what sort of man pops off leaving his wife and kid that short of the long green stuff? He was silent for a few moments then asked, 'What did your old ma –' hastily he corrected himself, 'what did your husband do for a living?'

'He was an RAF test pilot who tested one plane too many...and before you ask, he liked playing the horses...' she shrugged again. 'Unfortunately, the ones he backed seldom made it first past the post and we still hadn't got around to buying a house, or getting adequately insured when he was killed – it was not entirely his fault,' she was immediately on the defensive at Ryan's cynical expression. 'Insurance and mortgage companies tend to fight shy of test pilots you see. Either they won't play at all, or if they do, the premiums are too high. The RAF gives me a pension, but I still need to work.'

'That's tough.' Ryan commiserated. He took a sideways glance at her closed expression and wondered why she'd been celebrating, if that was the word, the birthday of such an unreliable character.

Almost as though she'd read his thoughts she gave him the

answer. 'Jamie was fun and full to the brim with life and I loved him very much. So much that I've not looked for, nor wanted, another man to take his place. No man could: he was unique.' She quickened her pace almost to a run. 'Now you've managed to wring that out of me and know I'm not up for grabs, you can just bugger off and leave me in peace.'

He stood on the path and watched her hurry away, her shoulders hunched under the jaunty red coat. Leaning against the end of the wooden beam above the lock he stared down into the water. *Well, smart-ass, there goes what might have been a beautiful friendship. Serves you right for hitting on a dame who does nothing for you except make you want to see more of her legs!*

Waiting until she'd had enough time to reach her car and begin her journey back to the dump in Battersea, he walked to where he had left the Jowett, already regretting the bread and cheese which seemed to have given him a nasty taste in his mouth.

Arriving back at Marlborough Street, he saw that number sixteen was still closed and silent and that some joker had parked in his space. There was a light in Charlie's hallway and space at her curb, but always careful to cover his tracks from Hannah, he left the car out of sight in the next street and walked back to the house on the corner.

11

MARLBOROUGH STREET, CHELSEA

October 1965

'I get the impression your weekend wasn't all you'd hoped for – or expected,' Charlie commented as he lay half-dozing in tired but euphoric post-coital content, an arm about her shoulders.

''Darned right it wasn't; all I got was a whole heap more questions I'm never going to get answers to.'

'For a literary man your sentence construction can be pretty lousy...' she ran a fingernail down his chest. 'Do you want to talk about it?'

'What, my sentence construction?'

'No, you idiot: your week-end.'

'Nope,' he rested his chin on top of her head. 'I kinda prefer my lady shrinks don't wear their professional hats in bed.'

'So you've had one before?'

She was sharp all right. He tried to pass it off lightly, 'Not in the Biblical sense and not so as you'd notice. Hannah tried to fix me up with one a few months back, but she had buckteeth. Buckteeth I can't take in any woman, let alone a shrink.'

'You don't really like – or at least don't really trust women, do you?'

'I love 'em,' he kissed her, 'especially lady shrinks with straight teeth.'

She laughed and sat up, reaching for her clothes. He fastened her bra then cupped his hands over her breasts, murmuring against her neck, 'Must you go?'

'Yes I must.' She twisted around to face him. 'Can I give a closet misogynist a tip?'

'Sure you can.'

'When you talk to a woman, don't look at her with those iniquitous blue eyes of yours, as though she is the most beautiful, fascinating and important woman in the world – that is, not unless you mean it, which seems to me highly unlikely.' She stood up, slipping her dress over her head. 'Now get out of that bed, go home, and treat your momma as though she's someone you like...you may not have noticed, but she's a woman too.'

Ryan sat on the edge of the bed and watched her walk towards the door. He said, 'Just one little thing, Doc ...' She stopped and looked at him enquiringly over her shoulder. He grinned and held up a wisp of nylon lace. 'You forgot your panties.'

She grinned back. 'Keep them as a souvenir you bastard!' she said over her shoulder and kept walking.

*   *   *

He'd scarcely taken his key from the lock and swung open the door of number sixteen, before Joel hurtled from where he was crouched at the foot of the stairs and flung his arms about his waist.

'Dad!'

Ryan was startled: such un-cool behaviour was something new. 'Hey,' he steadied him, 'where's the fire, boy...'

'It's Gran'ma – she's *sick* – real sick!'

Ryan's heart thumped; heeling the door shut he squatted down, holding Joel's shoulders he said quickly, 'Take it easy now...where is she?'

'Downstairs...dad, I been waiting and waiting an' you didn't come!' Joel's face was streaked with tears.

'OK, OK; I'm here now.' Holding him tightly to his side, Ryan almost fell down the basement stairs. The sight of Hannah, fully dressed and sat up against the pillows of her bed had his breath escaping in a relieved whistle. She was looking pale but reassuringly normal and smiled at his precipitate entrance, spreading apologetic hands.

'Sorry, honey if I scared the boy – just felt a little faint when we got home – too much walking about I guess.'

'Never mind about scaring the boy, you damn near gave *me* a heart attack!' He sat down beside her and Joel immediately scrambled onto his knees; Ryan put an arm about him and held him close. He took one of Hannah's hands in his. 'What happened exactly?'

She shrugged. 'Like I said, I just felt a little faint; thought it would be best to set Joel to watch out for you while I caught a little sleep.'

She was casual; too casual. He knew his ma, or thought he did. 'Horse feathers, I'm getting the doctor...' He made to rise but she stopped him.

'See, here, I want none of that fussing. I'm fine now. You go running for the doctor when there's nothing wrong and you'll get me a bad name.'

'At least let me get Charlie – '

'It's my feet that are tired, not my brain. You go on up and feed that boy and I'll be joining you when I've freshened up.'

Ryan gave her a long hard look, but she only smiled again. 'Stop fussing – sure, you're bad as your dada.'

'Don't you come on with that old Irish malarkey or I'll *know* there's something wrong.' But he had to smile and give in; this was Hannah as she really was, not some suddenly frighteningly sick woman. He slid Joel off his knees and stood up, careful to keep an arm around him. 'You see,' he told him with faint sarcasm, 'your grandmother was just tired. Old ladies get like that when they've spent most of the day tagging around after boys and their girl friends.'

'Ryan honey, you call me an old lady again and I'll *show* you there's nothing wrong with me!' She squeezed his hand. 'Now take that boy away and get him cleaned up and with some food in him. I'll be along in a bit.'

*   *   *

Joel sat on the worktop while Ryan cut bread, fried bacon and set him to stirring beans in the pan. He still looked anxious and asked suddenly, 'She isn't going to die, is she?'

'Nope,' Ryan made a snatch as the toaster shot out a couple of slices then shoved in a couple more while reaching for the butter, wondering how women managed to do half a dozen things at once *and* answer their kid's questions without going crazy. But then, as he knew to his cost, some of them didn't manage it at all…He hesitated, then gave his son what he hoped was a reassuring grin. 'Trust me: she won't be going anyplace where she can't tell *us* what to do!'

'She might, though – and Abby's an awful long way away.'

'She won't; and I'm here anyway.'

Joel didn't look at him, only stirred harder at the beans. 'You ain't hardly here ever anymore.'

Ryan sighed, 'Don't say ain't,' he corrected automatically but the guilt he'd been pushing aside since his arrival in the house kicked in hard; Joel was right, he hadn't been here overmuch; not since Hannah had arrived and relieved him of what had become the burden of being on call twenty-four hours a day. He had, he thought with some shame, most surely been culpable of neglecting both of them; hadn't given much thought to the fact that taking almost sole responsibility for a small boy and running a large house virtually single-handed would be

95

a sight more wearying for a woman in her mid-sixties than it had been for him.

What could he say now in reply to his son's simple, if baldly phrased reproach – that he was sorry; he'd been busy fucking a neighbour when he was needed but would make it up to them both later? He felt a sudden stir of disquiet, Joel wasn't a kid who frightened easily; Hannah might have been more than just a little faint and tired.

'Joel, leave the beans for a minute.' Ryan took his shoulders and turned him to face him. 'Tell me exactly what happened when your grandma took sick.'

Joel's face assumed the agonised contortions of a small boy thinking: 'Well,' he offered eventually, 'first we took Niki home, but Gran'ma wouldn't stay for tea or anything 'cause she said we should get back for you, but when she was opening the door she had a sort of pain and nearly fell over...she was awful white and trembly.' He relived the moment, his frightened gaze fixed on Ryan's face. 'You weren't here so she said I must let her have my shoulder to help her downstairs; then she told me to go back up an' wait for you...an' I waited a long time but you didn't come an' I thought...I thought she might be *dead* an' I was all alone.'

He began crying again, great fat tears that blobbed on his jeans and he scrubbed at the wet patches with angry, distracted hands wailing 'Where were you, where *were* you?'

Jesus! Ryan moved the pans off the hob and taking him in his arms sat in the old wooden armchair, hugging him close. 'I'm sorry; real sorry.'

Joel squirmed, burrowing desperately into his shoulder. 'I thought you'd only be a minute 'cause we saw your car was by the shops an' Gran'ma said you must have just gone for tobacco an' would be back before we knew it; but you weren't...'

There was a lump in Ryan's throat. 'Shh...it's OK.' *You bastard*, he cursed savagely: *you were in Charlie's bed while your mother was sick and your kid was going through hell.* He smoothed back the hair from his son's wet face, feeling for his handkerchief before he remembered he'd left it with Calamity Jane. *You're a great one for making people cry, aren't you?* he jeered in silent disgust. *You could maybe do it for a living...*

Gradually Joel's sobs lessened until at last he lay exhausted in his arms like a sodden kewpie fairground doll. Ryan took him to the bathroom and for the second time that afternoon washed his son's tearstained face. It had been, he thought as he towelled him dry, one

96

hell of a homecoming.

* * *

While he was setting the meal on the table Hannah appeared, freshly made up and looking almost her normal self. Refusing the bacon and beans she drank tea and ate toast with apparent appetite while chatting with a still subdued Joel about the visit to the museum.

Ryan watched her with vague misdoubt. He couldn't quite put a finger on it but knew something, somewhere was wrong; that nothing quite added up. Maybe, he thought, it had suited him not to question her reasons for suggesting she come to England to stay with them, but questions there most certainly were and he should have asked them before all this started.

First, why she would make the trip at all: she led a busy life, with a close circle of friends, a home she loved and wouldn't normally leave to live in an unknown country with a notoriously unpredictable climate. Then that she chose a sea crossing: Hannah, who always took the shortest and most convenient route between two points, who enjoyed flying and had no particular love of the ocean. Finally, and most telling of all, over these past weeks she hadn't been forever on his back: to go to Mass, to find a decent woman to be a mother to his son, to be the good, upright man she'd raised him to be. Sure, she niggled now and again, but mildly, jokily, as though she got some private amusement from it all and that none of it mattered overmuch, anyway.

He would, Ryan determined, get the bottom of it all sometime soon.

* * *

He did the honours that night and had an easy ride. Joel was still very quiet: he bathed, cleaned his teeth and got himself into bed in record time then as Ryan was about to tell him goodnight he asked 'Can I have a story...' he pointed to his bedside table, 'this one?'

'Sure.' Ryan picked up the book. Covered in dull red cloth and with faded gilt title it wasn't Joel's usual sort of bedtime reading. 'Hey, where did you find this?'

'Miz Frazier said I could have it. Nicole's granddaddy gave her a new one for her last birthday – a big one with a gold picture of the E'phlant's Child an' the crocodile on the front.'

How come, Ryan mused that Julia Frazier could succeed where

he'd failed, by getting his kid to read something other than Superman or Mutt 'n Jeff...?

'Which story do you want?' he asked.

Joel settled down, thumb in mouth, 'The Butterfly one.'

'My favourite,' Ryan said and turning to the last pages of the 'Just So Stories', began to read "The Butterfly That Stamped".

'This, O my Best Beloved, is a story – a new and wonderful story – a story quite different from the other stories – a story about The Most Wise Sovereign Suleiman-bin-Doaud...'

Ryan finished and closed the covers gently; he thought the boy was asleep but as he laid the book back on the table Joel murmured drowsily: '"*She* was Queen of Sabea, and *he* was Asia's Lord, but they both of 'em talked to butterflies when they took their walks abroad!"'

Well, thought Ryan as he made his way back downstairs, thanks to a kick-start from Calamity Jane he may, if he lived that long, see his son reading Racine one day.

*   *   *

Sometime toward the end of that night he half-woke, conscious of a bony back pressed against his. Struggling with sleep, his heart thumping he put out a hand, breathing: 'Niles?' then heard Joel's sleep-drugged response: 'Sing, daddy...' and realised he had real human company.

He whispered, 'Not now' and Joel snuffled a bit then wriggled further into his back. In the stillness and with that warm bony body pressed against his, Ryan lay staring at the dawn light filtering through the curtains, letting the past weeks unroll within his tired mind; realising with wonder and some dismay that events and people and places were forcing him to look at himself and at the world in general with different eyes. It was uncomfortable, even painful to find that old Ryan creeping back: the one who wasn't afraid to let himself care...maybe in time even let himself be seen to be caring.

But all in all he reckoned it didn't feel too bad. Not too bad at all.

*   *   *

As is sometimes the case, something poignant and tender – his dawn awakening, his penitential-son mood of the previous day, his own son's pleasing interest in decent literature and a consequent mellowing towards Julia Frazier, particularly the latter, degenerated into farce at breakfast the next morning when Joel, refreshed after his nights sleep, paused in his attempt to break the world speed record for eating a bowl of breakfast cereal to ask, 'Dad, what's a Call Girl?'

Ryan breathed '*Holy cow!*' under his breath and picked up his coffee cup, sipping thoughtfully and buying time. Eventually he said, 'It's the kind of lady that some guys will pay a whole lot of dollars to make them feel happy.'

Joel's brow creased. 'Gee, I thought they were something to do with telephones.'

Ryan suppressed a grin. 'I guess in a way they are. What made you ask?'

'Nuthin. Just something I read at Nicole's.'

'What do you mean: "read at Nicole's"' he was immediately alert, '*what* did you read?'

'Some magazine stuff,' Joel waved his spoon. 'There was pictures of these girls, see – one of 'em was sittin' on a chair with no clothes – well, I s'pose no clothes, 'cause it said 'Naked Temptress' but that was a lie because you couldn't see nuthin' because the chair was in the way an' she was a Call Girl an'–'

'Yeah, yeah – I get the picture. Feigning disinterest Ryan picked up his coffee. 'Now can it or you'll be late for school.' He was annoyed. Damn fool woman letting kids read a load of crap about a hooker and her fancy politician boyfriend.

Not to be deflected Joel spooned up some more cereal and offered conversationally, 'It said the other lady – the pouty one, not the one on the chair – 's a common prostitute who made her money outta men an' Nicole reckons she's gonna be one of them when she grows up so's she can get rich an' help her mum.' He looked up into Ryan's thunderstruck face and wrinkled his brow again. 'I thought I might be one of them too, although she thinks it's only for girls, but she'll ask her mum sometime what they do so it *might* be OK for me too.'

Ryan's coffee sloshed over; snatching at his napkin and mopping the spill he said tersely 'Get on with your breakfast and don't talk so much!'

Joel persisted. 'But dad, I been thinkin': if they c'n earn lots, why doesn't Miz Frazier be a prostitute and get the money for herself? Or she could be a Call Girl, couldn't she?' He began to enthuse. 'She's gotta telephone an' she smells great and she's real nice – I bet she could make a lot of men happy and get paid lots of dollars like you said – I bet she could even make *you* happy –'

'Joel,' Ryan restrained himself with an effort. 'One more word from you about call-girls and prostitutes and how Miz Frazier can get rich quick and you'll go to your room straight from school and stay there.'

'But dad, you *said* –'

Ryan raised his voice. 'You quit talking about it – NOW. You hear me?'

He muttered 'Yes, sir,' and stuck his nose back into his cereal.

Hannah appeared from the kitchen with a rack of toast. 'What's all the yelling about, Ry?'

She looked rested and fit and far too alert for Ryan's liking particularly as he was feeling neither. Yesterday's morning drive from Hampshire, followed by crossed swords with Julia Frazier for lunch, afternoon sex with Charlie and an evening of Joel's tears and his own guilt had him feeling limp as a wet sock. 'Nothing,' he answered shortly, 'just the boy talking dumb.'

'I was not!' Joel was indignant; Ryan glared at him and he subsided back into his cereal. Hannah raised an eyebrow.

'Sure sounded like you were doing a lot of hollering about nothing then.'

'I'm going into college early...' Ryan gulped the rest of his coffee and stood up, adding meanly, 'perhaps Joel should have a rest from spending so much time around at the Frazier's; he seems to be getting some mighty funny ideas.'

'How funny?' she asked. He opened his mouth to terminate any further questions but Joel got there first.

'I only said Nicole was gonna be a prostitute an' make a lot of money when she grows up an' Miz Frazier could be a call-girl right now if she liked an' maybe make dad happy...' he waved his spoon indignantly and droplets of milk flew over the table, 'how come *everything* I say makes him mad at me, Gran'ma?'

She gave a barely repressed yelp of laughter and began to butter her toast. 'Who knows? Maybe it's easier to be mad at you than be mad at himself.' Without looking at Ryan she added obliquely, 'Don't forget your car's parked right around the corner, will you, honey – saw it from the bus last evening!'

Ryan decided he'd had enough for one morning and left, slamming the house door behind him.

12

MARLBOROUGH STREET, CHELSEA
November 1965

The next few weeks passed without major incident or alarm, but with his senses sharpened by Hannah's still unexplained collapse Ryan watched her closely. If she was aware of his concern she made no sign, nor did she comment upon the fact that he was home more often. Although during the absence of Charlie's long time partner Ryan continued from time to time to enjoy the comforts of her bed, he made good and sure that he was home most evenings for Joel. Not that Joel always needed him that much as he in turn continued to make regular after school visits to Julia Frazier's alleged dump in Battersea, from which outings Hannah always collected him.

This irritated the hell out of Ryan because these collections always took place while he was at work. As time passed he found himself rather keen to meet up again with the elusive Mrs Frazier, if only to get even for the Call Girls, rile her a little and watch those dark eyes flash in anger. But no matter how much he might hurry home, Hannah had always left for Battersea before his return and his hints that she was tiring herself unnecessarily were met with a bland smile and the observation that she enjoyed the short journey on the bus and her little chats with Julia.

Apart from these journeys across the river a couple of times a week, Ryan suspected that his mother spent the larger part of each day in the house. Back in Boston he knew she would have been out and about – shopping, visiting, going to theatre matinees, playing bridge at the club and lunching with friends. Sure, she'd already made friends in Chelsea, but she did that anywhere, making friends was standard Irish custom, but it was gradually born on him that most of them came to *her* instead of the other way around, and that Sixteen Marlborough Street was the main venue for all the afternoon tea and bridge parties and gossip.

He figured there was a lot of the latter as she knew every damn thing that happened within a two-mile radius of the street. Certainly she knew he visited Charlie, though Ryan doubted she'd believe the main reason for those visits, unless the Archangel Gabriel himself told her. In Hannah's book well-bred professional women like Charlie just didn't do things like go to bed in the afternoons to have sex with anyone but their husbands. While she herself might have pursued a lifelong policy of flirting with any and every man, from the bus conductor to the parish priest, it would never have occurred to her to be unfaithful to his father.

For a worldly woman Ryan reckoned his ma could be pretty naïve.

*   *   *

'Hannah's bothering me.' he told Charlie when he dropped by one afternoon, on this occasion just for a chat between a couple of her private patients. 'It's half term and Joel's over at Calamity Jane's all day today, and for the first time Hannah's asked would I collect him: says she's got to visit some old dame across town this afternoon – one of her bridge buddies. When I offered to drive her she said no, she'd take a cab. I just don't get it.'

'I daresay she wants to stay independent.'

'Yeah, maybe.' Restless, he wandered about the room to fetch up at the window. Gazing at the trees standing black against the damp brick and stonework of the houses opposite, their branches bare and hung with great beads of moisture, he dove his hands in his pockets, grumbling, 'I'd forgotten how fucking awful London was in winter.'

'Cheer up. When you've had another gander at your Julia's legs this evening and she's got your pecker up, you won't notice the weather.' Charlie took up the little leather pouch she kept her grass in and began to roll a thin joint.

He scowled. 'Charlie, for a lady you can be pretty crude sometimes.'

'For a gentleman you can be pretty evasive; why can't you admit Julia Frazier attracts you?'

'Because she doesn't – and as she obviously couldn't give a rat's arse about *me* that's AOK.' He took a couple of drags of the reefer Charlie handed him and passed it back. He sat down, draping his long legs over the arm of the chair. 'Anyway, one woman at a time's my motto.'

She drew deep and sent a thin spiral of smoke ceiling-ward. 'You know, I'm beginning to ask myself why you spend so much time and energy hiding behind that macho façade of yours.'

'Hey – dump the analysis – you're between patients; remember?'

'Umm, I'm glad you reminded me, you'd better shift.' She

pinched the butt and placed it back in the bag. 'God, but I'd like to get into your head sometime!'

He said dryly 'Don't even try; you have no chance of making it with me.'

'I thought I already had, "in the Biblical sense", as you once put it.'

Ryan took an appreciative look at her: the long angular body with unexpectedly voluptuous breasts, the short curling ash blonde hair, the square, professionally clinical face, redeemed from severity by a pair of calm grey eyes and a generous mouth that always held the hint of a smile.

She met his gaze and raised her eyebrows. He turned his head away. 'Yeah, well, we make it pretty good together, so lets keep it that way – and why should I pay your indecent fee for an hour's soul-searching when I could do it in the confessional faster and for free?'

'*I'd* let you do it for free, but you won't, will you?'

'No – and I won't do it in the confessional, either.'

She laughed and threw a cushion at his head. 'OK, I'll leave your nasty little brain to simmer in peace: but you mark my words, one of these days you'll spill it all to someone. Good, caring men who don't, or won't, see how good and caring they really are always do. Sooner or later something, or someone will tip the scales and it will all bubble up to the surface.'

He was uncomfortable and covered by scuffing his shoe against the carpet, drawling with mock bashfulness, 'Aw, shucks, lady, you sure do say the darndest things...'

*   *   *

He may make a joke of it all, he mused as he made the short drive towards Battersea later that afternoon, but recently there had been times when he'd been tempted to take up Charlie's offer and have her plumb the depths of his mind, both conscious and subconscious. A kind of brain enema, he thought with a grin. It might do him a lot of good, but then again he might find the resurrecting of his past, and the reality of the sum total of his life to date, just too darned uncomfortable to live with.

He passed over Battersea Bridge and the old London hit him right between the eyes. He thought: back home Time and Newsweek may continue to enthuse that London was swinging, and certainly it swung pretty wild around their neck of the woods, with the Chelsea Drugstore knocking the eye out, Twiggy and Mary Quant setting the style in the Kings Road. Afghan coats, Military uniforms, trendy drugs and loon pants down Carnaby Street; Mick Jagger pouting and strutting, the Beatles telling how it was with Eleanor Rigby and David Bailey snapping them all.

But with only a mile or so and a bridge between, Battersea was like another country. The market that flourished down the Northcote Road brought a splash of life and colour to the drab thoroughfare each Saturday, but that one event apart, only the green stretches and flowerbeds of Battersea Park relieved the depressing sight of littered gutters, rows of Victorian villas and the lorries grinding up the Rise, spewing diesel fumes onto the damp dank sidewalks.

Ryan crawled along looking out for the inaptly named Lavender Sweep, and when he eventually reached it, located Julia Frazier's dump halfway along. He knew it was her place because in the lamplight he could see his son was sat outside of the house on the white-painted wall, between a small blonde girl and a Joel-sized black boy; all of them well zipped into their parkas, each clasping a half eaten apple apiece and looking like the three wise monkeys having a night off.

As Ryan climbed out of the car Joel stood up, a nicety of British manners he seemed to have picked up, along with quite a few others Ryan had noticed of late, and his companions followed suit, ranging in line to stand like diminutive soldiers drawn up for battle.

'I hope you haven't come to take Joel away,' the small girl spoke politely but firmly; she had, Ryan noted with some amusement, her mother's eyes and determined chin, 'because we haven't really finished playing yet.'

He bent to her level. 'That depends: what are you playing?'

'Truth or Dare.'

'Sounds dangerous to me,' he straightened, 'OK. I'll go talk to your mommy while you finish.' He tipped Joel a salute, 'Hi, there.'

'Hi there, dad.'

The black boy said 'Hi, there, man.' Ryan said 'Howya doing, man?' and gave him a high five and got a small pink palm across his own and a wide grin in return before all three hitched back up on the wall and resumed their game.

He walked up the path and made to knock on the door, but it was open and gave at his touch, so giving an introductory cough he stepped into the narrow hallway.

'If that's you, Nicole, tell Joel his grandma will be here soon...' Julia Frazier came from a door at the end of the passage, wiping her hands on a kitchen cloth. She stopped dead, the now familiar flush

104

staining her cheeks. 'Oh – it's you.'

'Sorry, but the door was open…'

'That's all right. Come in.'

With a self-conscious gesture she put the hand holding the cloth behind her back. 'You've caught me on the hop; I usually have him ready for Hannah when she comes.'

'That's OK. My fault: I'm kind of early.'

For a moment they stood awkwardly, she holding open the door to what was obviously the living room, Ryan hesitating, caught off guard by the sudden rush of pleasure he felt at the sight of her: flushed face, untidy hair, no make up and all automatically let his gaze rove downward and immediately the wary look was back in her eyes.

'Go on in and sit down,' she said quietly, that edge of steel showing. 'I'll make some tea.'

'Thanks.' he watched her walk back into the kitchen, then turned into the long room which, like that of the Marlborough Street house, ran clear through from front to back. For a minute he stood just inside the doorway looking around, both surprised and impressed. Outside the house may appear something of a dump, but inside it was a revelation; a testimonial to Julia Frazier's taste and talent that could make old and shabby look up-market and classy.

It was warm and comfortable, with a couple of unmatched but harmonious easy chairs and a long couch; the two alcoves either side of the fireplace shelved and filled with books; an eclectic collection of pictures on the walls; an old desk by the far window covered with papers and more books; some part-worked tapestry on a standing frame; a thick dusky pink carpet and matching heavy drapes. Behind the door stood an old but well-kept upright piano, the top littered with sheet music. Ryan crossed to the mantle on the opposite wall to look at the photograph in a silver frame of a dark, curly haired man standing beside a Hunter Jet, hands in the pockets of his flying suit, obviously in relaxed conversation with the fitter who perched above him on the cowling of the aircraft. This, he reasoned, must be the Jamie who had been full of life and laughter before he'd test-flown one plane too many…

Beneath the mantle a fire burned in the old-fashioned iron grate and in the background a radio played softly *Try a Little Tenderness* with Nat King Cole's smooth voice trickling the lyrics like warm chocolate sauce over ice cream.

It was one of those rooms that say 'Sit down; relax.…' and gratefully Ryan did just that. Sinking down into a worn but comfortable chair beside the fire he listened to Julia Frazier moving around in the kitchen and watched through the window the Three Wise Monkeys huddled together on the wall, deep in their private, no adults admitted, world. He tried to fit the spiky Julia into some kind of category, measuring her against the more notable women in his life, both sacred and profane but still unable to come up with an answer.

She wasn't beautiful as Claire, nor cutely pretty like Ellie; not laid back classic cool and sexy like Charlie; nor street smart, uplifted and Max Factored within an inch of her life like Maria, one of his more classy occasional women back home, but neither was she plain or devoid of sex appeal. No woman with eyes like *that*, he mused, could ever be plain, and sure, she had a complexion any woman would envy, while those legs and cute butt screamed out for something more descriptive than just plain sexy. She was, he thought with a smile, a brown woman: brown eyes, brown hair, brown skin like his own – except his was older and a deal more leathery – the kind of colouring that owed nothing to sun and wouldn't vary overmuch in tone between summer and winter...

She came into the room quietly, startling him out of his pleasurable daydream. As he made to stand she said 'Don't bother' and placing the tray she carried on a low coffee table before the fire, knelt and began to fill two mugs from an earthenware teapot.

Ryan could sense the wall she'd erected between them as clearly as though it had been lit up in neon lights. He took a deep breath. 'I'm sorry.'

She glanced up at him then away again. 'Sorry for what?'

'You know for what: for riling you the last time we met. And I hit on you again just now, but that's only habit, nothing personal.'

'A bad habit, but your apology is accepted.' As she still wasn't making eye contact he risked it and took another good look.

Today she wore a dark blue skirt of some soft material, a pale pink wool shirt and loosely knotted around her shoulders, a plain sweater that matched the skirt. Small gold studs glinted in her ears and during her absence she had brushed her hair and put on a little lipstick. She looked elegant and very top-drawer. He thought about the clothes she'd worn that first day and was puzzled as to why any woman with such obvious good taste should have been going around dressed like a Ruritanian peasant...

She handed him his tea. 'If you've quite finished looking,' she offered composedly, 'you might try drinking that.'

He said feelingly, 'I'll bet you scare the bejesus out of your pupils – or do you just reserve the put-downs for guys like me?'

She sat back on her heels and for a few moments studied him

gravely. Her mouth broke into a reluctant smile. 'You and all the other roving eyes, though I have a nasty suspicion that *you,* Professor Petersen, are not very easily put down.'

He took courage from the smile and ventured, 'The first time we met, you, er, well, you were dressed kind of odd – very nice,' he added hastily, 'but a tad... unconventional. I guess that just makes me look a little harder each time we meet.'

For a moment her expression was uncomprehending, a slight frown between her brows, then her face cleared. 'Oh, *yes* – I remember!' Suddenly she was convulsed with laughter. 'I'd got roped into helping with a 'Gypsy Camp Day' for the kids at the community centre; I hadn't stopped to change after because Nicole wasn't too well that day and I'd left her with my neighbour.' She wiped at her eyes with her fingers then gave another peal of laughter. 'Don't tell me – you thought I was some loopy groupie with a rock band!'

Resignedly he handed her his handkerchief. 'No, ma'am, I thought you were straight out of the chorus of *Carmen* – and don't you have a decent handkerchief of your own? You keep doing this every time I lay eyes on you I'll soon be clean out of them myself.'

She waved away his offer. 'Thanks, I only need one of those when I'm having a good snivel...and the one you loaned me is laundered and ready for return. Remind me before you leave.'

Ryan sat nursing his drink, feeling at ease with her for the first time. He gestured around the room. 'I like all this: it's friendly; welcoming. I can see why Joel likes coming.'

'I like to have him.' She hesitated a moment, stirring her tea although she hadn't used any sugar. 'There's something bothers me, though – I didn't like to ask Hannah, but...' she hesitated again then said in a rush, 'I've gathered from her that your wife died, but at school Joel's been telling the other children she's still in America. I thought you ought to know he's a bit mixed up about it.'

It was a real zinger; if she'd dropped a flat iron on his head she couldn't have fazed him more. For a few moments he just stared at her in total disbelief before he found his voice.

'But that's crazy. He *knows* she's dead.'

'Oh, I'm sure he does. Perhaps it's just a fantasy because he wants – needs – a mother.'

'Well there's not much I can do about that!'

He was badly shaken. Joel had never talked about Ellie; never asked a single question either before or after her death. He'd seen so little of her over the last four years of her life when she'd been in the clinic that Ryan had figured her actual dying had made little impact.

107

Belatedly he remembered Hannah urging him to listen to and talk with his son; that there were things that he needed brought out into the open.

Conscious stricken Ryan rubbed a hand through his hair. Shit, he thought, but I'm a self-absorbed bastard if I could miss what's been going on in that boy's head.

Julia said earnestly, 'Look, I'm sorry. Perhaps I shouldn't have said, but after half-term I'll be taking over Joel's class and I don't want to get it wrong.'

She sat quite still, watching him intently and he made a distracted brushing motion with his hand.

'It's OK. I have to think about it.' He was silent, mulling over her words. The most ridiculous thought began at the very back of his consciousness that he could, with a little persuasion actually tell this woman about Joel's mother; the fiasco of their marriage: why it had happened and how it had ended. Then he remembered how abrasive she could be and immediately dismissed the idea as sheer lunacy. The forthright woman he'd so far encountered may have just shown she had a softer side, but he wasn't about to take a bet that she'd keep to it if he embarrassed her by getting close up and personal; might even think he was making a play for sympathy.

He found he was gripping the mug so tightly it was liable to shatter; only their respective offspring bounding into the room at that moment relieved the tension. Letting go the breath he didn't know he'd been holding, Ryan thought he had never before been so grateful to be interrupted in any *tête à tête* with a woman. He shot a glance at Julia Frazier and saw she was regarding him closely, a puzzled look in those expressive eyes.

He steadied his hand and put down the mug. Joel hovered in the doorway but Nicole came straight over to stand in front of him, fixing him again with her direct stare. 'Hello?' he raised an enquiring eyebrow. 'Something I can do for you, cup cake?'

She appeared to find this encouraging and gave a great big smile; the kind little girls, and not so little girls the world over give to a man when they want something. She leaned confidingly against his knee. 'We are going to see my grandpa in Devon the day after tomorrow for three whole days. Can Joel come too?'

He answered her cautiously. 'I'm none too sure. How would your grandpa – and your mommy feel about that?'

'Oh, they'd be pleased!'

He glanced up at Julia Frazier. 'Would they?'

'Very,' she answered gravely.

He hedged, really just to test how she'd handle a refusal. 'It's a long way for three days.'

She responded quickly, giving another of her half smiles and he knew she'd already anticipated he might get awkward and had all the answers off pat. 'Only to Bran Tor: it's on Dartmoor, not all that far from Oakhampton, and I'm used to making the journey; I do it regularly. Nicole would love the company and if we leave early on Thursday we don't need to start back until Sunday lunch time.'

He asked dryly. 'What was it Hamlet said about the lady protesting too much? I only asked and I haven't said no...yet.'

She flushed and shrugged, 'Oh, well, it's up to you, of course.' she hesitated and added, 'I wondered if Hannah...well, she's looked a little tired lately. I thought she might do with the change. I was going to ask her today.'

Yeah, he thought, I bet you were – and wouldn't you just have locked me right up between the pair of you! Not that he would have refused anyway. With both Hannah and Joel gone that would leave the whole weekend free. If he could summon up sufficient courage he might return once more to that unfinished business in Hawksley, without the problem of leaving his son to fret that gran'ma might die on him.

'*Please*, dad.' Joel had left his post at the door and come to lean against his other knee, gazing up into his face in agonised supplication. Ryan saw he was expecting him to say 'no' and conscience hit him another blow. He'd been so busy testing and teasing Julia he'd forgotten his son was a part of all this sparring.

Belatedly he grinned and tweaked his hair. 'OK. I guess you've earned it,' he agreed then watched Joel's face break into the kind of smile every father should get from his son at least once in a lifetime.

'Gee, dad, thanks – thanks a million trillion!' and Joel hugged him. Just like that.

Over his head Ryan looked at Julia Frazier; now she raised an eyebrow and grinned with ill-concealed triumph. 'This,' he said laconically, 'is what I call a *fait accompli;* and I'll talk to you later – in fact, see me after class!'

'Would that be before or after half-term?'

'After. Over dinner,' he stood. 'I'll get Hannah to call tonight with her answer.' Tightening his upper lip over his teeth he paraphrased, '*Of all the joints in all the world, I had to walk into yours...*'

'You're welcome,' she said, 'but don't hold your breath about that dinner.'

She stood at the window, watching him walk to the car, his arm around Joel's shoulders. Just before he opened the door he glanced back, caught her looking and gave his sardonic two-edged grin. Bastard, she thought equably and gave him an answering and equally equivocal smile before stepping back into the room and closing the curtains. Ryan Petersen, she mused thoughtfully, was too confident, too attractive and just too damned disturbing to have around...

'I like Joel's daddy.' Her daughter offered from where she sat cross legged on the rug before the fire. 'His eyes go all crinkly at the corners when he looks at you, don't they?'

'Do they?' Julia picked up the tea tray and stood for a moment, balancing it on her hip. Nicole looked around and gave her gap-toothed grin.

'Yes, they do. Can I come with you when you go to dinner?'

'No.'

'Why not?'

'Because I shall not be going.'

Her daughter's lower lip jutted stubbornly. 'But you *have* to; he asked you.'

Julia thought: no he didn't he *told* me. She said, 'I expect he will have forgotten all about it by the time we come back. Now up you go and wash before supper.'

Nicole got slowly and grumpily to her feet. 'If he asked me, *I'd* go!'

Julia resumed her journey towards the kitchen, observing sweetly over her shoulder. 'Well if he ever does, you may.'

13

HAWKSLEY, HAMPSHIRE

November 1965

Ryan waved the old Ford away from the house in Lavender Sweep; Hannah in the front passenger seat, the two children in the rear; the latter well armed with comic books and a couple of empty cereal cartons, just in case...

Although not exactly crazy about them all travelling as far as Devon in her crappy heap, by now Ryan had enough faith in Julia Frazier's good sense to figure she wouldn't take any chance of being stranded again. She would at least have made sure the car was in good shape.

He watched them out of sight, then feeling unexpectedly lonesome drove back to Chelsea. As he hadn't bothered with breakfast he stopped at a café just off the bridge for what had to be the unhealthiest fry-up in London, before carrying on to Kings and a day's work.

Time dragged in the empty house that evening; Charlie was away to her parents for the weekend; he had no lectures or tutorials for Friday, and once he'd packed a small valise ready for an early start next morning he poured a drink, put the Rachmaninov Third on the Decola and stretched out on the couch.

Julia had shaken him badly with her revelation about Joel's fantasy mother, and for an hour or more he turned the problem over in his mind. Looked at from any angle, it was clear that he'd have to talk to his son, and that before very long. Just lately life seemed to be nothing but problems needing to be faced and sorted; he still hadn't yet figured out the whys and wherefores of the change in Hannah, and what, if anything, he should do about that.

The Rachmaninov was a bad choice, being the sort of heart-wrenching stuff guaranteed to send anyone into a major depression; when it finished he exchanged it for a John McCormack selection of Irish airs belonging to Hannah, which he always affected not to like, then putting both son and mother out of his mind settled down to read the latest James Bond, both music and book proving pretty good antidotes to depression.

111

*　　　*　　　*

He left the following morning while the roads were still reasonably clear; making good time out of town and onto the Great West Road. He drove carefully, mindful that despite Ian Fleming and John McCormack, he hadn't managed all that much sleep but spent a large proportion of the night figuring out what would be the best way to discover exactly what had happened to put the master of Hawksley Manor in a wheelchair, and why neither Claire nor Rupert appeared any longer to be part of the scenery.

The problem, Ryan thought as he manoeuvred the Jowett around Twickenham, was how to find the answers without going anywhere near Geoffrey de Lacy again.

*　　　*　　　*

By the time he stopped for a late breakfast at a diner just past Camberley he'd decided to stay again at The Bull in Stafford Ley. Although the Manor was a couple of miles away in the next village, the loquacious Eddie would probably be well informed about the happenings well beyond his own home ground, also, questioning him had the added advantage of not having to begin all over again with someone else.

Despite an initial determination to reach his destination and get the whole thing sorted and done with, Ryan found himself strangely reluctant to arrive. He took his time on the road, stopping again at a pub in Ower and lingering over a plate of shepherd's pie.

For these past months he'd pushed to the back of his mind that brief conversation with de Lacy, only occasionally allowing himself to worry and fret at the memory of it, like a terrier around a rabbit hole, always in the end drawing back, aware that the discovery of what had happened to leave the master of Hawksley crippled and apparently alone, might in the event be more painful than his present ignorance.

To allow the thought that Claire might have loved someone else more than she'd loved him, loved so much that she would do what Ryan had begged for in vain, left home and husband for him, could after all these years still stir the black and bitter jealousy he had once felt for the returning Geoffrey. Now as he drew nearer to his destination, an almost overwhelming feeling of apprehension was beginning to build, so that by the time he hit The Bull he was almost ready to turn tail and head back to the safety of Marlborough Street.

*   *   *

Walking into the empty bar he rapped on the counter and when Eddie appeared greeted him abruptly, 'Hi again, Eddie; a whisky – and make it a large one will you.'

Eddie gave a wide grin. 'Hey – it's Mister Petersen, innit?' He shook his head apologetically. 'I'm sorry, I can't serve you now, sir – me dad'ud kill me; it's past lunchtime closing.'

Ryan hefted his canvass grip onto a barstool. 'If I book a room can you bring up the bottle and a glass?'

'Aye, sir, I can do that,' he turned and took a key from the rack behind the bar. 'Same room as last time – that all right?'

'Yeah – and, Eddie, better make it the bottle and *two* glasses.'

'Whatever you say, sir.'

Eddie followed close on Ryan's heels as he took the stairs two at a time. Setting the bottle and glasses down on the small writing table by the window the barman stood, eyeing him uncertainly. Ryan broke open the Scotch and poured a couple of fingers into each glass.

'Grab a chair and relax, Eddie – I need to pick your brain before you get busy again.'

'Right,' Eddie pulled a chair to the table, 'now, sir; what is it you want to know?'

Ryan lifted his glass, emptied it in one then reached for the bottle to pour another. 'What do you know about Hawksley Manor – and its owner?'

Eddie looked puzzled. 'Only what everyone else knows; that it's open to visitors all season and Squire lives mostly in the old stable cottage – tho' I think he moves back into the big house in the winter, especially when Miss Sophie comes home.'

'And who the hell's Miss Sophie?'

'His daughter, of course...' He grinned and kissed his fingers, 'now there's a looker for you!'

'Oh, he has a daughter, does he?' Ryan frowned. 'What about the son?'

'Young Rupert?'

'Yeah,' he was impatient, 'young Rupert.'

'Why, he's dead, sir, along with young Mrs de Lacy. That would be, oh, more'n ten years ago now...' he screwed up his eyes in concentration, '... nineteen fifty-four it was, I remember now because it was around the time Bannister ran that four minute mile...'

113

Ryan sat staring stupidly at him as he rambled on. He felt as though he was looking down a kaleidoscope at a series of changing images, all whirling and merging into one another: Claire and Rupert, Samson and de Lacy in the wheelchair...de Lacy and Claire, Rupert and himself...

'WAIT!' He realised he must have hollered because Eddie stopped suddenly, caught in mid sentence, his mouth agape. Fighting for control Ryan gripped the edge of the table. 'How...why...' he floundered. '*What* accident?'

'Why, the car crash – I'm sorry, sir. I didn't realise...'

'It's all right.' Ryan's hands were shaking and he fumbled for his glass, spilling some of the liquid on the table. Reaching for a handkerchief, the one newly laundered by Julia, he mopped ineffectually at the spill then threw the sopping linen in the waste bin. 'I didn't mean to yell at you.' He swallowed at the painful constriction in his throat. 'It's just...I knew them; a long time ago...I hadn't heard.' Ryan looked at him helplessly. 'Tell me about it.'

'Well, they was all in the Land Rover – that is, Squire an' Missis an' young Rupert, on their way back from picking him up from his last term at school before Oxford; the little girl would have been with them but she'd had chicken-pox and was still poorly...' he stopped and took a long swallow at his whisky. 'Terrible it was.'

Ryan topped Eddie's glass and his own. 'Go on.'

'They was just crossing over by Worthy Copse – you know, sir, them crossroads at the bottom of the hill outside of Boxton – when one of them girt great French lorries come hurtling around the corner and straight into the off side of the Land Rover. Missis an' the boy was killed outright, and Squire, well, he was thrown clear like but was terrible injured – been in a wheelchair ever since; tho' he do get about on crutches, Mrs Peck says.' He shook his head. 'But he's not the man he was; no, nor 'as been since the day he come home from the hospital. Used to ride that girt great hunter of his through here an' out to the forest four an' five times a week he did, sometimes with Missis beside him, pretty as a picture on the chestnut filly he bought her after her old mare died. Had it put down afterward, he did...folk reckon he couldn't bear to be reminded, like.'

'Christ!'

Ryan held clasped hands against his mouth, digging his teeth into his knuckles. Remembered images of violent death rose in his mind's eye: the flaming torch that had been a Messerschmitt pilot falling from his plane; a French saboteur sagging at a firing post; a German soldier with his throat cut and his life blood running into the grass;

114

Ellie with the weed in her hair…Claire and that little tow-headed boy he'd carried on his shoulders: smashed and bleeding in a wrecked car…he reached for the bottle again.

'Anything I can do for you, sir?' Eddie's voice came from a long way off. With difficulty Ryan focused on his anxious face.

'No. It's OK; I'll, um, I'll…' distractedly he looked around the room. 'I think I'll maybe take a drive…'

'I shouldn't do that, sir – not after the whisky and you comin' all this way and having a shock n' all that. Why don't you rest for a while; I'll bring up some coffee later on.'

'Yeah; good idea…'

Ryan waited until Eddie left the room, discretely removing the bottle as he did so, then he heeled off his shoes and rolled onto the bed. Turning his face into the pillow he gave himself up to an orgy of anger and frustration. No chance now of seeing her again – even from a distance, no way of laying the ghost, of setting the record straight. A senseless bloody road accident had robbed him of even that.

Now there was just a long dark tunnel and at the end of it, through all the pain and heartache, the figure of Geoffrey de Lacy seated in that wheelchair…and very much alive.

Why Claire? Why Rupert? he thought bitterly, why not *him*? Why should lousy de Lacy have been the one to survive? Useless bastard; sitting there while they were six feet under in the graveyard…

*   *   *

By the time Eddie came up with the coffee a couple of hours later, he more or less had it together again, apologizing for giving the barman a hard time. 'That's all right, sir; we all 'ave our moments.' Eddie stood for a while, watching him as he sat on the bed and drank the coffee. 'You knowed 'em up at the Manor, didn't you, sir? My dad remembered you soon as he clapped eyes on you the last time you was here…used to see you ridin' past here with the missus he said.'

'Yeah,' Ryan said. 'I knew them, but only the two Mrs de Lacys – and Rupert, of course. De Lacy himself was still in North Africa then.'

'Arr – well, the old lady be dead as well, now; not long after the accident that were: folk reckon she never did get over the shock. Put great store by the young missus an' the little lad she did,' he made to leave. 'If that's all for now, sir, I'd best be getting back to the kitchen and help dad get the evening meals prepared.'

'Just a minute,' Ryan halted him at the door. 'You said there was a daughter?'

'That's right. Miss Sophie – she's down here right now with her father – going to be married she is; at Christmas. I daresay there's plenty to be doing before then so she'll be staying quite a while I should think – 'cause, *he* didn't want her to get married just yet, her being so young and still at University an' all – made her finish her studies he did, an' wait 'til this month when her turned twenty-one.'

Twenty one, Ryan thought and was again gripped with sudden jealous rage; the old bastard hadn't been *that* badly wounded then – hadn't lost any time getting Claire pregnant when he'd come home on sick leave back in 'forty-four. Hard on his heels he'd been, for sure. Ryan glanced at his watch then reached for his shoes. He had to get moving, get away from everyone and be completely alone for the next few hours if he was to go on walking and talking like he was real...He said 'Thanks for your time, Eddie. Reckon I might walk for a while now.'

'Be back for dinner, sir? Got a three choice menu tonight – steak n' kidney puddin', liver n' bacon, n' cod n' chips.'

Ryan's stomach heaved but he said, 'Sounds great,' and crossed to where his bag still stood unpacked on the floor. 'I'll just sort myself and clean up before I go out again.'

Ten minutes later, well dosed with seltzer he hit the road outside The Bull. Turning away from the road to Hawksley he crossed the village green and climbing the stile began to follow the footpath that curved around the edge of the woodland, to emerge eventually at the far side of Falcon Field.

*   *   *

He sat on the crumbling step of the control tower, aching with the terrible sense of loss for what had – and for what might have been. For the bright-eyed boy who had left his supporting hands one summer's day and splashed so valiantly across the lake shouting, 'Look at me, mummy – I can do it – I can swim all by myself!' while Claire with all her life before her watched from the bank, laughing and clapping her hands and calling 'Bravo!' The walk back to the house under the heat of the noonday sun with Claire's hand in his and body tingling from the cold water. Rupert running and leaping ahead of them in his red cotton bathers, a Labrador puppy, Ryan's present for his eighth birthday, bouncing at his heels...

*   *   *

The tears didn't come easily, but when they came they came with a vengeance. On that cold November day, Ryan Petersen sat amid the ruins of Falcon Field and with his head in his hands wept for those he had known, and loved, and now would never know again; wept as he had only once before, for Niles, that other bright star.

He had touched rock bottom more than once in his life but never so grievously, nor with such utter devastation of spirit as now. This then was the end; no need to stay longer; to question, to hope. Round and round in his head went the refrain he had sung so long ago, words that had meant so much:

S'ist wahr, s'ist wah, ich hab dich lieb...

Now there would only ever be the memory of that love.

*　　　*　　　*

Dusk was laying its blanket of winter mist over Falcon Field, when he eventually roused and retraced his steps to The Bull, where he quickly lost himself in the anonymity of the crowded bar, bypassing the enticement of steak and kidney pudding for the more potent pain killing condolence of the bottle; drinking steadily until 'Time' was called and he could weave his way up to his quiet room and the big empty bed.

*　　　*　　　*

His intention to take off next morning for the safety and sanity of London was thwarted by his resultant hangover. Crazy though he was to leave, he knew that in his present state he was unfit to be in charge of a bicycle, let alone a car. Eddie averted his gaze in sympathy as he served him with the jug of iced water, the strong black coffee and Aspirin he requested, disappearing into the kitchen while Ryan drank in great thirsty draughts while supporting his aching head on one hand, wondering if it was possible for a man to drink himself into permanent oblivion. No one, he thought mordantly, could say he hadn't tried from time to time...

Eventually he roused and going out into the raw cold of a misty winter's morning, began to walk, aimlessly at first then with more purpose, towards Hawksley Church. He would take just one look at their graves; rule a thick black line across the bottom of memory and go back to the land of the living.

117

He found them easily: mother and son, side by side in the shade of an ancient yew and close by the stone slab surrounded by rusting railings that was the old de Lacy family tomb. Ryan was glad they were not there in that dark crumbling vault, lying alongside other more ancient bones. For a long time he stood looking down at the twin marble headstones with the lettering picked out in gold, until the lifting of the heavy iron latch on the lych-gate made him aware that he had company. He drew back quickly into the murky depths of the laurels beyond the yew, as with quick light footsteps a young woman came along the path to stop before the two headstones. She wore a white raincoat, her head covered by a red woollen scarf, the tasselled ends thrown back over her shoulders. In her arms she carried a sheaf of cream and gold hothouse chrysanthemums.

Ryan stayed in the shadows as she bent to lay the blooms one at a time over both graves. Finishing, she rose to her feet and half-turning pulled off the confining scarf. Shaking her hair free she stood for a moment, looking across the churchyard and for the first time he saw her face.

If four months back the sight of Geoffrey had startled him it was nothing compared to the shock of coming almost face to face with Sophie de Lacy. For what seemed breathless minutes, but could only have been a matter of seconds, he stared at the sculpted line of her cheek and jaw; the long, wide-spaced sapphire blue eyes, a wing of the shining silver blonde hair that framed them falling over the straight brows, and knew there was no possibility on this earth that any de Lacy had fathered this particular child.

*　　　*　　　*

Afterwards he wondered how he had managed not to move, to let her know he was there, but he was quite literally rooted to the ground with shock. Perhaps had she lingered he might have come out of his trance; even spoken to her, but before he could gather sufficient wit or strength to move, she was walking away from him on long slim legs, the hair swinging on her shoulders like a silver bell.

Leaning back against the rough bark of the Yew, heedless of the damp seeping through his coat Ryan watched her out of sight. A daughter, he thought with a kind of petrified awe, he had a daughter! His hands were cold and his forehead burned; He felt light-headed and euphoric. But why, he thought feverishly, had Claire kept it from him

– and how the hell had she explained the small matter of her pregnancy to Geoffrey?

Then reason returned. Of course: his departure and Geoffrey's homecoming on sick leave had almost coincided; had in fact been uncomfortably close. When he flew that last mission Claire probably hadn't even known she'd conceived his child. Ryan felt a sudden stab of guilt at the distress he must have caused: not only to his love but also Marion de Lacy, who had been so unfailingly kind to him. For reasons he'd not entirely understood she had always chosen to turn a blind eye to their love affair, and while not actually condoning it, had certainly shown a remarkable degree of tolerance unusual for one of her generation and class. But how would even she have viewed the arrival of this obvious cuckoo in the de Lacy nursery?

And what of Claire...how had she felt about carrying his child? Had she even realised it *was* his until after the child was born – and even then would she have told Geoffrey the truth? She need not have done. Although her own hair and eyes were dark, Geoffrey, Marion de Lacy and Rupert were all fair-haired and the eyes of all three, if not of that particularly piercing blue, were at least in the same spectrum of colour. Would she, *could* she have kept her secret all those years?

I shouldn't have come, Ryan thought, in a silent agony of despair. *I shouldn't have come to this country at all. I should have stayed in the old planked house on Brackets Sound, driven to Boston each day, taught my students and let Abby continue to organise my life...*

But he had come; had opened this particular can of worms. In his head was an echo of Geoffrey de Lacy's mocking "It was nice meeting *you*, Mr. Petersen!" Of course the old bastard knew who Sophie's father was – and now Ryan Petersen knew as well.

So there was one more hurdle to take before he left Hawksley for good.

He had to see de Lacy one more time. Geoffrey might of course send for some brawny manservant and have him thrown out – or just freeze him with a polite brush off. Whatever, there was no way he was going to leave without telling that cold-eyed bastard to his face that he, Ryan Petersen, was proud to acknowledge Sophie as his own daughter.

*   *   *

At this stage he had no wish or intention to involve Sophie. Rocked as he was by her unexpected appearance and hungry to see her again, he knew he couldn't possibly risk the disruption it would bring to her

119

life were they to come suddenly upon each other, so that any discussion of her past and future would have to be between Geoffrey and himself alone.

She had to go out sometime, he reasoned, even if just to shop or visit friends. As he could hardly telephone and ask her when she might be doing either of those things, Ryan figured he would just have watch an await his opportunity, however long that might take.

Returning to the Bull he collected the Jowett, bought a packet of cheese biscuits, a bar of candy and a bottle of milk from the Stafford Ley mini-market and drove back to Hawksley. Arriving at the Manor he stationed the car about fifty yards along Sweetwater lane, where he could watch the gates without looking too obvious to any passer-by, or to anyone leaving the house.

It was well into the afternoon before his patience was rewarded. Cold, cramped and half dozing he almost missed the yellow Mini turning out of the gates and heading for the main road. It was being driven fast, but just a glimpse of a blond head as the car accelerated down the lane told him the coast was clear.

Wishing he had something stronger with which to ease his suddenly dry mouth he finished the milk, brushed biscuit crumbs from his overcoat, fired the engine and with a sinking feeling in the pit of his stomach, went to meet what he had a nasty suspicion might very well prove his Nemesis.

*   *   *

The woman who answered his knock was the one who had sold tickets on his last visit to this house. Ha, he thought with a certain sardonic amusement, this must be Mrs. Peck, de Lacey's housekeeper, who doubled up in the season as keeper of the cash-box; nothing like getting his money's worth...

'Yes, sir?' she was looking at Ryan with raised brows, a faint glimmer of something suspiciously like amused recognition in her eyes.

'Good morning, ma'am,' He summoned what he hoped was a confident smile. 'My name is Petersen; would you please ask Mr de Lacey if I can speak with him.'

'If you'll just step inside, sir,' she held open the door. 'I'll see if that is convenient.'

He stood in the centre of the big hall where she had left him and looked around. As it had been with The Bull and Hawksley village, nothing much had changed. There were the same wall hangings, the same vast stone fireplace, the long iron basket, the pine logs crackling and spurting tongues of blue flame; the gallery where the orchestra had played that New Year, the door in the corner leading to the long gallery where they had waltzed in the moonlight... *Lippen schweigen, 's flüstern geigen...*

The soft swish of tyres on the stone flagged floor alerted Ryan to de Lacy's presence, and he turned slowly to face him.

'Good afternoon, Mr. Petersen.' The remembered voice was edged with sarcasm. 'I've been expecting you to turn up again at sometime or other.'

'I only heard about the accident yesterday...' Ryan's control was on a knife edge, his voice low and strained. 'I'm sorry for your troubles.'

De Lacy stared hard at him then swung the wheelchair towards the drawing room. 'Come in here. Pru is bringing some coffee shortly; she thought you looked as though you could do with it.'

Ryan followed him in silence, taking the chair de Lacy indicated beside another crackling fire while his host stationed his wheelchair opposite him and continued to sit, also in silence, although his eyes never left his companion's face. Ryan gave him a full five minutes then said baldly, 'I was in the churchyard this morning. I saw your daughter.'

'Ahh...' It was more sigh than exclamation. 'I wondered what had brought you today in particular.' He rubbed his knuckles across his chin. 'Did she see you?'

'No. I kept well out of sight.' Ryan sat forward, resting his forearms on his knees. 'Not out of any great altruistic motive – I guess I was, to use a quaint old Yankee phrase, too discombobulated to move!'

De Lacy's eyes creased a little at the corners. 'And do you intend to stay "well out of sight"?'

'That depends.' Ryan stared into those pale blue eyes for several seconds, but they were giving nothing away. Screw you, he thought, and took the first shot. 'When did you know you were not her father?'

'From the day that my daughter was born, and make no mistake Mr Petersen, my daughter she is, in every real meaning of that word,' de Lacy spoke quietly, evenly, his gaze still fixed on Ryan. 'Any man can start a life but being a father, as I am sure you know, is an entirely separate matter. The first may be accomplished in a matter of seconds; the other requires a lifetime of love and commitment. *You* were not there to take on that task, I was.'

Strange how few words it can take to begin to change one man's

121

opinion of another. That he might feel even the slightest degree of empathy with de Lacy was, given the circumstances, pretty crazy. Was he, Ryan queried sourly, in danger of getting soft? First Hannah, then Calamity Jane and now de Lacy; if he didn't watch out he'd be up to his neck in retrospective guilt and over-compensating in all directions. Not the kind of scenario to exactly grab a man by the balls.

He reminded himself of how many years this man had been his *bête noire*, his King Charles head. Forever getting in the way, forever the unknown quantity in Claire's life: the barrier that had proved immovable and ultimately lost him his love. The hated Geoffrey de Lacy; that unsatisfactory, neglectful husband who had neither deserved nor cherished the woman he'd married. Now those few words spoken with such calm sincerity had kicked the bottom out of Ryan's world of festering jealousy.

He may have been no worse than I, he thought, better in fact, for in the end Claire must have been content; perhaps even more than content. Maybe he had loved her...maybe she had come to love him. Fragments of Eddie's half-remembered words struggled to the surface: "Missus riding alongside him...pretty as a picture...had her horse put down afterward...couldn't bear to be reminded..."

Wearily he closed his eyes and leaned back in the chair. 'Claire once quoted to me that the English lose every battle but the last, and I guess that's true. You won after all.'

'I might not, had you come back.'

Ryan opened his eyes. 'Oh, yes you would: you were always going to win. You had Rupert didn't you? You held the ace.'

He shrugged. 'Yes, I suppose I did – and believe me, if it had come to the crunch, I would have played it.'

There was a discreet tap at the door and Mrs Peck entered bearing two tall fine china mugs and a silver coffee pot, cream jug and sugar basin on a polished wooden tray. Placing the tray on a small table beside de Lacy's chair she smiled at Ryan. 'The coffee is my special blend, Mr Petersen, known as the Peck-pick-me-up!'

De Lacy grunted. 'Takes the lining off your stomach – be a good girl Pru and fetch over the whisky decanter as well, will you? This damned weather gets to my knees and the long streak over there looks as though he could do with a dram.'

She said, 'Any excuse...' she poured the coffee then added the whisky with a generous hand. 'Sugar, milk?' she queried and Ryan shook his head.

'Black and as it comes, ma'am, thank you.'

She left them and de Lacy raised his mug. 'Cheers!'

'Prost!' Ryan drank. It hit his gullet and rushed through his gut like a hot-arsed ferret. Tears started to his eyes. He gasped 'Kee-*rist*! What is this – corpse reviver? What in hell does she put in the stuff?'

'I've often wondered – never liked to ask. At a guess I'd go for coffee flavoured gunpowder.' De Lacy sat back nursing his own drink. 'Now, as we will not be disturbed again unless you go for my throat and I have to ring for help...' he gave his companion a long, sardonic look, 'and as both you and I have so many unanswered questions, this might be a good opportunity to air them. See what answers we come up with.'

Ryan hedged. I don't want this, he thought, 'What about your...' he hesitated, '...your daughter.'

'She won't be back until tomorrow; gone over to Oxford to stay with her prospective in-laws. Her chap's in the wine importing business and visiting Australia at the moment, so he's well out of all the wedding flummery – if he's any sense he'll stay out until his presence is required at the altar!'

'You don't want her getting hitched to this guy?'

'I've nothing against young Ben; thoroughly nice chap, but she's too young.'

'She's twenty-one. Down in Tennessee they could do it legally at thirteen.' He couldn't resist the jibe. De Lacy scowled and rose to it like a trout to a mayfly.

'Bloody pig-ignorant pederasts; ought to be strung up by the balls!' He finished his drink and put the mug back on the tray. For a few moments he sat pinching his lower lip between forefinger and thumb. Shooting Ryan a particularly hard considering look he took a coin from his jacket pocket. 'Toss you heads or tails for who goes first!'

Reluctantly Ryan called 'tails' – and lost. He swore quietly and de Lacy's teeth showed in a not altogether pleasant smile.

'Your call takes it. Let's have it straight, shall we: the whole truth, right from the beginning and no evasions to spare my feelings – or yours. You owe me. I came back to a different wife from the one I left in 'forty-two. I know *why* and I think I know what you meant to Claire; what I *don't* know is what she meant to you.'

'And after twenty years that matters?'

'Too bloody right it matters; so come clean.'

Ryan considered if there might be an option to this request, but there wasn't. He was acutely conscious that Claire's husband had told him nothing at all of what, or how much, he knew. Obviously Claire must have told him something, but had she been totally honest? Given her circumstances it would have been a temptation to admit to a 'brief encounter' type wartime romance: to have been taken off guard and fallen for some oversexed Yank without a conscience. De Lacy may have no idea of the length of their relationship, or of the intensity of their love.

He felt a trickle of sweat at his temples and brushed it away with his hand. Well, if the man wanted it straight, that was OK. Ryan was still too hurting and raw from the shock of Claire's death to dissemble, or try to make things easy for him.

'Not come this far just to fall at the first fence, have you?' de Lacy mocked. 'Come on, Mr Petersen, as your countrymen might say: "Let's hear it as it is!"'

Ryan stared him out. 'You'll hear it as it is all right. I just kind of like to gather my thoughts before I take a fence as high as this one.'

*   *   *

It wasn't that difficult to begin, to speak of their first meeting and the joyous, carefree months that followed, when they had walked, rode and made love at every opportunity. All the heat and the passion rose up from somewhere around Ryan's gut and he didn't spare his inquisitor; de Lacy got the lot, right up until the late autumn of nineteen forty-three, when one problem came upon the heels of another and the first clouds began to gather: clouds of loss, of grief, of a desperate, hopeless, clinging to love and an aching need to maintain hope and faith in a future seemingly devoid of either.

That was the point where Ryan Petersen really retreated back into the past...

14

FALCON FIELD, HAWKSLEY, HAMPSHIRE
September 1943

By September all the crews were suffering from too many missions and too little rest, but the pressure had to be maintained and from somewhere they dredged up undreamed of reserves of strength and willpower to carry them through. There were times when the whole station prayed for rain and cloud dense enough to obscure any target, so that the order would come to stand down, allowing them a precious day or two; to drink in the pubs, sleep – not always alone – and put the next mission on the back burner.

The tide of war was beginning to turn; in Russia the retreat had begun, the build-up to the invasion of Europe was gaining momentum and massed daylight bombing of Germany was the usual agenda for the B17s of Falcon Field. As their losses became heavier the crews grew harder. Boys became men, and men became old before their time as friends and comrades failed to make it back to base through the vicious barrage of the waiting guns and enemy fighters. Replacement 'planes were flown in and almost daily new faces appeared at the briefings. Several times the *Boston Babe* returned badly shot up, the fuselage pitted and holed by canon shell and tracer bullets; sometimes touching down with one or more engines out of action, once with part of their starboard wing almost burned away, half of it just a blackened and twisted steel skeleton.

But always they made it back, and gradually the myth began to build amongst his crew that every man in the *Babe* led a charmed life; that nothing could touch them or bring them down.

And sometimes Ryan almost believed the myth.

All through the summer of that year, whenever they were either stood down because of bad weather, or for a rare brief rest between missions, he left the base to meet with Claire. If it was a weekend or during the school holidays the meetings frequently included Rupert, who seemed to take in his stride the new man in his life, happy to be instructed in the finer points of baseball, or training his new puppy to retrieve, or learning to dive into deep water.

One evening toward the end of September Ryan slipped away

after dinner and took the path through the woods. Arriving at the five bar gate he vaulted it easily then crossed the meadow towards the rear of the house. Always after a mission and as soon as the de-briefing was over, he telephoned the Manor so that Claire knew he was back. Once assured of his safety she would wait and watch from the terrace for him to come to her.

Now, leading her through the French windows he wrapped his arms about her murmuring 'Ah, but I've missed you, my love, my love...'

Drawing him down onto the long couch by the fire she kissed his tired eyes, 'Bad trip?' She smoothed his hair and he nodded.

'Noisy, damn' noisy,' he admitted then forced a grin. 'Made my Air Medal today though; so did Hoagy. Thought once or twice we'd be getting them posthumously.' He looked around the familiar welcoming room. 'All right now, though.'

'Relax, darling.' She sat at one end of the couch and he stretched out to lay with closed eyes, his head pillowed in her lap.

'Should I go and say hello to Marion, or is it too late?'

'She's been in bed an hour or more with a foul cold; Nanny is visiting her sister in Corfe Mullen and won't be back tonight.' She smiled, tracing her finger over his mouth. 'So you and I, my darling, will be able to leave this couch in a little while and creep undisturbed to bed.'

'How long is a little while?'

'Another hour and we should be quite safe.'

He pulled her face down to his, kissing her lips, her neck, her breasts, groaning aloud as through the fine wool of her housecoat he felt her nipple harden against his mouth. 'An hour sounds one hell of a long time to wait.'

She gave a soft chuckle. 'It will give you time to gather your strength.'

'It's gathered already,' he turned his head, pressing into her, breathing deeply. Jesus, the sweet smell of this woman...

She held his head between her hands, murmuring, 'Darling; oh, sweetheart,' then was suddenly still. 'Shhh, someone is coming!'

Ryan sat up quickly as the door opened and Rupert, sleepy-eyed, in candy stripe pyjamas, crept into the room. 'I woke up and Nanny wasn't there...' his voice quavered. Claire went to him and knelt, putting her arms around him.

'It's all right, darling; did you have a bad dream?'

'No, but I woke and it was dark.'

She comforted him. 'I expect the bulb on your little nightlight

126

blew.'

He looked at Ryan. 'Can you mend it, Captain Pop?'

Ryan laughed. 'I guess so. Have a cuddle with mommy first, then we'll go have a look for another bulb and fix it.'

Claire lifted him on to the couch where he squirmed down between them, pushing his thumb into his mouth. Over his head they smiled at each other; Ryan mouthed: *Love you – love your son,* he ruffled the little boy's hair. 'Take your time, fella. The night is young!'

*   *   *

Twenty minutes later he carried a sleepy Rupert back to bed, Claire following with the new light bulb.

'My bed is cold.' Rupert shivered. Pulling the covers up to his chin he asked, 'Captain Pop, can you read me to sleep?'

'It's a bit late for that.' Ryan grinned at Claire as she tucked the bedclothes around her son's ears. 'My mommy always sung me and my brother to sleep; would that do you?'

He looked doubtful. 'What did she sing?'

'Old songs, Irish songs: close your eyes and we'll give it a shot.'

He murmured, 'OK, Captain Pop, give it a shot!' and screwed his eyes tight. Ryan smoothed his hair.

> *'The pale moon was rising above the green mountains,*
> *The sun was declining beneath the blue sea,*
> *As I strayed with my love to the pure crystal fountain,*
> *That stands in the beautiful Vale of Tralee...'*

Before he reached the end of the first verse Rupert was asleep.

*   *   *

Claire closed the nursery door quietly and took Ryan's hand, leading him to the end of the carpeted landing and the guest bedroom, which once the house was asleep became their own private place. Inside, with the door closed, Ryan undid the buttons of her housecoat and as it fell to the floor slid his hands down her body, pulling her hard against him. 'Shall I sing you to sleep?'

'Not yet.' She began to undo his jacket buttons. 'First things first, Captain Pop!'

It was almost dawn when he showed the yawning sentry at the guard post his ID, then skirted the silent airfield, heading for his quarters. His thoughts were still with Claire as he had left her: curled in sleep, one hand tucked beneath the pillow, the other still resting where it had lain across him before he eased away from her. When a form suddenly stood out from the shadows of a hut he jumped, his heart hammering. He swore aloud.

'What the fuck...'

'Now don't be like that, Ry!' reproved the chaplain. 'You gave me a bigger a fright than I gave you!'

'Excuse *me*, father, but what in hell are you doing out here?'

'Having a quiet pipe: I couldn't sleep. What are *you* doing?'

Ryan was terse, 'Trying to get to bed.'

The Chaplain asked, 'Left it a bit late haven't you?' and when Ryan didn't answer, added, 'Don't think I don't know where you get to until all hours – what you're doing isn't right, you know.'

'Save the sermon, father, I signed up for the Air Corps, not for sainthood.'

'Mebbe, but you should have signed up for not sleeping with another man's wife. You know that's a sin.'

Ryan gave a tired sigh. 'I respect you, father and I don't want to start any ecclesiastical arguments, but the Church can't have it both ways. You can't bless us and send us out to blow women and children to pieces then tell us it's a sin to love another man's wife and child.' Taking out a pack of Lucky Strikes he lit one, eyeing the chaplain over the glow of the match. 'And please don't tell me I'll go to hell; I do that every time I get up in that 'plane to bomb shit out of which-ever poor buggers we're targeting that day.'

'I'm sorry to hear you say those things, Ry.'

'Yeah, well I'm sorry to be doing them.' He took a long pull on his cigarette. 'Nothing personal, but if I haven't been to Mass these past months it's because I've kinda felt God has disconnected the phone and taken a holiday.'

'Don't bullshit me, Ryan.'

'Father, if you think I'm doing that, you don't know me at all.'

'Perhaps I don't know any of you anymore.' The chaplain's voice was suddenly bitter, 'maybe all those boys think that way, only unlike you, none of them say it to my damn face. You may or may not go to hell, Ry, but for now I wish you'd just go hit the sack; you make my head ache.'

*　　　*　　　*

Ryan woke to grey skies and heavy rain and knew there would be no flying that day. He glanced at his watch and saw it was still only a few minutes after seven, no wonder he was bushed. Two hours sleep before he'd had to leave after making love with Claire, another two since he'd crashed out this morning...reaching for cigarettes and lighter he propped himself against the pillows, prepared to laze away the hour before breakfast.

He had almost finished the smoke when he became aware that the building was unusually quiet; aware also that although he'd several times heard the approach of footsteps that slowed as they neared his door, the owners had paused, then after a brief hesitation hurried past. He sat up, crushing his cigarette butt into the ashtray, a puzzled frown etched between his brows. Sure, there was no flying, so most of the guys would be taking it easy, but it was darned funny about those footsteps; he could have sworn one set belonged to Hoagy...

He swung his legs out of bed and began to dress. Tying his tie he grimaced at his reflection in the mirror. Maybe there was something big brewing. Maybe, as it was pissing like Niagara out there and visibility down to zero, some lunatic thought it was a great time to invade Europe! He was just zipping his Eisenhower when the door opened and the chaplain came in. Closing the door slowly he turned to face him.

'Something's happened and nobody wanted to tell you, so they voted the old sky-pilot to do it for them.'

Ryan grinned and said flippantly 'What's the matter father – your altar boy gone on strike?'

'Sit down, Ry.'

Ryan looked at him sharply. 'Why?'

'Quit arguing and just do it.'

'Whatever it is, I'd rather be on my feet, so shoot, will you.'

The chaplain came forward and laid a hand on his shoulder. 'It's your brother, Niles. He's dead. I'm sorry, Ry.'

Ryan thumped down onto the bed. He said stupidly, 'What?'

'Niles is dead; he was wounded in an assault on the airport at Guadalcanal and died a few hours later.'

'Christ!' Ryan leaped up. Snatching his trench coat and cap he wrenched open the door.

'Wait: don't blow your stack. Come with me – '

Ryan turned on him savagely. 'What the fuck for – to pray? Tell you something, father, God just blew it.' Cramming his cap on his head and fighting his arms into his trench coat he flung out of the door. Heels ringing loud on the concrete floor he strode along the passageway and out into the rain.

The chaplain followed him as far as the steps, then stopped and raised his eyes to the leaden skies. 'Do me a favour, will you?' he asked, 'just see nobody lets him have a jeep while he's still going off half-cocked, 'cause I sure as hell don't want to have to read the Last Rites over that particular body today.'

*   *   *

Ryan didn't try for a jeep, didn't even go off base, but made for the hangar where the *Boston Babe* stood like some vast caged bird. Climbing to the cockpit he sank down into his seat and closing his eyes held his head between his hands.

*   *   *

A few days before Niles left for the Pacific and Ryan for Europe they'd climbed on their old boyhood roosting spot on the coalhouse roof; two tall young men with only a year between them; flaxen haired, wide shouldered and loose limbed, as alike as twins. Between them they'd smoked a packet of Camels and drunk a bottle of their father's wine. Lars had found it was missing after Niles left so he, Ryan, had taken the fallout. It was the last time he had seen his brother.

The only tangible things of Niles he had now were a few out of date photographs and a bundle of letters in his table drawer.

*   *   *

He didn't know when he started weeping, or when he stopped. Only that when he at last climbed from the Fortress his eyes were sore, his body cold as ice and a part of him as vital as blood or bone or sinew was gone forever. Returning to his room he locked the door. Swearing aloud he kicked his shoes across the room and rolled onto the bed.

'Fucking chaplain, fucking England, fucking war.'

*   *   *

The foul weather continued and late the next afternoon he drove to the hospital through a streaming downpour. Waiting on the forecourt for

130

Claire to appear he sat smoking and listening to the rain drumming on the canvas top of the jeep. Let it piss for a month, he thought, then the *Babe* could stay in the hangar and he could get stinking plastered every fucking night…

*   *   *

'Something's happened.' She climbed into her seat, twisting round to look at his face, 'darling, what's wrong?'

He fired the engine. 'Tell you when we get in out of this rain.'

'Do you want to go home?'

'Nope, neutral ground; somewhere where nobody knows us and we can talk without being interrupted, or overheard.'

She studied his set face for a moment. 'Beaulieu, then, The Montague Arms will be quiet this early in the evening.'

His mouth twisted. 'No questions?'

'No.'

He squeezed her hand. 'OK.' He turned right out of the hospital gates. 'What did I do to deserve a woman like you?'

*   *   *

They sat in a corner of the almost deserted saloon bar, their untouched drinks on the table before them while she held his hand, listening in silence as he talked of 'my bro'. Rambling a little; switching back and forth between boyhood and manhood; college, old friends, the hunting and sailing holidays they had spent together; the girls they had both fancied; Beth, the girl-next-door that Niles wanted to marry when the war was over…occasionally his voice would falter, then he would set his jaw, steady, and carry on.

So controlled, she thought, marvelling at the hard constraint he was imposing on himself. Over these months together she had seen him change, watched with sadness the easy, laughing young man gradually slip away, replaced by this tough disciplined man with the tired eyes. Only when they were completely alone together, when he made love to her with tender hands and passionate mouth, did that other young man return.

Now he was raw and fragile with grief and anger and despair; exorcising his agony in this anonymous, public place where he must keep control and mask his pain from everyone but her. When he was silent at last she brought his hand to her mouth and wordless, laid her lips on his fingers.

He stared at her, eyes brilliant in his drawn face. He said simply, 'I couldn't have borne it without being able to tell you. Now can we please get the hell out of here, go someplace else and make love?'

*   *   *

In the hours that followed she was the rock to which he clung, and willingly she carried the burden of his grief. At first, caught in a terrible vortex of anger and despair he was rough with her; a roughness verging on violent, but she wasn't afraid of him; didn't cry out or protest, but held him with a deep fierce compassion, yielding her body to his demands as he took her with a hard, ruthless, almost uncaring desperation, then afterward rolled away, his own body, despite his release, still tense as a coiled spring.

She wrapped arms bruised from his fingers around him and turning him to her again drew his head onto her breast, stroking his shoulders with gentle fingers until his body slowly relaxed. He laid his lips against her throat. 'I hurt you.' His voice was thick and hoarse. 'I'm sorry; so very, very sorry.'

She said nothing, but continued to caress him quietly until desire rose in him again and he made love to her once more with a deep and poignant tenderness.

When he left her bed in the early hours she lay half asleep, watching him put on his uniform, his only reference to the hours just passed a murmured, 'Thanks for listening, and for seeing me through the night...' then he kissed her and slipped away from the sleeping house.

*   *   *

The letters home were hard to write; he managed them somehow, writing several over the following weeks, although he thought they were poor offerings and would do little to assuage his parents' grief. He didn't know his father kept those letters; read and re-read them, and through them saw his eldest son with new eyes.

"They are beautiful," Lars said in wonderment to Hannah. "Why did he never show to his papa that he was such a man?"

She couldn't tell him in the midst of his pain that it was because father and son were so alike in the jealousy that made them antagonists that neither had been able to see the other as the person he really was, only as a rival for her love.

132

*   *   *

Now Ryan welcomed every mission. Only in the air and with the controls of the *Babe* in his hands could he blot out every thought and feeling and concentrate solely on the job in hand. When, with the approach of Christmas he was summoned to the Group Commander's Office, he went with a tightening of the stomach, a sliver of fear lancing through him. What now, he thought. Was the old man going to break some more bad news?

'Sit down, Ry.' Colonel McIllhenny took a cigar from the box on his desk and bit off the end. 'I got news for you: I want you to take over from Delaney as Air Exec.'

Jesus Christ, Ryan thought, now there's a nasty surprise.

'Delaney's got an ulcer – needs surgery so he'll be out of it for some time. Job starts tomorrow, *Major* Petersen.'

Ryan regarded his colonel with narrowed eyes. 'You wouldn't be trying to soften me up, then railroad me onto a desk job would you Deejay?' His voice was level but edgy with suspicion.

'Hell, no, soon as you're back on base you can go on flying and putting the fear of God up Adolf.' Colonel McIllhenny struck a match on his thumbnail and lit his cigar. 'You and your crew are grounded for ten days as from now; you leave for a rest camp in Dorset Monday morning; that'll give Delaney time to fill you in on the office work before you go. When you come back you got leave over Christmas, so's you can return here fresh and raring to go. The doc says Delaney can hang on until then.' He sent a puff of smoke wreathing towards the ceiling then looked at Ryan, whose mouth was beginning to set in a stubborn line. 'Now don't you start giving me hassle, Ry. The Group won't fall apart without you and it's my job to see when men need a break. Hell man, you and your crew and that damn ship are one of the few originals we got left here, and you're all in danger of burning out. With what's going to let loose some time soon I can't afford to lose old hands. Air Exec will give you a bit more paper work and a hell of a lot more responsibility but you'll still have time to fly – within reason.' He winked, 'and to go visiting.'

Ryan grunted. 'Thanks, sir, but I was doing just fine as I was!'

*   *   *

Claire didn't even try to hide her delight when he telephoned to tell his news. 'Darn it,' he said in response to her delighted "Oh, *wonderful!*" 'lady don't you know there's a war on – I didn't join up to fly a goddam' desk!'

'Well the war can just take a back seat – and you'll look wonderful flying a desk.'

'Maybe, but I have to spend a week or so down in some darn rest camp first.' He wouldn't tell her yet that he'd still be flying missions, he'd let her have a break from worrying about that for a while. 'Look, I'm on base pushing paper until I go Monday, so can you make the mess dance Saturday night?'

She gave her throaty chuckle. 'Dress or undress?' she asked.

'Both, if you're a very good girl!'

'Well, now,' she said, 'that depends what you mean by good...'

He put the 'phone down reluctantly. Hell, but he wished she were here right now. He tipped back on his chair and for a few minutes stared moodily at the unfamiliar office wall, then got to his feet and opened the door. 'Roscoe, where in this neck of the woods would I get flowers in November?' he asked the snub nose kid at the outside office desk.

Roscoe grinned. 'If I find 'em do I get to deliver 'em, major?'

He growled, 'Yeah, you find them, corporal, you can deliver.'

'Shazam! You got 'em, sir.'

Ryan made his way to the mess and leaning on the bar ordered a beer. A morning's pen pushing with Delaney breathing down his neck had given him a thirst. Listening to the rain drumming on the roof, he reflected that he may as well be shackled to a desk as lying on his bed waiting for the weather to clear. A few days at the rest camp, then Christmas spent with Claire would more than compensate for the new responsibilities that had been thrust upon him.

*   *   *

Grumble as he may, Ryan knew they all needed that rest camp, which turned out to be a rambling Tudor mansion in Dorset. The RAF's 'Bomber Harris' had promised that Berlin would be bombed until the heart of Nazi Germany ceased to beat, and back that summer when the first combined raids had really begun to hit; the RAF by night, the Eighth Air Force by day, the air and ground crews of Falcon Field had done their bit to help that promise along. Ryan and his crew had flown almost every mission: factories and oil depots, marshalling yards and cities – Regensburg and Schweinfurt, Dortmund and Hamburg, Bremen and Kiel. When news broke on that Christmas Eve that Eisenhower had been appointed Supreme Commander for the Allied Invasion of Europe, excitement on the base rose to fever pitch and all of Falcon Field responded with a party to end all parties, but by then Ryan was out of it.

*   *   *

For the ordinary, law-abiding British household rations were short. Conscious that his stay would be both a strain on resources and a temptation to gossip, Ryan shamelessly bought not only Mrs Buckroyd, the cook's gratitude, but her co-operative silence as well by arriving with his jeep laden with goodies from the PX. Tins of ham and butter and vegetables strange to English palates: sauerkraut and borsch soup; bacon rashers sealed in plastic, cookies and a big box of candy provided everything necessary to make sure that where Mrs Buckroyd and village gossip was concerned, discretion would be the name of the game. The extra boxes of candy stowed in his bag were for Rupert; the Max Factor make-up and nylon stockings for the comfort and pleasure of Marion and Claire.

Nanny Baines was staying with her sister over the holiday and with Marion de Lacy turning the blindest eye any woman ever managed to turn, the way was clear for Claire and himself to drop all pretence and let their relationship blossom openly.

But the deeper his love grew for Claire and Rupert, and the love he received in return, the greater his need for a settled future for them all. With only forty-eight hours before his leave ended, impatient to turn their long love affair into permanent commitment, he lay in the canopied bed with Claire in his arms and asked her to leave Geoffrey, and when the time came, to follow him to the States with Rupert.

She was silent for almost a minute and he waited, tense and edgy for her answer. When at last she said softly, 'Remember what I said when we first were lovers – that someday it would have to finish?' his mouth set in the straight stubborn line that presaged trouble.

'Yeah, but that was then; this is now and I won't, I can't, give you up; either of you, not now nor ever.'

'We still have each other.' She stroked the tight line of his jaw. 'No one can ask more than that, or try to plan a future while we are still at war.'

'You say you love me – now you're going back on that,' he accused.

'I do love you – God, *how* I love you.' Suddenly passionate she held his face between her hands. 'Ryan darling, don't do this to me; don't force me to choose between you and my son...'

'For Christ's sake – did I ever ask that? I want Rupert too; you

135

know I do. You can't really believe even *that* bastard would use him to blackmail you into staying.'

'Darling,' her eyes were full of tears, 'you don't understand...there is no way that Geoffrey would allow me to take Rupert away from this house.'

'This is the twentieth century – not medieval England,' he raged. 'What about your goddam wonderful British justice that's supposed to be so fair and impartial?'

'Not where a husband's right to his son and heir are concerned it isn't. Geoffrey might be prepared to let me go – after he'd fought every inch of the way *and* made things so hot for you that you'd be lucky to get out unscathed.' She was suddenly bitter. 'I can imagine how he would present his case: Returning war hero forced to see his ancient family name and unblemished reputation dragged through the mud by a randy Yank, who made love to his wife while he was away fighting for King and Country –'

'What d'you mean: unblemished reputation? You can bet he's screwed his way all around the Mediterranean.'

'He is allowed,' she returned with quiet irony. 'He's a man. For a woman the rules are different. To any divorce court judge he would only have been doing what came naturally; to the same judge I would be little less than a whore; a woman unfit to bring up her own child.'

He flinched, knowing she was right, but still he couldn't let it rest and the argument went back and forth, until at last, worn out and exhausted they slept, a space between them, each wrapped in their own cocoon of pain.

Waking at dawn Ryan lay watching her sleeping face, reproaching himself bitterly for the traces of tears on her cheeks. It had been their first quarrel and he felt a deep shame at the remembrance of his stubborn refusal to see any reason but his own.

Women adapted, saw and understood more than one point of view; put aside their own needs for those they loved. They did what men expected of them. They made sacrifices, changed their lives for husbands and children, whereas men... it simply never occurs to most of us, he thought with compunction, that *we* might change and adapt and sacrifice...

She frowned in her sleep and with tender fingers he smoothed the two vertical lines between her brows murmuring,

"When she sleeps, her soul, I know,
Goes a wanderer on the air,
Wings where I may never go,

136

Leaves her lying, still and fair,
Waiting, empty, laid aside,
Like a dress upon a chair ... ' "

Soft as his voice and light as his touch she awoke, opening her eyes slowly to gaze up into his shadowed face. He said, 'I love you and I want to be with you for the rest of my life; but I won't ever hurt you again, or try and force you to choose.' His mouth twisted in a painful grimace. '*Carpe Diem* – we'll seize the day, you and I, and to hell with the future...'

She raised her arms to clasp his neck and pull him down onto her. 'We will seize *all* the days,' she said, and he felt an icy finger of fear touch his heart, hearing again the happy, confident Robyn Graham, when they had walked through the snow together that first New Years' Eve.

"Not only for the day, sir: for all the days..."

*   *   *

The evening before the Big One he spent with Claire. In the morning he would fly the *Belle,* just one craft in the hundreds taking a massive raid right into the heart of Germany. The captains had already been briefed and knew where they were going, knew too that fuel and their flying time would be tight. Now was the time, if they hadn't already done so, to check that will and write that letter home.

'No soft bed tonight,' he said, after they had kissed. He pulled a wry face, 'Just head down on my own pillow well before midnight.'

She didn't ask why, but held his shoulders and kissed him again. 'When you said you were coming early I made some sandwiches and brought up the last bottle of Geoffrey's Single Malt.'

'Gee, isn't *that* a hanging offence?'

'Probably, but I'll worry about that later.' There was an odd note in her voice and her hands on his shoulders trembled a little. He looked down into her eyes.

'What is it? Are you cold?'

She shook her head. 'No; I've had a letter.' All at once there were tears in her eyes; he watched them spill over. 'It's Geoffrey: he's coming home.'

For a long moment he couldn't speak; then asked through tight lips, 'When?'

'Any day now.'

'Christ...' he sat, drawing her down onto his lap, holding her

137

against him.

'He's been wounded,' she trembled and he held her, rocking her slowly as she clung to him. 'Oh, God, darling, I know it had to come, but not yet; not yet...'

A log fell in the grate; the clock on the mantle chimed the hour. Ryan looked down into her face. 'I have to go soon.'

'Make love to me; now,' suddenly urgent she pulled him closer. His hands shaking he laid her back on the long couch and began to undress her, while she pulled at his tie then unbuttoned his shirt, whispering, 'I want you; I want all of you...' He dragged off his jacket, fumbling in the inner pocket and she caught his arm. 'No. Tonight you just leave all that to me...'

'You sure?'

'Yes.'

He shucked off his shoes, peeled off socks and pants then took her in his arms again. She drew him down onto her and as the liquid fire swept through his body one thought was racing around and around in his head: *This could be the last time, the last time...*

15

HAWKSLEY, HAMPSHIRE

November 1965

Ryan stopped speaking; the slate clock on the mantle ticked loudly in the silence. Geoffrey de Lacy leaned forward to take a log from the hearth and throw it on the fire. Ryan sat watching the flames leap up the chimney. He said, 'I had always taken such care of her; how could I have taken that chance?'

De Lacey sighed. 'Not your fault; nobody's really, Claire thought she was safe – or so she said, but I've often wondered...' he was silent a moment, then asked abruptly, 'How come you were posted missing, believed dead?'

Ryan shrugged. 'Because that's how it was.' He didn't quite add, *you stupid bastard* but it was implicit in his voice and de Lacy gave a mocking half smile.

'Oh, I think you have to do better than that, Mr Petersen. Very much alive pilots don't just disappear for months without a word, even in wartime. Your chaplain came to tell Claire you were missing. A month later one of your crew turned up. Said you'd been trapped and unable to bail out. He heard the plane crash and saw the flames while he was still in the air. You never turned up on any prisoner of war lists. So where *did* you get to for all that time?'

Ryan said quietly, 'I didn't want any of this; it was your idea. Anything I may say to you concerns only Claire. If you figured on getting the low down on everything you've picked the wrong guy.'

'Humour me.' De Lacy hunched forward in his chair, 'If you were a free man and not a POW, what happened to keep you in France? The Resistance were very good at getting grounded airmen home.'

Ryan shrugged again. Gee, but this guy was persistent – and what did it matter now anyway. It was all a long time ago. He answered, 'It was just a combination of things, bad timing for me and bloody good timing for you! I came down too close to the German Border to make getting home easy with a busted foot. When Claire had your letter to say you were wounded and on your way home, I guess we both knew it was the end, but neither of us could bear to say the words. I flew that last mission in the certainty that whatever happened, whether I came back or got blown out of the sky I had already lost everything and everyone who was important to me; above all, I'd lost the only woman I'd ever love. I'm not a gambler; I don't believe in luck and I don't believe in fate; never did, but if I had to I guess I'd have said that was just the day the number came up for both of us.'

He leaned forward resting his forearms on his knees, his gaze fixed on the fire, seeing it all unreeling inside his head. 'It didn't go so well that last flight. Although there wasn't a German fighter in sight the flack was bad all the way to target, the worst we'd ever flown through. We were in the tail going in over Bremen when the Fort took a hit smack on the engine cowling. By the time we'd got it together and found we were still airborne we'd missed the first target, which was well on fire anyway, so we went on and pasted the secondary. Then as we turned for home a shell exploded under the port wing and a second later the ship took another plumb on the landing gear. Five minutes after that the whole Fort was shot to hell with machine gun fire from the one bloody Hun fighter that showed that day. Within seconds my co-pilot, navigator, bombardier and upper turret gunner were all either dead or dying...' he stared into the fire, a sheen of sweat on his forehead as he relived the moment, 'God knows how the bastard missed me. By then the ship was down to two crap engines and there was no way we were going to see base that night. The best I could do with what remained of my crew was to get them as far as France, because by this stage of the bombing German civilians weren't fussy about honouring the Geneva Convention; unless the military got to them first any airman who dropped over Germany had a fifty-fifty chance of either getting beaten to death or lynched.' He gave a grim, reminiscent smile. 'Those old Fortresses were one hell of an aircraft you know; they could take punishment you wouldn't believe and still fly. The old *Babe* made it just over the French border, but by then we were losing altitude fast, so I told what was left of my crew to jump.'

He hunched forward, staring into the flames with unblinking eyes. 'I couldn't bail out with the others; I was stuck – literally – my dead co-pilot slumped across my knees pining me down and my left foot caught fast between the controls and the buckled fuselage. By then the *Babe* was flying so low it was almost brushing the tree tops and believe me, I was praying real hard. Suddenly the trees thinned and below me and in the dusk I saw this darn great field covered in what looked like fresh plough furrows.' His mouth twisted with grim humour. 'Not exactly the place I'd have chosen to drop a shot-up B17 with no landing gear, but I figured if I could put her down on her belly without standing her on her nose, and *if* she stopped before hitting the next lot of trees I had a chance.'

He looked up then and shook his head. 'It must have been raining for a week, I hit pure mud and the old ship did the longest belly-skid you ever did see... right the length of that whole darned field; then she slewed right around, what was left of the port wing smashed into the trees and she up-ended with her nose buried in the mud. I was told later I was out for the count, hanging arse-up with my head through the side cockpit window. I guess if a guy ever needed a little piece of serendipity, I needed it then – and got it. Seems I'd landed almost on top of a half-dozen French Maquis guys who were busy slitting the throats of a German patrol. A couple took time off to haul me out, busting my ankle in the rush, then lugged me into a ditch before the old *Boston Babe* exploded and was blown over several square miles of French countryside.'

He paused then gave a short laugh. 'It was one hell of a way for a guy to start taking French leave – all eight months of it before the boys in khaki finally arrived!'

Geoffrey asked incredulously, 'And you managed to stay hidden for all that time?'

'Only in a manner of speaking: one of the local guys, whose family were all in the Resistance, had been shot up by a patrol the previous night while he was out shoving detonators under railway tracks. He made it back home but died a couple of hours later. The family were shit scared their cover would be blown if the Germans came checking on missing persons, so when their pals turned up with me I was like manna from heaven. Before I was even halfway with it they'd dyed my hair brown, pasted my photo on forged papers and I had become Jean Phillipe Duval, farm worker, son of Claude and Marie Duval, who'd turned his tractor over and got concussion and a broken leg. The real Jean Phillipe was buried quietly under the hay barn. Poor guy, I hope they dug him up and did the decent thing after the war.'

'And you got away with it for all those months?' de Lacy gave a short bark of laughter. 'I wonder you weren't rumbled in days.'

'I spoke good college French: in a few weeks I spoke the local *patois* even better. The Germans came looking that first night, but I played unconscious then and they didn't cotton. Soon as I was properly with it again papa Duval made me some crutches and I just got on with the milking and feeding. When my ankle was mended I joined the Resistance in their sabotage efforts until one morning a company of your Green Howards marched into town. Ten days later I was back in the States.' He gave a grim, close-mouthed smile. 'I got me a purple heart and a Medal of Honour – just for being a hick farm hand for eight months; not bad for a Yank, eh?'

'No. Not bad at all,' De Lacy's expression was inscrutable, 'but if Claire really meant that much to you, I can't help wondering why after you returned home, you didn't at least let her know you were still alive.'

Ryan shook his head. 'Oh, no, you don't pin that one on me. I had plenty time to think in those few months and I guess I kind of ended up looking at things from a different perspective. You were back, Claire wanted to leave you, but not without Rupert, and you wouldn't let him go.' He spread his hands, '*Impasse.* You see, I couldn't blackmail her into making choices – I tried it once, but I loved her too much to put her through that sort of grief again. I figured it better she thought me dead: that way there were no choices to make. I finished my flying a long way from temptation in Burma and over Japan; then after *that* war ended, went home and tried getting my life back together. Not very successfully, as it turned out.'

When he finished there was a long silence; eventually de Lacy stirred. He reached for the tapestry bell pull beside the hearth and when Mrs Peck answered asked, 'Can you rustle up an extra place for dinner, Pru, and open up the Rose room. I rather think Mr. Petersen will be staying the night.'

Ryan said quickly, 'It's OK. I don't want to put you out – '

'I know, I know – and you have a room at The Bull. Pru will phone old Bob. He won't mind.'

Ryan asked suspiciously, 'How do you know where I'm staying?' and de Lacy grinned.

'Not difficult,' he said, 'you can't hide a big Yank around this neck of the woods for long without he's spotted. Not out of season anyway!'

*   *   *

Whether from sheer exhaustion or the culminate effects of a second shot of Pru Peck's lethal brew, followed by game pie and a good deal of late night drinking with his seemingly immune to alcohol host, Ryan slept deeply. Waking in the dark he laid supine and sleepy for a few moments then fumbled for the bedside light and pressed the switch.

'*Holy God*!'

Repressing a scream he screwed his eyes tight. He was in a

142

strange place; in a room only vaguely recognisable and someone had fried his eyeballs while he slept. Groggy with drink and sleep his fingers scrabbled for the switch, plunging the room back into merciful darkness.

Sitting up he clasped his head in both hands then rocked to and fro whimpering faintly. He had died, that was it: died and gone to hell. Risking one half-opened eye he squinted at the luminous dial of his watch: six forty-five! Falling back on the pillows he prayed for oblivion.

It took less than a minute to realise that a demanding bladder and thundering head meant he wouldn't sleep again. Turning slowly he sat on the edge of the bed. Lowering his feet on to bare boards and clinging to any available piece of furniture he felt his way across the room until he reached a wall; groping his way along until his fingers found the door to an adjacent bathroom he opened it cautiously and stumbled in.

A pity to jettison all that whisky, he thought, his forehead pressed to the wall above the lavatory, then groaning with relief and still disorientated by his surroundings, grasped the old-fashioned chain and pulled. The resultant uproar was horrendous. The cistern gave an almighty clang, followed immediately by a phenomenally loud cascade of water. Uttering curses that would make a hardened cowhand blench, Ryan crashed down onto the lavatory seat and hanging over the basin put his head under the cold tap and turned it on full.

Slowly and gingerly he began to re-orientate himself. This was a bathroom at Hawksley Manor, not his room at The Bull, and he had just passed the night as a guest of Geoffrey de Lacy. He groaned again. Hours they'd talked and drunk whisky and still the crafty old bastard hadn't told him all he'd come to find out. But maybe that was his own fault: too raw and disturbed by the re-living of old traumas, he had shied away from any discussion of what had happened at Geoffrey's homecoming. De Lacy had also avoided the subject, talking lightly of his own war and the decision, once it ended, to abandon his career as a regular soldier and stay at home to concentrate on running the estate. A wise decision as it turned out, when post war problems of heavy taxes and the rising costs of running expenses and repairs had made the stringent management of the farm and eventual opening of the house to the public a necessity.

Ryan felt for and found a towel to dry his hands and face. Vaguely, from the previous evening he remembered a strip light over the basin and above it a small wooden medicine cabinet. Cautiously he felt around again, located the pull cord and released a mellower glow of light than that flung by his beside lamp.

Neatly arranged on a shelf and still in their cardboard covers were toothbrush and paste, shaving soap, brush, a safety razor and a pair of beech-backed hairbrushes. Alongside these items a bottle of Aspirin and a glass.

'Ahhh!' he stood slowly. Propping himself against the basin and keeping his eyes half closed, he filled the glass with water, unscrewed the Aspirin and took a double dose.

*   *   *

An hour later, showered, shaved, dressed and feeling several degrees more human, he left his room and walked soft-footed along the corridor and down the staircase; avoiding the treads that creaked in the way he had avoided them twenty years before. The lock on the outside kitchen door gave sweetly and silently to the turn of the key, and taking a deep reviving breath, he stepped out into the early morning air.

It was a still cold morning, heavy with frost, a pale pink flush spreading across the lightening grey sky. Ryan walked slowly through the grounds, following the path taken on his first visit, stopping for a few moments when he reached the lake. In summer midges danced above the sparkling gravel-bedded and spring-fed water, dragonflies skimmed the surface and in the clear shallows minnows fussed busily around the banks. Now the water was black and faintly sinister, only the occasional sluggish rise of bubbles betraying the presence of fish deep beneath the surface and he moved on with a barely repressed shiver. A melancholy journey, he thought, and why was he putting himself through all this?

He reached the stables where Sampson came to the bars of his loose box, puffing clouds of warm air from his nostrils and whickering a greeting. Ryan smoothed his neck and rubbed his ears. 'Remember that first ride, fella? Remember the sun on the heather, the way we jumped the stream and raced the wind?'

And I held Claire in my arms and kissed her for the first time and started all this tangling of lives. He stared into the shadows of the stables; recalling a tall slender figure standing by two graves in the churchyard; all the grace of her mother in her stance and look, but the shining flaxen hair, the long blue eyes, the line of cheek and jaw, his and his alone…

Giving a last rub between Sampson's alert old ears he turned

144

away and took the path back to the Manor.

*   *   *

Returning to the house he found Geoffrey sitting at the kitchen table, a cup of coffee before him, Mrs Peck at the kitchen range frying thick slices of bacon and plump tomatoes in a huge black pan. They both looked up at his entrance, the housekeeper greeting him warmly, 'Well, hello, Mr Petersen,' while Geoffrey asked with faint sarcasm, 'Feeling better for your walk?'

'Marginally, although I feel I may have frostbite in some pretty odd places.' Ryan eased himself into a chair. His host pushed coffee pot and cup and saucer across the table.

'Help yourself. Meals in this house are generally informal; especially breakfasts. The kitchen is the warmest place first thing.'

Ryan poured his coffee then sat nursing the cup between his hands to warm them, vaguely aware that there was something odd about this domestic tableau. He looked around the room, bright now with early winter sunlight, trying to pinpoint what it might be.

Everything appeared unchanged from the previous evening, when he had helped the housekeeper to clear the dinner table and carry the china and cutlery back to the kitchen. Dresser, table and chairs, china and glass, pots and pans all occupied the same places: a fat marmalade cat slept on the warming rack above the range; nothing unusual there. Puzzled, Ryan turned his attention to his two companions.

This morning Geoffrey was seated on an ordinary chair, a pair of metal elbow crutches propped against the table, his folded wheelchair relegated to the back of the room. Freshly shaved, his thick white hair still damp from bath or shower, he was dressed in a tweed suit and chequered shirt under a cream sweater. He looked well groomed, alert, and every inch the country squire: an impressive achievement for a badly disabled man.

Now how the hell, queried Ryan silently, could he have got it all so together this early in the morning? If there were a manservant or nurse around to help then they sure as heck were good at keeping a low profile. Curious, he turned his attention to where Pru Peck stood relaxed and at ease before the range, looking more housewife than servant, while de Lacy leaned back in his chair equally at ease, a smile hovering around his mouth as he watched her deftly turn bacon and tomatoes onto a side plate.

Ryan's eyes snapped wide open. Geoffrey de Lacy, his guard down for once, was watching his housekeeper with the lazy eyes of a

145

quite unmistakably contented lover...

Hiding his own smile Ryan looked down into his coffee cup. Doorkeeper, housekeeper, nurse and bed-mate...well, hubba-hubba-*hubba* – how's about *that*!

*   *   *

Breakfast finished and cleared, Geoffrey pulled himself to his feet and taking up the crutches, nodded at Ryan. 'I'm off to Stable Cottage – want to come along?'

'Sure,' he rose, gave Pru a smile, 'thanks for a great breakfast.'

She returned the smile. 'I'll have a pot of coffee and a plate of flapjacks ready around eleven.'

'Sounds good to me, ma'am,' he held open the door for Geoffrey who, moving with remarkable speed on the crutches, swung through and into the passageway. 'Better get a topcoat,' Ryan suggested. 'I near froze out there earlier.'

He collected his own coat from the boot room then helped Geoffrey into his duffle. 'Thanks.' His host flexed his shoulders and settled his crutches, explaining, 'I had a level path laid between here and the stables. Mornings are better than evenings for me to get about on these things and I can manage the walk pretty well.' He gave a tight smile. 'All part of keeping mobile as long as possible: sit in that damned chair all day and my lungs will give up even faster than the medics threaten.'

Ryan gave him a swift look. 'Not a happy thought.'

'No,' de Lacy increased his pace to match Ryan's stride. 'Mrs Trump comes up from the village at nine each weekday morning to help Pru, it keeps me out from under their feet to get down to the cottage early – nothing worse than a man sitting around where they want to clean,' he gave Ryan a sideways glance. 'I thought we could finish our talk there.'

Ryan said soberly. 'I don't want to cause you any more grief: I just want to get a few things straight before I go back. I've spent twenty years wondering how it was with Claire. What kind of life you had together. If she was happy...'

'I like to think she was.' Seemingly without effort Geoffrey kept pace with him, but remembering the painful toll crutches had in the past taken on his own arms and shoulders, Ryan slowed and shortened his steps, eliciting another sideways glance. There was a long silence, which he was the first to break.

'Your Mrs Peck seems pretty unfazed by this guy who turns up out of nowhere, gets sauced out of his head and stays the night. I'm darned sure she recognised me from a few months back but she says nothing. That strikes me as kind of odd.'

By now they had reached the cottage; Geoffrey unlocked the door and motioned him inside, then waited until they had shed their coats in the small hallway before he spoke.

'When I left the rehabilitation centre ten years ago I didn't need a nurse as such, but I did need someone to run the house, keep an eye on Sophie during the holidays and give me a hand when and where it was needed. Quite a tall order it seemed and I got through a fair amount of housekeepers before Pru arrived on the scene, which she did just about in time to save me from cutting either my own throat – or one of theirs!'

He led the way into a small sitting room, simply but comfortably furnished with two easy chairs, a good thick Turkish carpet and heavy deep green velvet drapes. In the centre a highly polished table held a vase of flowers and half a dozen books; against the far wall was a handsome antique writing bureau, the flap down and covered with papers. Geoffrey sank down into one of the easy chairs, gesturing Ryan towards the other. 'Pru had looked after her older brother when he was left disabled by polio,' he continued, 'shortly after his death she saw my most recent advertisement in the *Times* and came to see me. That was eight years ago. For all her help, especially with Sophie, I shall be eternally grateful; alone I should never have coped.' He was silent a moment, watching Ryan's face. 'Sophie and Ben are to be married next month and will move into the Manor. They have plans to turn part of it into a Conference Centre, which seem to be all the rage these days. By then Pru will have become my wife and we shall live permanently in this cottage and leave the young people to get on with it.' He gave a faint grin at Ryan's lack of surprise. 'As you have obviously deduced, Pru is more than just my housekeeper. There is nothing she doesn't know about this family – and that includes your place in it. She knew who you were the first time you showed your face here.'

Ryan said slowly. 'How come either of you knew for certain?'

Geoffrey gestured towards the bureaux. 'In the third drawer down you'll find a photo album with Rupert's name on the cover.'

Ryan smiled in sudden recollection and understanding. 'You sent him a camera for his birthday that year – and I gave him a puppy! I remember now that he took pictures of just about everyone. Mary gave him the album to keep them in.' He shook his head ruefully. 'Guess I was pretty naïve to imagine he wouldn't show it you.'

Geoffrey said dryly, 'Oh, he showed it to me alright, and did nothing but talk about you for months, so Claire couldn't have kept quiet about you had she tried. But it so happened she didn't, she told me the truth straight off...that was Claire. I never knew her do or say a dishonest thing – apart from go to bed with you behind my back, that is. Seeing I'd been such a lousy husband I suppose one could hardly blame her for that.'

Ryan fetched the album from the bureaux and resuming his seat opposite Geoffrey, leafed in silence through the pages as the memories flooded back.

Claire, sitting on the gate and smiling down on him as he leaned at her side; Rupert perched on his shoulders, eyes screwed up against the sun. Marion de Lacy in the shade of the big cedar, tea things on a table spread with a white cloth; himself again, rolling with the puppy in the long meadow. Rupert, half elated, half fearful, seated before him on Sampson...the whole of that summer, captured and preserved intact within the album's faded fabric covers.

Eventually he closed the book. 'How did you feel when you saw all these?' he asked quietly.

'Completely floored; if it had happened a couple of years earlier I'd have gone through the roof, but like you I'd had time for reflection in what had by then become a very bloody war.'

He passed a hand over his face then gave a wry grin. 'I'd been in the Army since I was eighteen and apart from service in India in the early thirties, when rioting was the order of the day, I'd never faced an enemy or fought a war. When we first arrived in North Africa I had a damned good time– plenty of booze and plenty of girls – until I got caught up in the real action – leading a Long Range desert group. Very hairy, that: either tearing into the thick of it, shit scared with all hell letting loose around you, or hours spent lying doggo with nothing to do but think about the very real possibility of ending up dead. It gradually dawned on me then that I'd lived a pretty selfish life and if I bought a packet my mother would probably be the only one to shed a tear. As for Claire, I'd treated her abominably, so I'd hardly expected her to 'stand at my grave and weep'.

'All the same, I reckon she would have.'

'Maybe,' he was silent a moment. 'She was certainly good to me when I came back, despite her grieving for you – and my God, she did grieve; deeply, agonisingly, always in silence in a way that was hell to watch. You have no idea how much I hated you then.' He stirred, shrugging his shoulders. 'But she nursed and cared for me as though I was a half-way decent human being. I think it was then I began to love her; really love her; hope that some day she'd feel the same way about me, even though I knew you would always be there between us.'

He looked up at his companion's suddenly taut face. 'I wouldn't talk about you again...until she told me she was carrying your child.' When Ryan stayed silent he asked harshly, 'How much more do you want to hear?'

'Nothing,' Ryan's voice was rough, but steady. 'You loved and cared for her child; that tells me all I need to know.'

Geoffrey's mouth twisted and he said with sudden gentleness, 'Claire *was* happy, you know; eventually. It took time, but we managed to make a good life. When she and Rupert died I wanted to die with them, and I might have: but then there was Sophie.'

'Yeah,' Ryan gave a painful grin, 'then there was Sophie – and I guess I should get myself well away from here before she comes back.'

*   *   *

When they left the cottage he walked silently at Geoffrey's side, all the way letting his gaze rove over the familiar landscape. He knew now that he would not ever return to this particular beloved place, with all its memories and all its pain and felt a sad desolate ache deep inside to know he was seeing it all for the last time. When they reached the house he stood for a moment with his hand on the door latch. He asked abruptly, 'Does Sophie know?'

'That I am not her real father?' De Lacy's eyes were very straight. 'Yes, we never hid the truth from her. She grew up believing, as we all did, that you had died during the war.'

'Didn't she ever see the photographs?'

'No, by the time she was old enough to be curious Rupert was old enough to be discreet.' he smiled. 'After all, you were *his* Captain Pop and not to be shared.'

'And she was never curious about where I came from or who I was? Never wanted to know anything about me?'

De Lacy shook his head. 'I'm sorry, the answer has to be "no". I'm afraid she was only interested in the father she already had, not what might have happened to the one she never knew.'

Ryan winced, but his voice was even. 'Fair enough, I guess she's right at that – and you needn't worry; I'm not going to rock the boat; I'll not be coming here again.' He looked out across the gardens, the long wall that ran right around the Manor grounds, at the fields and the dark line of the pheasant strip. He gave a slight shake of his head, freeing himself from memory.

'I think this is where I leave.' He held out his hand and Geoffrey let go one crutch to grasp it firmly. 'Say goodbye to your Pru for me – tell her I'm sorry to miss the flapjacks...' he hunched his shoulders slightly. 'Guess there's nothing more to say, really: just that I wish you, all of you, a good life.'

He turned quickly, striding swiftly away down the side of the house and out of sight.

*   *   *

Geoffrey returned to the kitchen and sinking heavily into his chair leaned his arms on the table. Pru came to him and placed both hands on his shoulders.

'Has he gone?'

'Yes.' Geoffrey gave a faint wry smile. 'He said to tell you he was sorry to miss the flapjacks.' He put up a hand to cover one of hers. 'He's a good man, Pru. Any other time, any other place, I would have liked him in my life. I think he would have made a valued friend.'

'Will you tell Sophie he's been here?'

He shook his head. 'No. Too late for that and it would be too painful. He thinks as I do that this meeting must be the one secret we keep from her.'

'Well, I'm not sure that you are right, but for my money he's not the only good man around these parts.' She bent to place a very gentle kiss on his head. He squeezed the hand he still held in his own.

'Flatter me some more,' he said. 'After the past twenty-four hours I can do with all you have to spare!'

*   *   *

Ryan paid his bill at The Bull, said goodbye to Eddie and his knowing-looking old father, slung his case onto the back seat of the Jowett and turned the nose homeward.

He felt desperately, achingly lonely; it seemed incredible that in a little over forty-eight hours he had made a friend of an enemy and gained and lost a daughter. 'God help me,' he mused aloud as he gunned the car along the almost deserted Sunday roads, 'when the hell am I going to start saying hello instead of goodbye...'

With the closing of one chapter, at the back of his mind and now moving relentlessly to the fore was the unfinished business with Joel's

150

fantasy mother, so recently brought into the open by Julia Frazier. How was it, he questioned, that he could have been a loved and loving father figure to Geoffrey's son, then failed so abysmally with his own? Had he been so busy sorting his own problems that he'd had no time left for Joel? That he had neglected, perhaps even for a time rejected his son was an uncomfortable thought to have as his only companion on this journey back from the past.

Somewhere along the way he had gone badly wrong, quite where he wasn't sure: perhaps it had started when Ellie's illness had begun to occupy all his time and thought; perhaps when Abby came to Brackets Sound and he had taken the easy way, immersing himself in work, shifting the burden of caring for Joel on to her broad and willing shoulders.

He thought with a certain grim determination that one thing was for sure: it was time to relinquish the distant past and regain something of what he had lost in more recent years.

*   *   *

He had almost reached Holland Park when rain began to fall; rain that in minutes transformed into a lethal sleet that froze on contact with the windscreen. A car in front of him braked and went into a skid and Ryan slowed to a crawl, suddenly aware with a sickening lurch in his gut and something near panic that by now Julia Frazier, Hannah and the children would be well on the way back from Devon: on narrow country roads in a beat-up old car with tyres only three quarter the width of the Jowetts' and an engine with half the power.

All at once his hands on the wheel were clammy with sweat. Swearing beneath his breath he headed for Battersea and Lavender Sweep.

Part II

It had to be you, it had to be you,

I wandered around, finally found, somebody who

Could make me be true, could make me feel blue,

But even be glad, just to be sad, thinking of you……

16

CARTERS END, BRAN TOR, DEVON

Julia finished drying the last plate. Clasping the damp cloth between her hands she gazed out of the kitchen window of Carters End and thought about Ryan Petersen.

She didn't *want* to think about him and was both irritated and confused at the way he was increasingly intruding on her consciousness. All right, she conceded, he was clever, good looking and sexy, and you didn't get too many of those to the pound, but he had an acid wit and more than a touch of masculine arrogance. In addition to all that, he was obviously used being in control of things – and people. All the attributes she most mistrusted in a man.

But exasperating and dominating male that he was, he did have charm: lashings of it, and for a woman who had been too long without a man, that was proving very uncomfortable.

'A penny for them,' Alec Tawton came up behind and laid a hand on his daughter's shoulder. 'Who or what is it that keeps sending you off into a trance?'

'Nothing, nobody,' she turned, pasting a quick smile. She glanced at her watch. 'Lord, is that the time already...we have to go, dad. Will you be all right; got plenty of rations in if the snow comes?'

'You know I have, and yes, I'll be all right.' He squeezed her shoulder briefly. 'I'm not dead yet, even if I do look it first thing in the mornings.'

'Don't!' She caught his hand. 'I don't appreciate your mordant sense of humour.' She stared up into his eyes. 'Please come and stay with us – just until the spring. You know how this place is when winter sets in.'

He said dryly, 'I should; I've lived here for over half my life: but no, thank you. I'd rather stay on home ground.' He pushed her gently towards the door. 'Better round up your gang and get on the road.'

'We'll be down for Christmas as usual. Don't forget to order the turkey from Bovills farm – not too big or you'll still be eating it for New Year.'

His eyes glinted behind his spectacles. 'If I was to invite that little Yankee and the incomparable Hannah to come back down with you, I wouldn't have that problem, would I?'

She chuckled. 'No, but I'd have more than a problem with the Professor. I can't imagine he'd take very kindly to the idea of cooking his own Christmas dinner.'

'Then I'll invite him too,' he returned and watched the colour flood her face and wondered, could it possibly be the little Yankee's father who had been occupying his daughter's thoughts so much lately? He hoped so. Jamie had been a delightful fellow, but hardly the most reliable of husbands, so if Julia *was* interested in this new chap one could hope he was a nice stable American, like Jimmy Stewart or...now what was the name of that fellow in Mrs Miniver? Alec racked his brain: ah, *Pidgeon*, that was it; Walter Pidgeon...funny name, but if this Peterson was anything like either Jimmy *or* Walter, it might be a very good idea to encourage him...but Julia was already out of the room, flinging a scathing: 'He's not the jolly family Christmas type.' over her shoulder.

Ho, ho! Alec grinned. If she *was* finding the professor attractive she wasn't yet ready to admit it, even to herself. However, a few days under the same roof with him might be just the thing to sort that little problem...always supposing the professor was of the same mind. Metaphorically rubbing his hands Alec followed his daughter into the sitting room where Hannah was briskly and efficiently organising Nicole and Joel into their boots and coats for the return journey.

'How has your son been amusing himself while you've been visiting me?' he asked Hannah innocently.

She looked up from tying Nicole's scarf and gave her wide, knock-your-eye-out smile. 'Gone to look up some old friends, I think; but with Ryan you never know. He may just be sitting at home and behaving himself for a change.'

'Not found a lady friend in London yet?'

'Like I said; with Ryan you never know.' She winked. 'But I sure do keep hoping.'

Joel, watching this little scene scowled. 'I don't. It's bad enough back home with that stupid Maria: Abby says *she's* nothing but a – '

'OK honey, that'll do,' Hannah said firmly, 'Now make your goodbyes because I guess we are all set to go soon as Julia says the word.' She gave Alec another smile. 'Kids,' she said, 'notice how they come right out and say nothing they should and everything they shouldn't?'

'Umm,' he gave her a long calculating look, 'but they do have their uses – you know what they say: "Out of the mouths etc.'

He may have been getting his hopes up for nothing he thought gloomily, it sounded as though Julia's professor might turn out to be rather more Errol Flynn than Walter Pidgeon.

*   *   *

Julia glanced in her rear view mirror to where the two children shared a comic, her daughter arguing the merits of Pansy Potter over Dennis the Menace, while Joel poured lofty male scorn on her choice. Born fifty years earlier Julia thought, Nicole would have made a formidable Suffragette and Joel a successful Conservative politician.

The visit to her father had been a triumph of hope over expectation. On the way down she had been beset with fears that the children would be bored and bicker and squabble; that her father and Hannah might take an instant dislike to each other. But she need not have worried. Nicole and Joel, to all intents and purposes now joined at the hip, had amused themselves with the contents of her old games cupboard, while Hannah had positively charmed the hide off her father, who could be an awkward old cuss from time to time. Moreover she had proved more than a match for him at the card table and they had played obsessively, leaving Julia temporarily free to rid her lungs of London fumes and fogs with solitary, if freezing, walks over the moor.

She sighed, feeling her spirits dip in the way they always did on leaving Carters End; she was Devon born and bred and found London a poor substitute; but she couldn't impose on her father and the ordered life he had made for himself since her mother's death, and after all, the city was where the work was.

She flexed her shoulders and settled deeper into the driving seat. Only another four hours and they should be home; less than that if the traffic remained as light as it had so far. Then it would be back to the old routine of work and shopping and struggling to make ends meet. She turned the radio on low, not at all surprised to find that the BBC had already started filling the airwaves with Christmas Carols. Dreamily she let her mind wander over a pleasing if unlikely scenario of them all, Ryan Petersen included, seated around the table while her father carved one of Jeremiah Bovill's prize turkeys.

*   *   *

By the time they had bypassed Exeter, the snow that had begun falling as farthing-size particles an hour ago had changed to dense flakes the size of half-crowns. Julia increased the wiper speed. 'Good job I know

157

this road so well,' she said. 'Actually, I do the trip so frequently that this heap could probably find its own way home.'

Hannah laughed. 'Back home I leave the car in the garage when the snow starts. Go out to the store in sunshine for a loaf of bread in January and you could need chains on your tyres for the return journey!' She peered out at the swirling flakes. 'You get much of the white stuff in London?' she asked. Julia shrugged.

'It snows but doesn't usually last. I love being at Dad's when it comes and the moors look as though someone has spread a huge white blanket over them. That's when the farmers put out feed and the ponies come down from the moor. Dad always spreads bales of hay and straw and they come right up to the orchard fence to feed.'

Joel's enthusiastic voice sounded from the depths of his parka. 'We don't get ponies down at Brackets Sound, but oh, boy, you should just see the snow. Last Christmas when me and dad came back from Vermont we had to shovel for *hours* before we could get our path and sidewalk clear...an' Jake n' me made a snowman that lasted for *weeks*!'

Nicole said in a maddening grown-up voice. 'Well this Christmas all you'll have to shovel off the pavement is ice!' then added with little girl smugness, 'Me and Mum will be all right though, because we always spend Christmas with Gramps.'

'Now then,' Julia warned, 'don't start on the "my snow is better than your snow" lark or I'll stop the car and make you walk!'

Joel was silenced but Nicole whispered, 'Take no notice; she's always saying that but she never does.'

'Oh.' Joel snuggled deeper into his fur-lined hood. 'My dad's always saying he'll strap my ass, but he never does that either – whops me one with a slipper now an' again, but that don't hurt much.'

Julia repressed a snort of laughter and Hannah murmured, 'I sure must remember to pass that one on to Ryan directly we get back home, so that next time he whops a bit harder!'

Julia laughed outright. She rubbed at the windscreen with one gloved hand, 'I expect he's already back by now and toasting his feet at the fire. We may be a little later doing the same if this keeps up, although I daresay it will ease the nearer we get to London – at least let's hope it does.'

*   *   *

They had left Carters End shortly after lunch, but it was almost eight o'clock when, bone weary, cold and with aching eyes Julia stopped the car before her little house. She had driven at snails pace, almost without pause through first snow, then sleet and freezing rain, only stopping at intervals to phone Marlborough Street and hear the bell ring in an empty house. Now all there was to show for a cold and dangerous journey was a heavily iced car glowing eerily beneath the light from the sodium lamp across the frozen street. She glanced over her shoulder to where both children were huddled together, fast asleep. She said, 'The heating will be on but let's go in and start a fire before we move them.'

'And plug the kettle in,' Hannah added, unwinding the rug from around her knees. She smiled but her face was pale with cold with fatigue. 'Though I guess you deserve more than tea or coffee...Honey, I never saw anyone drive better. Guess we owe you for getting us all back in one piece.'

'Soon get you warm,' Julia said encouragingly and laid her hand on the door handle, but before she could open it, it was swung wide and a cool New England voice laced with a searing edge of vitriol enquired: 'Hell lady, what the holy, half-assed time of day do you call this?'

*   *   *

Inwardly Ryan was a mass of contradictory emotions: relief that they were home warring with anger at what he saw as Julia's recklessness in attempting the journey at all. With the memory of that other accident vivid in his mind, as the hours passed he had grown more and more frantic; at intervals driving to Chelsea in the hope they may go first to Marlborough Street, then slithering back fast over treacherous roads to Battersea. Hideous visions of a sudden skid and another vehicle ploughing into Julia Frazier's old heap had him sweating with anxiety; so that when at last he saw the familiar car pulling up outside the house, he was out of his seat and along the pavement in a violent rush of mingled anger and relief.

Gripping the door handle he fought to keep control of his voice as Julia stared up at him for perhaps a half minute in shocked and frozen silence. Then she exploded.

'Let go of my damned door, you uncouth, uncivilised, arrogant bastard!' She struggled out onto the pavement her legs almost too cold to support her. 'I've never met *anyone* who could be so bloody brilliant at saying the wrong thing at the wrong time to the wrong person,' her voice rose. 'Out of my way before I *brain* you!'

'Couldn't have put it better myself!' Hannah leaned across the

159

seat and spoke through the open door. 'Ry, honey, just come around this car and help me out, then maybe Julia can get into that house before she dies of cold.'

Giving the driver one more penetrating glare Ryan swung on his heel and strode around the car while fumbling in her pocket for the house keys, Julia marched up the path flinging a belligerent, 'Keep your bloody voice down and don't wake those two kids until you have to,' over her shoulder.

He crashed his heels and saluted, 'Yes *ma'am,* certainly ma'am. Then when I've carried out orders I suppose you'd like me to cut my own throat, ma'am!'

'That,' she returned from the safety of the open door, 'is probably the best suggestion I've heard all day.'

Despite feeling very much the worse for wear Hannah was shaking with silent laughter as Ryan took her hands and lifted her from the car. For a moment he held both hands tight and looking down into her eyes asked unsteadily, 'You going to go on frightening the bejesus out of me every time I leave town ma, or do I get to relax once in a while?'

For a moment she closed her eyes and giving in momentarily leaned against him. 'You always did lose your temper when you were scared. Now get me inside that house and be real nice to the woman who got us all home safe.'

*   *   *

He draped the car rug around Hannah's shoulders and once inside the house made her lie on the couch. Covering her with the rug he knelt before the hearth to light the laid fire. 'You stay put while I get Joel, then I'll take you both home, pronto,' he said.

When he returned to the car Julia was already there, struggling to lift Nicole from the back seat without waking her. He touched her shoulder and said evenly, 'Let me. I'll come back for Joel.'

Too tired to argue she watched him ease the sleeping child into his arms then closing the car door behind him led the way back into the house and up the stairs. 'There are twin beds in Nicole's room; put one in each, it won't hurt for them to sleep in their clothes for one night.' Her voice was as calm and even as his and he tried to ignore the fact that she had taken control again.

Once in the little blue painted bedroom he left her removing Nicole's coat and boots and went back to fetch Joel. Alone, Julia tucked the blankets around her daughter, kissed her cheek then

160

remained seated on the side of her bed until Ryan reappeared. She watched in silence as he eased the parka and short boots from his son's unresisting body before laying him on the other bed and pulling the covers up to his ears. For several seconds he stood watching Joel's sleeping face, then bent and kissed the crown of his head. ''Night, fella,' his voice was husky. 'Sleep tight.'

In the light from the bedside lamp his face was strained, the blue eyes weary. Impulsively she said, 'I'm sorry. It was a terrible journey and took so long; you must have been out of your mind with worry. We did stop a half dozen times to call Marlborough Street but there was no answer.'

'No. I was dodging to and fro; I guess I just missed you.' For a long minute he stood looking down on her pale tired face then bending kissed her gently, first on one corner of her mouth, then on the other.

Dumbfounded she stared up at him with startled eyes.

'What on earth made you do that?'

'Darned if I know,' he gave a lop-sided, embarrassed grin. 'I guess you just kind of looked as though you could use it, and I kind of felt I needed to do it!'

Flustered, and blushing as though he had suggested ravishing her on the spot, Julia got rather shakily to her feet. 'I think,' she said faintly, 'that the kettle will have boiled by now,' and bolted down the stairs. Ryan followed more slowly, wondering why on earth he had responded to her moment of weakness with such an uncharacteristic and impulsive one of his own.

Goddam, but that had been one crazy thing to do; he touched a finger to his mouth. Nice lips though, he grinned again and thought he'd probably go for a repeat if she gave him the chance.

*   *   *

But she didn't: by the time he reached the kitchen she was busy heating soup and making sandwiches, maintaining an aloof silence beyond a brief request that he should take a cup of fresh made coffee through to Hannah. Ryan gave a resigned shrug. OK if cool was how she wanted it that was how he'd play it.

Re-entering the sitting room he was in time to see Hannah tucking a small bottle into her handbag. He said, 'Coffee up,' and she looked around with a start.

'Just what I need to get me a little more pizzazz so's I can get up and go,' she answered quickly and took the cup with a bright, and to

Ryan's eye, forced smile.

'Ma, you crack me up; you really do.' He took a chair and hunched forward, watching her intently. 'I wasn't born yesterday; I can see you've been popping the Aspirin and are just about tuckered out, so maybe we ought to take a rain check on Julia's soup and sandwiches and I should get you home right now – '

From behind his chair Julia's cool voice interrupted: 'And maybe Hannah should stay here tonight and be spared another cold journey.' She put a tray with bowls of soup and a plate of sandwiches on the coffee table. Smiling at Hannah she said: 'You will be sensible, won't you, and take my bed for tonight?'

'Can't say I'm not tempted, Julia honey, but where would you sleep?'

'On that couch; as I have done on many occasions when there have been overnight guests...and very comfortable it is.'

'Wa-al then, I guess it would be kind of obstinate of me to refuse.' Hannah returned her smile, but her eyes were shadowed, her voice sounding only a faint echo of her usual vigour. She raised her brows at Ryan's sudden frown, 'That all right with you Ry?'

'Sure,' he said, shortly. 'That's OK with me.' He continued to stare, the vertical lines between his brows suddenly deeper, his eyes sharpening. Hannah didn't just look tired, she looked ill, and he was filled again with the deep sense of unease he'd felt the last time he had returned from Hampshire to find Joel in tears and Hannah recovering from some kind of collapse...*and I did nothing about it then, and nothing since,* he thought, *no more than I've taken the time to sort Joel out...*

Apparently unaware of his scrutiny Hannah had begun on her soup and sandwiches, chatting between mouthfuls about their time in Devon and how enjoyable the visit had been for all of them, while Julia assiduously divided her attention equally between Hannah and her own meal while managing to avoid any chance meeting with Ryan's eyes.

He sat back and watched in silence; beneath the surface he could feel his temper begin to simmer again. Damn the pair of them, he thought: Hannah for being one secretive aggravating, worrying woman...and Julia Frazier for being another.

*　　　*　　　*

When he woke the following morning he lay for a moment, wondering at the quiet house before he remembered the events of the previous evening. Not in the best of tempers when he'd left Battersea, he'd been in an even less charitable frame of mind on his return to an empty house; spending what remained of the evening nursing a bottle of bourbon and in reluctant solitary contemplation of the immediate future.

This morning it was still achingly cold with an icy wind, and once showered and shaved he dressed in the warmest clothes he could lay hands on: tweed pants, wool shirt and heavy roll neck sweater He stood in the kitchen eating toast without enthusiasm, wondering in which order to tackle the twin problems of Joel and Hannah. He supposed that as Joel's return to school after the half term was imminent, his needs must come first, but hadn't as yet the faintest idea of how to go about laying it on the line with his son. He made coffee while mulling over several scenarios, none of which had any immediate appeal, until glancing at his watch he saw it was almost nine-thirty and he had a tutorial at ten. Swearing beneath his breath he was halfway to struggling into his overcoat when the telephone rang in the hallway. Irritated he grabbed the receiver, growling, 'Petersen here.'

The voice at the other end of the line was cool, professional and female. 'May I speak to *Mrs* Petersen, please?'

'Sorry, she isn't home right now. I'm her son. Tell me who's calling and I'll get her to call back.'

'If you would do that…this is the Connaught Clinic and we have her test results. Mr Neville can see her to discuss these at ten-thirty tomorrow morning, or she could ring him this afternoon if more convenient.'

'Excuse me?' he stopped with his coat half-on, half-off, '*what* test results?'

'I'm afraid I am not at liberty to discuss those with anyone other than Mrs Petersen herself.'

With an effort he refrained from enquiring if she'd like to take a bet on that, but contented himself with a curt, 'OK. I'll leave a message…' Laying the receiver back on the rest he continued to shrug into his coat, turning the short conversation over in his mind. Who the hell was Mr Neville and what had Hannah been doing at any clinic here in London? "We have her test results", the cool voice had stated. What tests and when had she had them? All at once he remembered the day she had refused to let him take her across town to "visit a friend" and swore again. Goddam it all to hell, he'd known all the time deep down that there was more to that collapse than she'd let on…he banged a despairing hand against his forehead. It looked like

Joel was going to have to wait his turn.

Tearing a leaf from the notepad by the phone he wrote: *Hannah: The Connaught Clinic called about your test results – I'll be home early when perhaps you'll explain to me just what the hell is going on. And don't even think about cooking up some cockamamie story to put me off.'*

Picking up his briefcase he left the house with a vicious slam of the street door that sent the neighbour's Pekinese into an apoplectic ten minute barking frenzy.

*   *   *

Hannah scanned the note, raised half comical, half exasperated brows and passed it to Julia. 'Wa-al now,' she drawled, 'reckon that son of mine is going to be positively fizzing by the time he makes it home tonight!'

Julia was puzzled. 'What's it all about?'

Hannah said 'Tell you when I've brewed some coffee,' and made for the kitchen. Julia read the note for a second time, thinking Ryan Petersen certainly had a neat turn of phrase. Replacing it on the hall table she turned to deal with Nicole and Joel, who were making a great show of strength carrying Hannah's small valise and Joel's backpack in from the car.

'Leave those here,' she directed briskly, 'then upstairs and play, read or what you will. I shall be in the study talking to Joel's Grandma for a while so no getting up to mischief!'

Joel said, 'No ma'am,' but Nicole, more forthright and in less awe of her mother demanded, 'What are you going to talk about – us?'

Julia answered dryly, 'There are other things. Now do as I say and no ear-wigging at doors. Remember: school starts again tomorrow and you have *me* for lessons for the rest of this term!'

'Aw, c'mon, Nic, let's play Dr Who,' Joel was already halfway up the stairs, 'if you want you can be the Doc an' I'll be a Dalek,' he offered generously.

Julia winced at the shortening of her daughter's name, then thought, thank God for little boys who couldn't care less what grown-ups might discuss, and went to hurry along that coffee. The unpredictable Ryan might return at any time and she certainly didn't intend to be around when he did show up. Where that gentleman was concerned, self-preservation, she decided, was the name of the game.

*   *   *

His tutor group ended, Ryan sat at his desk swinging gently from side to side in the swivel chair. Now that he had had time to cool down, anxiety was rapidly replacing anger. Hannah probably felt she had good reason to keep her own counsel; after all, he hadn't been the best or closest of sons, nor all that willing to share his problems with anyone, not even Hannah; perhaps especially not Hannah, so why should she share hers with him?

A great wave of depression swept over him. He had determined to do his best to leave the past behind and make what he could of the future; counting on his own strength, his own innate commonsense to see him through and out of that long tunnel of remembrance. Now it seemed he was out in the light again but with a whole heap more trouble on his plate.

Propping his elbows on the desk he rested his head on his hands. If he took the familiar path he had travelled since his return from the war, he would continue to keep a distance from those who should be his nearest and dearest, eschewing any sympathy or advice, dealing with every problem logically and unemotionally. If, on the other hand he allowed the cracks that had begun to show in that particular philosophy to widen, he would be letting himself in for a very painful process indeed. He was too old to change course, he thought morosely, the habit of years too entrenched to alter.

But if Hannah really was sick where would that leave all his fucking brilliant detachment? Would he be able still to play the "keep your distance from me, ma" card as he had done all these years – and what about Joel? Was the need to invent a mother because he craved one and had been left with a father who couldn't or wouldn't show him all the love he needed, or didn't he care and was just fantasizing to make like he was the same as all the other kids in class?

Frustrated he tugged at his hair: if he couldn't go back then he had to go forward, but he had a pretty good idea that the something deep down inside him that had already begun to gnaw and hurt, was going to get a whole lot worse before he found the answers to all those questions.

As he stood to take his coat and scarf from the old-fashioned bentwood stand, he mused that if life was going to continue pitching shit hot stingers at him, he might just find himself forced to stop dodging and meet them head on for a change.

*   *   *

The house was unnaturally quiet for midday, except for the distant sound of music from above. For a few moments he stood in the hallway before his ears tuned into McCormack singing *Galway Bay*. Without stopping to remove his outdoor gear he climbed the stairs quietly and opened the door into the long sitting room.

Hannah was seated in a corner of the couch, leaning back on the cushions. At first he thought she was asleep until she opened her eyes and greeted him with a smile. 'Hi,' she said, 'I heard your car. No need to hush, I'm just resting my lids.'

'Seems you should have been doing a mite more of that than you have been,' he stood over her, still in his coat and scarf. 'Where's Joel?'

'Gone to the movies – Julia took them both to a matinee.'

He thought: that woman again! He asked, 'Ma, why didn't you tell me something was wrong?'

'Didn't want to bother you, I figured you had enough troubles.'

'I guess there's always room for a few more.' He hunkered down on his heels and took her hand in both of his. 'You've got to level with me, ma. Did you come over her to be with Joel and me because you thought you might be running out of time?'

'Something like that, a year seemed like an awful big slice out of my life without you both around.' She sat forward and with her free hand pushed the wing of hair from his forehead. 'But it's not so bad as that old fool Bart Friedland back home thought...getting me to cross on that damn' boat instead of flying; seems with the right medication I could get old enough to be a *real* nuisance to you!'

'Mom, will you cut the crap and tell me what's wrong and what these tests were for?'

Now she gave the kind of smile she'd given him when he was in trouble as a kid and she had him up against the ropes. 'Tell you what, Ry honey: I'll level with you if you level with me about why you've suddenly sat up and taken notice of your old mom after near on twenty years.'

He gave her a long, considering look. Oh no, you don't he thought, this time I'm not tossing any coin, this time I call the shots. He stood, peeled of his coat and scarf, tossed them over a chair. 'Your turn first, ma,' he said.

17

MARLBOROUGH STREET, CHELSEA

'Angina...that's serious isn't it?' Ryan rubbed a hand across his face, trying not to show how much her news had shocked him, still not sure if she was really levelling with him. 'Who's this Neville guy then and what is it with these latest tests?'

'Mr. Neville's a cardiac specialist. The tests were only a double check to make sure the pills were working fine. After I had that little bit of trouble a while back I went to him because Clarice – one of my Bridge partners, said he was the best. Now I've got it all sorted out and the right medication I'll soon be feeling a whole lot better. It's not *that* serious, Ry; not if I take on board all the advice he's given.'

'Which is?'

'Oh, to rest a mite more, not go parachuting out of airplanes or try to swim the channel; that sort of thing!' She smiled at his set face. 'Lighten up, honey. I'm going to be around for a while yet.'

He didn't return the smile, only said stubbornly, 'I should send for Abby. She'd know better than anyone how to look after you and make you mind what the guy says.'

'No, that wouldn't be fair: not on Abby nor the Elliots – especially since that pretty little Margery has had her baby.' Hannah could score over even Ryan when it came to stubborn. 'I'm not an invalid, so don't get any ideas about wrapping me in cotton wool.' He made to protest but she put her fingers to his lips. 'I mean it, honey. I'm pretty sure Doris will come more often than a couple of times each week if I ask. Apart from that I'll carry on as usual.'

He wasn't about to give up that easily and persisted, 'If you won't have Abby come then I think you should go back home to my place where she can keep an eye on you. I'm sure the Elliots won't mind.'

She said briskly. 'Now you just stop clucking around me like I'm on my way to the graveyard already, because I'm going to hang right in here until this job of yours is finished and we all go back home together; me to my place and you to yours.'

'Goddamn, ma, but you'd make a saint cuss!' he gave an unwilling grin. 'OK we'll play it your way – but I want your promise you'll take it real easy from now on and not spook me every time I turn around.'

'You got it.' She stretched lazily and gave his ribs a prod.

'Now how about you make us both a coffee then come and tell this old momma where about in your head you've been all this long time.'

*   *   *

He spoke calmly, if not easily at first. She could see the effort it cost him to expose to her of all people his vulnerability and helplessness, his open admission of the mistakes made over the years, the missed opportunities and the cruelty of rejection, both thinking and unthinking of those he should have loved but hadn't, and it caused her to look with new eyes at this son of hers: outwardly so big and competent, who fitted his skin as though he was all of a piece until one saw the hurt behind the façade, the pain behind the cool eyes.

His voice, sometimes measured, sometimes rough with emotion brought the past into the quiet room: Falcon Field, the thunder of take off, the fear of each mission: bearable because he could return each time to Claire. Riding through the Forest or walking Belstead Wood with her at his side in winter; swinging Rupert in his arms and rolling with his puppy in the long meadow in summer; the agony of Nile's death; his loss of faith, the pain of returning to the reality of shattered dreams to find himself facing the man he had hated for more than twenty years and now was almost able to view as a friend…

He fell silent then for so long that Hannah thought he must have told all, but something about the hands held so tightly clasped between his knees and the set of his shoulders registered that there was more, and she stayed silent, waiting for him to finish his story.

Eventually he stood and walked to the window. Leaning against the frame and looking down into the street he said baldly, 'I've only just discovered that I have a daughter who will be twenty-one this month. When I flew that last mission neither Claire nor I knew she was carrying our child. Her name is Sophie, I've seen her, just for a few moments,' he gave a twisted, painful smile, 'and she looks just like me, only a whole lot more pretty.'

Hannah caught her breath and thought briefly that if she was ever going to have a heart attack now was the moment. She exhaled very slowly. 'Did you meet? Does she know you are her father?'

'No, to both those questions; she's had the best of fathers in de Lacy and she knows virtually nothing about me…and that's how it's going to stay.' He turned, thrusting his hands into his pockets and hunching his shoulders. 'So you see, ma, I have a daughter and you've a granddaughter whom neither of us will ever know, and who will never know us. For that, and above all for shutting you out of my life for so long, I am truly, deeply sorry.'

She was silent for a moment, then got to her feet and went to him. She put up her hand to touch his cheek. 'A long way back,' she said with a smile, 'you were a whole lot of fun: so warm and smart: just so darned *nice.* Now I've got this crazy notion that with a lot of hard work you might be that way again. Want to give it a shot?'

He said with a dry return to levity. 'Sure, if you keep out of my hair and don't expect miracles. I guess I'll still be an all-fire pain in the ass most of the time but yeah, I'll give it a shot.'

She admitted, 'I didn't want you to come back to this country; I thought it was a mistake: that you'd been unhappy when you were here before and it could only make things worse, but I reckon in the end it's been all for the best.'

'Sure, ma, sure,' he turned her around and pointed her at the door. 'C'mon. Now I take you out to lunch and you can watch me checking the girl's legs – that should bring you back to reality pretty damn' quick.'

*　　　*　　　*

When the telephone rang later that afternoon Julia expected to hear Hannah telling her the coast was clear to return Joel; instead Ryan's laconic tones stated without any preamble, 'Hi, thought I'd save you a journey and pick up the boy. Half an hour OK?'

Huh, she thought, calling the tune again, Mr Petersen? She countered sweetly. 'Make it an hour. We've only just got back and they're playing Mary Poppins and trying to clear Nicole's bedroom by magic.'

To her surprise he answered amiably. 'Sure, gives me time to work on some papers before I leave.'

She chewed a fingernail then asked cautiously. 'Is Hannah all right?'

He drawled, 'She is so far as I know, ma'am. I fed and watered her before I left.'

So it was going to be one of those days, she thought. 'An hour it is then,' she snapped, and as she plonked the phone down could almost see his smart-ass grin.

But when he appeared on the doorstep an hour later and punctual to the minute, he was all polite charm. Proffering a box of Belgian

169

chocolates elaborately gift-wrapped in gold paper and tied with red ribbon, he said with a bow and a perfectly straight face, 'For services beyond the call of duty!'

Caught on the hop for the second time in less than twenty-four hours she struggled for an appropriate reply but he got in first.

'Reckon I owe you for my family's lodgings last night.' He waggled the chocolates enticingly. 'But this is just a peace offering for bawling you out when you got back – the payment for the lodgings will be that dinner you kind of refused a while back.'

Julia's power of speech returned. 'I'm afraid that not having a resident child sitter means I never go out in the evenings.'

'What *never*?'

She hedged, 'Well, hardly ever.'

Deadpan he observed, 'Sounds a bit Pirates of Penzance to me,' then grinned at her involuntary smile. 'I'll bet you played the love interest in your college production – come on now, admit it, you did, didn't you?'

'There's clever now,' she took the chocolates, 'but it still won't get you that dinner.' She held the door wide. 'You'd better come in. If you stand on the doorstep any longer the neighbours will think you're the rent collector and you'll have put them to the trouble of bolting their doors for nothing.'

He followed her into the sitting room; from up above he could hear frustration type yells and a lot of banging about. He raised an eyebrow. 'Guess Mary Poppins never showed.'

'You guess right. I've just told them to get on with clearing up the old fashioned way.'

'About that dinner,' he returned to the attack. 'I don't have any ulterior motives – it's just a friendly gesture.'

That wasn't entirely true, he thought as he watched her turning this one over in her mind; he was surprised that he still found this spiky woman interesting. And not only just interesting; she was also beginning to push all the right buttons for him. However, given her apparent low opinion of men in general and him in particular, anything more than dinner was unlikely, but his buttons being the way they were right now it *was* just possible. He shied away from the thought. Julia Frazier, he'd bet a year's pay, was not one-night-stand or uncommitted sex material; she was the type you'd have to take for keeps and taking for keeps wasn't yet on his itinerary; might never be. It was time he decided, that he got back to Charlie...

'Saturday,' she said suddenly then almost changed her mind at his startled smile, 'but I'd have to be back by ten-thirty,' she added repressively. 'Rosie next door likes to get to bed early.'

'OK.' He returned swiftly to deliberately casual, 'half after seven all right?' She nodded. 'I'll pick you up,' he said, 'but now I guess I should take Joel home.' He looked at her directly. 'I haven't forgotten about his mother. I'll talk to him soon, I promise.'

'I'm sorry. It must be difficult for you.'

'I'll survive; we both will.' He turned away and called, 'Joel, best get down here and into your coat; it's time to go home.'

There was a pause before Joel tumbled down the stairs to swing on the door handle. 'Do we have to go right now?'

''Fraid so, kid.'

He sighed. 'I'll get my things.'

What happened to a grudging OK, preceded by a Bolshie argument, wondered Ryan as he helped him into his parka, and a minute later turned away to hide a grin when, unprompted, the son and heir said a polite, "Thank you for having me, Miz Frazier, and for the movies and the ice cream and all that.'

Much more time spent around Julia and her civilizing influence, he thought sardonically, and Abby would be in for one hell of a shock when they got back to Bracket Sound.

*   *   *

'So where are you taking her for dinner – not The Curb, I hope.' Charlie ran her long fingers down his back. He grunted.

'Hadn't thought; where d'you recommend is OK for a romantic evening without the romance?'

She pondered, 'Hotel or restaurant?'

'No hotels. Just a suspicion I might have rented a room and she'd stab me with the steak knife. Have to be a restaurant –somewhere with a dance floor in case the conversation gets strained and I need the diversion.'

'Hmn, well now...' she considered, 'Do you or do you not wish to impress?'

'Excuse me? Impress Julia Frazier?' He was scathing. 'You have to be joking. The only way for me to do that would be to suffer spontaneous combustion and disappear in a puff of smoke!'

She was patient. 'I'm trying to help here. How do you want to play it – man of the world, or shucks, lady, I ain't been no place like this before...?'

'If we weren't in bed and I wasn't hoping for an encore I'd slap you for that.' He rose up on one elbow to gaze down on her

171

threateningly. 'Just cut the crap and tell me the right place to wine and dine a lady, will you?'

She closed her eyes briefly. 'You have a gift for words...try the Mirabelle in Curzon Street: classy, cosy, small dance floor, black tie but not *too* chic: should do you nicely...by the way, Bruce will be home in a week or two so don't burn *all* your boats with your schoolteacher, will you? I don't think three in a bed is Bruce's style.'

'That's bad news.' He kissed her. 'I'll miss you." He was sincere and she felt a small twinge of regret, but only for a moment.

'I could say I share your sentiments, but Brucie has first claim, besides I love him rather a lot and *this* time he is hot-footing it home to make an honest woman of me.' She grinned and tweaked his chest hair. 'Want an invitation to the wedding – you can bring Julia along!'

'I'll take a rain check on that. Brucie might mind having you invite your temporary bed-mate to his nuptials.'

'Why should he? I don't expect he'll have slept alone every night for all these months.' She stretched and smiled invitingly. 'So let's make hay while the sun shines, lover.'

He gave a theatrical groan. 'Christ, I reckon you both need a Psychiatrist! OK, just a quickie then.'

She said equably, 'I don't do quickies.'

He rolled her into his arms and bit her neck. 'Come to think of it, ma'am, neither do I...'

*   *   *

Walking back that evening he wondered why he hadn't confided any details of his last Hampshire visit to Charlie. Perhaps he had done all the telling he needed to Hannah; certainly there had been a lifting of his spirits since they had talked.

He walked slowly, the cold evening air nipping at the tips of his ears and nose. God, but he'd miss Charlie: for her no-nonsense approach to sex, her generously given time and patience – and all those post-coital reefers. Still, the times they were a-changing, and he must change with them. Although at forty-seven it was a touch undignified to have to move over for a younger man; life with Charlie had been fun while it lasted.

*   *   *

Opening the door of number sixteen he found Joel sitting on the stairs and fixing him with reproachful eyes. 'You said seven o'clock,' he complained, 'it's half after. Gran'ma says I have to go to bed now and I wanted you to show me that chess thing again.'

'Sorry.' Ryan hung his coat and ran his hands over his damp hair. 'I kind of got talking – you know how it is. Go take your shower and I'll read – or you could tell me all about the movie.'

'OK,' Joel began to trail up the stairs, 'but why do you have to go to Miz Lawrence to talk; why can't she come here?'

Ryan swatted at his behind with his scarf. 'Don't sass me or I'll come up and wash out your ears!' He watched him scramble giggling up the stairs, before turning into the dining room where Hannah was laying the table for dinner. 'Mom, what are you at? I thought we agreed I was doing all that now.'

'You're late and I'm hungry – and as you'd already gotten the meal ready to cook that left me nothing else to do but this.'

'Sorry,' he said a second time. 'Charlie had some good news to celebrate: her guy's coming home and they're getting married, how about that?'

She said approvingly. 'Now that's great. Maybe we'll see a mite more of you in the future.'

Ryan took a breadstick and chewed thoughtfully, wondering if Hannah was quite as gullible about the reason for his visits to Charlie as he'd supposed. She seemed a hell of a lot sharper than she used to be, or maybe *he* just hadn't been as perceptive as he imagined about what his mother was thinking. Retreating he said, 'You go and rest while I see Joel into bed,' and as he turned away caught the edge of a very knowing smile. He climbed the stairs slowly, finishing the breadstick. Either he misread that smile or Hannah was mellowing in the illicit sex department.

Maybe, he mused, there was something in all this English rain that kind of washed out some of the Boston starch.

*   *   *

Listening to Joel's blow-by-blow account of his trip to the movie: how Miz Frazier had bought ice-cream and not got mad when he dropped it down his shirt, how Miz Frazier had laughed so much at the penguins that she cried, how Miz Frazier understood about magic not working all the time but said it didn't hurt to try once in a while, Ryan concluded sourly that he was getting a bellyful of Miz Frazier this evening; that maybe he should by-pass the dinner and take *her* to the movies so's she could work a little magic on him. 'Better wrap it now and get to sleep,' he cut in when his son finally stopped for breath. Joel gave him an offended look.

'Don't you like Miz Frazier?'

Ryan scowled. 'What's that got to do with you getting to sleep?'

He persisted. 'Nothin', but *do* you like her?'

'Sure. She's OK.'

'I like her,' he lay back, staring up through the skylight. 'I like her a lot an' she likes me.'

'It takes all sorts.' Ryan said laconically, 'I sure didn't go ape over any of my schoolteachers at your age, but then they were all nuns and pretty handy with the paddle!' Joel didn't comment, only hunched his shoulders and kept right on staring at the rain drizzling down the glass. Ryan wondered if this was a good time to clear the air. He gave it a minute then said firmly, 'Joel, we have to talk.'

Joel turned apprehensive eyes on him. 'Why? I haven't done anything bad.'

Ryan took the plunge. 'You've been telling the kids in school your mommy is alive and back home. Why?'

Joel flushed scarlet and stuck out his bottom lip. 'Now you're mad at me.'

'No. I'm not, and you can't wriggle out of answering by pretending I am.'

He turned away, pulling the covers up over his head. 'I'm tired. I want to go to sleep.'

'Sorry fella: I can't let you pull that one either.' Ryan detached the sheet from his grasp and sat him up; keeping hold of his arms he said sternly, 'you're not the only one it's ever happened to are you? Nicole's daddy is dead but she doesn't pretend he's still alive.'

Joel wouldn't look at him. 'That's different. S'all right for Nic; she can tell everyone his 'plane crashed and they all think he's a hero.'

'So? You haven't got to spill it all, have you? All you need say is your mommy died. You've got to level with me Joel, and tell me why you can't do that.'

He mumbled, 'Kids might ask questions.'

'What kind of questions?'

'I dunno. I s'pose they might like they do back home, when they ask about how your mom died, and how d'you *know* she's dead if you never seen her for ages and can't remember properly what she looked like?' he twisted his head away. 'I don't want to talk about it.'

Ryan persisted. 'What else do the kids back home say?'

'Like she was poopy an' flaky…' all at once the tears were pouring down his cheeks, 'and she was, wasn't she?'

'Come here.' Ryan hauled him bodily from beneath the covers and onto his knees; holding him close he said firmly, 'Now you listen to me; your mommy was sick, real sick. With some people it's their body that gets sick and hurts; with mommy it was her mind. She couldn't help that, any more than folk can help getting a fever or a bad heart.' He used the corner of the sheet to mop at the cascade of tears. 'Hell, even you or I can't help feeling bad in the head sometimes – like when you want to yell at me and play up, or when I get mad at you.'

Joel was inconsolable. 'But Jake's brother told him she was a mush-head and jumped in the river on purpose ...did she, did she do that?'

For a moment Ryan was rocked back on his heels. Recovering swiftly and with an effort keeping his tone reasonable and comforting he admitted, 'Kid, I don't know the answer to that; she might have, but it could have been an accident and she just fell in; no one will ever know. But Joel, one thing is for sure, your mommy wanted you and loved you more than anything else in the whole world; she just was too sick to be able to take care of you, that's all.'

He wailed, 'I can't say that to the guys in school!'

'I see that; but *you* know and that's what matters. When we get back home, if the other kids start pushing again, you just have to tough it out and not let what they say get to you.' He shook him gently. 'But you had a fresh start over here, where nobody knew about your mommy; now you've kind of mussed it up and we have to find a way to put that right, don't we?'

'I guess.' He didn't sound either convinced or happy. Ryan persisted.

'How about I have a talk with Miz Frazier and see if between us we can figure things out: will you do as we say and get it all straightened?'

'Yeah, OK.' He scrubbed at his eyes and blew his nose on the sheet.

'Heck,' Ryan winced and hastily put him from his knees. 'You go wash your face and I'll get that in the laundry bag before your grandmother sees what you've done to your clean linen.'

By the time he had changed the sheet Joel was back, pink-eyed but ready to bargain, his first words, 'I don't want to do out loud prayers now; I'm too old. Nicole says so.'

Ryan grinned. 'There's a girl after my own heart.'

'She says when she remembers to do them at all she does them lying down and in her head.'

175

'Makes sense; reckon a one to one chat when you feel like it beats a whole lot of hollering,' said Ryan. Joel heaved a sigh of relief and dived under the covers. Ryan ruffled his hair and leaned to switch off the light. 'Night fella,' he said and Joel answered primly, 'Goodnight daddy. Thank you very much!'

'Don't push your luck,' Ryan gave his rump a backhander through the bedclothes, eliciting a stifled giggle in response. The tone and accent had been unmistakable – pure Julia Frazier to a tee.

*   *   *

In her pyjamas and determined to delay bedtime as long as possible, Nicole sat crossed-legged on her mother's bed and watched Julia sort through her wardrobe, giving gratuitous and not very helpful ten-year-old-going-on-nineteen, advice.

'On a first date and for a funeral,' she offered, 'it's best to wear black – it said so in Verity Robinson's mother's Nova Magazine.'

'This is just dinner; not a first date *or* a funeral,' Julia frowned repressively, then remembering a very loud demand for an explanation about call-girls and prostitutes made in the middle of M & S one Saturday morning a while back, added sternly, 'and I've told you before about reading grown-up magazines: mine, Mrs Robinson's or anyone else's.'

Nicole remained uncrushed and undaunted. 'If it's a posh place you should wear long.'

Exasperated, Julia ordered. 'Bed, now. I'll be in to see you in ten minutes.'

With much muttering of 'It's not fair' and dragging of feet Nicole departed. Once free of her daughter's critical eye Julia gazed in despair at the meagre collection of dresses, none of which could be even remotely considered suitable wear for dinner with Ryan Petersen, who even in old cords and a sweater always managed to look well dressed.

Standing before the long cheval glass she posed, holding each garment against her in turn.

One blush pink organza, long, dated and highly unsuitable for the Mirabelle, where she had once been wined and dined by a fellow officer and friend of her late husband. The ultimate in a string of uninspiring dates, and one that had ended with her practically fighting for her honour in the cab on the way home while vowing never to let another man into her life: a vow she had managed to keep for the past two years.

She poked moodily at the inevitable little black cocktail dress: rather more the thing, but if dancing on the Mirabelle's miniscule floor was likely to be part of the evening's entertainment, and it probably would be, the dress was cut much too low in the back. What Ryan's warm brown hand resting on her bare skin might do to her libido was something she would rather not think about, she found him quite disturbing enough without that.

She sighed and dropped the black dress back on the bed. If he didn't habitually rub her up the wrong way at least once each time they met she could quite like him, she mused, but he *was* the most aggravating man. Take his reaction to her question when he had called to tell her the venue for the dinner. Feeling it tactless to say she had been to the Mirabelle before, when she asked if a short dress would be in order, he had answered with that phoney Southern drawl, "Well, ma'am, ah surely don' know 'bout you-all, but *I'm* gonna be warin' ma pants as usual!" Bloody man...

Reaching into the wardrobe again she unhooked her penultimate possibility: a slinky red, knee-high shift: a genuine original Mary Quant and ruinously expensive, even from the Dress Agency in West Ken. *God no*, she tossed it hastily aside: wearing that would be tantamount to saying "I'm available: come and get me!"

That left only one tenable choice. Opening the long drawer at the base of the wardrobe she took out a shallow cardboard box. Removing several layers of tissue paper she shook out the folds of silk and laid the dress across her bed. Part of my past, she thought, part of the pain and the longing, unworn now for five years, the last time at a mess dance just a week before Jamie crashed. She stood smoothing the silk with an unsteady hand. Could she bear to wear it again for another man...an uncertain little smile touched her lips: after five years, would it *fit*?

She peeled off her sweater and skirt, took a deep breath and pulled the dress over her head. With a whisper of silk it slid down over her body, covering her neck to mid-calf; settling over her small breasts and narrow hips as though it had just been delivered from the hands of the wizened little Chinese tailor in that Singapore back street. Slowly she fastened the high collar and the diagonal loops across the breast then turned to view herself in the long mirror: Julia Tawton, in the cream silk cheongsam that had been her wedding dress.

She turned this way and that: admiring anew the pale silver embroidered dragons writhing sinuously through pink almond blossom and golden chrysanthemums then paused to peer more closely at her reflection. Hell, but those side slits were high – surely she had never walked down the aisle showing all that much leg? She supposed she must have done. Now she came to think of it, that particular dress always had drawn more than the occasional wolf-whistle at station dances. She gave an apprehensive shudder. If she actually found the courage to wear it tonight, would that obvious legman Petersen think she was making a play for him?

She looked again at the pink organza, the little black dress and the screaming red come-and-get-me and gave a defeated sigh. She would have to risk it; leg or no leg, memories or no memories, it would have to be the cheongsam and bugger the consequence.

*   *   *

The following evening she saw Nicole safely settled in front of the television with Rosie-from-next-door and repaired to the bathroom, where a long soak in a verbena scented bath settled her nerves. Afterward, wrapped in a housecoat she sat before the dressing table mirror and made up with more than usual care. Finally she slipped the cheongsam over her head then brushed her hair into a sleek shining cap.

Finishing with a subtle spray of preciously hoarded *Joy* and taking a last look in the mirror, she gave a small sigh. Well, this was it then: Julia Frazier all done up like a dog's dinner and stepping out on the town with a man she wasn't even sure she liked; a man who, although undressing her with his eyes at every meeting, showed no other sign of interest in her as a woman. Gathering her long wool cloak from the bed she folded it over one arm. At least, she thought, she would make sure she was well wrapped in *that* before he arrived.

Stepping light heartedly down the stairs she threw open the door to the sitting room and pirouetting on one foot, flung out both arms with a theatrical: 'Well, girls, how do I look?'

The sole occupant of the room turned from examining the picture over the mantle. 'You look,' said Ryan Petersen, an expression of unholy joy lighting his sapphire eyes, 'abso-fucking-lutely *bodacious*!'

Her immediate reaction to the sight of him that it wasn't fair, no middle-aged man had a right to look *that* good in a dinner jacket, gave way rapidly to embarrassment at being caught on the hop – again. 'I *beg* your pardon?' She bristled to cover her confusion. '*What* did you say?'

With an exaggerated bashful gesture he clapped a hand to his mouth. 'Sorry, just a slip of the tongue,' he apologised. He swept both hands down and out in an attitude of humble supplication. 'But ma'am, you surely did take ma fuckin' breath away!'

Belatedly she flung her cloak around her shoulders, clasping its lopsided folds tightly about her. 'If you use that word once more I am going to stay right here...' despite her best effort her voice wobbled and she fought to control the bubble of laughter that rose in her chest. Solemnly Ryan placed a hand over his heart.

'Ma'am, my lip is buttoned.'

'Good.' She regained her self-control. Keep it light, she admonished herself, and he might forget you've just demonstrated you are a complete idiot. 'What have you done with Rosie and my daughter?'

'Well, they kind of got tired of the TV and went to pop corn in the kitchen.'

She stared. 'We don't have the sort of corn you pop.'

'You do now.' Easily he took the collar of the cloak she held bundled around her, shook it out then draped it over her shoulders, and amazingly she let him. For a moment he held her shoulders between his hands. 'Great, dress, great perfume, great woman,' he said softly; then the light of mischief was back in his eyes as he added, 'and I surely am beholden to you, ma'am, fer cleanin' up so nice and purdy, jest fer me.'

She asked scathingly, 'Are you going to keep that up for the whole evening?'

'Nah, just getting it off my chest!' he grinned and took her arm. 'Guess we should go say goodnight to the corn-poppers before we get right out there to light up the town.'

18

He drove fast but not, she noticed with grudging approval, with any unnecessary flourish. After a few minutes pondering what had caused him to make, and her to accept this invitation in the first place, she said curiously, 'I'd like to know the real reason you asked me out tonight.'

'We-el, now, I didn't know you'd want a reason, but I guess it *had* occurred to me that if you could be a friend to my mother and son, maybe I should make the effort to get in line too.' He flicked a sideways glance at her face. 'Except that you surely don't like me very much, do you?'

She flushed. 'I don't know you well enough to either like or dislike you.'

'So how about you loosen up and we get to know each other better?'

She gave an indignant squeak. '*Me* loosen up, when most of the time *you* are halfway up your own – '

He gave a bark of laughter and spun the wheel to slide into a parking space a few yards from their destination. 'That's Service talk if ever I heard it – and from a lady too!' He killed the engine and twisting around to face her gave his slow-burn smile, 'We've got more in common than I thought.'

She sighed and shook her head. 'I'd be seriously worried if I imagined for one moment that might be true!'

*   *   *

Quite a few heads were turned, not all of them male, as they were shown to their table. Julia thought the women were interested because she was with a man who looked as though he could stand-in for Lawrence of Arabia, Peter O'Toole version; Ryan knew the men were interested because he was an older man with a younger woman who quite simply looked good enough to eat.

He had to admit she'd knocked him sideways when she had made her dramatic entrance. He smiled at the remembrance of that little pirouette and her spiky self-consciousness. In the car she had been defensive as usual, but now seemed all at once poised and confident, and he thought, well aware of the attention she was drawing. When they were seated he smiled straight into her eyes and said. 'It's quite a while since I took a lady to dinner and even longer since I've had so many men wish they were in my shoes.'

She hoped he wasn't going to continue to keep his gaze riveted on her face in that fashion; the onslaught of his smile was as disturbing as it was unexpected, as was his rapid change from provocative tease to admiring escort. An aggravating acerbic Ryan she could deal with, but one now putting out quite such a concentration of beguiling charm was a horse of a different colour. The response of a maidenly blush would probably please him no end, she thought crossly, but then again, he had never struck her as a being a connoisseur of blushing maidens...quite the reverse in fact...

She was saved from making a response by the appearance at their table of a waiter, who offered the wine list with a lofty, 'Madame, M'sieur: la carte des vins. Souhaitez-vous un apéritif?' Dragging her gaze away from Ryan's she snatched at the only word she'd understood and studied the list of aperitifs.

While the man hovered with the haughty expression of every wine waiter he'd ever clocked Ryan anticipated what she would choose, a medium sweet sherry, and uttered a mental *ouch* when she said crisply, 'A dry Martini, please, with very little ice.'

The waiter bowed, 'Certainement, Madame.'

He handed the list to Ryan, who eyed him speculatively then passed it back instructing, 'Faites que deux, tout de suite, s'il vous plaît.' A banknote changed hands, some of the hauteur left the man's face and with a bow and a further 'Certainement, M'sieur' he wafted away. Ryan waited until he was out of earshot then raised an eyebrow. 'I had you down as a medium sherry!'

She grimaced and shook her head. 'I've had too many of those in too many messes where women are supposed to know their place.'

He grinned. 'I remember some of your British brass could be pretty stuffy.'

'Well, they aren't all like that, although Jamie had one Group Captain who was straight out of a 1940's stiff-upper-lip-chaps movie. Given the honour of sitting next to him at dinner you instantly became a Little Woman who was expected to listen attentively and be flattered witless by an excess of My Dear's and a lot of avuncular knee patting.'

Ryan laughed. 'I'll bet you just loved that,' he sat back as the waiter returned with their drinks and the menus. He flashed the man a smile. 'Est-ce que nous en dix minutes, cela passera commande est. OK?'

He bowed, returning the smile. 'Parfaitement, m'sieur.'

Julia looked after the waiter's retreating figure. She'd been with men before who had aired their French in just such a situation as this, usually loudly and to impress; Ryan's exchange with the waiter had been quiet, matter of fact and without a trace of self-consciousness. Intrigued, she asked, 'How did you know he was French? That accent could be phoney; most of them are. He could have been born in Bermondsey.'

'Na.' Ryan twirled his olive around his martini. 'He's the goods all right. No guy from Bermondsey could roll his r's like that.'

She asked with a hint of sarcasm, 'But a guy from Boston can?'

'Sure. I learnt the hard way.' Abruptly he changed the subject. 'I said ten minutes before we order because I wanted to get some business out of the way first.' He tasted his drink, nodded appreciatively. 'Um: great.'

'What business?'

'Joel. I talked to him last night. He didn't say much: cried a lot, though.' He put down his glass and hunched forward. 'He knows he has to put it right; thing is, I'm not too sure how to help him do that. I guess I hoped you might have some ideas.'

She gave the suggestion a lot of thought. 'Well,' she was business-like and slightly bossy: a typical schoolmarm, he thought. 'First off, he will have to stop telling porkies...'

'Excuse me?'

She sighed. 'Porkie-pies – lies: your lot didn't invent slang, you know.'

He said dryly, 'I remember now: apples and pears; plates of meat: titfer-tat and all that jazz!'

She ignored him. 'It will probably be better for him to keep quiet and off the subject of his mother for a while,' she said, 'if someone asks he'll need to just tell the simple truth and say she is dead now. I think he'll manage because he has guts, your son.'

'Yeah, and he'll need plenty. They could tear him to shreds if they find his weak spot.'

'Not necessarily, nothing holds their attention for long you know; it will all fade away pretty quickly. In the meantime I'll pass the word in the staff room to keep an eye out for any sign of trouble or Joel getting distressed.'

'I'll talk to him again; suggest he just quits talking about Ellie for now and see what happens. Like I've already told him, if he gets asked he has to tell it like it is, then just tough it out.' He was silent for a few moments, looking down into his glass and twisting the stem between his fingers. Eventually he looked up again to ask bluntly, 'What has my mother told you about my wife?'

She hesitated. 'Not much: only that she died about a year ago but you were on your own quite a while before that.'

He almost smiled. Yeah, he thought, good old Hannah...just dropped enough to get your sympathy and let you know I was available. Much as he hated the idea, he knew the time had come to really level with Julia Frazier. If Joel was to be helped out of his present trouble she had to know the truth. He leaned forward propping his forearms on the table. 'You've said you'll help Joel, but I don't think you can do that without knowing what happened to his mother. The truth is that she drowned a year ago. It may have been an accident, but it's more than likely she took her own life.'

He saw the shock in her eyes but she didn't, as most would, say she was sorry or commiserate in any way, and he was grateful for that. With only the briefest pause he continued. 'Everyone back home knew about Ellie and some of the neighbourhood kids gave Joel a rough time of it...' He paused again, then said flatly, 'He barely knew her; she'd been mentally unstable since before he was born and in a psychiatric clinic for the last five years of her life. When we came here seems he couldn't handle a whole new lot of people finding out his mother was crazy, so he lied.'

Julia said swiftly. 'Please, you don't have to say any more if you'd rather not.'

He shrugged. Julia felt she was beginning to know that shrug: it was the give-away to his feelings...it could be defensive, irritable, embarrassed or defeated. Now it was weary. He said, 'It's because I've been avoiding it that Joel's gotten himself into this mess. It didn't all happen overnight.'

A few musicians and a male vocalist had appeared on the small rostrum at the far side of the dance floor. Obviously, in this elegant place the Stones and the Beatles wouldn't have a prayer and the repertoire began with *In the Still of the Night.* Ryan threw a glance in their direction. 'Great,' he smiled his close-mouthed smile. 'Confession to Cole Porter!' he said then very quietly, keeping his eyes fixed on hers, accurately and economically he sketched the story of his marriage.

'When my war was over I returned home to Boston and the girl I left behind – or at least, that's how Ellie saw it. She'd worked in my dad's pharmacy since finishing college and we'd dated a few times, although I was quite a bit older and already teaching at the university by then. But she was around and available, and I kind of slipped into

183

the routine when I visited home, of taking her dancing or to the movies, then necking in the car afterwards. I volunteered for the Air Corps early in 'forty-one when it was obvious the US was going to have to join the war eventually. I wanted to get in ahead of the draft and do what I wanted to do, which was fly. When I was sent overseas in 'forty-two Ellie said she'd wait for me – and so she did; trouble was, I didn't wait for her.'

Absently he took up his fork and began to trace patterns on the tablecloth. 'While I was over here I had a very committed love affair,' again the shrug, 'but that's another story. I finished my war in the Philippines and when I got back home again I thought, well, what the hell. I tucked everything that had happened over the past four years away into a nice dark corner of the closet, closed the door and married Ellie.' The fork drew four straight parallel lines then left them going on into infinity. 'It was a big mistake. I was twenty-eight, battered and tired; all I wanted was a home, a woman and peace and quiet – lots of peace and quiet. Well, I got the home and the woman so maybe two out of three wasn't bad. Ellie was twenty-three, young and fresh; maybe a little wild but hot to settle down, be a housewife and raise lots of babies...' he paused. 'Boy,' he said softly and with a tinge of regret, 'when that gal sparkled, she really sparkled, but when she went ape, which she did pretty often, then she was hell in gingham!'

'So it all went wrong?'

'It sure did.' He lifted a hand; ran it through his hair. 'She wanted a baby right away after we married; I wasn't that keen but, well, she was determined and got pregnant pretty soon; always did. Trouble was she never went full term. Six late miscarriages in nine years had her depressed as hell. Then at last, after all the disappointments there was Joel.'

'Didn't that help?'

He shook his head. 'No, she'd been getting more and more flaky but after Joel she went downhill fast: postpartum depression, they said; I tried my best and did everything the experts told me to help her get back to normal, but nothing worked and she kind of slipped into a full-blown psychosis.' His voice was flat, devoid of expression. 'I guess it didn't exactly help that she loved me and I didn't love her, although I did try.' Neatly, the fork drew another set of lines then executed a four-pronged full stop.

'I guess that's about it: we ran the usual gamut of more specialists and supposedly better drugs; then in and out of clinics, until finally, for her own safety, she was committed permanently to a psychiatric unit. Shortly after that I was granted an annulment to our marriage.

Her parents took off and left me on my own with Joel – said they never wanted to see the boy or me again; can't say I blamed them.'

There was more, she knew, but guessed accurately that when a man like this said that was all, for the present at least it was.

As he finished speaking another waiter appeared; 'M'sieur, Madame, vous inquiéteriez-vous pour passer commande maintenant?' with a flourish he produced two menus, each the size of a memorial wall, then withdrew to hover at a discreet distance.

Over the top of his menu Ryan raised a sardonic eyebrow at his companion. Deadpan he murmured, 'Now that one *is* Bermondsey, through and through!'

* * *

The food, when it came, was good; they ate their way through the entrée, main course and a sweet of spun sugar and cream while chatting with increasing ease about work and leisure and who liked what.

Ryan, Julia discovered, had an eclectic taste in music, ranging from Grand Opera to Louis Armstrong; he had a passion for the First World War English poets and had written his PhD thesis on Wilfred Owen. Hitchcock was his favourite movie director; he liked watching baseball from the bleachers, sailed and swam in summer and skied in winter.

Julia, Ryan ascertained after a good deal of probing, was a ballet fan, read crime novels in bed, was crazy about the poetry of Stevie Smith; watched any old films, swam only if the water was very warm, thought playing any kind of game a waste of time and energy, but confessed to watching cricket at the Oval when she had time to queue for a cheap seat.

'Cricket?' he was straight-faced, 'that's kind of like baseball, only slower, isn't it?'

'Shhh!' she glanced around in mock terror, 'in a place like this, that sort of remark could get you hanged!'

In the atmosphere of expensive luxury, mood music and a Ryan who had somehow managed to metamorphose from unpredictable protagonist to easy, entertaining companion, Julia let herself drift on a pleasurable tide of well-being and content. When they had finished the last of the wine and he asked if she'd like to dance, relaxed enough to ignore the warning bell ringing faintly in the far recess of her mind, she answered, 'Why not?' and stepped unhesitatingly into his arms, as though it was something she'd been doing for years.

185

*   *   *

Julia Frazier, Ryan had reluctantly to acknowledge, was having quite an effect on him, so that *Mack the Knife,* a good up-beat number unlikely to tempt anyone to smooch, had come at just the right moment, when the easy exchange of likes and dislikes were about to segue into an intimacy which could lead to all kinds of confidences and revelations that he might later regret. Getting the temporary hots for this woman was one thing he told himself firmly, opening up his life to her something else again.

Caught up in their exchange of confidences he hadn't registered that one dance followed almost seamlessly upon another, so when Kurt Weil and *Mack the Knife* progressed with only the barest pause to Jerome Kern and *They Didn't Believe Me*, he was taken completely by surprise.

For a moment he stumbled and lost step, then recovered swiftly, with a muttered 'Sorry' in answer to Julia's quick, inquiring glance. He knew the intelligent thing to do was make an excuse, however embarrassingly feeble, and leave the dance floor immediately, but was simply unable to summon the will to do so. His heart began an uneven thud and his hands developed a tremor he couldn't suppress; worse, the evocative words and music triggered automatic memory and for a few breathless dizzying seconds he was back in the great hall at the Manor with Claire in his arms...

With an effort he wrenched himself back into the present; to London nineteen sixty-five. The hell with it, he thought: this is a real warm flesh and blood woman and goddam it, I'm only human. Drawing Julia closer he rested his head against hers, dancing as he hadn't danced for more than twenty years.

*   *   *

The slight vibration of Ryan's hand against her back sent a shaft of something Julia refused to put a name to swooping through her body. Big mistake she thought, to get this close to a man who, while apparently not particularly attracted to her or she to him, had, at close quarters, an uncanny ability to reduce her legs to jelly.

She had known instinctively, if not from their first, but certainly by their second meeting, that despite the lazy, provocatively sexual air that hung about him like an aura, he managed at the same time to give off a very clear and unmistakable message of *"Noli me tangere"*; but if he wasn't over eager to let any woman close, why should she now

186

have the feeling that she was quite definitely being held in the arms of a lover?

Even more disturbing: why was she enjoying it?

The dance ended and the orchestra swung into a quickstep. For a long moment Ryan stood on the dance floor, Julia still held close in his arms, until a passing couple jostled them. Releasing her and placing a hand on her shoulder he guided her back to their table. 'Coffee?' he asked, avoiding her eyes and when she nodded her agreement, summoned their waiter and gave the order.

Julia waited until the man was out of earshot then asked directly, 'What happened?'

Ryan raised an eyebrow. 'Excuse me?'

'Out there – while we were dancing: something happened,' she twisted a finger at her temple. 'You went right off the edge...'

'Nothing happened.'

She flushed at his deliberately blank look. 'You know damned well what I'm talking about...' She had a sudden startling flash of intuition, remembering how his eyes had, just for a few moments turned opaque; looking through her to something, or someone else. 'You came on to me, and you didn't really know you were doing it, did you?' she demanded.

Ryan, shaken by that slip into *déjà vu*, and even more disturbed by the realisation that out on the dance floor he had felt and was still feeling something a great deal more than a passing moment of lust for this challenging woman, struggled to maintain an expression of impassive non-comprehension.

''Fraid you've lost me there.'

'In that case perhaps when we have had our coffee it might be a good idea to lose each other,' she returned tartly. Much more of this, she thought, and she'd go to the Ladies, climb through the window, if she could manage it in this damned dress, and take a cab home. The infuriating thing was that despite his maddening, unpredictable switches of mood, he was really beginning to get under her skin.

Perhaps it had been his frank admission of his shortcomings, both as husband and father that had tipped the balance in his favour; perhaps the intriguing glimpse she had caught of what lay beneath the façade of indifference, or perhaps it was the way he had held her and the feelings he had aroused when they danced.

However, there was no way she would let him see he had found a chink in *her* armour; not when he was once more making it clear that one glimpse of the real Ryan was all she was likely to get; now, or at any time in the future. Once you had known heartbreak, she reflected, you didn't set yourself up for another dose.

Ryan glanced at his watch, the hands at only a quarter to ten o'clock. This was one hell of a way and time to end the evening he ruminated, and wondered how he could get back to where he was before Jerome Kern had wrecked the whole shebang. The knowledge that he would quite definitely like to have Julia in his arms again, on the dance floor or anywhere else was disquieting, but the surety that would be the last thing she would want kept him in his seat, with the table between them. He had, he considered pensively, not a snowball's chance in hell of ever getting under *her* guard: moreover, he'd be a fool to even try; setting himself up for another doomed love affair wasn't in the cards, now or ever...

'Votre café, m'sieur, madame.' Both snapped out of their separate reveries as their waiter appeared and setting down his tray poured their coffee. When the man had left the table again Ryan offered the sugar bowl and when she silently refused it, sat back and cleared his throat. 'I suppose it's some kind of progress that we managed a whole couple of hours alone together before we fell out!'

Forgetting her resolution to end the evening at the first possible moment, she gave a faint smile at this handing of the olive branch; he gave his own brand of knock 'em dead right back and she blinked under the force of it. 'Perhaps if we tried a little harder we could manage another hour or so,' she suggested.

How come Ryan wondered, that he'd never noticed before how her mouth tucked in at one corner and her eyes crinkled right up when she smiled? He asked, 'Haven't you to be home by ten-thirty?'

'Oh, I think I could probably stretch it to eleven.'

'Shame on you to think of keeping Rosie from her bed!' he raised his coffee cup; looking at her over the rim he suggested tentatively, 'How about we finish this then go take a walk along the Serpentine?'

How about I get home right now? Julia thought, but that would be just too gauche and exactly the sort of reaction to paste a cynical smile right back onto that handsome face. 'A walk would be fine,' she agreed, 'but the last time you invited me to stroll by the water you said if I liked I could kick you in. Does that offer still hold good?'

He grinned. 'I'd rather take a rain check on that, at least until summer!'

*　　　*　　　*

He drew her arm through his as they left the Mirabelle and crossed Park Lane to walk towards the Serpentine. Tonight London was at its winter's best: the air still, the grass crisp with frost, soft lamplight reflected in water lying motionless under a star-studded sky. Despite the cold it was a night for dreamers and lovers thought Ryan, glancing at his companion's face, finding it composed and calm but definitely neither dreamy nor lover-like. A pity he mused, if she hadn't been wearing that Keep Off sign around her neck he would quite like to kiss her. Not necessarily a passionate kiss as a prelude to sex, but just a nice warm friendly one...he grinned to himself. Gee, but he *must* be getting old!

They had walked, mainly in silence for perhaps ten minutes when he felt her shiver and realised that his tuxedo and Crombie overcoat were considerably warmer than her silk dress and wool wrap. Stopping beneath a lantern he took off his coat to place it around her shoulders, shaking his head decisively when she began to protest.

'Just slip your arms into this and don't argue: my suit is a sight warmer than all you have on combined – even if you were wearing long-johns, which you sure as hell are not.'

She pushed back her wrap and drew the coat, warm and comforting from his body heat, over her cold arms. 'How would you know? I might be.'

'Trust me: those slits in your skirt go way too far up your legs to allow for any long-johns worth the name!' He turned about and began to retrace their steps, suggesting, 'If you like we could find somewhere to get another coffee to warm up.'

'No – take me home and I'll make us both a hot toddy.' The invitation was out before she could stop herself. Damn', she should be thinking of a polite way to end the evening, not finding ways to extend it. Hastily, she added, 'You don't have to; if you have lectures first thing I expect you'd like to get to bed in reasonable time.'

He grinned. 'I never get to bed at a reasonable time, and being as how it's Sunday tomorrow, I don't have a single lecture either.'

She flushed. 'Of course; I'd forgotten...'

The blue eyes gazed down into hers with deceptive innocence. 'Ma'am, if you can forget what day it is, maybe you've had a real good time after all.'

She stopped dead, fixing him with her own dark gaze. 'Will you *please* stop calling me ma'am like that, or any minute now I'll be saying, 'La, sir!' and hitting you with my fan!'

He threw back his head and laughed; the sound of his mirth sweeping like a wind over the quiet water, eliciting a murmur of muted protesting quacks from some nearby ducks. 'I say,' she demurred, 'it wasn't *that* funny.'

'It was coming from a gal wearing my overcoat and looking like she kind of wished I'd fall in the pond!' Still chuckling he took her hand and began to walk briskly back towards Park Lane.

*   *   *

As she settled herself beside him in the Jowett he felt that familiar kick-in under his ribcage and wondered should he have accepted her invitation to a hot toddy? He was sure it had been made innocently and on the spur of the moment and probably already regretted. But if he made an excuse now and left her at her door she might be offended or embarrassed: maybe even both; if he stayed there might be a return to the intimacy of the Mirabelle, and God only knew where that might end. Probably, he thought wryly, with Ryan Petersen getting his face slapped.

The warmth of her beside him in the journey back to Lavender Sweep didn't help much and he surreptitiously flicked the switch that sent a draught of cold air directly onto his face. You are, he reminded himself testily, a forty-seven year old man spending a polite and gentlemanly evening with your son's schoolmarm, so for the love of God pull yourself together and act the part.

*   *   *

When they reached the Battersea house Rosie-from-next-door was half-dozing on the couch. Rousing to greet them with a wide smile, her perfect teeth gleaming white in her black face she asked in a rich West Indian contralto, 'You two had yourselves a great time then?'

Ryan grinned. 'Yeah, how about you?'

'Watched Steptoe and some damn' fool talent show.' She gave a peal of laughter and stood, smoothing her dress over hips too fragile-looking to have cradled any child. 'I see more talent than that down the club any night of the week!'

Julia said quickly, 'Stay and join us in a drink, won't you – I've promised Ryan a hot toddy.'

'No gal: better I'm away to me bed – me cleanin' job down the Town Hall starts seven am sharp an' I don' want gettin' me pay docked for bein' late.' She hugged Julia, blew Ryan a kiss, swung her coat over her shoulders and was out of the door like a miniature whirlwind.

'Does that little pixie really scrub office floors?' Ryan asked incredulously, following Julia into the kitchen. 'She looks like a good blast of wind would snuff her out.'

'Don't you believe it, she's tough as they come; she has to be. Earle doesn't earn much on the buses so Rosie needs the work.' Julia filled and plugged in the kettle, then assembled glasses, whisky, lemon and sugar with practised ease while Ryan leaned against the doorjamb, watching her preparations with an amused eye.

'You work in a bar or something?' he asked as she began slicing the lemon, 'or did you learn all that in Teacher Training?'

'Neither.' She grinned. 'My dad showed me how at an early age.' She flipped a finger in his direction. 'Spoons are in that drawer there; then could you see if the fire needs more wood?'

'Yes, *ma'am*,' Ryan clicked his heels, found the spoons and exited followed by her gurgle of laughter. So far so good, he thought as he crouched before the fire and fed a couple more logs to the flames. She had given him the lead of friendly co-operation, so that was the way he'd play it. It might be pleasant, he reflected, to have Julia Frazier as a halfway friend rather than a halfway foe. A little frustrating perhaps, but he could go along with that.

At least, he thought he could.

*   *   *

He finished his drink, reckoning hazily that this was where he should get out of this comfortable chair and go right on home. But a quick bourbon to fuel his resolution before starting the evening, then that Martini followed by something rather above his fair share of their wine, and finally one of Julia Frazier's daddy's toddys which, he reminisced, had been every bit as lethal as Pru Peck's gunpowder coffee, had left him a little weary and off balance. Making a determined effort at control he put down his empty glass.

'Thank you, but I think it's time I left.'

She fixed him with an expert eye. 'Perhaps coffee first – black, I think. You don't want to end up in the Battersea Nick, do you?'

'Not particularly,' he agreed. 'But then I'd sure hate to ruin your reputation by staying any longer.'

She said coolly, 'I think my reputation will survive another ten minutes.'

'OK,' he levered himself from the chair, 'but only if you let me help with the coffee.'

'That isn't necessary.'

He put out his hand and drew her from her own comfortable seat. 'It is if I'm to stay awake to drink it,' he assured her gravely,

She laughed. 'In that case perhaps you should come into the kitchen and drink it standing.'

'That would be safer.' He stood looking down on her then raised the hand he still held to brush his lips across her fingers. 'Thanks for a great evening.'

She quickly pulled her hand from his and turned away. He followed her to the door then watched her as far as the kitchen. Suddenly he was overtaken by an almost irresistible urge to follow her, turn her around and kiss that inviting mouth. He swallowed hard.

'Miz Frazier,' he said with careful sobriety, 'I kind of think I should leave right now; seems to me the chance of a night in a cell might be a darned sight less risky than staying for that coffee.'

He gave her a tense unsmiling look and taking his coat and scarf from the newel post where she had hung them, went swiftly from the house.

*   *   *

She stood indecisive, one hand on the doorframe, the other held palm up in automatic protest, then her shoulders slumped and she stared miserably at the closing door: oh great, this time she really had blown it!

Faced with a sleepy, slightly inebriated Ryan she had felt a ridiculous, crazy need to cosset him; to delay his departure until, caught wrong-footed by the touch of his lips on her fingers, she had reacted with immediate instinctive retreat.

'Damn, damn, damn!' She turned and switched on the kettle; then leaning her hands on the warm handle let tears of disappointment and self-recrimination slide down her burning cheeks.

*   *   *

For a few moments Ryan stood on the pavement, pulling on his coat and looking hesitantly back at the house, then he shrugged and unlocking the car door slid into his seat and fired the engine. From a long way back he heard Mike Hogan's rueful voice giving the GI Joe's comment on an unsuccessful end to a hoped-for amorous night out: "*Situation Normal and All Fucked Up...*"

'Yeah – Snafu!' he said out loud then letting in the clutch drove carefully back to Marlborough Street, regret crawling over him like an army of invading ants.

19

November

In the days following that evening Ryan thought a lot about Julia Frazier, always coming to the same conclusion: that despite the temporary nature of his job in this country, his own reluctance to become involved in anything more than a casual liaison with any woman and bearing in mind the lady's apparent indifference to him as anything other than Joel's father, none of these obstacles could prevent him feeling hot as any pimply youth at his first school prom, longing to hold the first girl he'd danced with in his arms again.

Sitting idly between lectures or seminars: driving to and from the university or lying waiting for sleep at night, he played the last scene of that evening over and over in his mind, wondering what might have happened if he had stayed for that coffee instead of getting cold feet and walking away from temptation.

Had he wanted her?

Yes.

Might she have wanted him?

Unlikely.

Did he care enough to look beyond the immediate satisfaction of having sex with her?

Maybe.

Could he imagine she might ever do the same?

Not a chance.

Impasse, he thought wryly. Not a prayer. He was discombobulated and going nowhere.

How the heck, he brooded, had he let himself step into this particular heap of crap, and why the hell couldn't he get the damnable irritating woman out of his mind?

*　　　*　　　*

Hannah left the house early for her journey to Battersea, determined not to be beaten by Ryan, who would insist he fetch Joel and save her the bus ride. He was getting a little too over anxious about her – probably making-up for all those past sins of omission, she thought with an inward chuckle. She may be way the wrong side of sixty and with what the jocular Mr Neville described as a 'dicky-ticker' but she was no way near ready yet to being measured for her coffin. Besides, she wanted to know what her close-mouthed son wouldn't tell her: how the evening at the Mirabelle had gone.

*   *   *

Julia knew quite well why Hannah had arrived early and was determined not to give away any of her innermost thoughts and feelings about Ryan and the unsatisfactory ending to that evening. Having those thoughts was bad enough, handing them over to Hannah as possible ammunition against her son's resolution to resist another canter down the aisle was unthinkable, but she greeted her arrival warmly.

'The children are at Rosie's. Noah's daddy made him a boat and they're sailing it in the bath.' Leading Hannah in to sit by the fire she said, 'Make yourself comfortable while I get the tea.'

But Hannah was too wily to be side-tracked. She followed her into the kitchen and before Julia was halfway through filling the teapot had her admitting Ryan had told her all about Ellie's probable suicide and his failings as husband and father.

At this Hannah made a sound halfway between a sigh and an exasperated sniff. 'I never knew a man blame himself so much for something out of his control. Perhaps he shouldn't have married Ellie when he didn't love her, but I'm telling you honey, that he spent ten years of pure hell trying to keep her on an even keel before Joel was born, then another five being both mother and father to the boy while Ellie got steadily more unstable and harder to handle.' She shook her head, adding softly. 'Poor kid, she'd always been a mite high strung; she couldn't help what happened to her, but the only relief my boy got in damn' near twenty years was when she went permanently into that clinic.'

Julia sipped thoughtfully at her tea. 'No one should marry without love. Sometimes that's all that keeps a person going when problems arise.'

'I guess he'd already given all he had in that department to someone else, and thought he could manage without the second time around.' Hannah gave her a shrewd look. 'Didn't tell you about that, did he?'

'He touched on it.'

'Well, I think it must have gone real deep and hurt so bad that

194

when he came home he dug a great big ditch to keep everyone, including his momma and poppa – and Ellie, from ever getting close to him again.'

Julia was silent. *I know all about that, because I've been there, done it. Suffered the sleepless nights, the longing for arms that will never hold me again – and stepped back from any chance that I might be persuaded to go through it all a second time.*

Hannah watched her for a few moments then said gently, 'Doesn't matter how deep a ditch a person digs, or how high a wall they build around them, sooner or later they got to love again and risk the hurt. That's what living in the real world is all about.' She gave a little huff of laughter, her expression lightening. 'Now Ryan, he's just struggling back into that world and I guess finding it mighty confusing, judging by the way he keeps blowing hot and cold!'

Julia sipped her tea, her expression pensive. 'I can't get on his wavelength for more than five minutes at a time,' she said, 'he and I got off on the wrong foot right from the beginning. He puts my back up every time we meet; which makes me bossier than usual and him even more determined to be top dog; so we are never likely to see eye to eye – especially when *his* are so busy getting down to my bra and pants...' embarrassed she broke off suddenly, conscious that it wasn't the sort of thing you said to a man's mother, but Hannah only laughed.

'Guess you're pretty good at dealing with that,' she answered, 'he's a bad boy alright, but the right woman could do a lot with what's behind those 'let's get laid' eyes.'

This conversation, Julia decided, had gone on long enough; she said coolly, 'We should both hope he finds the right woman then, before he *really* gets himself into trouble.'

Hannah was in no way put out. 'Could be,' she said composedly, 'he already has only neither of them knows it yet.'

'You mean he's seeing someone?' Julia knew she should be relieved, but instead felt a pang of regret. Did Hannah mean that the Charlie Joel was always complaining his father spent too much time with was of more significance than she had thought?

'Seeing someone?' Hannah repeated. Her eyes crinkled. 'Oh yeah, he's doing that all right: in a manner of speaking.'

'Serious, do you think?'

'Will be when he realises what's happening to him. When he does he'll either fall or fly!'

'Oh, well.' Julia finished her tea. 'That's all right, then.'

And you, she told herself severely, can just get yourself back to normal and stop thinking that because a man gets a little flirty once in a while it means something, when with that particular man it actually means bugger all.

At that moment the telephone began to ring and relieved, she hastened to answer it.

*   *   *

Ryan, Hannah and Joel arrived at number sixteen simultaneously: the former in the Jowett, the latter two by taxi. Leaping from the cab Joel greeted his father excitedly.

'Dad, dad: Miz Frazier's daddy called just before we left an' asked would we like to have Christmas with him. We can, can't we? It'll be much better than here an' he says there'll be a huge turkey, just like at Thanksgiving at home an' that we'll go carol singing an' feed the ponies if it snows an – '

'Hold it!' Ryan's voice was sharp and Joel stopped, his excitement abruptly curtailed.

'Miz Frazier's daddy's awful nice,' he ventured, 'and Nicki will be there so we can play together and I won't be a nuisance...'

Ryan controlled his irritation with an effort. Unlocking the door he ordered quietly, 'Inside,' and as a deflated and crestfallen Joel slipped past him, turned to Hannah. 'Did you know about this?'

'Not until about twenty minutes ago.' She finished paying the cabbie and giving Ryan a sardonic look stepped past him into the house. 'You sure put a damper on that boy quicker than a bolt of lightning hitting a tree.'

'I don't like being met by a *fait accompli* – '

She interrupted. 'You weren't. The boy was excited and anxious to tell you about the invitation, that's all. Seems like you might have paid him more attention and heard him out 'stead of snapping at him like that.'

Tight-lipped, he threw his briefcase on the table and stripped off coat, scarf and hat in a swift over-controlled sequence. 'I'm beginning to wonder what, or who, gave someone I've never met and you barely know, the sudden notion he'd like three extra house guests for Christmas.' He began to mount the stairs after Joel's retreating form. 'I think I'll just go find out a little more about...what's the man's name?'

'Alec Tawton, and I can tell you all you need to know.'

'I'm darned sure you can, but right now I think I prefer a Joel's eye view!'

Joel was seated on the edge of his bed swinging his legs, but when Ryan appeared he jumped up and stood shifting from one foot to the other as though ready for flight.

'Hey, I'm not going to eat you!' Ryan sat down in the place his son had just vacated. Joel's lower lip trembled.

'What did I do? What did I say wrong?'

'Nothing, you just kind of took me by surprise.' Ryan took him by the elbows, pulling the boy towards him. 'Tell me about Nicki's Granddaddy.'

'He's nice but old and sort of creaky and Miz Frazier fusses over him a bit. He tells good stories and likes to play cards with gran'ma...' Joel's brow furrowed in the effort to explain. 'When we were leaving I heard him say she should ask us for Christmas only she said...she said...' he hesitated, shooting Ryan a wary look, 'I forget what she said.'

Ryan hid a grin. He said sternly, 'Oh, yeah? Why don't you just try telling it as it was?'

Joel wriggled. 'I gotta go to the bathroom.'

'Tell me first.'

'Dad, I really gotta go take a wizz!'

Ryan persisted mercilessly, 'You can do that when you tell me what Miz Frazier said.'

Joel's squirming reached an agonised pitch. He gabbled, 'She said you'd be trouble an' wouldn't come because you weren't the jolly family Christmas type...*now* c'n I go?'

'OK, then come back; I haven't finished with you yet.' He let go and watched as Joel bolted for the bathroom in what he was sure was a mythical need to relieve his bladder.

So I'd be trouble, would I? Ryan thought grimly, *I'm "Not the jolly family Christmas type" aren't I? In one way or another Julia Frazier, you're asking for a whole bundle of trouble from this guy...*

When Joel returned, ostentatiously zipping his pants, Ryan asked, 'Do *you* want to go to Mr Tawton's place for Christmas?'

'Yeah lots.'

'Why? We could have a good time on our own; we always have, haven't we?'

'Yeah, but it won't be like home when we can go skiing – and I like being with Nicki, it's fun to have someone else around all the time – did you know we're almost twins 'cos her birthday's only two days after mine?'

Ryan said dryly, 'She must be quite a gal to have you willing to spend so much time with your schoolteacher.'

'Miz Frazier's OK.' Joel corrugated his brow again. 'She's not like a teacher out of class. She hugs real nice.'

Ryan raised his own brows. 'How would you know?'

'She hugs Nicki lots an' sometimes she hugs me too.' His freckles merged into a deep copper blush. 'She's all nice an' soft!'

Oh, Jesus, Ryan struggled to keep a straight face. 'Abby hugs you and grandma too. Aren't they soft?'

He mumbled, 'S'not the same as when *she* does it.'

Now he was so red that his skin was in danger of clashing with his hair. In sudden compunction Ryan leaned forward and gave him a bear hug and Joel screamed in mock terror. Releasing him Ryan said briskly, 'So that's a real hard hug from me! Come on now and you can help get supper.'

Joel was swift to improve the shining hour. 'Can we go to Mr Tawton's for Christmas, then?'

Ryan stood and dropped a hand on his shoulder. 'I'll think about it.'

Joel looked up, his face apparently devoid of guile. 'Say yes and maybe Miz Frazier will give you a hug too!'

Ryan looked back with narrowed eyes. 'Now don't you get fresh with me or you'll be spending Christmas right here in your own bedroom, you hear me?'

'Yes sir.' Joel hopped down the stairs before him singing: 'Praise the Lawd, praise the Lawd, clap your hands an' praise the Lawd...' in a good but treble impersonation of one of Abby's revivalist hymns, with which her rich tones often regaled their household of a Monday morning after Sunday spent at the Gospel Hall.

Hannah was standing sentinel at the foot of the stairs. She watched Joel hop towards the kitchen and raised an enquiring eyebrow at Ryan, who placed both hands together in an attitude of prayer, saying humbly, '*Mea culpa.* Sorry, I jumped the gun.'

'So does that mean we accept Alec Tawton's generous offer?'

'I'm thinking about it ma,' he was blandly nonchalant, 'I'm thinking about it...'

*   *   *

The following afternoon he left the university and drove straight to Battersea. His ring on the bell brought Nicole to the door; gravely she looked him up and down then peered behind him. 'Oh,' her disappointment was evident, 'where's Joel?'

'Back home, I hope.'

She sighed. 'I suppose that means you want to talk to mummy about something private and *I'll* have to go upstairs – *again*.'

Ryan grinned. 'It's a tough life.'

'Mummy's gone next door for a while to help Mrs Rosie with some sewing. I'm not supposed to let anyone in but as it's you I expect that will be all right.' She held the door wide. 'Would you like a cup of tea? I have to finish my homework but I could make you some first.'

Ryan's mouth twitched. 'Maybe we should wait and see if your mommy thinks I deserve it.'

She watched as he took off his coat and scarf and hung both over the banister rail; she asked, 'Why do Americans say mommy instead of mummy – and tom*ay*to instead of tom*ar*to?'

'I guess we're just funny that way.'

She said 'Oh,' again and led the way into the long living room. Ryan sat in one of the chairs by the fire and she sat opposite, watching him in silence for a few moments before inquiring politely. 'Have you come about Christmas?'

Ryan was amused. 'You got a crystal ball somewhere, cupcake, or do you just eves drop when your mom's on the phone?' She put both hands over her mouth and giggled and he raised one eyebrow. 'I thought you were supposed to be finishing your homework.'

Her mouth went down at the corners. 'It's a long poem. I can't learn long poems. I keep forgetting what comes next.'

'What is it?'

'Some blooming thing called *Isle of Innisfree*. It's rubbish!'

He stifled a grin. 'That's not so long; nor so hard.'

'But it doesn't make sense: first its beans and beehives, then its crickets and birds then water and pavements...how can anyone remember all that stuff?' She broke off to glower fiercely at him. 'It's all right for Joel. He always gets it right.'

'He does?' Ryan was startled. 'Joel gets *poetry* right?'

'Yes, every time. Last week Mr Collins made him stand up and recite in front of the whole school and he did *Paul Revere* right through without a single mistake, the rotten little swot!'

In her indignation she looked so like her mother that Ryan laughed out loud. 'Hey, come on, you're not going to let Joel beat you at anything, are you? Get your book and let's see if we can sort it out.'

She looked doubtful. 'Mum might think that's cheating.'

'You think so?'

199

'Umm; she's like that.'

'You don't say. Must be hard being in school where your mom is teacher.'

She nodded vigorously. 'Yes, it jolly well is!'

'Tell you what,' he settled himself back in his chair. 'I'm a teacher too, sort of, so I guess we'll go right ahead, then, if there's any flack, you duck and I'll take it.'

*   *   *

Julia saw his car parked behind her own when she left Rosie's and her heart plummeted to somewhere around her knees. Damn Alec and his invitation! She'd take a bet Ryan was here to argue about Christmas... of course he wouldn't accept. Why oh why hadn't she phoned him last night and got it over with then?

Because you're a coward, she answered herself, *and avoiding the inevitable brush-off for as long as possible.*

She let herself into the house quietly. From the living room she could hear Ryan and her daughter deep in conversation. She moved forward soundlessly and opening the door a crack, eavesdropped unashamedly.

'...Now you've got the words – more or less,' Ryan was saying, 'just close your eyes and imagine you've had a hard day at school: teacher's been mad at you, it's raining and you've got to walk home when where you'd *like* to be is in a little cottage right by a lake, where you can just sit in the sun and dream...so off you go. If you forget a word or line don't stop; just keep going and it'll come right the next time.'

'IwillariseandgonowandgotoInnisfree...' Nicole gabbled furiously through Yeats' immortal verse, finishing with a gasp for breath. Ryan chuckled.

'You see, you can do it. Now lets take it slower; see, it's a bit like music...you need to hear the rhythm. Tell you what, I'll conduct and you do the words in time with me.'

Julia pulled the door to again soundlessly. Going quietly into the kitchen she put the kettle to boil and began to set a tray with mugs, milk, sugar and the big brown teapot. 'Hidden depths,' she mused aloud, breaking open a packet of Nicole's favourite Bourbons and topping up the biscuit barrel, 'the man has hidden depths!'

And only just managed to stop thinking that she wouldn't mind plumbing a few of those depths herself.

*   *   *

Nicole was seated on the arm of Ryan's chair, her head close to his, her face absorbed and intent as he read aloud 'Tarantella,' so engrossed that she didn't notice her mother's entrance with the tea tray. Ryan raised his eyes; Julia shook her head, miming, 'Don't stop' and he lowered his gaze back onto the book. When he came to the end of the verses he paused for a moment then looked up again to where she still stood in the doorway. With a wry provocative expression he asked, 'Do *you* remember an Inn, Miranda; do *you* remember an Inn?'

She gave him back look for look. 'Only too well.' she said.

He rose to his feet and taking the tray from her hands placed it on the low table. 'Me too.'

'Oh, mummy,' Nicole could barely keep the disappointment from her voice. 'Now we shall have to stop.'

'Since when did you ever have a passion for poetry?' Julia enquired.

Ryan winked at Nicole then looked at his watch, 'The way I figure since about half an hour ago.'

Julia observed dryly, 'Perhaps more persuasion than passion!' She knelt on the floor as she had that first time and began to pour the tea. Nicole swung her leg.

'Joel's daddy has come to talk about Christmas.' She looked confidently at Ryan. 'That's right, isn't it?'

He answered, 'Right on the button.'

Julia blushed. 'I meant to ring you last night,' she said, not quite truthfully and knew without looking that he was giving his irritating grin. 'Dad really enjoyed the extra company the other weekend and as we always spend Christmas with him he thought all of you might like to join us.'

Ryan asked mildly, 'Was that before or after he heard I wasn't the jolly family Christmas type?'

She passed Nicole her tea with a steady hand. 'Two biscuits only,' she said, 'eat them in the kitchen or upstairs. Professor Ryan and I need to talk.'

Nicole sighed and gave him a resigned look. 'I told you so.'

'You're a smart girl.' He picked the book from the chair and handed it to her with a smile. 'Knock 'em dead in class tomorrow.'

She gazed at him in a considered silence for a moment, then asked, 'Do you kiss Joel goodnight?'

'Sometimes: when he lets me.'

She gave him a long look from beneath her lashes and asked innocently. 'Boy's don't like kissing, do they?'

'This one does!' he bent to kiss the top of her head, 'and in case I don't see you again this evening, goodnight, Miss Nicole Frazier, and sleep tight.'

He waited until the door closed behind her then sat down, cradling his mug in both hands and stretching his long legs to the fire.

'Little flirt,' he said.

Julia looked down into her tea. 'It takes one to know one.'

*   *   *

She sat back on her heels before the fire, waiting for him to speak again but when he remained silent she offered stiffly, 'I'm sorry if you had my father's invitation sprung on you, but you need not feel obliged to accept.'

'I don't. Feel obliged, that is. It's very kind and thoughtful of your father and I am grateful to him for his offer.' He sat forward, putting down his mug. 'If I seem a bit cautious it could be that I'm not too sure how *you* might feel about having this particular spectre at your feast.'

She looked round at him, her mouth curved in a reluctant smile. 'You are rather too real to be a spectre at anybody's feast, and *I* should feel grateful if you would just say 'yes' or 'no' and stop fencing with me.'

He held up both hands up in surrender. 'OK then, it's 'yes' – although as I guess you'll want to spend most of the holiday with your father, we'll leave you in peace once Christmas is over.'

She was momentarily flustered by this unexpected capitulation, but ventured, 'I think he would feel he was being a bad host if you didn't stay for at least a week, that's if you can bear to leave Chelsea for that long.' She added silently *...and if you can tear yourself away from the fascinating Charlie's bed.*

'Well now,' his eyes teased, 'I guess I can cope if you can.'

'Oh,' she answered him dryly, 'I'm a great one for coping.'

'I had noticed.' He stood. 'I must go or Hannah will be on my back. Please thank your father for the invitation; accepting it may make me shine a little brighter in my son's eyes.' He gave his sudden devastating smile. 'By the way, I kind of shanghaied your daughter back there into letting me help her with her homework; I promised I'd take any flack on her behalf.'

She felt her insides do that disturbing sideways slip again, and rising hastily to her feet, preceded him from the room. 'I'm glad you did. It was kind of you to take so much trouble.'

'It was a pleasure and I take my pleasures where I may.' He

202

pulled on his coat; stood looking down on her for a moment, then bent and kissed the top of her head in much the same manner as he had with her daughter, murmuring in a thick French accent, 'Thank 'eaven for leettle girls – and beeg ones. Goodnight, Julia: you sleep tight as well.'

She closed the door quickly behind him then leaned back against it. Hell and damnation, but she would feel a lot safer at the prospect of spending a week under the same roof with him if he had retained more of his former rude and irritating manner. If these sudden about-faces continued then Christmas could prove something of an ordeal. There might be a limit to how much of that lethal charm she could deal with, and while it doubtless meant little to him, the danger signals were certainly flashing for a possible end to *her* peace of mind.

She wondered again about the unseen Charlie and whether he went to bed with her, or if they were just good friends and Hannah's hope that Charlie might turn him into a faithful husband prove to be just an illusion. For another self-indulgent second or two she considered what going to bed with Ryan Petersen might be like then quickly dismissed the traitorous thought. It would, she reckoned dourly, need a bloody miracle to bring that about.

* * *

Caught up in the late afternoon traffic Ryan drove nose to tail down Battersea Rise and over the bridge, content for once for his journey home to be a slow one, affording him time to mull over his latest brush with the enigmatic Julia. What was it with that woman, he wondered, that had him feeling all kinds of emotions he had thought long gone.

Common sense told him that the shock of hearing of Claire's death and the re-awakening of old passions might be the reason for his present confusion. An appreciation of any woman's physical attributes and just plain lust he could deal with, he'd had plenty of practice in that field, but to find he was actively seeking this one particular woman's company with an almost forgotten desire to hold and touch with tenderness as well as passion was disturbing. Given any sort of encouragement he might easily go overboard for Julia Frazier...

But I'm kind of old, he thought wryly, to go down that road again. Loving meant letting someone get in close. Although he could now manage that to a degree with Hannah and Joel, to do so with Julia could be courting disaster, her inevitable rejection hurt just too darned much. And rejection there was bound to be. After all, what woman in her right mind, and Julia Frazier was very much in her right mind, would take on a middle-aged academic with too much turbulent past and not enough peaceful future and who, like Beatrice's Benedict, had rather more bad parts than good?

He thought about the return next year to Brackets Sound and his old aimless existence. To sporadic sex with others whose feelings were as shallow as his own. He felt depression settle over him as a big grey blanket. But if he didn't want that ...he saw a gap in the traffic and turning swiftly down a side street took the longer but less congested way back to Marlborough Street...then what did he want apart from his home, his boat and his work? Someone to love who would love him and be a mother to his son...?

Dream on, he thought, he couldn't shake off the past that easily, nor could he hope to ever love, and be loved, as he once had. But if he couldn't have love then what was the point of either wife for him or mother for Joel? Maybe they were better off with just each other.

Wearied by his thoughts he reached the corner of Marlborough Street. Slowing down as he passed Charlie's door he saw a sleek, unfamiliar Jaguar was drawn up behind her Volvo, and two large suitcases and a flight bag stood in the open lighted doorway. While he watched a tall, dark haired man appeared, picked up the cases, lifting them effortlessly into the hall before returning for the flight bag. Ryan's mouth went down at both corners.

Home was the sailor, home from the sea, and the hunter home from the hill!

He shrugged and murmuring 'Cheers, Brucie,' drove on to his own parking space outside number sixteen.

20

December

Even though they would be in Devon for Christmas, Joel begged for the house to be decorated and Ryan was only too glad to leave that task in the capable hands of Hannah and the indefatigable Doris, while he researched a paper he was writing on Rupert Brooke. In the intervals between University and home he shopped, he hoped imaginatively, for presents, enjoying the student-free if not work-free vacation.

He spent an inordinate amount of time over choosing a present for Julia, settling at last on a soft Liberty silk scarf in shades of brown and gold to match her eyes; a not too intimate gift, and one that should not raise the hackles of even that unpredictable woman.

The coming trip to Devon he viewed with a mixture of pleasure and mistrust; on the one hand was the bonus of getting to know Julia better, on the other that it was one hell of a long way to go with no assurance that the venture would prove a success for anyone other than the two children. Julia was indefinable and her father an unknown quantity. At the back of his mind was the uneasy thought that if Joel and Nicole were busy doing their own thing, and Hannah and Alec Tawton welded to the card table, then he and Julia were liable to find themselves very much in each other's company.

Which may, or may not, be a good thing.

Another cause for anxiety was the weather. This wasn't New England where the seasons changed more or less according to plan; where houses and cars and people were built to withstand hard winters, but good old unpredictable England where a single night's snowfall could create chaos on the roads, stop trains running and freeze the asses off the eighty percent of inhabitants who still hadn't discovered central heating. Four years spent up in the sky and long periods since at the helm of the *Dancer* had made him as aware of the weather as any professional weathercaster, and as the time for their journey drew nearer he could smell and feel that certain something in the air that hinted snow was not far off. He remembered seeing aerial photographs of the vast, sparsely populated and inhospitable terrain of Dartmoor, taken during the first flush of an early summer, and had thought then how bleak and dangerous those high moors would be in the grip of winter.

'I sure hope Alec Tawton keeps a warm house,' he commented to Hannah as he prepared to leave Marlborough Street one morning, a few days before the proposed journey. He knocked a finger against the glass in the banjo barometer hanging in the hallway. 'While Joel may be praying for a White Christmas I'll be content with a temperature a whole lot higher than freezing.'

'Don't you worry about that; the cottage is real cosy with log fires and bottle gas heaters in the bedrooms...a darned sight more snug than this place.' Hannah handed him his scarf. 'Are you out all day today?'

'I guess; but I'll be home in time for that afternoon tea you've gotten so keen on.' He kissed her cheek. 'Stay cool, ma; don't overdo it.'

*   *   *

Apart from taking a quick break at midday he worked in the library until around three o'clock. It was only when he finally closed his file and was screwing the top back in his pen that he glanced up at the tall windows and realised how dark and threatening the sky had become. By the time he reached his car an icy rain was falling and the wind rising fast. Pulling his coat collar about his ears he fumbled with the lock, hands already stiff with cold, then once inside fired the engine and sat for a minute or two to let it warm.

'Perfect; just the weather to be thinking about spending a week on fucking Dartmoor,' he muttered. Shivering he hunted for his gloves, eventually finding them screwed into a ball under the dash, a half-sucked sherbet lemon adhering to one finger. Making a mental note to bend Joel's ear about his anti-social habits, he dropped the sweet into the ash tray, turned the wipers to maximum and drove out into what promised to become a stormy end to the day.

If Goldie the Eagle was still AWOL from London Zoo he thought feelingly, then the poor damn' bird was in for one hell of a rough night.

*   *   *

The second he opened the front door he knew something was wrong; not only was Joel seated on the stairs awaiting his return, a sure sign that he had either a complaint or a problem, but Nicole was sharing a stair with him, a fraught expression on her small face.

'Hi, kids.' He looked directly at Nicole, who was quite clearly battling against an imminent attack of tears. 'What gives, cupcake?'

'My grandpa is sick – Mr Proverbs from the farm rang mummy and she's gone to see him – '

Joel interrupted, 'And gran'ma said Nicole must stay here with us until her mommy gets back, so she's brought her toothbrush and everything.'

'That's all right, then,' Ryan was deliberately calm, although his mind was racing like a ferret on uppers. Shit! That crazy woman was driving over two hundred miles in *this* weather and in the dark? He hunkered down in front of the little girl and took her hands, feeling them cold as ice. 'What time did your mommy leave?'

'I don't know.' She twisted her fingers in his. 'After Mr Proverbs called she 'phoned Joel's grandma at once, then we came here and mummy left right away.'

'That's pretty clever of you to remember all that. Now you go right on up to the sitting room with Joel and stay warm while I talk to his grandma.' He raised an eyebrow at Joel. 'Where is she?'

'Makin' a bed for Niki in my room...can we watch TV?'

'Yes. I'll talk to grandma first then one of us will bring you a hot chocolate; is that OK?'

'Yeah, c'mon, Nic,' Joel encouraged, 'hurry up or we'll miss Deputy Dawg!'

Ryan took off his coat, shook it and hung it to dry on the hall pegs. Following the children up the stairs he saw them into the sitting room then went on to the top of the house.

'I guess you heard the news.' Hannah looked up from beating a pillow into its case. 'And don't ask why didn't I stop her – I tried, but reasoning with that gal when she's hell bent on having her way is like trying to stop a charging buffalo by shooting peas at it!'

'Any idea how serious it is with her father?'

'Sounded like he might have broken something; seems they already got a lot of snow there and he slipped coming back from the shed with a load of wood. She didn't stop to tell me more: just lit out like crazy.'

'How long ago?'

'An hour or more past.'

'Right,' he ran a hand through his hair. 'Ma, can you make those kids a hot drink and fill a flask for me while I change – '

'You thinking of going someplace?' she interrupted.

'Yeah,' he answered through gritted teeth, 'you bet your sweet

207

life I am; straight after that crazy woman and see she gets there in one piece. You wouldn't remember what route she drove you the other week?'

'Sure do. You change and simmer down while I make you up some food and drink to take, then I'll write you directions so you can map it out before you start,' she walked past him, throwing over her shoulder, 'You're crazy too but I got enough sense not to try stopping two charging buffalo in one evening!'

*   *   *

He changed into wool shirt, thick crew neck sweater, lined sweat pants and fur-lined boots, then from the top of the robe took a heavy lumber-jacket and fur lined leather cap and gloves; standard wear for the snowstorms that swept New England in winter. On the way back downstairs he looked in on Joel and Nicole. 'I'm going to see if I can help your mommy.' He smiled reassuringly at her pale pinched face, 'so you just stay right here with Joel for now. Joel,' he ruffled his son's hair, 'you take real good care of Nicole and mind what grandma tells you. OK?'

'Sure dad, I'll see to everything,' Joel made a big effort at nonchalance and almost made it, then spoiled the effect by asking anxiously, 'you gonna be long?'

'Not sure: depends how things turn out.'

Nicole asked bravely, 'Will we miss Christmas?'

'Heck, no,' Ryan gave them each a brief hug. 'We've got five whole more days before you hang up your stockings. I'll be there and back in good time to take you all down for the best Christmas you've ever had.'

He had his doubts about that, but what the hell...he restarted the Jowett's still warm engine. There was no sense in making them miserable before time.

*   *   *

Once clear of London's suburbs and out into comparatively open countryside, despite the rising wind and unremitting sleet he drove fast, perhaps a little too fast for safety. Although sure that Julia's progress in the old Ford would be slower and probably much more cautious than his, and that he would eventually catch up with her, how long that might take him and just what he expected to do then wasn't at all clear in his mind. She would probably be mad as a wet hen with him for following her, he thought moodily, that would be par for the course where Julia Frazier was concerned, but she couldn't stop him following close behind until she reached the safety of her father's house.

He made good time for a little over an hour; but that was before the wind began to rise; another hour into his journey a gale was blowing in earnest, tearing small branches from the trees and bombarding the car with flying debris. Cursing out loud he was forced to slow down. Fixing his aching eyes on the road ahead, headlights on full beam and alert to the constant hazard of fallen branches he was unwilling, despite his increasing pangs of hunger to take a break even to eat the sandwiches or drink the coffee Hannah had prepared for him.

*   *   *

He left Exeter behind and turned to follow the signs to Oakhampton. By his reckoning he could now be less than thirty miles from his destination, but relief in having made it this far was tempered by anxiety that soon he would be leaving the main road to begin a journey across unfamiliar country, in search of an isolated cottage of which he'd never so much as seen a picture. He could be in real trouble…and where in hell, he demanded of the unresponsive air, was Julia? He ground his teeth. Given the start the hot head, cantankerous woman had on him she'd probably been ahead of the storm and was by now sitting snug in front of a fire sipping a hot toddy with her miraculously recovered old man…

Past Oakhampton snow began to dot the windscreen; by the time he turned off the main road for the less civilised route across the moor the fall had become heavier, with snow plastering the windscreen almost as fast as the wipers could clear it. At least, Ryan thought morosely, it had to be a bonus that there were no goddamned trees now to hamper his progress.

Twenty minutes later, with terrifying suddenness the wind rose, howling around the car obliterating the way ahead. 'Jesus *God:* what have I done to deserve *this?*' he stared hopelessly at the blinding wall of snow and automatically reached out to turn off the engine, then snatched his hand back. He couldn't stop; mustn't stop. Sweat gathered at his hairline; there must be ditches either side of the narrow road and at any minute the car might tip into one…

He remembered this road on his map when he had plotted his journey; how it snaked for some five miles across the moor to

Broadhampton and Alec Tawton's cottage. Letting the car creep on, his mouth dry and his heart jumping around in his chest like a crazed racoon, he realised with an enormous lifting of his spirits that although the snow continued to fall, the wind seemed to have spent itself in that sudden burst of savage fury and was slowly dying. If he kept his gaze riveted on the clearance afforded by the sweep of the wiper blades he reckoned he had a good chance of making his destination all in one piece.

It was due to his unwavering concentration that he managed to stop without hitting the shape that loomed suddenly in the beam of his headlights. Although only a white hump, half on half off the road, it was just recognizable as a car; the front end dipped at a crazy angle down an incline, the back reared up; wheels inches from the ground. For a long minute he sat immobile, wondering when and where before he had felt this heart-stopping, totally immobilising funk; then with sudden vivid recollection he was back in the cockpit of the *Babe*, hearing the *whump* of the exploding shell and his bombardier screaming in agony.

'Oh, Christ, no...' he tore himself out of his trance, flung open the door and heaved from the car, feeling his feet sink and the snow seep over the tops of his boots. Ploughing through the intervening few feet he reached the hump and wrenched open the offside door of what he now recognised as a horribly familiar car.

Julia Frazier, blood streaking her face and seeping over the front of her white duffle from a long gash on her forehead, lay across the seats her eyes closed and her back hard up against the passenger door. For a few heart stopping seconds he hung petrified in the doorway, his breath rasping in his throat, too overcome to speak. 'Julia,' he managed at last, his voice a harsh croak.

To his relief she stirred and looked up at him through partially closed eyes. 'Well, bugger me; if it isn't John Wayne...' her voice was vague and unworried, 'lost your bloody horse, have you?'

He wanted to slap her then; yell and demand what she thought she was at, tearing off into the night like some fucking moron and near sending him out of his mind, but he knew shock when he saw it. Mentally he consigned all his pent up fear and fury to a convenient corner of his brain to be vented at a later date. Wedging his bulk into the doorframe he knelt on the edge of the driver's seat.

'Lie still. Don't try to move.' He took off his gloves and pushing up her slacks gently felt her legs from ankle to knee, wondering all the while how long she had lain like this. The blood on her face and coat was already drying and she was icy cold from shock. Unhooking her duffle he made a careful exploration of her neck before feeling cautiously around her ribcage, back and hips. She gave a croaky giggle. 'Trust you to get fresh!'

He smouldered. 'Just tell me where it hurts.'

'Don't know…all over.'

'Can you move your head?'

She yawned. 'Think so.'

'Try – and for Christ's sake do it slowly.'

Obediently she moved her head sideways from right to left then left to right. She giggled again, 'Tick-tock.'

He said 'Fuck,' under his breath and she wagged a finger.

'I heard that!'

'You'll hear a damn sight more in a minute if you don't shut up.' Awkwardly he slid one arm behind her back and the other beneath her knees. 'I'm going to move you and I give you leave to yell good and loud if anything, anything at all hurts – you got that?'

'Yes *sir.*' She went to salute, hit her nose, said 'Oh, God; bed I think,' closed her eyes and slumped against him. He swore again.

'Christ almighty! Stay awake, damn you – you hear me? Stay awake.'

She slurred, 'Bloody bully. Should think the whole damned county can hear you.'

He began to inch her across the seat, grunting with the effort. 'Lady, right now and compared with the average bully I'm a pussycat, but you keep right on being a smart mouth and see how quick I change.'

Once free of the car he settled her in his arms and began the treacherous trudge back to where the Jowett stood: engine still running, the headlights guiding him.

He made it without dropping his burden, despite the fact that she now had his neck in a stranglehold and was croaking *The Last Time I saw Paris* completely off key, which he figured was bad news for a music teacher. With a sigh of relief he slid her into the passenger seat, where at once her eyes closed again and she slumped forward. Exasperated he shook her arm. 'For God's sake woman, stay *awake*…you can sleep once I've got you thawed out.'

'Go 'way: 'm *tired.*'

She sounded like an aggrieved child. He sighed. 'I just know I'm going to regret saying this…but talk to me, will you, and keep talking.' He located the flask of coffee under the dash; unscrewing the cup he filled it and held it to her lips. 'Drink,' he ordered.

She obeyed grumbling. 'Shudup – keep talking – drink…make up your mind...you know what,' she squinted up at him, 'you're a bastard.'

'That's me.' He waited for her to finish then refilled the cup. It might not be quite the thing for shock, but it sure as hell hit the right spot for him he thought gratefully, as Hannah's strong, whisky-doctored coffee slid down his throat like a benediction. 'Now,' replacing the cup he tucked the flask in the door pocket, 'talk to me; talk all the way across this blasted heath.'

'Wa's'l I talk about?'

'Something...anything,' he slipped the gears into second and set the car crawling forward again, 'your husband...tell me about your husband.'

She peered at him owlishly. 'I don't talk 'bout Jamie.'

'You should.' He spared her a fleeting glance. 'Five years of not talking sounds enough to me. I didn't talk about someone for over twenty years and I've only just gotten around to seeing that was twenty years wasted.'

She said truculently, 'Well bully for you, buster.'

He persisted, 'Where did you meet the guy?'

'Singapore...Went on a two-year teaching job...Jamie stationed in Kuala Lumpur flying bandit strikes...met him on leave...' She yawned hugely, 'Wanna sleep now...'

Desperate to keep her awake he goaded, 'One of those flash RAF fighter boys was he? I remember them from the war: top button undone; Victory Roll; Tally ho...goddamned show-offs, the lot of them!'

She glowered fiercely.

'Well they bloody saved our hides while *your* lot sat on the fence faffing around and wetting your pants at the thought of actually fighting.' Tears began rolling down her face to mingle with the blood; she looked awful and wonderful at the same time. 'Jamie was lovely and special, the life and soul of every party...' she wailed, then paused and gulped loudly, 'totally effing *useless* as a provider...but I *loved* him and now he's gone and nothing will ever be the same...'

'Ever thought it might get better, given time?'

'Huh!' She was truculent again. 'You ever been a young – well, almost young widow?'

'No-o, can't say as I have.'

It couldn't be far now surely, he thought desperately; much more of this and his concentration would be all shot to hell and they'd both end in a ditch.

She answered belligerently. 'Well let me tell you it's not much fun. You go out with a chap for an evening...' she gestured extravagantly and Ryan dodged, 'you think he's being kind and caring to a poor widow woman when all the time the bugger's just waiting to get into your knickers because he thinks you're dying for it.'

*Jesus...*Ryan stifled a laugh; *I just hope she doesn't remember any of this in the morning...*

The longest thirty minutes of his life later Alec Tawton's thatched cottage loomed out of the snow, crouched like some sinister beast under the lea of a sheltering tor. With misgiving Ryan saw that it was in complete darkness. Bringing the car to a halt as close to the gate at possible he touched Julia's shoulder. 'Looks like we're here – do you have a key?'

She sat up and peered through the windscreen, 'S'on the ledge – over the door.'

'OK, just stay in the car until I've opened up.' Despite the fact that during the latter part of their journey she had begun to shiver violently and her face beneath the congealed blood remained deathly white, he noted with relief that her speech was almost back to normal and she had become several degrees more lucid and alert.

He found the key and pushed open the door onto total darkness and absolute silence, and knew at once the place was empty of any human presence. His fingers found the light switch and he clicked hopefully, but without result. *Shit*, that meant the electricity was out. He felt in his pocket for his Zippo and snapped it, then holding the flame before him advanced a few paces into the room towards a table on which he could just make out an old fashioned oil lamp, a box of matches and a sheet of paper held fast under a glass paperweight. Lighting the lamp he bent to read the message written in a firm flowing hand.

Julia,

Electricity and phone lines down so have taken Alec to hospital in the Land Rover. Probably won't return tonight, so stay warm until it's clear enough for us to make it back safely. Don't worry: he seems to have nothing worse than a fractured wrist and a few bruises, so no need for you to make any mercy dash to Exeter!

Bob.

PS: Fire laid; plenty more logs in boot room; food in 'fridge.

Ryan said aloud. 'God bless you, Bob, whoever you are!' He crouched before the deep fire basket to put a match to the laid paper and kindling then built a careful cradle over the leaping flames with a

213

half-dozen tinder dry logs taken from the stack at the side of the hearth. Once the fire was burning steadily he heaved the huge cumbersome shabby velvet sofa in closer to the warmth and went to fetch Julia.

*   *   *

Although she still couldn't stop the shaking Julia no longer felt cold. She had only the haziest recollection of why or how she had arrived at Carters End, but was quite content to lie wrapped in blankets before a blazing fire, the remains of Hannah's coffee coursing through her veins and a warm body seated beside her on the couch. A faint protesting moan escaped her as deft fingers began sponging away the caked blood from her forehead. Forcing her eyes open a fraction she saw Ryan's taut concerned face above her.

'Hmm.' His voice seemed to come from a long way off. 'What that gash needs is some antiseptic and a band-aid – a big one. I wonder where daddy keeps them...'

Julia opened her eyes a fraction wider. 'Bathroom cupboard: first left at the top of the stairs,' she murmured.

The blue eyes above her sparked with sudden brilliance and his mouth broke into a smile. 'Back with me, are you? Hang on in there.'

She closed her eyes again. 'Don't be so bloody daft; I haven't *been* anywhere.'

'Oh yes you have...' he continued to work the damped cotton wool swab over her face, 'Hell,' he said, 'darned if you don't look like some kid whose been let loose with the ketchup!'

She felt him patting her face dry with a towel then he moved, leaving a cold spot on her side where his thigh had rested. She turned her head into the cushions and hoped he'd come back quickly and warm her some more...

*   *   *

'Wake-up – I didn't get that pre-historic kitchen range going to cook this so you could pass out again before I've fed you.'

Ryan put his hands beneath her shoulders and she sat groggily while he supported her with one arm. Squinting up at him she mumbled, 'What's going on?'

'I'll fill you in on that latter. Now eat.' He put a forkful of scrambled egg to her mouth and she took it obediently.

'Mmm...lovely.'

214

She gave him the kind of smile that told him she was on her way back and he felt the tension of the last hours flow from him as though a lock gate had opened in his chest. 'Shit,' he said, 'but you gave me one hell of a fright.'

She took the plate and fork he offered and began to eat ravenously, only pausing to wrinkle her brow in concentration and ask, 'I turned the car over, didn't I?'

'Yeah, something like that.'

'It was a pony – or maybe a deer – seemed to come out of nowhere. I had to brake.' She stared up into his face. 'What on earth are *you* doing down here?'

He was laconic. 'When a dame like you takes off half-assed into the father and mother of a rising storm, a guy like me thinks he ought to do something about it…I lit out after you soon as that little pixie of yours told me where you'd gone.'

She put a hand up to the dressing on her head. 'Is this all I got away with?'

'That and a few bruises.' He watched remembrance dawn in her eyes; she clutched his arm. 'My father!' her voice rose. 'Where is he – is he all right?'

He said calmly, 'He's OK – your neighbour took him to hospital. He only has a busted wrist so he probably looks a darned sight better than you. Guess he'll be back tomorrow if the roads are cleared enough.' He gestured at her plate. 'Now will you just shut up and eat?'

'Don't you tell me to shut up – '

He interrupted tiredly. 'Lady, I've been telling you to do that half the night, so don't start in to hassle me now. If I'd known you were going to be this cantankerous I'd have stayed home by my own fire.'

'Oh.' Suddenly deflated she flushed and bit her lip. 'I'm sorry – I can't remember things all that well. Have I been awful?'

His mouth twisted. 'You could say you got just a mite sassy.'

'Did I say anything foul; swear at you – anything like that…' her blush deepened. 'I'm always scared of having an anaesthetic in case I come out with something really disgusting!'

'Well now,' he gazed thoughtfully into the fire. 'Come to think of it you did say quite a few things I'd rather forget and a hell of a lot more I'm too much of a gentleman to repeat…'

She swallowed the last forkful of egg, handed him back the dish then slid down beneath the covers. She turned her back. 'If you were really a gentleman,' she said, her voice muffled, 'you'd just go now and leave me to die of shame.'

'Then it's good I'm not that much of a gentleman because I'm staying right here for what's left of the night.' He lay down beside her and pulled a rug from the back of the couch to spread over them both, then anchored himself with an arm tucked about her blanket-swaddled waist. He said, 'Just look on me as your friendly neighbourhood hot water bottle and sleep safe in the knowledge that I'm just too darned bushed to be anything else!'

*   *   *

Julia awoke, warm and once again in complete control of her body and senses. She could see Ryan kneeling on the hearth feeding more logs onto the glowing embers. He wore only singlet and trousers and as the wood took fire his long lean body was outlined against the flames. She felt a swift lick of desire snake through her when she remembered that body lying along her back on the big old chesterfield and how his warmth seeping through the layers of blankets had stilled her shivering and lulled her to sleep...she closed her eyes quickly as he gave a slight grunt and sat back on his heels. Would he come back to the couch? She waited a minute then opening her eyes again a fraction peered through her lashes.

He was seated on the floor now with his back to the fire, bare feet dug into the sheepskin rug, knees drawn up, his arms around them, watching her with his unswerving blue gaze. She saw his mouth give a little sideways twitch and knew that *he* knew she was awake. She said with a fair attempt at nonchalance, 'It's very draughty on that floor; you *can* come back to the couch you know.'

'No, I can't.'

She struggled into a sitting position, aware that somehow and at sometime her slacks and jersey and bloodstained coat had been replaced by her father's old dressing gown. A surreptitious feel beneath it assured her that both bra and knickers were still in place. Pulling the gown more tightly around her she asked, 'Why not when you've already been here half the night?'

He smouldered. 'Because if I do I shall make love to you and right now I'm not in the mood for a broken jaw.'

She giggled then was silenced by the look on his face. She had never actually had a man smoulder at her before. It was exciting: more than exciting, it was sexy, very sexy. 'Hmm,' struggling to control her thoughts she eyed him with an expression that held a hint of *schadenfreude*. 'I notice you've managed to get down to my essentials in perfect safety but perhaps that was because I was unconscious

216

when you stripped me!''

In one swift movement he was on his feet and looming over her. 'You make one more crack like that and I'll do a sight more than take off a few clothes,' he threatened.

She saw the temper in his eyes, heard it in his voice. If she could have run she would have, but with no avenue of escape open to her she did what she did best: she fought back. 'You are,' she said succinctly, drawing herself up, unaware that the movement slid the overlarge gown off her shoulders, '*the* most fucking arrogant bastard I've ever met!'

Ryan drew a very deep breath then with lightening speed pushed the gown right down to her waist, immobilising her hands and arms. Taking her shoulders between both hands he dragged her towards him and forced her lips apart with his own.

Emotion and feelings long dormant roared into life; an indescribable heat shot through her chest to descend with a crash between her thighs. With her ears roaring and every nerve end vibrating she freed one hand and grabbing him behind the neck pulled him down, catching him off balance so that he fell on top of her, almost knocking the breath from her body.

There was an electrifying silence as a pair of hot and passionate blue eyes blazed down into hers. Then: 'For sweet Jesus' sake woman,' he hissed through clenched teeth, 'if you *wanted* to be ravished, you only had to *ask!*'

*   *   *

He lay breathing heavily, his face buried in her shoulder. She stroked his hair; she said, 'I don't do this sort of thing.'

'You could have fooled me. If that wasn't doing it I don't know what is.'

She said inconsequentially 'I'm thirty-five and I haven't had sex for five years. I suppose I was ripe for it.'

'I'll say you were,' he was convulsed. 'I'm forty-seven, I haven't had it for a month and I was hot as hell!'

She sucked in her lower lip. 'I have stretch marks; they don't show in the firelight.'

He passed a hand over her belly. 'No teasing now – how come you know I'm crazy for stretch marks?'

'I don't trust this personality change.' She narrowed her eyes. 'Any minute now you are going to start being rude to me again.'

He propped himself on one elbow, resting his head on one hand while with the other he traced her collarbone from throat to shoulder. 'I can be a downright ornery pig I know, but for you, Julia Frazier, I could try real hard to reform.'

'Not too much.' She smiled suddenly. 'I think I'd quite like a spot of downright ornery piggery once in a while!'

He gave a silent chuckle. *All these months and I'm only just seeing the real woman...*but then that made them pretty well even, because until tonight she had never seen the real man. Wasted time, he thought, what a lot of time they had wasted between them.

'What happens now?' she asked after a long and comfortable silence. He moved his hand to her breast, caressing her with his thumb. 'Give me another ten minutes or thereabout and I'll show you!'

She covered his hand with her own. 'I mean after tonight – you: us.'

For a moment he was silent, then looked up at her, his eyes very straight and cleared now of laughter. 'I don't know what to do about the way I feel about you – or what you want me to do.' He lifted her hand to his lips; kissed the palm. 'Something I never thought would happen again has. I've fallen for you, Julia Frazier; how, when or why I don't know, but now I've found you I'm not letting go...'

I've said this before, he almost winced at the sudden pain, *but this time I don't fuck-up; this time it has to come right.*

'But it's impossible – an hour ago and we were still fighting; besides, you go back home in a few months; I have a living to make and a daughter to bring up...for heaven's sake, Ryan, we don't even *know* each other – '

He stopped her, laying a finger on her mouth. 'Julia Frazier, do you love me?'

She said wildly. 'Of course I do – I don't know any more than you why or how, although I *do* know it's certain to be a complete catastrophe, but yes, I really do love you, blast it!'

'Then that's easy: we get married before my exchange finishes then you and Nicole come back to the States with me.'

Was he really saying this? he wondered; up to an hour ago he wanted to get married like he wanted to be back in the cockpit of a B17 again...

'We *can't*: there's my father.' All at once there were tears in her eyes. 'He's a walking disaster: this isn't the first time he's fallen and broken a bone or two you know. He's never really recovered from being a prisoner in Burma during the war: he came back from the camps weighing about five stone and with both legs half eaten away by jungle ulcers; he should use a stick but he's too proud.' She almost wrung her hands. '*Nothing* comes more stubborn than my father. Since mother died I've spent half my life running up and down, seeing he's all right. I can't just up and leave him now – '

He interrupted. 'OK, I get the picture. No problem.' He took her restless fingers and kissed them again. 'He comes with us. I've a big house; there's plenty of room.'

She gazed at him in despair. 'That sort of idea makes me wonder what you smoke in that pipe of yours! For forty-seven you're bloody naïve if you think he'd agree to *that*. The stubborn old fool won't even live with me in London, never mind about America.'

'Lady when you're talking stubborn, you just watch this boy.' Ryan wrapped his long arms about her and knew that this was something he would be happy to do for the whole of the rest of his life …if she would let him.

21

CARTERS END

They bathed together in the big iron bath; Julia, drowsily compliant lay back against him while he soaped her aching limbs and washed her matted hair, afterwards towelling it dry before wrapping her in a bath sheet and carrying her to her own bed.

'Too much lovemaking and too little sleep,' he said, drawing up the covers. 'I guess it isn't really standard medical practice for accident victims to be doing what you have most of the night.'

She half-closed her eyes. 'You seduced me,' she murmured.

'I did?'

'Yes, you did, and you weren't exactly unprepared, were you?'

With cheeks flushed from the warmth of the bath, her hair damp and curling about her head like a boy, she looked about eighteen. He felt an almost painful protective surge around his heart. Stooping he kissed the band-aid on her forehead. 'Standard Air Corps stuff...I've never been a guy to find himself without a parachute, even if I wasn't expecting to fly! Anyway, I think maybe we kind of seduced each other.'

She acquiesced, 'Maybe we did.'

'Now it's light I'll get down to the woodshed. We keep that fire and the range going the way we have and your friend Bob's logs will be gone by this evening.'

'Darling, I love you naked but don't you think you should put on some clothes first?' She smiled, but he could see she was already halfway to sleep. He kissed her again, then after checking the bottle in the heater held sufficient gas for several more hours' burning he turned to go downstairs and retrieve his clothes from the hearthrug; as he reached the door she murmured in a passable Yankee drawl, 'Nice ass, fly boy!'

He paused; looked back at her over his shoulder. 'Yeah,' he said, 'and yours is pretty cute, too.'

*　　　*　　　*

After he'd gone she lay for a while, drifting between sleeping and waking, watching the patterns the fire made on the ceiling and thinking over the hours just passed; scarcely yet able to grasp how her life had changed, and with such breathtaking speed. She thought about Jamie and found she could remember him without that instant stabbing pain she had become so used to feeling. He had indeed been her first, her greatest love, but he had also been her greatest anxiety, even at thirty-five still the eternal boy. Still filled with youthful enthusiasm, chock-full of confidence, ready to take a bet with anyone about how fast he could drive from one point to another; the next horse he would back, the poker game he would win, the next plane he would fly... Now suddenly here was this big, competent both-feet-on-the-ground-man taking over her life and making love to her with a skill that told of long and probably reprehensible practice. A man who had driven his car steadily and safely through that terrifying storm to find and tend and calm an injured and doubtless abusive and witless woman; a man who could scramble eggs to the standard of a Savoy chef; or at least, that was how they had tasted at the time.

That he could also domineer and demand and tease to distraction were character faults that might have presented as an insurmountable problem, if those same defects hadn't proved to be quite so potently arousing between the sheets.

She stretched luxuriously, remembering their first lovemaking: fast and furious and absolutely wonderful; of the hands and mouth that had roused her to new and dizzy heights of passion; waking her body and numbing her mind; remembered also the long, slow, sweet and infinitely tender, but no less erotic later follow-up to that rampant lust-filled overture...

Sighing with contentment, she turned on her side and slid into a long, dreamless sleep.

*   *   *

Ryan stepped from the cottage into a world dazzling to the eye; the white moor stretching before him into what seemed infinity; Bran Tor rising above the rear of the cottage a thing of beauty and awe. There was no other house in sight and absolute silence reigned. No birds sang; no sound of machinery disturbed the still air; the gale of the previous night might never have been, only the trees around the cottage heavy with snow, the hedgerows sculptured and hidden beneath fantastic blue shadowed shapes, bore witness to the capricious, swirling storm that had formed them.

With dogged determination he made his way through a foot of

snow towards the shed adjoining the end of the cottage and found a neatly stowed large wheelbarrow, a broad snow shovel and a yard broom. Further exploration revealed at the far end of the long garden a stone and timber building filled with a winter's supply of logs stacked three deep the length of two walls, the pile almost reaching an open hayloft full of straw bales and sweet hay.

An hour and a deal of hard labour later he had dug a pathway from gateway to porch and around the house, then made a clearing on the other side of the boundary wall where a small group of shaggy ponies were patiently gathered. Returning to the wood store for a bucket he broke the ice on a water butt, then halving one of the bales from the loft carried it and a brimming pail of water back to the ponies.

'There you are, guys: get your teeth into that!' he shook the hay over the cleared patch then wedged the bucket against the fence, securing it with bailer twine. He didn't know if this was customary, or if the absent Alec Tawton would approve, but could no more have ignored the animals' obvious needs than he could have passed by a hungry child.

After barrowing several loads of logs to the cottage he filled the log basket to capacity, stoked up the living room fire and the kitchen range, stripped off coat and boots and slumped onto the couch to fall into a sleep of total exhaustion.

Julia found him there hours later, when, rested and refreshed, she dressed and came down into the silent house. With his long rangy body sprawled across the couch, tousled hair falling over his forehead, his strong regular features softened in sleep, he looked much younger than his acknowledged forty-seven years. He must have been quite beautiful in his youth she thought; even now, asleep and with the lines around mouth and eyes deepened with exhaustion, he was still a seductively attractive man.

For a few moments she stood by the couch, marvelling that they had progressed from protagonists to lovers so swiftly, and with such ease. What if her father had never fallen she wondered? If there had been no storm; if that unidentified animal had not sent her skidding off the road and if Ryan had not followed her, would they have ever come to this?

Possibly, she thought. No, not possibly, probably. Even without the catalyst of the storm, sooner or later they would have come together. Although neither had realised it at the time she knew now that the die had been cast at that first meeting. All it had taken to set the wheel of fate in motion and bring two opposing characters together had been a broken gearbox.

Stirring the fire into life she piled on more logs then walked soft footed into the kitchen.

When she returned, carrying a tray with coffee, buttered toast and a bowl of fruit, he was awake. Swinging his feet to the ground he sat ruffling his hair and easing his shoulders. 'Hi,' he greeted her with sleepy, wickedly knowing eyes, 'are you the woman I slept with last night?'

'There is no polite answer to that kind of question.' She put the tray on the floor and sat back on her heels. 'Actually, the last time you "slept" – if that is the word – with me, was about six o'clock this morning. Although it's now midday I thought we should start off with the breakfast we missed.'

He grinned and sliding down beside her kissed her mouth. 'Did I tell you that I loved you?'

'You did; several times.'

'Did I ask you to marry me?'

'Yes,' she gave an explosive giggle, 'you did that several times as well: once, when you were in a *very* compromising position!'

He began to butter a slice of toast. 'Goddam,' he said thoughtfully, 'what are we going to tell our kids when they ask where and how I proposed – and how the hell do I explain you to all my other wives?'

She gave him one of her narrow-eyed looks. 'What was that line you shot last night about changing for the better? There's about as much chance of you doing that as there is of my father agreeing to set foot in the good old US of A!'

*   *   *

Later as they lay companionably together on the couch, his arms about her, her head against his shoulder, they began tentatively to speak of the future, and when and how they should tell both parents and children that all their lives were about to be irrevocably altered.

'Let's get Christmas over first,' Julia suggested. 'After that we shall either *all* be in love with each other or ready to commit multiple murder!'

'Couldn't have put it better myself; but I sure as hell don't look forward to sleeping alone for a week, with you half a mile away down that freezing passage.'

'Umm, can't say that appeals to me much,' she made a rueful face. 'God knows when we'll ever be able to make love again – even *after* Christmas, with our two kids and your mother watching every move.'

He grinned. 'I'll bribe Rosie to take Noah and our two out someplace a couple of times a week.'

'Why do I get the feeling you've done this sort of thing before?'

'That's fighting talk; I've never bribed anyone to mind my kid while I made love to a lady.'

'Hmm, I suppose you didn't have to bribe Hannah when you were bonking Charlie.' She waited for his denial, but he only laughed and wrapped his arms more tightly around her. 'Louse,' she nipped his neck with her teeth, 'so you *were* going to bed with her.'

'Yeah, of course I was,' he confessed, 'but that finished a while back and I wasn't in love with you then. Now it's our future that interests me, and we haven't exactly settled that yet have we?'

Julia sighed. 'Ryan, you know how much I want to be with you, but how can I leave dad? He may not be all that old but he *is* disabled, and Nicole and I are all he has left.'

'What about your in-laws; don't you all keep in touch?'

'God, no,' she shuddered. 'They live in a draughty great granite pile in the Scottish Highlands – and a bloody good job too! They are the most terrifying shower; the whole family has hated my guts for snitching Jamie away from the bride Mama and Papa Frazier had handpicked for him – a big strapping wench named Shauna McDonnal, who might *just* have got off a horse long enough to marry him if *he* hadn't been scared witless of *her*. I think I happened along just in time. Sending Nicole a cheque on her birthday is as far as the grandparental duties go. If they thought I might go to America they'd probably send the fare!'

He snorted, 'Tough shit. I guess we just *have* to persuade your father to move Stateside.'

She sighed again. 'Take my word for it, he won't.'

They continued to talk around a problem that seemed impossible to resolve. Surely, Ryan thought in silent despair, all his enthusiastic determination beginning to crumble, they weren't going to find their whole future put in jeopardy by one old man. He struggled to be reasonable, to see Julia's point of view, as he had once struggled to see Claire's; but he had never been close to his own father and found it hard to understand the bond that made it so difficult, if not impossible, for Julia to leave hers.

'At least let me talk to him,' he pleaded, 'maybe we'll hit it off and he'll agree to come. Stranger things have happened.'

She shook a rueful head. 'And I thought you were the man who didn't believe in miracles! When *we* have only just stopped fighting each other how can I ask *him* to put his future at risk for a man he's only about to set eyes on for the first time: a man whom I'm only just beginning to know and who barely knows me?'

He grumbled, 'I hate logical dames.' He began to unfasten the buttons on her shirt, 'so let's be illogical and make love again.'

*   *   *

Conscious that Alec might return at any time and put an end to another night alone together, they moved from each others arms only to stoke the fires, cook their meals, and from time to time try the lights and telephone; delighted as naughty children when their half-hearted attempts to change the status quo proved unsuccessful. Although the sun had shone for most of the hours of daylight and there had been no further snowfall it had remained desperately cold. With the approach of darkness each gave a guilty sigh of relief that while the roads remained impassable Carters End was theirs alone, at least until the morning.

That night they lay together in Julia's bed and made love; slept, woke to make love again then finally satiated, slept at last, curled about each other in total contentment.

*   *   *

It was the faint but insistent sound of heavy machinery that woke them, sending Ryan from the warm cocoon of bed to gaze down from the window on to a world still shrouded in white. In the far distance, glimpsed between gaps in the snow-heightened dry-stone walls, he could see plainly the top of a snowplough making ponderous but steady progress towards them.

'*Our revels now are ended!*' he sent a wry smile over his shoulder to Julia where she lay watching him with sleepy love-filled eyes. 'Better get up and dress,' he advised, 'seems like the cavalry is here and a naked woman before breakfast could be kind of a shock for the man in charge.'

'Just as well that doesn't worry you.' She sat, stretching out her arms and letting the covers slip to her waist. 'Once more, darling...?'

He looked at her bare breasts then back at the snowplough, gauging the distance it still had to travel before it reached the cottage. 'OK,' he said and dived for the bed. 'Once more it is!'

225

*   *   *

'They do be saying the road to Exeter is open and the GPO are out mending the lines – probably them an' the electric'll be on be this afternoon,' the driver told them over coffee and toast. 'Still,' he grinned, 'up here I reckon you'll be a'keepin' the snow until gone Christmas and beyond – into February even…'

They stood together, waving him on his way. When he had gone they returned to the warmth of the fire. Despondent, Julia sat down on the couch.

'I expect dad will be here by midday.' She smoothed her fingers over the cushions. 'I'll ask Bob to tow my car in then I can get at my suitcase for a change of clothes.' She raised her eyes to catch his smile. 'With you around I haven't needed to bother much about those, have I?'

'Only from time to time, and you sure look cute in your daddy's shirt and trousers.' He knelt beside her and took her hands in his. 'I'll leave soon as you have company. I guess Hannah will have been getting pretty anxious.'

'If the 'phones aren't working before you leave I'll keep trying and soon as they are I'll call and let her know you are on your way.' She freed one hand to push the hair from his forehead. 'I love you, Ryan Petersen. I shall miss you terribly.'

'I love you.' All at once the laughter had gone from his voice and he laid his head down onto her lap, but not before she had seen the sudden shine in his eyes. She pushed her fingers through his hair, stirred by his tenderness, the unexpected vulnerability beneath all the arrogance and teasing. Nothing about this man was simple or easy, she suspected that nothing ever would be. He was that sort of man.

Unsteadily she asked, 'Will I ever get to know you?'

He kept his head bowed. 'We'll get to know each other. We have time.'

'Have you ever loved, really loved, before?' She caught her breath, 'I'm sorry, I shouldn't have asked.'

'Yes, you should, and yes, I have; it was a long time ago.' He raised his head, his eyes brilliant. 'And you, did you love Jamie like that?'

'Yes.'

He brushed his lips across hers and smiled. 'Second time around,' he said, 'I guess it's up to us what we make of it.'

*   *   *

226

Around mid-day and when there was still no sign of Alec Tawton they both braved the cold to carry more hay and straw and fresh water to the ponies. 'Dad will be pleased you fed them,' Julia brushed husks of straw from her father's Barbour. 'They usually make their way down from the moor when the snow comes: they know there's always food here.' She looked around at the sparkling white landscape. 'In town the sun would have melted most of this by now, but here, as the man said, a heavy fall in these temperatures can stay for weeks before it finally disappears. It's nothing to be completely cut off for days at a time if we get two or three big falls in January and February, so the ponies get through a fair amount of hay.'

'Joel will go ape – I think he expected Christmas in England to be wet and gloomy.' Ryan put an arm about her as they returned to the cottage. 'Back home we have some pretty heavy falls, although these last couple of years I've taken him up to Vermont to ski and give Abby a break. He'll blow a fuse when he sees all this.'

She scuffed her boots through the snow. 'Tell me about your house; about Bracket Sound.'

'I guess the house is nothing special: just an old board place painted white and standing at the end of the bay. A good size,' he grinned, 'not big enough for the Waltons maybe, but roomy enough for a decent size family to have their space. Most of the ground floor is one big family room, with a woodstove in the centre and steps up a raise into the kitchen. Off that there's my office, next to that a den for anyone who wants to get away from it all. Then there's an open wood staircase to the bedrooms – there are five of those – a couple of bathrooms and a shower room. Out front's a lawn and trees and a covered porch; out back and overlooking the beach is a deck with cane chairs and a swing seat. There's a small harbour pool built at the other end of the bay where some of the bigger boats moor until late in the year when they come out of the water...'

She paced beside him, listening to his deep warm voice conjure the small town for her: the stores along Main Street, the old houses round the bay, the new houses clustered on the hill above. The long sun-drenched summers when the water was filled with children and dogs and boats, the beauty of the fall; the shutters put up in winter when the gales blew and snow piled high on the sidewalk; the relief when spring came and he could sail again. The fishing, the picnics, the shopping trips to New York at Christmas with Santa Claus on every corner, ringing hand bells and ho-ho-ho-ing themselves into apoplexy...and she laughed and hugged his arm and thought how wonderful it would be to share those things with him, and tried not to think about the impossibility of leaving her father alone at Carters End.

Later she perched on the big scrubbed pine table, while he made hash with tinned bully beef and onions and potatoes from a sack in the cellar; enchanted by the novelty of watching a man being so competent in a kitchen, guessing shrewdly and accurately that those skills had been honed during his long and difficult marriage.

'We lived on this stuff during the war,' he said, tossing a handful of chopped tomatoes into the pan. 'Perry Manaserro, my rear gunner used to swear they filled the shell holes in his cockpit with it!' He grinned over his shoulder at her. 'Sure hope this'll taste better than some of the stuff the army cooks came up with!'

*   *   *

'Hang on a minute, Bob,' Alec Tawton leaned forward in the Land Rover's passenger seat and stared intently at a white hump at the side of the road. 'Someone's put their car over the edge. We'd better take a look; see if anyone's still in it.'

'If there is I should think they'll be a gonner by now, judging by the amount of snow over it.' Bob stopped a few feet from the car and pulling up the handbrake heaved himself from his seat. 'Take it easy if you're coming – I'll not be driving you all the way back to Exeter if you fall arse over tip again and break the other arm!'

They left their own vehicle, walking cautiously over the covering of packed snow left by the plough. As they drew nearer Alec recognised the abandoned car. His skin turned the colour of parchment. 'It's Julia's!'

'Steady,' Bob Proverbs caught Alec's good arm as he swayed. He pulled open the door. 'See – empty. Someone must have come along and rescued her.'

Weak with relief Alec looked over his companion's shoulder. 'If they did they left her case on the back seat: better take that with us,' he gazed around at the deserted moor. 'Don't like leaving the car though; if someone does come along after dark they might be on it before they realised.'

'Ar, it's a bit of a hazard.' Bob swept snow from the Ford's windscreen and side windows with his gloved hands. He asked doubtfully, 'If I hitches up a tow and pull her out, d'you think you could steer with one hand if we take it very slow?'

Alec gave a contemptuous snort. 'Do I look senile? Of course I can bloody steer.'

228

'You know Alec, sometimes you can be a real grumpy old bastard!' Bob grinned. 'Stay here while I fetch the tow – and keep her straight when I start pulling.'

Between them they manoeuvred the car back onto the road, then Bob switched the rope from back to front and they resumed their interrupted journey. As Carters End came into sight Alec craned his head to get a better look at an unfamiliar car parked right across his gateway. It certainly didn't belong to anyone in the area, so whoever had rescued Julia was apparently in the cottage. His heart began to thump in painful apprehension. God, but he hoped it was someone decent who'd found her. Suppose some nut case had come across her when she was helpless – or badly injured? Whoever it was, in that storm and with all the lines down there would have been no help for them to call upon, medical or otherwise...

As the Land Rover stopped he pulled on the handbrake of the Ford and not waiting for Bob, scrambled down from the car and pushed open the gate, checking momentarily at the sight of the cleared paths before limping up the pathway to thrust open the door.

The warmth hit him as he stepped into the house: firelight glowed, there was a smell of cooking in the air and from the battery radio came soft music. On the couch drawn up before the fire lay Julia, fast asleep, a large Elastoplast on her forehead the only visible sign of injury. He crossed the room to bend and peer closely at her face. 'Thank God she seems to be all right,' he whispered as Bob reached his side, 'only took a bang on the head by the looks of it.'

'Well, *someone* put on that plaster and as I don't believe in fairies I imagine it was the owner of that fancy car patched her up.' Bob rubbed his hands, holding them out to the warmth of the fire. 'Thing is, where the hell is he now?'

'He's over here!'

As though some unseen hand jerked a string they both swung around together, confronting a man who had appeared silently at the open door to the kitchen. A tall broad shouldered stranger who stood very still, thumbs hooked into his belt, a wary look in his eyes.

For a moment silence and suspicion hung in the air then the stranger smiled and came forward, holding out his hand. 'Sorry, I was stoking that range and guess I missed hearing you arrive. My name's Ryan Petersen,' the smile broadened as Alec took the proffered hand, 'and you must be Julia's father – I recognise you by that busted arm!'

Putting aside for the moment the desire to demand what and how the hell his daughter's far from favourite man came to be alone in this house with her, Alec returned the firm handshake and gestured at his companion. 'This is Bob Proverbs, our nearest neighbour and my temporary ambulance driver.'

'Glad to know you, Bob. That must have been some drive you made to the hospital the other day.'

Conscious of the sleeping Julia they all spoke softly, but even so the sound of their voices must have penetrated her sleep and she awoke, stretching and rubbing her eyes and yawning widely, then before anyone could speak again asked clearly and succinctly, 'Why sneak off and leave me all alone, lover boy?'

Ryan coughed loudly and she sat up, her face a comical mixture of delighted recognition of her father and horrified disbelief at her damning utterance.

'Oh, my *God...*' confused and fuddled with sleep she looked from the bemused Alec to Bob, then twisted around to where Ryan stood with both hands raised as though facing a loaded pistol while a slow unholy grin spread across his face.

'Damn you Ryan,' she yelped, 'don't stand there sniggering; have you no respect and compassion for an injured woman?'

Ryan murmured, 'Glad to hear you're back to your old self, ma'am!' Then figuring this was one time his presence could only complicate matters, returned to the safety of the kitchen, leaving Alec to deal with his truculent daughter.

22

Ryan escaped from the house and what looked like being a fraught half hour or so to give a last feed to the ponies, reflecting that there must be the equivalent of jungle drums in this part of the moor as their numbers had now increased to at least a dozen and a half. He heard the Land Rover start and waved to Bob Proverbs as he passed by the boundary wall, then collecting more wood from the store returned to the house to stack it by the range.

From the next room he could hear the murmur of voices, relieved that whatever the content of their conversation it appeared to be amiable enough. Remembering Julia's sleepy greeting he gave a snort of laughter. She might as well have stood on top of the tor and yelled, "I've had sex with Ryan Petersen," right across Devonshire!

He was standing before the open store cupboard, wondering should he make Alec Tawton a meal before he left, when the man himself came into the kitchen.

'Seems my daughter got off lightly,' Alec pulled a chair from beneath the table and sat down. 'It also seems I owe you a very big "thank you" for looking out for her; you probably saved her life. She's pretty tough but she wouldn't have made it on here without you.'

'I just happened along, sir and did what I could.'

'Now I don't think that's quite the truth of it, is it?'

'No, not quite,' Ryan closed the store cupboard door and pulled out another chair. Straddling it he leaned his arms on the back and faced Alex Tawton.

'Sir, I guess I don't need to tell you that your daughter is one hell of a headstrong woman,' he said feelingly. 'Soon as she knew you were in trouble she took off like crazy. By the time I discovered she'd gone and where she was heading it was on the way to blowing a gale, so I figured someone ought to go after her: see she got here OK.' He shrugged. 'If you're thinking I followed just to get holed up here alone with her you're riding the wrong horse. It just happened that way.'

'I know, she told me; in fact after Bob went she told me rather a lot.' His eyes crinkled. 'You may be a tad early for getting what I'm sure was an unexpected Christmas present, Professor, but I doubt that either you or my daughter were exactly broken hearted I wasn't here to prevent you enjoying it!'

Ryan took a grip on the chair back. 'Mr Tawton, Julia and I had a pretty rocky relationship up until forty-eight hours ago, in fact ever since we met we've fought like hell and I guess there's no guarantee we won't go on fighting from time to time. I'm no saint, and like I said, sir: she's one hell of a headstrong woman, but I love her very much and I think you should know I don't give up easily.'

Alec Tawton gave a grunt of laughter. 'Sounds like you're two of a kind! She takes after her mother, don't you know. Never could be sure of what Adele would do next: keeps a man on his toes, though.' He held Ryan's gaze with old and knowing eyes. 'I'm Julia's father, not her keeper. She's a grown woman, and for the past few years a very lonely one. If I thought for one minute you'd taken advantage of the situation, busted wrist or no busted wrist I'd have my twelve bore off the wall there and run you right back to that car of yours, but since she tells me that you were *almost* a gentleman, and she wasn't quite a lady, I don't consider anything that may have happened here to be any of my business.'

'That's mighty understanding of you, sir, but I guess it *is* your business. See, I want to marry your daughter and that needs an awful lot of thinking about – not for me; I know what I want, and I *think* I know what Julia wants, but then there's Nicole and my boy and Hannah – and you –'

Alec cut him short, 'Plenty of time to talk it through when you get back. You should leave here soon and not keep your family waiting and worrying for another night.' He jerked his head towards the store cupboard, 'and now that's been got out of the way, shall we get some food on the table before you leave, Professor?'

Ryan let out a pent up breath. 'Ryan, sir,' he said, 'I feel more comfortable with Ryan.'

'And I feel more comfortable with Alec.' The old man held out his hand. 'You are very welcome, Ryan.'

*   *   *

Shortly before he began his journey home the telephone lines were restored and he was able to ring Hannah. She hid any worry about the past few days beneath a veneer of cheerful unconcern, but acutely aware of the ordeal it had been for her to wait with two anxious children for news of any kind, he could hear the strain behind her blithe greeting. Although he'd been in no position to lessen her anxiety he was filled with guilty remorse.

'I'm real sorry to have taken off like that, ma, but it was a good job I left when I did. Julia ran her car off the road and was in a bit of a mess – I'll tell you all about it when I get back. She's OK now and Alec has just got home; she can't leave him yet so I have a list of things to fetch from Battersea for her and Nicole. We can bring those with us Wednesday.'

She sounded doubtful. 'How are the roads there now – you sure it's safe to travel?'

'They're reasonable; nothing I can't manage and there's no further snow forecast so far. Of course,' he added lightly, 'we may get snowed in over Christmas and have to stay for a couple of months!'

She gave a little chuckle. 'That sure sounds comforting.'

'You sure you're all right, Ma; not getting overtired or anything?'

'I'm just fine and everything's OK – got these kids organised so as I've had an easy time of it.'

'I wish I could believe you. I'll see you get plenty rest over Christmas,' he promised. 'Is Nicole alright?'

'She's managing. Been a might worried about her granddaddy and missing her mommy.'

'And Joel?'

'He's missing you.'

'Tell them both I'll be home before bedtime. You be sure and take care; don't overdo things.' He hesitated, said, 'I love you, ma,' then quickly put the phone down. He looked at Julia, who was perched on the arm of his chair. She smiled.

'Well done!'

He was embarrassed, covering it with a grin. 'She says your daughter is missing you. I should have held the line so she could talk to you.'

'I'll call her myself in a minute. She's in safe hands,' she slipped down onto his knees and put her arms around his neck. 'So am I. You're a pretty nice man when your guard is down, Ryan Petersen; you should let it down more often.'

'I'm working on it, sweetheart.' He smiled into her eyes. 'I'm going to be missing you too, over these next few days.'

She kissed him, a kiss that went on for a long time; when she finally let him go she said breathlessly. 'On your way, professor; you don't want to miss reading the bedtime story, do you?'

'No ma'am,' he put her from him and stood, shrugging into his jacket and pulling on his gloves. He gave a Bogart lift of the lip. 'Guess I'd better leave before I start in gettin' all those clothes off you again!'

Her reply would have been unrepeatable in any company. He sucked his teeth and drawled, 'Well, I'll be doggoned, ma'am, I'll sure look forward to *that*,' and he left, his stomach doing a slow segue right around his spine and back again.

He thought about her invitation quite a few times as he drove through the crisp snow of Devon and the wet slush of more temperate byways. They had both come a long way from the smart-arse Yank and the snooty piece in the broken down car, he reflected as he turned into Lincoln Street and parked before number sixteen. Chuckling he made a bet with himself that she'd never done anything with any man in her whole life before like she'd suggested doing with him after that sizzling farewell kiss.

*   *   *

Joel flung himself at his father; clinging on tight before allowing Ryan to pull him up and into his arms and kiss him before he blushed furiously growling, 'Hey, that's girl stuff – let me down!'

Ryan hugged him hard and let him go. 'You'll learn,' he said and scooped up the waiting Nicole, who didn't struggle and was in no hurry to be let down.

'Reckon you've arrived just in time to tell them goodnight,' Hannah nodded at Nicole, who was clinging like a limpet around his neck, her head buried in his coat collar. 'That one sure isn't slow letting you know what she wants!'

Ryan said cryptically, 'Like mother like daughter.' He put his finger under the limpet's chin and raised it to smile into her peaked anxious face. 'It's alright, cupcake,' his voice was warm, reassuring, 'I'm sure your mommy told you she's fine. She just has to stay and help your grandpa because he has his arm in a sling, but by the time we all go down he'll be almost good as new.'

She said, tremulous but determined, 'I'm not going to cry, you know.'

'Sure you're not. So is it alright if you stay with us 'till then?'

She nodded vigorously. 'Yes.'

'That's OK then.' He put her down and flipped a backhander on the seat of his son's pants. 'Now you two get right on up and ready for bed – not both in the bathroom at the same time and flood the place! Ten minutes, then I'll come read you a story.'

He watched them scramble up the stairs, the release of tension and fear erupting into an outburst of shoving and excited laughter. Putting his arm about Hannah's shoulders he led her into the living room.

234

'I've more to tell you about how Julia put her car in the ditch, but for Pete's sake don't let any of it out to those two just yet.' He sat beside her on the couch, hunching his shoulders, giving his wry crooked smile. 'Just to put you in the picture; I, that is Julia and me, have had quite a time of it down at her daddy's place...'

*   *   *

While Ryan was spelling it out to Hannah, Julia was arguing with Alec.

'Don't expect me to forget I have a father and just swan off – especially a father like you, who is incapable of slowing down and acting his age.' She stuck her chin out, a sure sign of battle. 'I owe you, dad: I couldn't have gone on after Jamie without you holding me together and I'm *not* putting an ocean between you and me, and that's flat.'

He said mildly, 'Well you can't expect that man to cut all his ties and move to this country just to accommodate your whims.'

'*Whims*, who said anything about whims,' she was outraged, 'since when have you been a whim – you're my *father*, for God's sake!'

'Don't I know it,' he looked at her over his spectacles. 'Do you love him?'

'Of course I bloody do!'

'Do you want to marry him?'

'Yes.'

'Then do it.' He gave her a look of exasperated affection. 'Ever heard of airplanes – you, know, those things that fly over the moor and scare hell out of the ponies? I'm not so hard up I couldn't buy a ticket to visit once in a while.'

'Who are you kidding?' she asked with biting sarcasm, 'you hate flying; there's more chance of me dancing in the Bolshoi Ballet than you getting into a 'plane. But, dad, look what's just happened; you can't go on living here without some back up, especially through the winters, it isn't fair to Bob; he and Jess worry about you as much as I do. It's only just bearable when I'm on the end of a 'phone and a few hours away. I can't fly back across the Atlantic every time something happens.'

But as she'd told Ryan, Alec could be stubborn as the proverbial mule and she could batter against him all day and night and not make any impression. Still, she carried on, trying every twist and turn of argument, but with as little chance of resolution as she and Ryan had

had the previous night. Eventually, weary beyond words, she gave in.

'I'm through trying to fight you dad, and now I'm past even thinking straight; all this has happened so fast, come so completely out of the blue. Let's leave it for now and give us all time to settle down.' *And,* she added silently, *give me the chance to drop it in Ryan's lap when he returns, because I've just about had it right up to the back teeth!*

*   *   *

Armed with Julia's list Ryan drove the following morning to Battersea to pack a couple of bags and collect the already wrapped and labelled box of presents.

Mindful that Hannah needed a break he took Joel and Nicole with him, intending to keep them out for most of the day. Perhaps it was just the release of tension making both children awkward and irritable, but listening to their incessant bickering, Ryan wondered if they might be happier and less of a pain back at the house rather than out on London's cold streets. When he had loaded the car boot he asked, 'Would you like to get back home in the warm?'

'No, thank you,' said Nicole.

'No, thank you,' Joel echoed.

'Where would you like to go then?'

'The Science Museum,' said Joel.

'The British Museum,' said Nicole.

They scowled at each other.

'Then we'll split the vote in my favour and make it the Natural History Museum,' said Ryan firmly and decisively and they both scowled at him.

*   *   *

He parked the car near South Kensington tube station. As they began to walk towards the museum he became aware that now some kind of silent war was being waged between his son and Julia's daughter. They had stopped snarling at each other and instead had begun to vie for attention in other ways. If Nicole held his right hand Joel seized the left; if she dragged him to look in a shop window Joel immediately directed him elsewhere. By the time they had walked to the Cromwell Road and turned in at the museum gates, he realised with amusement tinged with apprehension that something like sibling rivalry was beginning to show its face.

236

Hell, he thought as he ushered them up the steps, what the heck would it be like if and when they really became a family? Like every other family, he guessed: some good days, some bad – and an awful lot of so-so in-between ones. Did he want that, he questioned? More, would he be any good at dealing with something of which he had absolutely no experience? Might it mess up the new and rather tentative relationship he was finding with Joel? Would he be the kind of father Nicole needed? Could he keep the balance right, could he cope?

He fast-forwarded a few years; thought about orthodontist and college fees and puberty and hormone-driven teenagers and sex...then his mind leapt to Julia and the feel and scent of her. He groaned inwardly as the familiar ache started in his groin and spread. He'd damn' well have to, he acknowledged savagely, because he needed her like crazy already and he was never going to be able to do without her, ever again...

Inside the great cavernous hall they stood in silence, staring up at a group of three elephants. Eventually Joel said, 'That one looks bigger than last time.'

Nicole said, 'It can't be, stupid.'

Here we go again Ryan thought and sighed.

Joel shoved out his lower lip. 'It might be, dumbo.'

'Dumbo yourself,' she tried to glare but suddenly her lip trembled, 'I wish my mummy was here now.'

Joel said 'So do I.'

'Me too,' Ryan said, 'then she could sort out the pair of you.'

They both looked up at him, their faces breaking into almost identical smiles, as though surprised and almost pleased to find they were all in agreement about something. With an effort he stayed unmoved. 'You two argue any more,' he said sternly, 'and I'll make you walk home.'

'My mum says that,' said Nicola.

'Yeah, her mum says that,' echoed Joel.

'I know.' Ryan said, 'the difference is, I mean it.'

Nicola whispered, 'Does he?'

Joel nodded, half convinced. When his father looked like that he could be bad news and it was better not to push it. 'You'd better believe it,' he said. Anxious to put a distance between them and any possible trouble he grabbed her hand. 'C'm on,' he urged, 'let's go see the dinosaurs.'

Ryan followed them at a leisurely pace. He couldn't think what he'd been worried about. Really, there was nothing to this family thing; nothing to it at all.

*   *   *

The letter arrived the evening before they left for Devon. Ryan, his heart thumping at the sight of the postmark above unfamiliar writing, scooped it from where it lay in the hallway and slipped it into the inner pocket of his jacket, leaving it there through the day until the rest of the house was sleeping and he was alone in his bedroom. Even then he sat for an age by his window, turning the envelope in his hands, reluctant to open it. Eventually he roused himself from his indecisive torpor and running a thumb beneath the flap, took out the single sheet of paper and spread it slowly, his eye going first to the signature at the end, then swiftly up to scan the rest of the page.

> *Dear Mr Petersen,*
>
> *Geoffrey does not agree with me, but knows I feel strongly that you have the right to at least see, even from a distance, Sophie on her wedding day.*
>
> *She will arrive at Hawksley village church at 2.30pm on Wednesday the 29th December. There is a yew tree at the front left hand corner of the churchyard that offers a very good vantage point from which to see, but not necessarily to be seen. I expect there will be quite a crowd of onlookers, all of them concentrating on the bride, so providing you cover that rather distinctive hair of yours you should be quite safe!*
>
> *Sincerely,*
> *Pru de Lacy*

He was aware he had been holding his breath: he let it go suddenly then caught it again. Crazy, he thought, crazy to even think of going, but as he folded the letter into the envelope and placed it back into his pocket, he was already calculating how long it might take to drive from Carters End to the little church at Hawksley and arrive on time for his daughter's wedding.

*   *   *

He said nothing to Hannah about the letter, but all the way on the drive to the West Country he could feel it lying against his heart. He drove swiftly, automatically down through Surrey and Hampshire, Wiltshire and Somerset, only slowing as they neared the Devon

238

border and met the snow covered fields either side of the main road; snow that became deeper the further they drove. When finally he turned on to the high road across the moors he heard Joel's long whistle of amazement and Nicole's composed, 'See, I *told* you there would still be *loads* left for snowmen and tobogganing!'

'Gee, dad,' awed Joel hung over Ryan's shoulder. 'I never knew England had this much snow – and look, they even got a little *mountain!*'

Nicola corrected him graciously. 'That's not a mountain, it's a tor.'

'A tor then; but dad it's 'most as good as Vermont, isn't it?'

'Better,' said Ryan, 'we never had Miz Frazier waiting for us in Vermont!'

23

For Julia time never passed more slowly than the forty-eight hours before Ryan's return to Carters End. Although she was kept well occupied with cooking and cleaning and making sure her father behaved himself and didn't try fetching in logs or carry hay to the ponies, when the day's work was finished and they sat by the fireside reading or listening to the radio, and most particularly when she lay in her bed at night, she missed him; longed for the feel of his mouth on hers, his arms about her, his body close and his voice soft in her ear.

The awakening of passion after so long had been cataclysmic; any inhibitions or doubts she may have had totally demolished by that first explosive coming together. Now the nights that had seemed so short when they were alone together were unbearably long, while the prospect of spending the forthcoming week in the company of their respective father, mother, daughter and son began to assume the aspect of an approaching nightmare.

If they couldn't find *somewhere* to make love during those seven days, she thought distractedly as she slapped icing on the lop-sided fruitcake, one of her less successful culinary efforts, she would undoubtedly end up a frustrated gibbering maniac.

*   *   *

When Ryan arrived in the doorway of Carters End loaded with luggage, aware of the watching eyes, four old, four young, she greeted him with a bright, 'You made it then?' and blushed at the inanity of her question and his perceptive, tucked in smile.

'Yeah,' he dropped his canvass grip, Hannah's suitcase and her own capacious bag on the floor and showing no inhibitions whatsoever, put his hands on her shoulders and kissed her on the mouth. Nicole giggled and Joel said 'Yuk!'

Ryan lifted an eyebrow at Nicole, 'Watch it, cupcake,' he said, then to Joel, 'and you just button up junior.'

His son dragged up a winsome smile, 'Look at the great tree, dad.' He waved an expansive hand at the fir taking up a whole corner of the room. 'Nicole and me get to put the things on it soon as we've all had tea. That's right, isn't it Mr Alec?'

'Absolutely,' Alec waggled a thumb towards the cellar door. 'You

240

can go down now and fetch up the decorations – Nicole knows where they are. Bring all the boxes – but only one at a time.' He grinned at Ryan. 'You any good with tree lights – damned things never work for me.'

'Don't know as I'm an expert but I'll give it a shot,' he answered absently, without taking his eyes off Julia. Hannah nudged him gently.

'Ryan honey,' she reminded, 'there are a whole heap more packages still in the car.'

'Oh, sure...'

Julia said quickly, 'I'll help,' and took a coat from behind the door. Alec hid a grin and moved towards the kitchen; Hannah followed him.

'We might fix that tea now,' she said, 'and give those two some time to touch ground before we all start eating!'

*   *   *

Ryan unpacked his valise in Alec's study that night, stowing his few clothes in a large brass-bound chest, glad of these few moments alone to order his thoughts. He had a lot on his mind, quite apart from figuring how in hell he and Julia were going to find time to be together and without an audience over the next few days.

Since receiving Pru's letter he had been torn between the need to have Julia with him when he watched Sophie arrive for her wedding, and an unwillingness to confess that long ago love affair and its resulting repercussions. He shrank from causing any hurt by speaking of Claire to the woman who had so unexpectedly taken her place.

But if this new relationship was to work, if he and Julia were committed to making a future together, she had a right to know all about his past. There should be no more secrets or half-truths between them now. But the opportunity to make a full confession was hard to find in a house brimming over with anticipation and the preparations for Christmas Day. This evening there had been the decorating of the tree and carols around the piano. Tomorrow a snowman to build in the garden and toboggan rides down the lower slopes of the tor, snowball fights to be waged to the death around the trees in the orchard and a mammoth turkey plucked, drawn and stuffed; all such diversions making it impossible for lovers to be alone together.

That night he lay awake in his designated bed on the long couch in the living room, aching for his love and unable to find release in sleep until, in the deepest part of the night, she came to him. Flitting

241

soundlessly down the dark staircase and across the room, she slid under the covers and wound her arms about him, whispering, 'I couldn't sleep, could you?'

'No.'

He could see her eyes above him, deep liquid pools caught in the dull glow from the fire. She said, 'I need you'. With a deep sigh he drew her beneath him and in a charged and trembling silence loved her and drove her and took her over with him and, when the moment came, covered her mouth with his to hush her final passionate cry.

Holding her close as they began the slow slide down into quiet content he murmured, '"*I do love nothing in the world so well as you: is that not strange?*"'

She brushed her lips across his. 'Not strange at all...'

She left well before dawn; he watched her melt into the darkness as noiselessly as they had melted into each other. Turning his head into the pillow he smiled and breathed in the lingering perfume of her hair.

He slept deep and dreamless until roused by Hannah with coffee and the news that it was a fine and dandy Christmas Eve, with still a whole raft of things to do before evening.

*   *   *

That night, when both children had hung their Ryan-sized socks on the bedposts and hopefully were fast asleep, Alec and Hannah settled at the card table and for the first time in forty-eight hours the lovers were free to walk alone in the white moonlit garden.

'At last,' Julia tilted her head to gaze up at the stars. 'I suppose we ought to go to the midnight service but oh, how I need to get away from people and have you just to myself again.'

Ryan clasped her hand and knew the moment had come to speak of Claire and the daughter he had never known; who thought him dead and who, for Geoffrey's peace of mind, must never know any different.

She listened in silence as he talked, pacing beside him over the crisp ground, and when he was finished asked quietly, 'How could you be so sure the first time you saw her, that she was yours?'

'I couldn't miss it, nor could anyone else who knew us both.'

They had reached the boundary wall beyond the orchard. She stopped and, clearing snow from the top, leaned her arms on it and he leant alongside her. Thoughtfully she said, 'If you hadn't had that letter, would you have told me?'

242

Without hesitation he answered. 'Yes. Perhaps not now: but soon. I need to start with a clean slate, not have something creep out of the woodwork sometime in the future.'

'You could have told me before: I would have understood.'

'I guess I didn't because I thought I might cause you hurt; if I spilled it all straight away I might even lose you...and I wanted to look good in your eyes.' He grinned a little awkwardly. 'See, I feel Jamie is a hard act to follow; there's one hell of a big gap between that good looking young fighter pilot who will always stay that way in your memory, and the reality of this beat-up old ex bomber pilot turned professor, who probably won't be the easiest guy to live with.'

'Oh,' she smiled without looking at him, 'I shouldn't worry too much about that. As you may have noticed, I'm not exactly up there with the saints, am I?'

He said, 'I've never been a saint man myself,' and she laughed.

'No, more of a leg man, I'd say!'

He smiled then sobered again. 'So will you come with me to Hawksley next week?'

'I would,' she answered truthfully, 'come with you to the world's end if you asked me nicely.'

'Does the world's end include Connecticut and that house on Bracket Sound?'

For a moment her eyes clouded then her chin came up. 'It has to,' she said, 'one way or another.'

'With or without Alec?'

She shook her head. 'That's a hard one. I've done my best. He just says, "Go"'.

'I'll give it a try: talk to him soon as I get the chance.'

She sighed. 'I suppose he has to be allowed the right to refuse you as well as me.'

'What we need,' he said, 'is a miracle. Maybe we should go to that midnight service of yours.'

She teased. 'I though you didn't go in for all that!'

'I don't go for the whole shebang,' he gave an awkward grimace, 'though I've never tried your lot.'

'OK; you're on,' she took his hand. 'Let's leave the car; it's less than a mile to walk. We have time and it's a wonderful night.'

Hannah looked surprised and Alec amused at their decision. 'Rather you than me, sitting on a cold pew at midnight,' he said, 'that church is like a tomb in winter.'

Hannah gave a dry sniff. 'Guess it's better than nothing, but leave me out. If I can't do it properly, I don't do it at all!'

The church had been built by the Normans and still retained the original stone flagged floor along with a dozen rows of carved and worn oak pews, each seating no more than six of the faithful at a pinch. It was cold as charity and getting his knees on an embroidered hassock about as close as any part of Ryan came to comfort. As a service it wasn't bad, he acknowledged, although he missed the colour and theatricality, the incense, the statues with the votive candles burning before them, and wondered why the English church had taken Christ from off the altar cross.

But the crib was familiar and the candlelight and choirboys reminded him of Niles and him, all done up in cassocks and lace surplices, singing *Adeste Fidele* at the Midnight Mass. All pure nostalgia; he mocked himself gently. Still, he enjoyed the singing.

'That was kind of nice,' he said as they began the walk back to Carters End.

She laughed. 'I don't make a habit of it but Christmas is special: better and more meaningful than New Year.'

'I guess.'

He remembered Robyn Graham: *"Not only for today, sir, for all the days..."* and was sobered and walked in silence for a while, then in a sudden burst of confidence told Julia about that long journey through the snow on an evening such as this. She didn't answer, but he saw the shine of tears in her eyes and said quickly, 'When you come with me to Hawksley we must stay at the Bull in the next village. There's a barman called Eddie who knows everybody's business, and a four-poster bed with an awful lot of that shiny flowery material in the drapes.'

'Chintz?' she hazarded and he nodded.

'That's the stuff: big flowers; makes your eyes water!'

'I can't wait,' she said.

*   *   *

Shivering and clutching their spoils to their chests, Joel and Nicole crept down the stairs and made for the banked up fire. Joel whispered, 'Poke it a bit – *quietly,* you dummy!' The flames spurted and he cautiously laid more wood on top. 'There,' he sat back satisfied from the blaze.

Nicole gave an exited bounce 'Now we can open these in the warm.'

'Pipe down, you dork, or you'll wake dad.'

Ryan watched them through half closed eyes; the hands of the clock on the mantle stood at five-thirty. Little brats, he thought, then remembering another Christmas when he and Niles had plundered the goodies almost as soon as their father had taken their empty stockings and replaced them with the knobbly exciting ones, he stayed silent and continued to watch and eavesdrop.

Joel was scrabbling excitedly, 'Gee – I gotta James Bond Aston Martin...look, this gun thing comes out,' he made *sotto voce* ratta-tatting noises. 'What you got in that square box?'

She tore off the wrapping. 'Crumbs, it's a Slinky! I've wanted one of those for *ages,* but mum said they were a waste of money.' Ryan grimaced inwardly. It looked like he'd put up a black there with Julia...

'Bet you get it all messed up first time you let it go downstairs.'

'Bet I won't.'

'Bet you will.'

Ryan growled, 'Bet you get my hand on your asses if you wake the whole darned house!' He sat and looked sternly at the two startled and guilty faces. 'Do you two kids know what time this is?'

Nicola looked at the clock. 'Almost morning?' she ventured.

Joel said defensively. 'It was cold upstairs. We didn't mean to wake you. Can we get in – my feet are froze most off.'

'Mine too.' Nicole made her eyes very big and soulful.

'What makes you think I want your thirty cents worth of cold feet in my bed?' They looked crestfallen and Ryan sighed. 'OK: in the other end both of you – and keep your feet to yourselves.'

They scrambled beneath the covers and continued with their plunder. Nearing the end nuts and tangerines were tossed aside until finally Joel thrust his hand into the toe of his sock and gave a joyful whoop, 'Chocolate money!'

'I've got a giant sugar mouse,' Nicole licked experimentally then gave Ryan one of her under-the-lashes smiles, 'if you like you can bite the head off this one,' she offered generously.

'Think I'll take a rain check on that offer, cupcake – '

'What *is* going on?' Julia appeared behind them, wrapped in her eiderdown and with rumpled hair. She looked accusingly at Ryan. 'Did *you* tell them they could stay out of bed at this hour?'

Joel sprang to his defence. 'He didn't. We were cold; we just came down ...ma'am.' he added with an ingratiating smile.

Ryan grinned. 'My counsel for the defence,' he said. 'Now stop giving us grief woman and get in – we've just got to the sugar mouse,

245

chocolate and tangerine stage.'

'Yes, get in, mummy,' Nicole urged.

Ryan lifted the cover invitingly. 'You heard the lady; there's room for one more.'

'Not sure there is without we go missionary!' she murmured. 'Budge over then,' she said aloud and dropping the eiderdown slid in beside him. He put an arm around to anchor her and Nicola beamed.

'Isn't this nice,' she said, 'all in one bed – just like in the Sound of Music when there was that storm!'

'Yuk,' Joel made sick noises and ran his Aston Martin across the back of the couch. 'First one starts singing I quit!'

*   *   *

When two sets of toes digging into his calves and Julia's thigh nudging his became too much, Ryan retired to the kitchen to fix an early breakfast, which they ate seated on the floor before a fire now blazing merrily as a fire should on Christmas morning. 'Back home,' Joel hinted, leaning comfortably against Ryan's shoulder, 'we have tree presents directly after breakfast.'

Ryan slid an arm around him, 'Not when breakfast is at half after six we don't.'

His arm wasn't shrugged away and he got an immediate and ridiculously warm feeling of pleasure at that; pleasure which was intensified when Joel smiled up at him and said simply, 'This is great, isn't it, dad?'

'You think so? Better even than Vermont?'

'Yes *sir*! A million trillion times better!'

Nicole edged in on Ryan's other side. 'What's it like in Vermont.'

'Lots of snow like here and cold enough to take your breath away on the ski slopes,' he answered, 'but mighty pretty. See, over there we have lights outside as well as inside our houses – even up in the trees, and when they are all lighted up, well...' He spread his hands

'...it just knocks your eye out!' finished Joel.

She gazed up at Ryan, her eyes like two shining brown chestnuts. 'I *wish* I could see all that.'

Ryan caught Julia's wry smile. 'Well now,' he put his free arm about Nicole, 'I guess we'll have to see what we can do about that, won't we?'

*   *   *

When Hannah and Julia had taken both children up to bed that evening and were occupied in bringing the excitement of the day under control with a long story session, Alec fixed Ryan with a faintly sardonic look and suggested a retreat to his den for a glass of the single malt Ryan had given him. As he followed his host into the little study at the back of the house, Ryan mused that this could be where it all got kind of hairy.

Alec lit the gas-fired stove, then poured their drinks and settled into one of the fireside chairs, while Ryan took the other. In silence they both drank: the younger man looking into the fire and the older one lying back with half-closed eyes. In a minute, Ryan thought desperately, he's going to fall asleep and I'll have missed my chance. He felt a light film of sweat break along his hairline and taking a long pull at his whisky broke the silence abruptly. 'Sir,' he began and Alec Tawton opened his eyes, giving him a dry look.

'It's been Alec all day, so why so formal all of a sudden?'

'Maybe the occasion calls for it.'

'Umm...watched you working up to it all evening, so whatever it is you want to say, say it; don't beat about the bush.'

Ryan held up his pipe; he asked, 'Alright if I smoke?' and when Alec nodded, took out a tin and began to shred the tobacco. 'Like I told you before,' his long fingers pushed the shreds down into the bowl, 'I'm in love with your daughter, and for some unaccountable reason, she seems to be in love with me. Now that means we want to get married before I'm due to return to the States...' he flipped his lighter and held it over the bowl, looking up at his companion over the flame, 'problem is, she doesn't want to leave you on your own here when we go.'

'Well I'm not likely to go with you, if that's what you're angling for.'

'Not even when you know she'll worry like hell when she's there and you're here – and do you really think you can go it alone through another winter?'

'Huh,' Alec gave him a long unblinking stare. 'Suppose I was to say I might not *be* on my own?'

Ryan was startled. 'How come?' he asked and watched the creases around the old man's eyes deepen. Realisation dawned and the corners of his own mouth quirked into a grin. 'You telling me you got a woman hidden around here someplace, Alec?'

'Could be...'

Ryan turned this unexpected news over in his mind for a moment; he sighed faintly. 'OK, supposing you *are* all fixed up here; how does it leave you feeling to know your daughter and granddaughter are way over in New England?'

Alec's eyes shifted fractionally from his; he said without conviction, 'As I've already pointed out to Julia, there are such things as aeroplanes. I could fly over, couldn't I?'

Ryan studied him for a moment in silence. 'Ye-es,' he said eventually, 'but just look me in the eye, *sir*, and tell me you would be prepared to fly over often enough and for long enough to satisfy everyone: say a couple of times a year. Or would you keep putting it off and just wait 'till it was time for us to come to you?'

Alec glanced at his sceptical expression then looked away. 'You're pretty astute, aren't you?'

'Don't know about that,' Ryan said equably, pulling on his pipe, 'but I sure do know bullshit when I hear it!'

Alec gave a disgusted grunt. 'Julia been talking has she? Told you I hate flying?'

'No: I just played a hunch.' Ryan grinned. 'Don't let it be a problem: a couple of tranquillisers and a good woman to hold your hand and you'd be fine.'

'I'll remember that,' he was dryly amused, 'matter of fact, if I get the woman I'm after I could probably do without the pills.'

Ryan raised his glass. 'Here's to her then; whoever she is.'

Alec tipped his own glass. 'I'll drink to that.'

Ryan blew a plume of smoke ceilingward. 'How's about levelling with your future son-in law then, and give with a name – one of your neighbours, is she?'

Alec looked sly and refilled their glasses. 'Mister,' he said, 'my answer to that is short and sweet: you can damn' well wait and see!'

24

HAWKSLEY

Julia was seated at the end of the couch listening to Ryan, who lay stretched out full length, stockinged feet propped on the end, his head resting in her lap. He spoke with his eyes closed, a hand resting on the open book that lay against his chest. When he finished she looked down on his face with frank disbelief, listened for a moment to check that Hannah and her father were still in the kitchen preparing the supper, then prodded him with an ungentle finger. 'What do you mean, he's got a woman?' she hissed.

'He's got someone lined up alright.'

She said flatly, 'I don't believe it; he's never shown the slightest interest before in anyone around here.'

'Maybe he's advertised in the Lonely Hearts columns,' he opened his eyes. 'You've been holding out on me, haven't you? You didn't tell me he's got a thing about flying; anything else I should know about while we're at it?'

She ran her hand through his hair. 'Probably, but no woman should tell a man everything, even one who buys his fancy bit a Liberty scarf for Christmas!'

'Hope that goes both ways and my fancy bit won't be expecting a full confession in return for this,' he tapped the book then turned his head to smile up at her. 'I chose that wrap because it matched your eyes.'

'And I chose that book because it matched *you*.'

He picked it up, turned back the buff paper wrap and ran a finger over the black buckram and gold lettering on the front cover and spine. 'The Collected Poems of Rupert Brooke,' he opened it, leafing the covering tissue from the frontispiece. 'This 'photo's a new one to me...great portrait – a real handsome English gentleman poet. Where did you find it?'

'In one of those dusty little old bookshops off Charing Cross...but getting back to dad,' she returned to the attack, 'didn't he give you a clue?'

'Nope,' with one finger he pushed an invisible Stetson up his forehead.

'Aren't you curious?'

'Nope.'

'Do you *know* how aggravating you can be?'

'Yup.'

She gazed at him broodingly. 'I can't think what I see in you.'

He took her hand, turned it and kissed the palm. 'I've been thinking that we should tell our children about us before you and I leave for Hampshire on Tuesday. Give them time to mull it over while we're out of their hair.'

'Um, yes,' she sounded unsure, 'but what if they hate the whole idea and play merry hell? I don't fancy leaving dad and Hannah to take all the aggro.'

He sat up swinging his feet to the ground. He put an arm about her. 'What is it with you that you have to meet trouble half way?'

'It's easier than waiting for it to find me.' She tightened her lips in vexation when he smiled. 'Don't you worry about how Joel and Nicole will take it?'

'Sure, I can worry with the best of them, but I have to believe it will all come right in the end; that something of what we feel will brush off on them; that they'll grow up knowing what it means to have parents who love and care for them – and for each other.'

'Now I know what I see in you,' she gave him a small, crooked smile, 'but while we're on the philosophical bit can you explain to me how, without breaking her heart, I tell Nicole that she will be leaving her grandfather behind?'

He said, 'You've got cold feet, haven't you?'

She sighed, 'Yes,' she admitted.

'About us?'

'No, of course not *us,* but you see when Jamie died I was the one who had to tell her. I wouldn't want to see that look on her face ever again.'

He turned his head away, 'I know,' he said quietly, 'I know.'

She put her hand up and touched his cheek.

'You had to do that, too, didn't you?'

'Yes, but now we do it together.' He stood, pulling her to her feet. 'Come on; before we take that jump off the high board we'd better let Alec and Hannah know that come tomorrow morning, the third world war could break out ...'

*   *   *

Joel demanded incredulously, 'You're gonna get *married*?'

Ryan hitched onto the arm of Julia's chair and took her hand. 'That's the general idea, junior.'

'What – to each *other*?' Nicole's voice raised a couple of decibels.

Ryan felt Julia's hand tremble in his but she answered bravely, 'Well, yes; of course to each other.'

The two children exchanged glances before both gave her a look of deepest suspicion, 'When?' they demanded in chorus.

'Not right away, but sometime before Joel's daddy is due back home; then we can all go together.'

Nicole was clearly bewildered. 'You mean you and me are going to live in *America* – with *them*?'

Ryan gave Julia's hand a final squeeze then left his perch to squat down before the couch, where both children sat side by side. 'Sure thing: that's all part of the package. You don't want to stay behind, do you?'

'No, but…if you're Joel's daddy,' she picked at her lower lip, 'does that mean you're going to be mine as well?'

'I guess: same as your mummy becomes Joel's. That's the way it works.'

For a moment she was silent until Joel said with the incautious callousness of the ten-year-old male, 'Sounds OK to me…'

If Julia's eyes could flash fire, that was nothing to what her daughter's achieved. Outraged, she snatched at Joel's hair, grabbed his cowlick and pulled hard, yelling, 'Well you can't have her; she's *mine*!'

With deadly swiftness and accuracy Joel deadheaded her arm with his fist. Tears started to her eyes and letting go his hair she squealed, 'Pig! You pig! That hurt!'

'Great,' his face was dark with fury. 'If I don't get your mom, then you don't get my dad!'

Nicole launched herself at him again, making another grab for his hair. 'I hate you!'

He deadheaded her other arm. 'And I hate you!'

She screamed. Ryan roared, 'QUIET!' and catching an elbow of each held them apart while Julia muttered an inaudible 'Oh, my *God*' and wondered if anyone would notice if she left the room.

Ryan stood, hauling both children up with him as they continued to spit insults. 'I said, '*Quiet*, both of you…*now*!' His voice held a menace that created instant silence from both protagonists. 'Let's get something straight,' he grated through set teeth, 'the only slapping around here gets done by *me*.' Eyes like twin chips of ice bore down on their now apprehensive faces. 'Joel, you don't hit girls – *ever.* You hear me?'

Shaken, Joel muttered 'Yes, sir.'

Ryan eyes pinpointed Nicole 'And you can cut out making like an alley cat and behave like a lady. Do *you* hear me?'

But Julia's daughter was made of sterner stuff. She stared him out in silence for a moment before she gave tongue. 'I'm not saying "yes, sir" to *you*,' she made it sound like an insult. 'Not even if you smack me hard I won't.'

Ryan gave her an even colder eye. 'I don't hit women, and that includes real sassy little kids like you – but you'll say it when you rile me real bad, and you're doing that right now.'

'Oh.' She picked at her lip again and looked at Joel, who made a Dracula face back.

'I'm waiting,' Ryan prompted softly.

Swiftly weighing up the ignominy of giving in now, with the possibility of something worse to follow if she didn't, she conceded victory. Making a swift transmission to the helpless female she gazed up at him, pitiful and doe-eyed, 'Yes, *sir.*'

His mouth twitched briefly and he let go of her arm. 'OK, subject closed.'

Ostentatiously she rubbed her elbow and treated him to another Little Orphan Annie look. 'What am I supposed to call you the rest of the time then?'

He hesitated for moment then gave a faint smile, 'A boy I once knew used to call me Pop. I guess that would do for starters.'

'Pop,' she shaped her lips around it. 'Pop.' She nodded slowly, 'all right.'

There was a silence. Joel, released from Ryan's grip sat down quickly and began to examine his sneakers. Nicole, her expression suddenly unsure glanced from Ryan to Julia and back again. She swallowed hard. 'What about grandpa,' her voice wavered, 'will he come too?'

Behind him Ryan felt, rather than saw, Julia stiffen; he said quickly. 'No, he won't do that. It wouldn't be right for him, would it, when he's lived here for so long? But he will visit us, and we shall visit him.'

'When?'

'In the holidays: maybe he could spend most of the winter with us and we could spend some of our summer vacations here. Then if you like, and when you've gotten a little older, you can come over and visit by yourself.'

'Do you promise; absolutely *promise* that?'

'I sure do.' He crossed his heart then wetting a finger passed it across his throat. 'Cross my heart and hope to die. If I have to swim all the way with you on my back, you'll get to see your grandpa!'

'Very well,' she said graciously, 'but I'll have to talk to grandpa about it.'

'Sure. You could do that right now while he's out back getting up the hay for the ponies.'

'OK.' She jumped up, giving Joel a friendly push. 'Hurry up, 'cause grandpa will need us to help carry the hay.'

Joel leaned an elbow nonchalantly against the arm of the couch, 'In a minute. I gotta think.'

Julia had dreaded the moment when *she* would be the one to confront Nicole's distress, perhaps deal with an angry tantrum; but when Ryan was the one her child had decided to challenge she had withdrawn from the contest, observing with professional admiration the juggling of his considerable authority with an enviable ability to bargain – and winning on both counts...

Quite a *tour de force*, she thought with an inward grin as her daughter left the room, defeated but with her pride still intact. She glanced across at Ryan but he was watching Joel, who sat alone on the couch, his expression closed and reserved. It was a childish version of Ryan's when he was unsure of what to do next and she was suddenly deeply moved. She longed to go to Joel then, hug him tight and tell him how Nicole really would love to have him for a brother once she'd got used to the idea. Unfortunately, despite all these months of close comradeship with her daughter, Joel didn't now appear particularly to want her as a sister, nor was he showing any sign of needing to be hugged. Indeed, she thought, beginning to despair, it was difficult to tell whether he was upset or angry or even on the verge of tears.

With her eyes she sent an agonised signal for help to Ryan, who only raised an eyebrow in return, then moved to the hearth and began feeding more logs onto the already blazing fire, his back giving out the unmistakable message: *I've taken care of your problem; now you take care of mine!*

Bastard, she thought, then gathering together her courage and all the skill honed over fifteen years of teaching just such small boys as this one, sat down beside Joel in the space Nicole had left. 'Would you like to go away somewhere quiet to have your think, Joel?' He shook his head, his gaze fixed on Ryan's back.

'No ma'am,' he sounded preoccupied, 'I'm just working out about

Nic and me when we get back home. See, most times I like her and I don't mind about her coming with us – and you too, of course, but I can't have a girl hang around all the time...' he went pink, 'they can get kind of drippy an' that...'

'Can they? How?' she asked gravely, aware of a slight tremor in Ryan's turned shoulder.

Throwing a furtive look toward the door Joel wriggled his skinny body back onto the cushions. 'She *says*,' he confided in a penetrating whisper, 'that she wants to marry me later on, when she's old enough.' He knit agonised brows. 'She reckons fifteen or so will be OK.'

'Holy *cow*!' dropping the log he held Ryan turned around. 'Reckon you've got something wrong there: no girl could even think of marrying a guy who eats his cereal the way you do!'

Joel scowled. 'Well *she* does – an' just suppose she tells the guys back home all that stuff about getting married?'

'She won't be able,' Ryan sent Julia the merest flicker of a wink, 'when Julia and I are married that will make her your sister, and brothers can't marry their sisters.' In this case that wasn't strictly accurate, but he'd sort that later...

'Gee, is that so...she sure is going to be mad about that!' Joel thought about it for a moment then looked pleadingly at Julia, 'you going to tell her, Miz Frazier, or will dad?'

'Oh, I think we'll let him do it, don't you?' She smiled sweetly at Ryan. Landing him with the task of shattering Nicole's pre-pubescent dreams of matrimony would damned well serve him right and equal the score of leaving her out on a limb with Joel. She turned away from Ryan's sardonic look and put a casual arm across Joel's shoulders, 'By the way, Joel, could you think of something to call me other than Mrs Frazier – out of school, that is?'

He looked blank. 'Like what?

'Like...oh, I don't know...' Faced with the question, she realised she didn't have an answer to give him. He'd never bring himself to call her Mummy, that was for sure, and Mom or Mommy was just too dire. Not even for Ryan could she bear *that,* not yet anyway. She hesitated, 'Julia, perhaps...?'

'No *way*!' the tips of his ears glowed fiercely, 'Abby 'ud *kill* me!'

Ryan said mildly, 'No need to get all fired up. You'll think of something,' then added straight-faced and with only the merest hint of malice, 'I should go on calling her ma'am for now. She likes being called that; kind of makes her feel like a queen!'

'Is that right, Miz – ma'am?'

He so looked relieved that Julia postponed for the moment an immediate and urgent desire to strangle her lover. She said weakly, 'Yes, that will do fine for now.'

'That's OK then; can I go now? Nic 'ul be waiting.'

'Yes, of course.' She gave his shoulders a hug, feeling his scapulas like sharp fledgling wings against her arm. She imagined that was how his father had been as a boy: all bony and brittle...dreamily she recalled the feel of Ryan's naked muscular shoulders beneath her hands and began totting up in her mind how many hours there were still to go before they left for Hampshire and the erotic delights of another whole night together...

Letting go of Joel she looked up and catching the full force of Ryan's perceptive slow burn smile felt herself blush and begin to melt at the edges. How does he *do* that, she wondered, had he perhaps some kind of extra sensory perception that let him know when she wanted him?

Joel leaped up with the alacrity of an arrow released from a bow and Ryan ruffled his hair as he passed. 'No more fighting, now,' he warned.

Joel paused. 'Aw, dad, not even if she starts it?'

'She won't, she's not all that tough – and you've plenty of hair left, haven't you?'

'Yeah, I suppose,' he sighed, 'I better go else she'll start hollering...' Reaching the doorway he paused again and hunched his shoulders. 'Heck,' his voice was deeply tragic. 'Women!' he said.

'Yeah,' Ryan grinned, 'but don't you just love 'em when they get real mad!'

*   *   *

Julia stared at him with narrowed eyes. 'That was too easy. I do hope you realise they are going to continue belting hell out of each other from time to time, *and* trying to play us off against each other.'

'Sure they are; but they're intelligent kids, aren't they? They'll soon figure out how not to make waves.'

'The trouble with you,' she said, 'is that you always have an answer to everything.'

'Ain't that the truth!' he took her hands, pulling her up into his arms and wrapping them around her. 'You going to smack me one for dropping you in it?' he asked.

'Not right now, later perhaps, unless you can make me change my mind.'

He captured her mouth with a long slow kiss then asked, 'How am I doing?'

'Getting there,' she answered, and pulled his mouth back onto hers.

*   *   *

Nicole paused on the way to the orchard to press the snowman's nose harder into his face. She said, 'I've changed my mind. I think I'd rather marry your dad than you.'

Joel hitched up his wedge of hay and gave a contemptuous sniff, 'everyone knows you can't marry him when he's your *father*, you dumb broad!'

'Oh well, then,' she dusted the snow off her woollen gloves. 'Perhaps I'll marry you after all.'

He whistled through his teeth, 'Like heck!' he returned and began to trudge through the snow to the orchard fence where the ponies were waiting for breakfast.

*   *   *

Ryan and Julia left mid morning the next day, waved on their way by Alec and Hannah, the two children already about the serious business of dragging the sled up the nearest hill for a thrilling and frequently spilling swoop down over the frozen snow. Alec watched the car down the lane then turned to Hannah.

'Darned if trying to get some time alone with you isn't worse than in my earlier courting days,' he complained, 'then it was parents, now it's always our own kids, or theirs, under our feet.'

She linked her arm comfortably in his. 'Well, we've a couple of days to talk things over...not that we really need to do much talking about it, do we?'

'I don't. Knew what I wanted the first time I clapped eyes on you...didn't think I'd get you, though!' He drew her back into the house; shutting the door he put his arms about her. 'You sure you want to take on an old wreck like me and live here in this place?'

'Never been surer of anything in my life,' she smoothed a hand over his thinning hair. 'You and I will manage just fine...two old wrecks together, looking after each other.'

'What about leaving all your friends behind...there's not much in the way of theatre and the cinema and dancing down here.'

'We can go to Exeter and take in a play or a movie once in a

256

while…and we can dance right here in this room. 'Sides, you sure are the best card player this side of the Atlantic, Alec Tawton, and I'm not passing up on *that* for anyone.'

He asked soberly, 'How's that son of yours going to take it?'

'Hard to say, you never know with Ryan. He'll likely cut up rough for a while.' She rested her head against his, suddenly sad. 'I sure hope Joel doesn't take it too hard.'

'We'll manage to make it right for him, like your boy did for Nicole.'

'I guess,' she took out her handkerchief and wiped her eyes. 'Will you look at me, snivelling like some teenager leaving home for the first time,' she summoned a smile. 'What about your Julia?' she asked.

He grinned, 'No idea. Probably think it's a hell of a laugh!' He held her a little away from him for a minute then gave a deep chuckle. 'Never did have a woman tall enough to look me straight in the eyes before. Suppose we celebrate this time alone together with a glass or two and nice cuddle on that couch our kids are so fond of?'

She said, 'Suppose we do just that – just to remind ourselves that life doesn't end when your knees begin to creak!'

*   *   *

Ryan drove in silence for several minutes, his mind busily engaged with interpreting the exchange of looks between his mother and Julia's father as they had stood waving them away from Carter's end. Odd, he thought, almost they had been the intimate relieved glances of two people waiting for the moment they could be alone together.

He ruminated silently on his conversation with Alec and the old man's sly hints of another woman in his life, and slowly the incredulous thought began to form that Alec and Hannah were…no, he amended, his mind skidding away from the thought; that was just too crazy. That awkward old stick insect Alec with his talent for breaking bones and feisty Hannah, with what she chose to call her "dicky-ticker," were hardly the most likely pair of lovers; but all the same, that had been some look…

Suddenly he hit the steering wheel hard enough to bruise his hand, making Julia jump and give a yelp of surprise. 'They *are;* they're fucking going to do it!' He swore with a profanity that made Julia blink.

'Stop giving me a heart attack – and watch the bloody road!' she glared at his contorted profile. 'You really do have an incredible range of foul language. Who is going to do what?'

He snapped, 'Your father and my mother, that's what. The old bugger wasn't kidding about his secret bit on the side...' he saw the entrance to a farm track and jammed on the brake, 'and we've just left them a clear field!'

'Are you still on that old chestnut?' She gave an incredulous laugh. 'He's never looked at another woman since mother died – as for it being *Hannah*...for God's sake, he's only known her for about five minutes.'

'Well he's a bloody fast worker then,' Ryan let go the brake, backed into the farm track and swung the Jowett into a tight turn.

'Will you stop this,' she thumped his arm, 'for a start nothing's going on and we shall look complete idiots if we go back now and you start a row.' When he ignored her she thumped him again. '*Listen to me, you bastard!*'

'I'm listening but I'm not stopping.' He sent the car surging forward, taking the first bend in a side-long skid. 'I'm not aiming to challenge or maim anyone, I just want to *know*.'

In less than five minutes they slid to a stop a few yards short of the gate.

Repressing a nervous urge to giggle Julia followed him along the path. From the living room came the murmur of voices and Hannah's unmistakable laugh. Still seething with anger but feeling like the worst kind of *voyeur* Ryan stepped to the side of the window and took a swift, half shame-faced peek, while Julia peered around his shoulder.

Alec and Hannah were seated together on the couch before the fire; his arm was around her waist, her head against his; both were smiling and raising glasses in what was an unmistakably convivial toast.

With one accord Ryan and Julia stepped back and out of sight. '*Shit!*' he ground through clenched teeth, and at the look on his face Julia's desire to break into hysterical giggles almost overcame her.

'Please,' she begged in an agonised whisper, 'can we just get the hell out of here right now...'

*   *   *

They argued, on and off, for the entire journey. Ryan, confused by the strength of his own jealous reaction to the sight of Hannah and Alec together was furious with Julia, who couldn't contain her hilarity at the remembrance of those two figures cuddled up on the couch. By the time they stopped for a late lunch his smouldering anger and her unsuccessful attempts to control her laughter meant they were barely on speaking terms.

'If you think it funny,' Ryan gritted over their apple pie and custard, his voice controlled but eyes hot with temper, 'that my mother, who has a heart condition, is on the point of climbing into the sack and apparently ready to live in the boonies with a man who has a gift for falling over and busting his bones, then sister, you have one strange sense of humour – '

'And you have none at all,' she interrupted, stung at last out of laughter and into retaliation, 'if I'd known what an unreasonable, jealous, wrong-headed moron you could be I'd have stayed home and given them my blessing.'

'Christ,' he pushed away his plate with a barely controlled fury, 'some daughter *you* turned out to be.'

Giving a final contemptuous sniff she retreated into silence. They completed their meal then still in silence resumed their journey, the air between them vibrating with repressed anger.

*   *   *

Arrived at The Bull, Ryan jerked their bags from the boot and strode ahead of Julia into the bar, leaving her to follow. Just like an old married couple, she thought gloomily, all her mirth now completely evaporated, Hell, what on earth was she doing out here in the middle of nowhere with a moody unreasonable swine like Ryan Petersen? Heavens...Alec and Hannah living happily together, loving and mutually supportive...it was the answer to a prayer. Why couldn't the blasted man see the positive – and the funny side of it all?

Inside Ryan's head the old unreasoning boyhood jealousy was raging. Just when he was getting closer to Hannah and making some headway in being a halfway decent son again, here was Julia's father taking over and shutting him out, just as Lars had always done. Chickens coming home to roost with a vengeance, he thought savagely, as love and anger and resentment fought with shame and guilt for all the years that he had shut Hannah from his own life.

He made a conscious effort to return Eddie's greeting, but left him to take their luggage and gallantly escort 'Mrs Petersen' up to their room, while he stayed in the bar, adding to his lunch time beer by sinking in quick succession the two double whiskies served him by old Nathaniel; who wasn't all that ancient but seemed to enjoy playing the gnarled old countryman.

If their whole time in Hampshire wasn't to be a complete disaster something or someone would have to give…morosely Ryan put up a finger to Nathaniel for the third double he knew he shouldn't have. Julia was *not* going to give an inch: it wouldn't surprise him if she got the next train back to Exeter although, he thought, with a certain grim humour, being the woman she was she'd be much more likely to pinch his car and leave him the train.

* * *

When Julia came down into the bar and saw the three empty glasses before him and a fourth already half empty in his hand, her heart gave an apprehensive sideways lurch. Months ago Hannah had told her about his occasional bursts of heavy drinking and now she could tell from his eyes that he was well on the way to getting very drunk indeed. Jamie may have had his failings but drinking to excess had not been one of them and she was conscious of treading unfamiliar ground. It was probably her fault for not taking him seriously, she thought miserably, and now she had absolutely no idea how to deal with him, drunk or sober.

She didn't need a degree in psychology to know that this was no longer the Ryan who laughed and teased and made love to her; the Ryan who might, on occasions, unleash a whiplash of controlled temper but always turn back swiftly into the tender, charming lover. This Ryan looked like he'd be up and raring for a fight any minute now. Well, she thought, suddenly resolute, he wasn't going to have it with her.

She took a seat opposite him at the small table and said flatly, 'I am not going to try to talk to you because I don't know how to; drunks, particularly filthy-tempered drunks, are something right out of my experience. If, when you are once again sober you wish to talk to me that's fine; if you don't that's fine too, but I think you should know that if you get too pissed to walk, *I* shall not slip a disc helping you to bed.'

'Anything else you got to say while you're at it, honey?'

'No. I just thought I'd tell you how I feel.' She stood. 'Now I am going to bathe and change, after which I shall have dinner and an early night. Whether you join me or not is entirely up to you.'

He tilted back on his chair, hooking his thumbs in his belt, 'Wa-al, thanks for the invitation, ma'am,' his out-of-focus eyes were mere slits in a face about as friendly as that of a wounded mountain lion, 'but I guess I'll take a rain check on that bath 'cause the tub up there

260

just ain't big enough for the two of us!'

Sticking her chin in the air and without affording him another glance Julia walked back up the stairs to their room.

*   *   *

Ryan watched her legs disappear around the turn in the staircase, then finished his drink and walked unsteadily to the bar. Beckoning Eddie, who was busily engaged in polishing glasses and trying to look as though he hadn't heard a thing, he said, 'One more double, Eddie, and when the lady comes down to dinner tell her I've gone for a walk and not to wait up for me.'

Eddie looked doubtful. 'You sure that's wise, sir – walking around in the dark like?'

'No, I'm sure it isn't, but right now it's one hell of a lot wiser than staying here.' Ryan watched Eddie pour the drink, downed it in one, and thumped the glass back on the counter. He squinted at the clock above the bar, the hands at seven-thirty. He said earnestly, 'It may be a long walk, so if I'm a bit late will you leave that little ol' side door unlatched again?'

Eddie raised enquiring brows at his father, who gave a sharp cackle and nodded agreement. 'Yes, sir, we'll leave it if you'll just make sure you lock it afore you goes to bed,' Eddie answered soothingly, thinking privately that if the Yank wasn't back by chucking-out time his missus would probably want to call the police and organize a search party. Watching Ryan weave his way between the tables Eddie argued quietly with his father, 'We shouldn't let him go like that, dad; if he stops long enough to think what he's doing he'll fall flat on his bleedin' face!'

Old Nathanial snorted his contempt. 'He'll be alright...knows around here like the back of 'is hand, he do; he'll be back soonest he's walked it off.' He gave another cackle. 'Sh'em got his measure all right though, un't she? Right sparky fer a little 'un, she are.'

*   *   *

Worn out from the long fraught journey and anxiety about where in hell Ryan had got himself to, by ten-thirty Julia was so weary she could scarcely keep her eyes open. Seizing a moment when Nathaniel was calling a half-hearted 'Drink up now, gen'elmen, *please*' for the fourth time to a bar full of unheeding locals, she slipped into the kitchen where Eddie was washing-up.

'Eddie, I *have* to get some sleep but I'm so worried about Mr Petersen. You've known him for a while, has he done this before...' she hesitated, 'you know: got plastered and just taken off.'

'Blimey, I'll say – he got hisself in a right old state a while back: tanked up to the eyes he would have been if I hadn't taken the bottle away when I did. Even then I 'ad to get him to sleep it off and feed him coffee before he were fit to go out the door!' Leaning back against the sink and wiping his hands on the tea cloth Eddie tried to look and sound encouraging. 'See, he'd 'ad some real bad news and just went off... gone hours he was, but he come back safe an' sound in the end.' He gave her arm a little pat, 'now why don't you go right on up, Missus, and don't you worry. He'll be back, bye an' bye.' Adding under his breath a fervent 'I hope,' as she thanked him and went up to bed.

She thought she wouldn't sleep well, but despite the revving of cars and motorbikes beneath her window and the final convivial farewells called by the departing customers, she was deeply asleep in less than five minutes.

*   *   *

She woke slowly, knowing even before she was fully awake that he was back. Opening her eyes she could see a match had been set to the laid fire she'd been too tired to light earlier. In a cushioned wicker chair drawn up to the bed Ryan sat in shirt and trousers, his hair damp as though he had run it under the tap: probably she thought to help clear his head of the drink. The shadows flung by the fire sculpted the fine bones of his face and the mixture of strength and vulnerability in that face moved her almost to tears. He looked tired to death but sober. When their eyes met he gave a faint, wry smile.

'Hi,' he placed a hand over hers where it lay on the coverlet.

She asked, 'How long have you been sitting there?'

'Quite a while; about an hour or so I guess.'

'Why not come to bed?'

'I liked watching you sleep.'

She sat, shivering and pulling the covers up against the chill. 'Where have you been until...' she glanced at the clock on the bedside table, 'until three o'clock?'

'Out on Falcon Field; walked right around it,' he rubbed a hand over his face and through his hair. 'Very cathartic, that old field; brings it all back ...' he looked away. 'A lot of dead people around there... ghosts. My crew...all those other boys who didn't make it back to base; and Robyn Graham, the old sky pilot – they got him in Korea, did I tell you? – Niles, Claire, Rupert...dozens of them to weep for...' he tailed off, was silent a moment then rolled his shoulders as though shedding a burden. 'Think I laid most of them to rest tonight, sure hope I did. Can't see my daughter go to her wedding with my head all cluttered up.'

He took her hand again, lacing their fingers together, resting them against his cheek. 'You were right and I was wrong to mind about Hannah and Alec. Guess I'm getting a little too old to be jealous about who besides me gets to love my ma.'

She said, 'Well you didn't have to be *quite* such an ornery old pig about it,' and saw the smile begin behind his eyes.

'And you didn't have to laugh quite so much.'

She lay back against the pillows. 'If I say I'm sorry too, will you stop talking and come to bed?'

He stood and began to unbutton his shirt. 'When a gal like you makes an offer like that, I guess a guy like me just has to say, yes...but take it easy; I haven't got this sauced for months and my head still feels kind of loose.'

On the verge of sleep he murmured, '*In your arms was still delight, Quiet as a street at night...*' he yawned. 'Rupert Brooke – remind me to tell you the rest of it in the morning.'

She said: 'It is morning.'

He murmured, 'Shut up smartass and go to sleep...' and she smiled and curled closer into his arms and slept.

* * *

The next morning Julia came into the bathroom while he was shaving. Putting her arms about his waist and looking over his shoulder she asked, 'How's the hangover?'

He drew the razor carefully around his chin. 'Punishing – like someone's been hitting my brain with a baseball bat.'

'That's no more than you deserve.'

'Tell me something I don't know.' He wiped his face. Looking at her reflection beside his he gave a lop-sided grin. 'My New Year's resolution – "Don't do it again."'

'Is that a hand-on-heart promise?'

'Yeah, I'm sorry about last night.' He turned, wrapping his arms about her and resting his forehead against hers. He said, 'Over at the field last night I really hit the wall; for a while I thought I wasn't going to make it back...scared the bejesus out of me.'

263

She breathed in the clean, early morning smell of his skin. 'You scared *me*...but you shouldn't take all the blame on yourself: I was pretty insensitive too.'

'Sure,' he was laconic, 'and you put me in the doghouse didn't you? Right there in the bar, in front of everyone. I remember that!'

'I thought you were going to make a fight of it, so I got in first,' she sighed. 'Am I always going to get up your nose?'

'Probably, but I don't mind all that much now. Guess that's what love does to a man.' He kissed her lightly. 'Better get out of that wrap and take a fast tub; I smell bacon frying, and I'm mighty hungry after missing supper last night.'

*   *   *

'Will you show me the airfield?' she asked when they finished breakfast and had returned to their room, 'I'd like to see it – but not if it bothers you,' she added hastily.

'Sure. It's not a problem...' he was brushing his sleeve absently around the brim of a black homburg, bought from a Jermyn Street hatter for the occasion. Julia stifled a snort of laughter.

'That will double for funerals for years!'

'The guy in the shop called it an Anthony Eden: sounds classy.' He chuckled. 'Pru told me to cover my hair and somehow I thought my hunting cap would look kind of out of place at a wedding.'

She asked curiously, 'Has your hair always been that sort of silvery blonde?'

'Yeah, just one of the things Niles and me – and Sophie, inherited from Pa, tho' mine's one heck more silver than blonde now. I think seeing Geoffrey's girl and me look so alike Pru thought it might be the final give-away.'

'Let's walk to the airfield now,' she said impulsively. 'On the way you can tell me about Sophie: how you feel about today...and having to stay back and never let her know who you are.'

'Not sure I know how I feel,' he confessed as they climbed the stile and began walking along the bridle path, 'pretty sad, I guess. Seems like today I'm closing a book I never really got to read. I'd have liked a daughter, you know. Still,' he squeezed her hand, 'I've got one now, haven't I?'

'Yes, I rather think you have. I hadn't realised how much Nicole needed, or wanted, a father until a couple of days ago, when you laid down the law and she gave in without much of a fight.'

'She's a way to go before she catches up with you, because I sure

264

as hell didn't see you giving much ground last night.'

She stopped and looked at him gravely for a minute. 'Don't you know yet,' she asked, 'that it's a woman's lot in life to keep a man in his place? *Ouch*!' She rubbed the seat of her jeans. 'What was that for?'

'That?' he smiled amiably, '*that* was for always being right!'

*   *   *

It would have been great, he thought, to have watched his daughter arrive at her wedding when there was snow on the ground and enough sun to make it sparkle. But the morning was sharp and bright and Sophie sparkled more radiantly than any snow. She stepped from the bridal car on to Geoffrey's arm, a vision in close-fitting white satin; a veil of sheer voile floating about her bright head. When someone in the crowd about the lych-gate spoke to her she laughed and putting her hands beneath the veil, swept it up for a moment, holding it over the small silver tiara that kept it in place.

Ryan took in a deep breath; his hand closed on Julia's, almost crushing her fingers. *I shall remember this moment for the rest of my life.* He watched Geoffrey fumble with his crutches then straighten and smile at Sophie. She kissed his cheek and lowering the veil back over her face, took his arm to begin the long walk along the pathway to the church door.

'Wow!' breathed Julia, 'I see what you mean.'

Ryan's eyes followed the two figures until they reached the deep porch and were lost to sight, then as the organ sounded the first notes of Mendelssohn's March, put an arm about Julia's shoulders and led her through the churchyard to the quiet place beside the old tomb.

Standing before the two flower-decked graves he said, 'It's their day, too, don't you think?'

She was silent a moment. 'What are you feeling now?' she asked.

'I'm not sure: sad, empty; resigned, I guess.' He smiled, his slow warm smile, 'but happy for Sophie.' Gently he squeezed her shoulder. 'Here is yesterday; it's time now to take out the marker; close the book...'

Silently, each lost in their own thoughts, they walked back to resume their vigil under the tree and wait for a last sight of Ryan's lost daughter.

The wedding peal crashed from the belfry; the well-wishers at the gate readied their first handfuls of confetti. Without conscious volition Ryan moved forward a pace, his gaze fixed on the church porch as

Sophie stepped into the sunlight, her hand on the arm of the tall, dark-haired, pleasant-faced young man who was now her husband.

Smiling and radiant she looked around the crowd now spilling over into the churchyard to line her route, then as if prompted by some inner instinct, raised her eyes and smiled straight across the expanse of lawn to where Ryan stood beneath the yew. For the length of a heartbeat their eyes met; then Geoffrey and Pru appeared, followed swiftly by a dozen guests. Sophie and her husband stepped forward, the confetti flew and the moment passed.

Ryan gripped Julia's hand again. She caught her breath. His face was illuminated, as though a light blazed from within and all at once she wanted to weep. Still smiling he turned his eyes to hers. 'That's it,' he said, and bending kissed her mouth. 'Let's go.'

'Are you sure?'

'I'm sure.'

He led her through a tangle of bushes to the rear of the church then through the iron kissing gate leading on to the narrow lane where he had parked the Jowett, out of sight of the lych-gate and the waiting crowd.

'Back to the Bull?' asked Julia as he fired the engine. He shook his head. 'Just a little detour first,' he said.

*   *   *

Mindful of the Jowett's suspension he drove sedately down the rutted lane and past the weed-covered brick foundations of the guard post, then crossed the grass to the start of the long central runway. Turning the car so that it faced the far belt of trees he sat unmoving for a long moment, feeling the quiet, deep-down ache that would always be Claire, then, shaking his shoulders as a dog will shake off rain, he smiled down at the woman beside him. 'When I say goodbye,' he said, 'I say it good.' Julia flinched at the light of pure devilment in his eyes. 'So, fasten your seatbelt sweetheart; it's going to be a bumpy ride!'

Driving his foot hard on the gas pedal he let go the clutch and the Jowett took off, heading straight down the runway for the forest of trees at the end. Above the protesting roar of the engine and scream of tyres the voices sounded clear in his head.

Jesus, Ry, that was a close one…
You are clear to land, sir…
That's my Rupert…

Not only for today, sir, for all the days…
Tell me a story, Captain Pop…
Mayday, Mayday, Mayday…
Lippen Schweigen 's flustern Geigen, Hab Dich lieb…

Ryan eased his foot off the throttle and the car rolled to a halt before the trees. Switching off the ignition he turned to look at Julia, who sat white faced, her hands still gripping the hanging strap. 'I needed that. How was it for you?' he asked and wasn't surprised when she hit him. He put up a hand to massage his jaw. 'I guess that closes the book real tight,' he said mildly. 'Now, how about we get home to our family and give Hannah and Alec a real hard time?'

Firing the engine again he turned the car towards Stratford Ley and the first stage of their long journey back to Bracket Sound.

By the same author

A Year Out of Time

A Year Out of Time is the story of one twelve year old girl from a "nice" middle-class background and a "nice" private school (where her mother hoped she might learn to be a lady) who, in the Autumn of 1940, finds herself pitched into the totally foreign environment of a small Worcestershire hamlet.

For the space of one year her life revolves around the village school and its manic headmaster; the friends she makes, notably Georgie Little the "bad influence"; the twee but useful fellow evacuees, Mavis and Mickey Harper, whose possession of an old pigsty proves the springboard to some surprising and sometimes hilarious happenings; and Mrs 'Arris, the vast and formidable landlady of The Green Dragon Inn.

In the company of Georgie Little she awakens to the joys of a new and exhilarating world: a secret world which excludes most adults and frequently verges on the lawless.

The year comes to an explosive end and she returns unwillingly to her former life – but the joyous, anarchic influence of the Forest and Georgie remains, and sixty years on is remembered with gratitude and love.

ISBN 978-0-9555778-0-2

Available from Sagittarius Publications
62 Jacklyns Lane, Alresford, Hampshire SO24 9LH

By the same author

And All Shall Be Well

And All Shall Be Well begins Francis Lindsey's journey through childhood to middle age; from a suddenly orphaned ten year old to a carefree adolescent; through the harsh expectations of becoming a man in a world caught in war.

Set mainly against the dramatic background of the Cornish Coast, it is a story about friendships and relationships, courage and weakness, guilt and reparation. — *The first book in a Cornish trilogy.*

ISBN 978-0-9555778-1-9

**Chosen as the runner-up
to the Society of Authors 2003 Sagittarius Prize**

"The author has succeeded to an extraordinary degree in bringing Francis to full masculine life. The storyline is always interesting and keeps the reader turning the pages. All in all it is a good novel that can be warmly recommended to anyone who enjoys a good read."
– Michael Legat

"Seldom do I get a book that simply cannot be put down. The settings and characters are so believable, the shy falling in love for the first time and the passion of forbidden liaisons written with feeling. Many of the sequences left me with a smile on my face, others to wipe a tear from my eye." – Jenny Davidson, The Society of Women Writers and Journalists Book Review

"A beautifully written novel. Eve Phillips' writing is a pure joy to read and her wonderfully graphic descriptions of the Penzance area of the Cornish Coast made me yearn to be there."
– Erica James, Author

Available from Sagittarius Publications
62 Jacklyns Lane, Alresford, Hampshire SO24 9LH

By the same author

Matthew's Daughter

Matthew's Daughter is the second book in a Cornish Trilogy and follows Caroline Penrose, as she returns from her wartime service in the WAAF to her father's flower farm in Cornwall. But once home she finds a number of obstacles and family conspiracies impeding her path to peace...

ISBN 978-0-9555778-2-6

The Changing Day

The Changing Day the final book in a Cornish Trilogy, begins in 1940, when a meeting between WREN Joanna Dunne and Navy Lieutenant Mark Eden is the start of a love affair that at first seems unlikely to stand the test of time. She is 22, single and an Oxford graduate; he is 36, married and in civilian life a country vet. She is attracted but not looking for romance, he is attracted but not looking for commitment and, as Joanna soon discovers, he is the black sheep of his family and has a very murky past.

ISBN 978-0-9555778-3-3

Available from Sagittarius Publications
62 Jacklyns Lane, Alresford, Hampshire SO24 9LH

By the same author

A Very Private Arrangement

In the spring of 1934 fourteen year old orphan Anna Farrell is transported from a life of drab, penny-pinching, genteel poverty with her cousin Ruth, to the elegant, affluent Bloomsbury household of distant cousin Patrick Farrell, owner of a successful antique gallery, and his manservant, Charlie Caulter. Naïve and young for her years, Anna is at first blissfully unaware of the well-hidden secret kept by the two men, until a meeting with the quasi-charming Madame Gallimard and her sons becomes the catalyst that threatens to tear her world apart

Against the backcloth of WW2 and a diversity of places and people; from Bloomsbury to Berlin, Army comrades to Polish partisans, with her beloved Patrick and Charlie to smooth her path through the inevitable pitfalls of first, second and last love, Anna matures from naïve young girl to confident young woman, well able to cope with the men in her life – and some of the women in theirs.

ISBN 978-0-9555778-4-0

Available from Sagittarius Publications
62 Jacklyns Lane, Alresford, Hampshire SO24 9LH